I0601760

Praise for *Ursula Major*

"Written so well that it is easy to suppose that it is a genuine piece of autobiography. Related with a mixture of humor and pathos that is a joy to read."
— Frank Parker, Rosie Amber's Book Review Team

"A winner! Nails the combination of lyricism and readability. Ideal Book Club material. Conklin's signature is utterly convincing writing. The strange life of childhood is immediately recognizable, told in language that is straightforward and beautiful."
— Fiona Forsyth, Author, *Poetic Justice*

"The writing manages to place readers right in the center of the action, so that we experience events with all our senses, sharing what the narrator sees, hears, smells, tastes, and feels. The characters are fascinating and feel true to life."
— Olga Núñez Miret, *Just Olga*, #TuesdayBookBlog

"Loved it! An intriguing exploration of nostalgia for a 1970s childhood, told by a most unreliable narrator. Conklin's is a persuasive voice and Jeremy's tales have an almost hypnotic quality, immersing the reader in the details of his lost childhood."
— Elaine Graham-Leigh, Reedsy Discovery

Ursula Major

ALSO BY THIS AUTHOR

An End to Etcetera
Soft as Water

Ursula Major

B. ROBERT CONKLIN

Skip the Preface
publishing

Columbus, Ohio

This is a work of fiction. Names, characters, places, and incidents are products of the author's imagination or are used fictitiously and are not to be construed as real. Any resemblance to actual events, locales, organizations, or persons, living or dead, is entirely coincidental.

URSULA MAJOR
Copyright © 2025 by Robert B. Conklin

All rights reserved. No part of this book may be reproduced in any form or by any electronic or mechanical means, including information and storage retrieval systems, without written permission, except by reviewers, who may quote brief passages for a review.

ISBN: 979-8-9922225-0-0 (Paperback)

Library of Congress Control Number: 2025907596

Cover art:
Front: Irina Usmanova | ID170200475 | Dreamstime.com
Back: Personal archive (author with younger sister)

A condensed version of chapters 1–3 was published as a short story titled "With Electra Comes the Dawn" in *Blue Moon Literary & Art Review*, issue 13, 2018.

First Edition

For more information, visit:
www.skipthepreface.com

For my sisters, of course!

"How do people make it through life without a sister?"

—Sara Corpening, author

Chapter 1

My sister was born in the back of a bus. At least, this is how I remember it. She was already a minor celebrity at birth. My mother, too, from the moment of delivery. We only had the one car, which my father used for work, so we resorted to taking the bus to run errands. Our town was big enough to maintain an old clunker of a converted school bus, a skoolie that prowled its route like a restless elephant in a zoo, just not a hospital with a maternity ward.

We were coming home from a trip to the Salvation Army when her water broke suddenly. Very suddenly. I heard a sound like a popgun shooting its cork (muted backfiring of the exhaust?), then a gush of water like a urinal flushing (slow hiss of the airbrakes?). My mother stood up and looked down between her legs. I looked down, too. There was a puddle of water on the floor.

"Mama?" I cried, feeling afraid and embarrassed. She was wearing a dress, and I thought she had peed her underpants.

"Oh, dear God," she announced, "my water just broke!"

The bus driver took charge of getting us to the nearest city with an ER in record time, but Ursula popped out just as we arrived. It was a momentous event. Where was I? Still in my seat, trying to puzzle out how water, which I knew to be a liquid, was capable of breakage, which I knew to be a property of solids.

Over the previous nine months, my parents had been gradually preparing me for the arrival of a baby by asking me variations of a single theme: How would I feel being a big brother?

The year was 1974. I was four years old. I didn't have too many thoughts about the matter. I suppose I thought it would be fine as long as I wouldn't have to share my toys.

And now, here she was already.

My mother lay in the aisle with her legs raised. I could never look at her face again without picturing it as it appeared in the compressed intensity of those several moments. It all happened very quickly. I sat quietly. I don't think I looked at my mother for long. A single glance had been enough.

Disembarking the bus, I became somewhat of an afterthought as I followed along behind the gurney, shepherded to the emergency room by someone's guiding hand, presumably the bus driver's.

At some point, my father showed up from his job behind the seafood counter of a local supermarket wearing an apron smeared with fish guts and smelling like a giant carp. I never wanted to go fishing after that. I didn't let him hug me for weeks.

"Jeremy Hilary Jones, you have a new baby sister," he said, sitting next to me in the lobby. He often enjoyed calling me by my full name—first, middle, last—and I admit, there is something rhythmical in the way the names all blend together. He was tall and thin. His face was sallow. He tended to have a slant-eyed look, as though he was always trying to figure out a new angle on life.

"I saw," I told him, "I already saw," although I hadn't—not really.

And here is another memory that isn't so much false as misguided. At the time, with the blood all over my father's apron, I developed the impression he had single-handedly delivered my baby sister from the bowels of my mother. Of course, I wouldn't have known about the intricacies of female anatomy that had made a C-section necessary. But the connection between the blood on my father's apron and what I found out later was an emergency operation to save my sister's life imprinted itself on my mind. The umbilical cord, it turned out, had become wrapped around her neck, causing distress. There had been only minutes to spare. Later, in the postpartum room that she shared with a distraught woman and her bawling newborn, my mother showed me the incision, a vertical rift descending from a point below her belly button, like the slash of a scimitar held together with a railroad track of stitches—a mixed metaphor, if ever there was one.

"Oh, I do hope the scar tissue goes away," she would sigh. "They've ruined me forever with this crazy stunt they had to pull just to get your sister out."

Somehow, though, I sensed she was pleased with this outward sign of a difficult birth, maybe by the way she held my hand after the stitches were removed and had me trace the visible portion of the scar over and over with my forefinger, as though to make it deeper, the way I might dig a small trench in the wet sand of a rain-soaked sandbox.

And so I have two memories, as though superimposed on each other: the one a distinct vision of my sister being born on a bus, the other of my being told of an operation called a Cesarean section to save her life. Had my sister been born twice? Had they put her back inside my mother just so they could cut her back out again? Or had there been two sisters, twins, only one of which survived?

In any case, they had already named her Ursula by the time she was born—"Ursie" for short. Like a constellation, she was to become my mother and father's "Little Bear," *Ursa Minor*, home to Polaris, the fixed star in the heavens about which all of the other constellations revolve. Although too little to know the names of stars, I already formed a presentiment that Ursie was to become the focal point of my parents' attention.

My father brought me back to the room where my mother was nursing my sister. After I inspected the red, tiny, wrinkled organism that was supposed to be my new sibling, I picked up a magazine that was lying around. I remember the advertisement for Hawaiian Tropic suntan lotion on the back cover. It was the middle of March in Ohio—in fact, the very Ides, Ursie's birthday and Julius Caesar's death-day occurring on the same date.

My mother took it as a bad omen. My father didn't believe in them—omens, that is—and told her so.

"Maybe when your mother is better, we'll take a vacation," my father said, looking over my shoulder at the beautiful tan model stretched out on a beach. The thought of a vacation seemed to intrigue him as an alternative to late nights staying up with a baby.

I've been told that the giving-birth-on-the-bus part of this story didn't actually happen the way I remember it. This all came out in a therapist's office after hours of idle chitchat about being and nothingness. And then, somewhere in there, I began to realize that many of my memories from this period are manufactured. I had—and have—a difficult time separating what's real from what's not so real. At least, this is what my therapist has told me, and I've come to believe her. This episode falls into the latter category. For proof, my therapist, an earnest young intern fresh out of her master's degree program, produced an archived news article from the Marietta Times, *all of 50 years ago, that she located through a remote library search on her phone.*

It's true my mother's water broke while we sat side by side on the bus. And it's true she pulled the cord for the next stop. Instead of getting off, she calmly informed the bus driver of the situation, and after ejecting all nonessential passengers, of whom there were two, the driver veered off course to deliver us to the closest hospital, which happened to be a forty-five minute drive upstream along the Ohio River to Marietta Memorial. Apparently, she did lie down in the aisle, but it wasn't to give birth, only to shift her body into a more comfortable position as she went into labor. Once we arrived, medics quickly wheeled my mother to the emergency-room entrance.

So much for facts. In my memory, I recall news reporters with microphones and the bright lights of cameras chasing my mother like a mob of hyenas.

But my therapist has cast doubt on this recollection as well. Granted, the article, "Woman in Labor Rushed to Hospital by Bus," made front-page news of the local paper, but there were no accompanying photographs of the bus's arrival, and all quotes—of bus driver and mother and attending doctor—were reported after the fact. If the incident had been broadcast on local TV news stations, the video footage was probably lost to history.

"Too bad this all happened in an era before smart phones," my therapist observed. "You would have gone viral."

In my mind's eye, though, my mother and I were celebrities. We were stars.

Chapter 2

We didn't go to Hawaii for a vacation, not that my parents could have afforded to. In fact, we didn't go on a vacation at all. But we did go to Indiana to visit my mother's cousins. Or at least this was my parents' intention.

We waited until little Ursie was two months old to make the trip. We had been there once before, although I couldn't recall the visit. I wouldn't end up recalling this one either, mainly because we never made it to our destination.

It should have been only a five-hour trip across the state and into the boot of Indiana, down along the Ohio River. Mom's cousins maintained a small cottage on a bluff overlooking a shaded tributary. I'm told I attended the funeral of their mother—my mother's aunt—and that this had been the occasion of my first visit.

With Ursula in the car, it took nine hours and forty-three minutes. This allowed for seventeen pit stops—I kept count—and a half-hour break for lunch. The reason I know this is that my father let out a sigh when we exited what was to become our final rest stop. "Nine hours and forty-three minutes," he said. "Can you believe it?" And that was only to get to the point where we had our big accident.

I could see the dashboard clock through the space between the front seats, but I was too young to keep time. As I mentioned, I was only four years old. Still, I knew my numbers, and I watched the numbers change sequence as we traveled. The number on the right, I observed, changed faster than the middle number, and it seemed the number on the left hardly changed at all. If I stared at it, it almost never changed. Only when I woke up from a nap or looked away and back toward it, did it change from one number to the next.

Case in point: my therapist has informed me that even this detail has been distorted through a process she calls additive memory. The first digital clocks came out in the form of wristwatches in 1972. Only after this inno-vation did digital clocks in car dashboards follow suit, and our car was a '69 Chrysler. Clearly, she had done her homework. However, if it was indeed an analog clock I was watching, I would only have been mesmerized by the steady, even ticks of the second hand. I was too young to have learned to tell time the traditional way.

In any case, my job was to keep Ursie from crying, which was often. When she wasn't crying, she gurgled, cooed, hic-cupped, burped, and chirped at times like a bird. My parents seemed to enjoy these sounds much more than the sound of her cries. I had any number of toys piled around me with which to entertain her. Her favorite was a small stuffed giraffe with a bro-ken wire neck, whose name, I recollect, was Ollie.

When she wasn't crying or playing with Ollie, she tended to stare at me. This was easy for her to do since she was facing backward and I was belted into my seat facing forward. Her bas-sinet was the vintage type that was loosely anchored in place with giant hooks that fit over the back of Dad's seat. This was before car seats were in vogue or required.

I can still remember the car. It seemed as big as a motorboat. It drove like one, too, surging on bad struts along the freeway like a boat skimming along a series of waves. These undulations gave my mother motion sickness, and from time to time, she would wave to my father to stop so she could lean her head out and retch onto the shoulder of the road.

The windows were rolled down a crack, so as not to create

too much wind for the baby, except when my father lit up a cigarette. Then he and my mother rolled the windows down all the way, letting a cyclone of chilled May weather circulate streams of smoke through the car. I suppose they thought this was allowing proper ventilation for the children in back.

I don't really remember the accident. There's a void in that part of my memory, every time I try to recall it.

The story goes that my father dropped a lit cigarette onto his lap while attempting to pass a John Deere tractor and juggle a cup of coffee at the same time. He passed the tractor but lurched back into his lane to avoid collision with an oncoming pickup truck. The sudden movement made his coffee spill, and he turned the wheel too hard. The front passenger tire skidded across the gravel shoulder and caught the lip of a drainage ditch that paralleled the side of the road. The car flipped end over end before landing upside down in a cow pasture. Apparently, it was all very dramatic. He never recovered his cigarette—a source of anxiety until we were safely removed from the car.

We were only twenty-two miles from our destination.

The tractor stopped, as did the pickup truck that had been traveling toward us.

"Is everyone all right?" my father asked plaintively. Never one to wear a seat belt—he claimed they would trap you inside your vehicle if it were ever to catch fire—he had been tossed around like a load of laundry in a dryer. Later, we found out he had broken his collarbone. "Where's Maddy?"

It turned out Mom had been flung from the car. She had unbuckled herself to turn and insert a fresh bottle into her Little Bear's mouth. She ended up hanging by her heels from the limb of a large oak tree.

When we found her, she was singing "Jesus Loves Me."

She wasn't the only family member with an inverted view.

This is what I remember: the aftermath. I remember hanging upside down in my seat, held in place by my seatbelt. The world outside seemed upside down, too. The face of the tractor driver peered into the car upside down. The driver of the other vehicle appeared behind him, also upside down. They reached inside for the baby. Then they helped pry my father from the car. I was the last one to be freed.

We all gathered around the trunk of the oak tree and looked upward, listening to my mother sing. She had a soft, feathery voice, a compelling *a cappella*. If the trunk had been smaller, we might have been tempted to join hands in a circle. As it was, my father had both of his hands occupied holding my sister, despite the pain he must have felt from his fractured collarbone.

Ursula, I'm happy to report, was unharmed. Like me, she had endured her very first lesson in the art of seeing the world upside down. My mother, too, was experiencing this lesson in her own special way. I'm not sure my father ever caught on.

Flying through the air, my mother, as she would tell us later, over and over again, had a vision of being carried by an angel.

Not an ordinary angel.

He was more of a biker. Instead of a chariot, he rode a motorcycle that spewed flames from two chrome exhausts. His hair had a burnished sheen, as well, long and sleek, a greenish blond, as though from having spent too much time in an over-chlorinated pool. His arms were covered in tattoos of crosses and hearts.

"But no wings," she would add, frowning and losing that wistful pucker of her lips, perplexed by this deviation from the norm, as if the biker outfit was ordinary angelic attire. "I always thought angels had wings."

Out of her description, my father was most perturbed by the mention of blond hair. His own complexion was dark and Neapolitan, as was my own.

—

This is how she found religion, and how religion found her.

After her experience in the tree, she went looking for it.

Reports would come in of a Madonna appearing out of nowhere: in the corrugated rust of a tin roof in a town in Alabama. In the flaking paint of a water tower in Oklahoma. In the profile of a fresh rock outcropping following a mudslide in some distant part of Brazil. In a misshapen pancake preserved under glass in Marseilles.

No, she didn't take us to these faraway places, much as she wanted to. She would cut out the newspaper or magazine article, though, and tape it in a scrapbook.

After so much time, her scrapbook became fairly thick with clippings.

"Look," she would say, paging through it some sunny afternoon with my sister snuggled in on one side of the settee and me on the other, both of us leaning in for a better look. "Wouldn't you like to see this tree? Look how the lightning struck it just so. Why, it's the perfect outline of our Lord and Savior." She tilted it this way and that toward the light, squinting her eyes. "Wouldn't you like to leave right now and see it? It's only a short ways away."

"What about Dada?" my sister might ask, glancing anxiously across our mother's lap to catch my eye. "Wouldn't Dada like to see it too?"

"Mommy, where is Argentina?" I might ask. "Is that a short ways away really?"

Having completed first grade, I was quickly outgrowing my library of Golden Books and proud of my mastery of the big words our mother's scrapbook articles introduced me to.

Our father had a different view of our mother's scrapbook.

"Look," he would say, setting me in a giant red comfy chair, while Ursie was dressing her dolls or drawing pictures on the walls.

He drew up a hardback chair so I would know he was serious.

"Your mother isn't right," he said, looking off to the side.

"About what?" I asked.

"In her head," he said, tapping his temple. "Ever since the accident. The accident changed her somehow. She isn't the same woman I married."

"Not the same?"

I was starting to feel alarmed by the possibility that my real mother had been kidnapped and was being held for ransom somewhere. I imagined her tied to a chair in a dark basement. I imagined pirates at sea.

"Take care of your sister," he said from time to time, patting me on the head as if saying farewell to the dog he wouldn't permit us to own.

"You're not going anywhere?" I would ask, half afraid. By now it was 1977, and I was afraid of a lot of things. Arrivals, departures, but especially departures. My parents had taken me along to three funerals in a row one summer. One was an old aunt of my father's. Another was an old uncle of my mother's. The third was the head librarian who had fallen asleep at his desk where my mother had part-time hours. He regularly kept his door closed and locked, so no one knew he was dead for two days.

I thought maybe my father had a terminal illness.

But he never answered my question—not directly.

"Just promise to always take good care of her. Okay?"

He'd give me that little nudge on my cheek with his knuckles that I was too timid to tell him I never cared for.

And so I started looking out for her, as though following a prime directive. I became my sister's keeper in a way.

At the time, though, it seemed it was my mother who needed the most watching.

Chapter 3

You hear about these people. They go about their lives seemingly as rational as a syllogism in logic. And then they throw themselves in front of an oncoming locomotive or jump from a hotel balcony. All very spur of the moment without leaving as much as a Post-it note behind to explain their motive.

"Post-it notes came out only in 1980," my therapist informs me, glancing up from the factoid she has brought up on her phone. "Yet your memory is set in 1977. Don't you think your analogy somewhat anachronistic?"

True, but did she know the idea *of it had come about six years earlier when a 3M employee used his colleague's adhesive as a bookmark for his hymnal? Which raises the question: What is more important? The idea or the execution?*

It's always someone else, of course. You never think it's going to be someone close to you. Or even you yourself—you can't imagine any fracture in your ordinary existence bringing you remotely close to such a life-altering act. There are many lines in the sand which most of us are unwilling to cross. But then there are always those few—the ones you read about. Their minds are made differently from the norm, you think, as a way of reassuring yourself before turning a page of the paper or clicking on a different link or recharging your phone. Their minds are made of metal, whereas the rest of us have brains of ordinary sponge.

Our mother's case was different. She put her life in danger while completely asleep. And not just her life. As part of her waking dream, she roused us from bed—my sister and me—and took us with her on what seemed, at the time, a marvelous adventure.

I'm not sure where she was taking us, or where she thought she was going. We were both in bare feet on a frosty November night. I remember holding Ursie by the hand and pulling her along past darkened houses with lingering remnants of Halloween: pumpkins rotting on porches, cardboard skeletons dangling on strings, toilet paper hanging from eaves. I tried reassuring her by singing her favorite bedtime song. Or rather humming it to her: "Twinkle, twinkle, little star ..." It became a sort of mantra, as we went along with our mother in her nightgown and her children still in their pajamas.

She herded us down one side street after another, keeping us always in front of her, picking up Ursie from time to time when she stopped and raised her little arms. Does this mean she was conscious of her actions? Or just that her mind was in a different realm? There wasn't a moon, and the pavements were all rain-slicked, wobbling with reflections of street lamps. We could have fallen through puddles into other worlds.

"This way?" I would ask whenever we came to an intersection. I was trying to goad her into a circle—or rectangle rather—by suggesting a series of left turns that would lead us back to our house. She wouldn't answer except to smile and nod or shake her head.

We avoided main roads and highways. She must have had a protective instinct, even in her waking dream. Subconsciously, she knew to avoid roads with too much traffic so as not to expose us to the gaze of motorists. It would have looked strange, I'm sure, to see a mother and her children stumbling along the berm of a thoroughfare past midnight. Maybe they would have offered a ride or maybe only slowed down. Maybe they would have called the police as soon as they found the nearest payphone. Or maybe they would have just thought us homeless.

"Which way, Mommy? This way?"

She was carrying Ursie now on her hip and looked confused. We had come to a railroad crossing where she led us off the road and down a set of tracks instead of the direction I was pointing.

The cinders were hard and pointed against my bare feet, so I hopped from one wooden tie to the next, preferring a chance of splinters instead.

"Ow! Mama, my feet hurt!" Ursie complained. Unlike my sister, I had graduated from "Mama" to "Mommy" the previous year.

When I turned, I saw our mother had set her back down on the bed of the track.

"It's not much farther," she said lightly. These were the first words she had spoken since she had woken us, and it was then that I realized she might have an actual destination in mind.

"Where are we going, Mommy?" I asked.

"Somewhere wonderful," she said.

"Argentina?" I asked.

It seemed possible she was intent on taking us to see one of the Madonnas. Either that or the Ohio River, based on the gradual downward slope of the rails. I wondered what would happen when we reached the river. I feared crossing the trestle bridge to the West Virginia side. I was sure we would fall through the ties and end up drowned.

Our town was christened Bellerophon (pronounced Buh-LAIR-uh-fahn) after the Greek hero who had tamed Pegasus and slain the Chimera, a monster with a personality disorder in the form of the three separate heads: a lion's, a goat's, and a snake's. The town itself was much duller than the myth, with the heart of it perched on bluffs overlooking the Ohio River, and the rest of it sprawling out on roads like the veins in a bloodshot eye. And now it seemed our mother was trying to bypass the town altogether.

Far down the tracks, a light appeared—a single headlight,

cutting through the gloom. On either side of the tracks was a steep embankment of cinders and ash leading on the left into a thicket of brambles and on the right into a thicker thicket of brambles, from what I could trace of their silhouettes.

The rumbling of an engine was still far off. The train seemed slow-moving, but as it crossed an intersection in the distance, it brought a clanging of bells and a flashing of red lights on the arms of the gates that swung down. A long, mournful wail of a siren rang like the underbelly of a baritone in a church choir, making me jump.

The look on our mother's face was a mingling of confusion and doubt.

She was holding Ursie by the hand.

"This way, Mommy."

I pulled at the edge of her nightgown and led her off the tracks. We descended the embankment in bare feet, ending up, as I knew we would, in the pincushion of a thorn bush.

The train moved past as soon as we reached bottom. The engineer's window was lit up, and I waved to attract his attention. The horn sounded again, deeper, louder, pushed down the track as the train went by, pulling a long string of gondolas heaped black with coal. The wheels clacked like hammers, making little Ursie hold her ears.

I held my ears, too.

Our mother looked perturbed, indignant at losing right—or is it rite?—of passage to something so large and long and unstoppable as a train.

It must have been the engineer who radioed the police. By the time we reached the intersection where the gates had been lowered, two police cruisers were waiting with their lights on, rotating beams of red and blue.

"Pretty," my sister remarked.

"Very pretty," I agreed. "Like Christmas."

Our mother seemed attracted like a moth to the lights, but the police were interested in meeting her halfway, just to be sure she was led to one of the cruisers.

Ursie and I were placed in the backseat of another.

A policeman sat in the front seat behind a cage. He seemed as big as a bear, and so I thought of him as I would an animal in a zoo. He was the one who was trapped, not us.

But he gave us candy—passing it through a rectangular space in the cage—small squares of a Nestle bar. And hot chocolate that he poured out of a thermos. My sister and I shared the plastic cup that also served as its lid. I wondered about the hot chocolate. It seemed strange that a man his age would be drinking it. But maybe it was his job to be on the lookout for little kids on the loose at night. And so I thought we shouldn't drink it all, in case he found other children being led astray by their parents.

———

After our mother's sleepwalking incident, a woman came to visit. She was middle-aged, somewhat squat, as though she worked out with barbells in her spare time, but pretty with a thin smile and a cold, calculating eye that made me think the smile wasn't genuine. She interviewed us separately—Ursie first, then me—at the kitchen table with our parents out of the room. At least, "interview" was the word she happened to use. I wasn't quite sure what "interview" meant at the time. It hadn't been on the vocabulary list for second grade. To me, it seemed we were only having a friendly talk.

She asked a lot of questions about my mother and father, and about my mother and father together, and about Ursie and how they treated her, and what I liked to play with, and if I had imaginary playmates, and if there were any places on my body that hurt or that I was afraid to show her. And then she wanted to know if there was anything I wanted to share with her, and I told her there was half a baloney sandwich in the refrigerator my mother had put away for later because I hadn't eaten all my lunch and she was welcome to it, if she liked baloney, because I wasn't too keen on it really.

With everything I said, she made little scribbles in a notebook she held at an angle so I couldn't see what she was writing. She made one final checkmark with her pencil, and that concluded the interview with a snap of her notebook.

After she left, my parents took charge of Ursie and me in the living room.

"What did you tell her?" my mother wanted to know.

"Tell us what you told her," my father insisted.

They both seemed very worried.

I tried to give them encouragement. I told them about my offer of the half-eaten baloney sandwich.

My mother smiled at this and ruffled my hair. I was subjected to a lot of hair ruffling in those days.

Chapter 4

At nights, my father took to sleeping in an easy-chair recliner near the front door. It was a type of guard duty. He thought he could prevent my mother escaping the house in her dreams.

"Daddy? What about the back door?" I asked him one evening as he leafed through the newspaper.

I was still young enough to call him "Daddy." "Dad" would come in a few years. Ursula—their Little Bear, as our parents liked to call her—was still sleeping in a crib in the room I shared with her, like a cub in a cage, even though she had outgrown it the year before. Apparently, my parents couldn't afford her a bed of her own. As a night watchman, she would be of no use at all.

My father turned a couple of pages without answering. He was the type of father who was slow to answer. It was obvious he hadn't given much thought to the back door.

My family had moved into a small house next to a fast-food restaurant the year before. The drive-thru was right outside my bedroom window. All night long, I heard the loudspeaker, squawking like a mynah bird: "Welcome to Burger Daddy, can I take your order?" And then I would hear the customers try to make up their minds or change their order or ask what comes with the combo. This was only during the summer with my window open to let in the breeze. My mother put a ban on air conditioning. She claimed she was allergic to recycled air.

In winter, with the window closed, it wasn't so bad. The voices sounded muffled, as though wrapped in scarves—and maybe they were. In any case, Ursie never complained. It's possible that her crib, positioned against the far wall to avoid drafts, was out of range of her hearing. I never tested it to hear for myself.

The drive-thru, named in honor of the restaurateur's deceased father, who had left her enough money to start her own franchise, was the first of its kind in our town. It was a sensation that drew in long lines of cars just for the novelty of it.

"Did you know the first drive-thru restaurant with an intercom opened in 1948?" I tell my therapist, just to preempt her conducting a Google search on her phone with which to correct my narrative.

My therapist is young, mid-twenties, approximately 30 years my junior: Gen-Z to my Gen-X, with a whole generation of Millennials in-between. She is small and petite, swallowed up in her cushion chair across the room. She wears her hair short, a tidy bob around her ears with bangs cut straight across her eyebrows. It's her eyebrows that are her most distinctive feature. They are Frida Kahlo eyebrows, as they appear in the great painter's self-portraits, thick and dark. They furrow and arch like a drawbridge, narrowing or widening the space between, as though to constrict or permit the passage of her thoughts. I admit it is her eyebrows and not her eyes that I focus upon during our sessions.

One other thing you should know: she is always in possession of her phone. It is omnipresent. She claims her intermittent flourish of thumbs is her way of taking notes in lieu of pen and paper, but I can't help suspecting ulterior motives: texting, Instagramming, playing Candy Crush. *This should annoy me, but it doesn't, mainly because she is always attentive, quick to pounce on any part of my memory that doesn't jibe with her notion of objective reality. These reality checks are like life buoys, tossed to a drowning man. At times, though, they feel more like anchors.*

"It's only temporary," my father would say to forestall any complaint. "We'll move somewhere else soon." I wasn't complaining, though. To me, at that age, my father *was* the Burger Daddy—a man who would take the family out for hamburgers once a week as a special treat. Of course, he didn't have to take us very far.

Our house was one of those shoebox-size houses on a slab of cement that were built after World War II to house ex-GIs and their families on the cheap.

Aside from the two bedrooms, there was a living room with just enough space for my parents to sway in a tight circle to their favorite song that had been the soundtrack to their "first dance" at their wedding: "A Whiter Shade of Pale," which always made me wonder just what color that could possibly be. There was an adjoining kitchen with enough elbow room to throw plates at each other across the table. It just depended on their mood whether they danced or fought. Tight finances, I observed at a very young age, can do that to a couple, make them blissful romantics one moment, furious contenders the next.

The drive-thru loudspeaker worked its way into my dreams each night. Many of my dreams were of being welcomed into strange worlds: "Welcome to …" Some worlds were wonderful, made of cotton candy and ribbons of red licorice. Some looked like Disney World, although I had never been there, and doubted I would ever have an opportunity to go, given the state of my parents' finances. Still, in my dreams, Mickey or Pluto was always there to greet me.

Other worlds weren't so inviting. They were nightmares with crooked entrance signs affixed to leaning posts with rusting nails. Old men pushed wheelbarrows down dark paths through graveyards collecting bones that lay out in the open under an orange moon encircled with bats.

I would wake up in heaving sweats, hollering for my mother. She used to bring me a glass of milk and a square of chocolate to help me go back to sleep. My father was usually at work already. He worked early hours to be there when the truckload of fish arrived so as to tackle it fresh. He would have approved of the chocolates, I think. He was very lenient that way.

My father was an ichthyologist. At least, that's what he liked to call himself in funny moments. He had gone to a community college for two years and earned an associate's degree in natural resource management. He had been the first in his family to attend college, a fact he brought out in the open from time to time as though polishing a pocket watch. It wasn't that his family was poor. They just weren't that interested in higher education. If colleges offered courses in drag racing, moonshining, lottery playing, and general horsing around, all of his brothers and sisters—my aunts and uncles—would have attended, I'm sure. He came from a small town along the West Virginia side of the Ohio River, and most of the men and a few of the women worked in, near, or for a coal mine.

"The smartest fish cutter this side of the state line." This is how my mother referred to him in company, sometimes with a comradely nudge, other times with a snide raising of her lip, so I never knew if her joke was meant to please or offend—possibly both. This was after he lost his job with the Department of Natural Resources and ended up working behind the seafood counter of the large supermarket that had opened on the outskirts of town. Budget cuts, he was told.

And so we stepped down—not a big step, but a step nonetheless. And it seemed we started descending a ladder one rung at a time ever since.

———

Voluntarily, I began sleeping at the back door—even though I missed being able to hear the drive-thru loudspeaker—just in case my mother tried to escape through this exit. My father didn't know about my vigils. If he had, I'm sure he would have sent me back to my room. Or else he might have set up a cot. He did neither, so I doubt he knew.

My father had changed the locks and kept the keys to both front door and back in his possession. Locking the doors, I should add, seemed a strange precaution, since we lived in a town that generally left its doors unlatched day and night. The crime rate for burglary was low enough to let people think themselves safe. A handgun in a nightstand or a rifle under the bed was considered all the protection one needed.

The only loophole in the arrangement was that my mother discovered the keys' hiding place—in a potted fern that hung from the ceiling in front of a south-facing window in the kitchen. It's possible the fern got too much sunlight, because it had become a brown, shriveled thing that my sister and I both felt sorry for. I named it Pete, and he became a sort of scapegoat for my private woes. Whenever something wasn't going right in my life—a poor report card, a rap on my knuckles with a ruler at school, a forgetful Tooth Fairy—at least I could say, "No worse off than Pete." Pete hung around, literally, for years, until the last of his strands of tiny leaves withered away and my mother threw him out. But, at the moment, he was the guardian of the keys.

Why didn't my father simply keep the keys on his person? His explanation, after the fact, was simple: his pajamas lacked pockets.

So every night for I don't know how long a period—possibly weeks—I would take my pillow and blanket and curl up near the back door on a bench in the mudroom. It was a small room off the kitchen—with a washer scrunched in a corner with hoses and spigots, and a bench lining the other wall with a row of brass hooks from which jackets and scarves were hung, waiting to make sure that spring had arrived to stay. The bench was hard, but I endured its hardness, enjoying the peacefulness of nights spent in relative solitude, sleeping in what I came to think of as a room of my own.

It was the noises of the night that took getting used to, however. I could no longer hear the drive-thru speaker. Or if I did, it sounded more distant, more muffled, than usual—a low garble of sound that could have been pebbles sliding through a cardboard tube.

I could hear my father snoring from the living room, so loudly at times he woke himself up with a snort. Then a rustling sound as of a bird settling into its nest.

From our bedroom. I could still hear Ursie turning fitfully in her crib, the mattress squeaking as she rolled this way and that. She rarely woke, but at times, she cried out for her "Mama." At other times, she broke into laughter, and I wondered what sort of dreams went through her head that she found so amusing.

As I lay there, I timed my heartbeats to the ticking of my watch. It was a vintage 1955 Davy Crockett wristwatch that had been my dad's when he was a kid. His passing it down to me as a gift on my eighth birthday that January had seemed an occasion of supreme importance. It had a picture of the frontiersman wearing his coonskin hat and perpetually aiming his rifle at 2 o'clock. Amazingly, it still told the correct time two months later, with Ursie about to turn four years old.

Any other watch I had worn would have stopped telling time by now because I would forget to keep it wound. But the Davy Crockett I remembered to wind daily, turning the tiny, ratcheted knob back and forth, back and forth, until it felt tight, but not too tight. You didn't want to overwind it!

I would hold my watch next to my ear and feel my pulse with my thumb. Eventually, my heart would either slow down or speed up to match the tick-tick-tick of each second. I considered this a perfect heartbeat: sixty beats a minute. One beat per second. It seemed an important goal to attain, and I was happy when I attained it. It gave me a feeling of control.

If I could control the beating of my heart, I reasoned I ought to be able to control my thoughts. They were worrisome, fearful, fretful thoughts—full of envy and spite. I imagined my classmates must be leading better lives. Their families must be better off than mine, their parents more normal—saner. They would be sleeping in their beds, not on a hard wooden bench in the mudroom.

My therapist believes this is a feeling I have superimposed on this episode from a later period in life. It's the kind of attitude more likely to be that of an alienated adolescent than an anxiety-ridden second-grader. Nevertheless, I know I had this attitude at some point. It might as well be now, so I don't forget to record it later.

One night during my watch, I woke up to find the back door wide open, the wind blowing through with a chill that had frozen me in my sleep.

"Mommy?"

I was in my pajamas and bare feet. To find a robe and slippers, I would have had to go back to my bedroom, and I was afraid of losing her track. So I went out into the backyard. It was a small yard, bordered by a low wire fence that served no distinct purpose since we didn't own an animal that would need to be fenced in. To one side, there was the late-night drive-thru, but its loudspeaker was silent, its windows dark. On the other side was a house, small as ours, looking like an oversized milk carton in silhouette against a milky-white glow of streetlights that made the low-hanging sky a smothering quilt.

"Mommy?"

The back gate had been opened. I padded across mats of wet leaves left over from the previous autumn that my father kept promising to rake and crept into the narrow alleyway that ran behind our house. I looked in either direction and thought I saw her pink robe at the far end of the alley where it led to a small park. The other direction opened right away to a main thorough-fare where the streetlamps were brighter, and I didn't think these would attract her in her sleep—if she was, in fact, sleepwalking. So I chose the way that led through the park to the railroad tracks. I already knew she was magnetically attracted to rails.

Walking down the alley was a delicate matter of balance and judgment. The asphalt was all crumbly and broken, and with bare feet, it felt like walking on bits of broken glass. In one backyard, a dog followed along the fence until I reached the edge of the small, detached garage. There, it decided I was a threat and began barking. A light went on in a house, but I kept walking. It seemed to take an eternity to reach the park.

All it had going for it was a rusted-out merry-go-round that creaked when you pushed it, a rusted-out sliding board that stuck to your bottom whenever you tried to slide down it, and a swing-set with rusted-out chains. And this is where I found her, sitting on a swing, pulling on the chains and leaning back, staring up at the sky.

"Mommy?"

She turned her head slowly, then sat up straighter in the swing. Unlike me, she wore a robe and slippers. Her hair was down around her shoulders. Usually, she kept it in curlers over-night.

"Jeremy? What are you doing here?"

I took a seat on the swing beside her.

"Looking for you," I answered truthfully. "What are you do-ing here?"

"Dreaming," she said, dreamily. She started swinging back and forth, pushing off with her feet.

"Mommy? Are you still asleep?"

"Oh, no," she said. "I'm awake."

"But don't you need to be asleep to dream?"

"This is a different kind of dreaming," she answered. "It's the kind you do when you're awake."

"Oh," I said, thinking about this as I would any new concept.

"I was waiting for the stars," she said, leaning back in the swing again. "I thought maybe the stars would come out tonight. This is the best place for looking at them. The sky is always so dark through the trees."

I looked up at the opening in the trees above our heads. The clouds were still low and thick.

"I don't think there will be any stars tonight."

"No," she said, slowing down, letting her feet dangle. Then: "Look at you! Out and about without a coat or shoes."

She got out of the swing. She took off her robe and put it around my shoulders. Then she removed her slippers and placed them on my feet as I sat on the swing.

"I was worried," I said.

"You shouldn't be," she said. "I've thought of something so you won't have to worry anymore."

She lifted me up in her arms.

"My, my, you're getting so heavy," she said. "How much do you weigh now?"

"Fifty-eight pounds, don't you remember?" The family doctor had just weighed me the week before for my annual checkup.

"Come on, let me carry you back, before you catch cold."

She was right about the cold. I woke up with one the next morning. It kept me out of school that day. I didn't mind not going, though. Usually, whenever I was sick, my mother had to take off working at the library. But this time, she didn't have to call in, and when I asked her about it, all she did was smile as she sponged my forehead with a wet washcloth.

In the evening, it was my father who put me to bed, who took my temperature one last time, who gave me a dose of pink medicine that tasted like bitter cherries.

"Where's Mommy?" I asked.

Was it this night that I found out? Or some other night? In my memory, it was this very night that I heard her voice, lulling me to sleep from outside the window. Or trying to lull me to sleep. Her voice, sweet as it was in person, was edged with static from the loudspeaker of the drive-thru.

"Go to sleep, little Jeremy," she crooned, as though into a microphone on a stage. It was a song she had made up years before. She hadn't sung it in a long time, but now it came to me through the pane of the single window in my room, closed against a nighttime chill. Instead of putting me to sleep, it woke me up with a start. I leapt to the window and raised it until it got stuck, as usual, about an inch from the sill. Across the yard, I could see her in the drive-thru window.

She smiled in recognition.

"Go to sleep little Jeremy," she continued to sing through the loudspeaker. "Go to sleep my little dear."

She gave a slight wave, and I waved back.

And then a car pulled up, and the song cut off as though lifted from a turntable with a jerk.

"Welcome to Burger Daddy," she said into her headset. "Can I take your order?"

A man with a mustache and white food-service cap of the kind my mother was wearing came up behind her in the drive-thru window. I found out later it was her manager when she introduced him to me one Saturday when our father took us there for dinner. He coached her on ringing up the order that came back at her through the loudspeaker. She was in the process of being trained. It was her first night of work at her new job.

Chapter 5

When our mother started doing hospice work, she made us dress up in Sunday clothes even if it wasn't Sunday—and it usually wasn't.

For Ursula, it wasn't so bad. She was still only four and looked oh so cute with her long blonde hair done up in a bow and clad in dresses (she preferred dresses to shorts) that came down to her knees, mostly plaids—the dresses, not her knees. Our father had a new job as a traveling salesman. He worked a regional route that took him through most of southeastern Ohio and even into West Virginia, which always seemed like forbidden territory, somehow, as it lay on the other side of the river. (Our town was too small to deserve its own bridge except for the railroad trestle.)

We were still a one-car family, so we had to walk to wherever our mother was assigned that day. This gave any number of passersby—generally retirees taking their walk around the block—opportunity to ooh and ahh over my sister. I must say, she ate up the attention as though she were stuffing her mouth with jellybeans. She liked being a star from an early age.

I, on the other hand, wasn't so lucky. In our town, you either lived in the seedier, cheaper top-of-the-hill neighborhoods, or the nicer, posh neighborhoods at the bottom of the hill in the old part of town along the river. We lived at the top of the hill. Our destination was at the bottom. Our town was too small to support actual gangs, but each rectangular block was ruled by a bully—sometimes more than just one. And there were at least twelve blocks we had to traverse, which meant keeping a wary eye out for neighborhood toughs. So on these walks with our mother on her hospice visits, I tried to shrink down as low as I could by scrunching my shoulders and bending my knees and curving my spine, wishing I could be magically transformed into something as impervious to physical harm as a turtle.

Alas, it was no use. I was bound to be noticed if only because of the clothes I was forced to wear—Sunday clothes, as I mentioned. Picture a prim and proper eight-year-old wearing a short-sleeved white shirt with black polka dots and a striped clip-on tie and black dress shoes polished to a sheen. My shoes weren't the only things that were shiny. Before going out, my mother always applied a generous amount of gel squirted out of a gray bottle that was meant to resemble a rocket ship with a pointed yellow nozzle for a cone. Then she would slick my hair away from my forehead in a loop that within minutes was cemented in place so as not to be ruffled by the strongest of breezes.

As soon as we stepped out, there would be a couple of boys across the street who would spot me and point. They would follow me, as I walked with my mother and sister, down our street and around the corner and down another street until we left their block behind. But a strange thing would happen. Instead of stopping at the boundary of their block and returning to whatever they were doing, they would keep walking. And, as we entered new and, to me, unfamiliar territory, they would be joined by another couple of boys from the next block over. And so on, block after block, as we descended the hill into the more historic part of town and reached our destination, by which time we had quite a posse of kids trailing us only a few yards behind.

Ordinarily, top-of-the-hill and bottom-of-the-hill neighborhoods were separated by wealth and class, as well as the main street (called, appropriately, Main Street) paralleling the Ohio River that functioned as a boundary. However, I discovered I was the lowest common denominator, as in a math problem, capable of binding the rival bullies and toughs and roughnecks of all walks of life together in a common cause.

What was the cause? you ask.

Simple harassment.

They took turns pelting me with pebbles, clods of dirt, chips of sidewalk cement, crabapples—anything handy that would serve as a projectile. One kid would sneak up and blast my back with a pressurized squirt gun that soaked my dress shirt with the force of a cannon until the water ran out.

"Did you know the 'Super Soaker' was the first of its kind?" my therapist interrupts me with the instantaneous result of a Google search. "It didn't hit the stores until 1990, when it was first known as the 'Power Drencher.'"

"I stand corrected," I reply somewhat peevishly. "Whatever it was, it drenched me. It still felt ice cold down my back."

The attacks were intermittent and subtle enough for my mother not to notice. I found myself zigzagging like a nervous gosling in her wake, but my attempts at evasion only added a level of competitiveness to their game. Bets were made as to accuracy. Stakes were raised as to body parts called out and hit. Muted fights broke out over the type of projectile used. My mother seemed oblivious. She sauntered along, hand clutching her small white purse, hem of her skirt fluttering like a flag with the briskness of her steps, eyes straight ahead, focused on her destination.

Sticks and stones can break bones, as the saying goes, but names really can hurt. Outside my mother's range of hearing, they took turns hurling insults in my direction: *nerd, dork, putz, fag.* Initially, I made the mistake of turning my head, which brought on the comeback line of "Made you look!" followed by a burst of laughter.

To ask for my mother's help would have meant outright ridicule. To stop, turn, and confront the herd of boys would have meant certain annihilation. I had no choice but to keep moving.

Unfortunately, on the very first day of her hospice duty, she thought it would be a good idea for Ursie and me to remain outdoors, since the weather was unusually sunny and calm for a Saturday morning in April with large cumulus slowly drifting like sails through an aquamarine sea.

"See what shapes you can make out of the clouds," our mother suggested, turning at the threshold while waiting for someone to answer the doorbell.

"But, Mom," I protested, feebly, half-turning to bring into my peripheral vision the horde of Huns and Mongols that had assembled in a fan-shaped formation behind me.

"Oh, don't be silly," our mother scolded, gently. "It's simply too nice to come inside. Besides, there wouldn't be anything for you to do, I'm sure. So be a good boy and take good care of your sister. See? You even have boys your age to play with."

And with that, I was physically turned around like a puppet to face my audience of sneering, jeering, leering kids. Not all were bullies, I should mention. Many were merely spectators. In any case, my mother prodded me down the front steps the way she would a wind-up toy to set it in motion. And so, taking Ursie by the hand, I slowly walked down the steps to meet my doom.

As soon as the door closed behind her entrance, my adversaries surrounded me, hemming me in like the Persians did the Spartans at Thermopylae, which I wouldn't learn about until high school. Little as I knew about military strategy, I could see quite clearly that I was not only outnumbered but outflanked.

Most wore holey jeans and grungy tees. Some were missing teeth—naturally or through internecine warfare I couldn't say.

Several were mashing the fist of one hand into the palm of another in the way Pueblos grind corn with mortar and pestle.

What could I do in such a situation? What would anyone do?

Instinctively, I took the offensive, taking one step downward to ground level.

"So, what do you fellows want to play?"

"Play?" one of the Mongols sneered. "Did you say 'play'?"

"Yeah, you know, like tag, hide-and-seek, capture the flag?"

"Capture the flag would be fun," my sister said from behind. I wasn't sure how she knew about "capture the flag." I doubt she had ever played it.

"Listen to this," another Mongol said, "Mama's Boy here wants to play."

"I have a game he would like," another suggested, although I didn't take this as a positive direction in our discourse, even though he and his group were better dressed than the others in Izods and Chinos. I felt I was losing my tenuous upper hand.

"Sure, how 'bout Ring Around the Rosie?" one of his comrades agreed through some sort of gang osmosis.

"Yes, yes," Ursie cheered, jumping up and down, clapping her hands, and starting to sing, "Ring around the Rosie, pocket full of posies ..."

As she sang, the larger and tougher kids closed the circle around me and began pushing me from one part of the circle to another. My sister was safely outside the perimeter, as I was batted around.

Eventually, they all grew bored and wandered off, breaking into their separate groups and going their separate directions.

I was lying on my back, staring up at the sky, trying to make the clouds stop spinning first clockwise, then counterclockwise.

My sister's face hovered into view with wide blue eyes.

"That was a pretty rough game," was her comment.

I reached up a hand.

"Help me up," I beckoned, although I knew, being twice her age and weight, I couldn't expect much assistance. Still, her small hand tugging my fingers was the encouragement I needed.

At that point, our mother emerged from the house, the door closing behind her.

"Oh, that Mrs. Darnell," she said, "such a nice woman, and so very, very Christian. She—oh, my Lord, Jeremy, what happened to you?"

I must have looked a sight. My dress pants were torn at the knees, my underwear was pulled up above my belt line, my shoes were scuffed—one of them lay beside me, the other I held to my ear like a telephone receiver—plus I could feel a wound on my forehead oozing blood and a patch of my hair had been scalped.

"You need to learn to take better care of yourself," she lectured me on the way home, after it was determined I was able to walk. "If only your father were around more often to teach you how."

But our father was who knew where, selling who knew what, out of the trunk of the family car.

It wasn't until we were halfway home that I realized my beloved Davy Crockett watch was missing—lost in the scuffle or stolen. I was never to see it again.

Chapter 6

Fortunately, we entered a rainy spell that last two weeks. I discovered that, mean as they are, bullies are often repelled by rain. But not so my mother. I begged her not to dress me up in my Sunday best. It was only Wednesday, for Heaven's sake! But did she listen to my pleas? She was as deaf as God, who never did grant my prayer for a new three-speed bike with high-rise handlebars with hand brakes and a banana seat.

All the way to Mrs. Darnell's, I kept looking over my shoulder, watching my back, as it were. But our only entanglement was when, arriving at the front steps, our mother caught strands of Ursula's hair as she folded the umbrella.

She got to her knees, to work out the tangle.

"I'm so sorry, dear. Here, let me—"

"Mommy, no! You're making it worse!"

"Yes, I can see that, but if you were just to hold still. It's the last thing I want to do is hurt you."

My sister thought about this for a moment as her hair was being unbraided from the metal ribs of the umbrella.

"You mean, you want to hurt me?" she asked, working it out in her mind.

"Of course not, dear. I wouldn't want to hurt you."

"But you just said hurting me was the last thing you wanted to do."

"That's right."

"So you want to hurt me last?"

"No, no. That's not how it works, my Li'l Bear."

And here she gave her a hug with the rain pouring even harder. I wanted to point out that no one had yet rung the bell and we were now all three of us getting as wet as herrings in sauce—which was a delicacy of Dad's, in fact.

"But you said—"

"Well, I know that's how it sounded. Oh, Jeremy, you explain it to her, won't you?"

Our mother rang the bell, and before I could untwist my sister's logic, the door opened with that slow, sinister, creaking noise you hear in horror movies.

The man who answered the door was tall—very tall. I craned my neck to look up at him the way I would tall buildings whenever we visited a city like Pittsburgh or Cincinnati, which was practically never. He had a terrifically wide forehead, embellished by a wave of thick black hair cemented in place the way mine was. He wore thick, black-framed glasses and had a hesitant way of smiling, as though he needed more practice with levity.

We soon found out that this wasn't the butler, as I suspected, but rather the dying woman's grown son, Walter, who had moved back home. The reasons were murky, but they had something to do with a nervous breakdown he experienced in California while working for Howard Hughes. I wondered if he worked for him personally, but my father, who always had an explanation for everything, said no, when I mentioned this facet of his resume. It must have been only one of Howard Hughes's subsidiary companies.

I'm guessing my father felt in competition with other men who had better educations or actually worked in the fields for which they were trained.

"Besides, by that point, he'd been dead for two years," my therapist informs me, producing the date of the eccentric millionaire's demise literally from her fingertips with a swipe of her phone "So your dad was probably onto something."

"Enough about my father," I tell her, admittedly somewhat testily. "Let's go back to Walter."

Walter was an odd case. He treated my sister and me as equals but not because he raised us to his level and acted as though we were little adults. Instead, he stooped down to our level and acted like a small child. He found everything about us fascinating, from my sister's Barbie doll to a secret decoder ring I had fished out of a cereal box and showed him how to use.

The house was enormous. The foyer ceiling rose to a dizzying height. Immediately, one suspected dozens of rooms and passageways, as we were led up a double flight of stairs with a wooden banister. On the second floor, we were led down a hallway and told to sit on a small bench against a papered wall.

"Do you like marbles?" Walter asked when he caught up with us, our mother forging ahead. "I have marbles if you like to play."

I didn't have any objection to marbles.

"There's a physics to marbles," he went on, shifting his voice so it sounded more adult. Apparently, he had been a brilliant engineer, and I could believe it, listening to him discourse about marbles. "It's in the angles," he explained. "You need to take into account the angle of incidence in combination with the angular momentum of the marble's spin when you're aiming your shooter, which, by the way, is one-eighth inch larger in diameter than the other marbles. You shoot from the pitch line, which is a line drawn tangential to the ring, and the object is to shoot your marble toward the lag line …"

And so it went on and on. I discovered when you got Walter on any subject involving mathematical formulas or geometric principles, it was hard to get him to stop. I kept wondering where his "off" button was located.

Our mother had ordered us to stay put, while she went to attend to Mrs. Darnell, but she soon returned and gently prodded Walter away from us.

"Walter, your mother wishes you to remain in the study while the children are here."

This was said so formally, so slowly, each syllable so impeccably accented, that I wondered what sort of schoolmarm spirit had temporarily taken over her body.

Walter rose and gave us a meek, crooked smile before shuffling down the hall toward the staircase.

And this is how it generally unfolded, visit after visit, two visits a week.

On sunny, pleasant days, we waited outside, fending off harassment by the amalgamated gang of neighborhood toughs, although, little by little, I was starting to win them over. At least, I was getting less beat up and bruised by the end of an hour's session. Sometimes, we played kickball, other times tag. More often, we crouched behind bushes and threw crabapples at passing cars. My sister was a particularly accurate shot, winning accolades from the toughest of the bullies.

My aim was terrible, as usual. After one dismal performance of my projectile skills, a gang member remarked that I couldn't hit the broad side of a barn. I was thankful there weren't any barns around to prove the point, until one of the kids, a small boy named Squeaky—too small to be anything more than an apprentice bully, a tough in training—piped up with an ironically baritone voice, "A garage would do, just as well." So I was herded toward the back of Mrs. Darnell's house—which was a very big house—and made to face the doors of her garage—which was proportional in size to the house. In fact, the garage was somewhat larger than my family's own domicile. I was handed three rocks and ordered to fling them one at a time at the garage.

"Rocks?" I queried. "Can't we stick with crabapples?"

"Crabapples are for sissies," one bully pointed out.

"Yeah," my little sister repeated, "crabapples are for sissies."

I wasn't sure I appreciated her lack of support.

In any case, I took aim and was both elated and horrified to see my rock crash through a garage-door window. I crept up to the shattered glass and peered inside on tip-toe to see what further damage the rock had caused in its descent, but it was too dim to make out anything except the hulk of a sedan with an indistinct color that might have been black, gray, green, blue, or brown.

"Nice shot," Squeaky said with his gravelly voice.

"Yeah, nice shot, bro," Ursie added.

But when I turned around to accept further compliments, I discovered all of the boys—even Squeaky, whom I was starting to consider a friend—had fled, and only my sister—whom I was starting to suspect of being a secret honorary member of the bullies—well, only she remained.

"Boy," she said, "are you going to be in trouble."

"Not if we don't say anything," I told her.

"What'll you give me? A quarter?"

"Sure, a quarter."

"How about two quarters? I'll keep quiet for two."

"Okay, two."

Now I just had to save my allowance for two whole weeks to replenish the two whole quarters I had handed over to my sister. It was 1978. My allowance hadn't caught up with the inflation rate yet. A quarter was still considered adequate compensation for helping with the garbage and the dishes (we didn't have a dishwasher—almost no one in our income bracket did) and the laundry (which involved hanging up clothes, since we didn't have a dryer).

But at least my sister kept her mouth shut.

Chapter 7

Forget disco. Forget bell-bottoms. Forget lava lamps or mood rings or pet rocks. For me, the '70s were about attending Sunday school and church service right after. Once a month, the Lord's Supper unsettled me with its vague threat of cannibalism and vampirism, making me thankful I was too young to partake. My mother assured me it had nothing to do with actually eating the Lord's body or drinking His blood—that they only turned into flesh and fluid for Catholics. Our father remained silent on the subject. I think he attended church only out of courtesy to our mother. He never had anything of substance to contribute toward our religious education.

Except when one of my Sunday school teachers was killed. This was a young man with long hair tied back in a ponytail who asked us questions about what we thought was true about God, Jesus, the Bible, Adam and Eve. He challenged us to think through contradictions and paradoxes—although he didn't actually use those terms. The class was only for second-graders, after all. But I do remember him discussing free will and whether everything we did in life was predestined. To protest this notion, he raised his fist and shook it at the ceiling, talking directly to the Almighty in threatening terms: "Let's settle this once and for all. Do you have it all planned out or don't you?"

Of course, there wasn't an answer, but two weeks later, he was killed in an auto accident when his Volkswagen Beetle spun off the road in a hailstorm at night and crashed through a guardrail, plunging headlong into a gorge.

"Let that be a lesson to you," our mother said on our way home from the funeral, addressing me directly, confined as I was by a seat belt in the back seat. "There's no challenging God's will."

"Oh, for Christ's sake," our father said suddenly out of the side of his mouth, "would you stop all this lecturing about God's will? What do you know about what God wants or doesn't want anyway?"

Our mother didn't appear offended—just obstinate, her lips compressing as though she had braced herself against this onslaught before.

"I know what I know," our mother said, "God's will is final. There's no changing it."

"Yes, and if the poor guy had survived, you would have said that was God's will, too, and what a miracle it was that God saved him from death."

"But he didn't," our mother was quick to point out. "He didn't save him. It was God's will that He didn't."

"But you always have it both ways," our father persisted, "so you always come out ahead. It's rigged so that you always come out on the right side of God. A tornado sweeps through a neighborhood, leveling houses, and that's supposed to be God's will. That same tornado goes on to narrowly miss another neighborhood, and that's God's will too."

"God picks and chooses whom to spare and whom to save," our mother said calmly.

But it was clear our father was perturbed. He tended to speed up the car when perturbed, and then the conversation would change as abruptly as the shift from third to fourth gear.

"Slow down, Henry! You're going to kill us all!"

"Not if it's God's will that I don't," our father said, rebuffing her. At this point, he surprised us all by letting go of the steering wheel.

"Henry, for God's sake, what are you doing?"

"God's *wheel*," our father said. I should mention he was fond of puns—especially at the most inappropriate moments.

"God's what?!"

"If it's God's 'wheel' we should get home in one piece, I'm sure he'll do the steering for us."

Our mother made a move to grab the wheel, but our father was too quick to grasp her forearm. We were driving along a two-lane highway past farm fields.

"Henry, have you lost your mind?"

"Free wheel or God's wheel," our father replied, somewhat calmly given the circumstances. "You can't have it both ways."

"All right, all right," our mother relented, as the car veered left of center toward a ditch reminiscent of the one that had catapulted our family sedan into a cow pasture. "Have it your way."

Our father brought the car back into its proper lane—but without using his hands. And then I saw his trick. Our mother noticed it too. He had been guiding the car all along with upraised knees pressed against the steering column.

"Oh, Henry, you're impossible!" Our mother slapped him hard on the shoulder—hard enough to make him wince. "Playing your little game and scaring the children like that." She turned back to consider the children. "Wasn't that not so very nice of your father, scaring you so?"

Ursie seemed anything but terrified.

"Cows!" she said, turning her head toward a pasture.

I was too petrified to know if I had been frightened.

"Speaking of petrified," my therapist interjects. "You may not believe this, but when I was younger, I had a pet rock."

"You're right," I remark with a grin, egging her on, "I don't. A little before your time, wasn't it?"

"It was my mom's actually, from when she was a girl. She passed it down to me. It was still in its original box with airholes and a bed of straw.

I redecorated her with googly eyes and purple hair and took her on walks and ..."

"Her?"

"Oh," she says, her cheeks darkening into a blush. "I gave her a name: Shirley."

"Sounds like you were pretty close."

Her face takes on a perplexed frown. "Now that I think of it, I wonder what ever happened to her." She gives her shoulders a shrug. "Ah well, knowing my mother, she probably gave her away at a yard sale."

"Do you want to talk about it?" I ask, putting on a deadpan face of my own. "That kind of loss—it must be devastating."

"I think I'll be all right," my therapist responds with a smile. "Now where were we? Talking about your father, weren't we?"

"Oh, right," I recall with reluctance. "My father."

———

As the summer progressed, he was gone for longer and longer stretches of time. At first, his sales trips took him away for overnights. He would pack up a small traveling case with shaving cream, aftershave lotion, razor, deodorant, and other sundries with just a change of underwear for the return journey.

I would watch him readying his face in the bathroom mirror. I had miniature versions of everything he packed except for the razor, although he had given me one without a blade for use in my pretend world of manhood. The miniature colognes and aftershaves came from the Fuller Brush Man—a dapper salesman in a frumpy suit and tie with a carrying case of samples—who would drop by unannounced about once a month. Only our mother was home to entertain him, which she did royally, because she rarely had anyone at the house to entertain, except for my sister and me. One way she entertained us was by opening the family Bible at random and picking out quotations by pointing to a page with her eyes closed. Thus, the idea of randomness was instilled in my still developing brain. We were supposed to extemporize on whatever verse her fingertip happened upon.

The contrast between my mother pointing out scripture and my father pointing out his sales route on a map seemed significant. My mother used a delicately trimmed and self-manicured fingernail, painted typically a rosy pink, whereas my father bluntly traced red and black lines of highways and county roads with his middle finger. Was this done purposely? Was it some secret signal? I wouldn't become aware of the usefulness of the middle finger for gesturing, especially in traffic, for a number of years. So if there was some arcane message my father was trying to convey, it was lost on me. Usually, I was the only one in the family interested to see where he was going.

We were aware of our father's bouts of anger, but we weren't sure what he was angry at—only that he was angry. He took out his anger in a peculiar way, by clipping the small hedge that lined one side of the walkway to our front door. Whenever he needed to let off excess emotion, he would grab the shears and start snipping. Eventually, the hedge began to take on attributes of a line of bonsai trees. Sometimes, he would be outside in the middle of the night, and I could hear him snipping away at the thing, taking an inch off the top in the way he would instruct our barber to do the same with my biweekly haircut.

Was it our mother's religiosity?

Or was it our family's worsening financial situation?

Or was it his lack of success as a salesman?

Remember, we still didn't know what he was selling, only that he was bad at it.

"It's because you lack confidence in what you're selling," our mother chided him as gently as she could, rubbing her fingernails along his spine, which always made our father flinch, shrugging off the affection the way a dog might scrunch its shoulders at the persistence of a flea.

"I believe in what I'm selling," our father countered. "So, no, I don't think that's the problem. It's the buyers. They just aren't buying."

Our parents took their "discussion" into the living room, while my sister and I remained in the kitchen, where we emptied the metal lunch pails we used as carrying cases onto the linoleum and engaged in animal warfare of a most dangerous and violent sort. My sister's army comprised plastic zoo and farm animals: kangaroos, elephants, and cheetahs mingled freely with horses, cows, and goats. On my side of the battlefield I arranged plastic-molded dinosaurs and prehistoric beasts into columns and rows. Up front—the sacrificial pawns of my army—were dodos and duckbills and extinct crustaceans. Behind these, operating as artillery, was a rank of triceratops, ankylosaurs, and stegosaurs. Held in reserve was the fiercest cavalry I could assemble: allosaurs, T-rexes, and saber-toothed tigers.

We each took a turn rolling the die. The higher number was the first to initiate attack. In this case, it was my sister. She flung a wildebeest at my infantry, wiping out a brontosaurus and two giant ground sloths. What luck! My turn didn't inflict as much damage, I was sorry to see. All my triceratops did was flatten a penguin. Such is the fickleness of warfare. And so it went back and forth, until the last animal standing determined the winner. However, to the victor did not go the spoils. We simply packed the carnage away in our lunch pails to await another battle date.

This time, our battle was perfunctory. We were barely paying attention. All because we had one ear on the conversation in the living room.

"Did you ever think it might be you?" our mother said, using that same, gently prodding voice she would use to suggest, for instance, that I undertake a disagreeable chore.

"Me?" our father almost shouted. All right—he actually did shout. But it was a shout of surprise, not necessarily the anger that would drive him back out to the hedge.

"You need to believe in yourself, dear," our mother instructed. "It's the cardinal rule of selling. Always remember, it isn't the product, it's you, yourself, that you're selling to the customer."

Our father took a moment to digest this bit of advice. Even to my small ears, it sounded reasonable, although I wondered how our mother had come to have it to dispense. As far as I knew, she hadn't sold a thing in her life. Maybe she had learned it by interacting with the Fuller Brush Man or the Avon Lady, who also came by from time to time.

"My self," our father mumbled. "Sell my *self*." He grabbed his hat and suit coat from the rack and walked through the door, slowly, as though entranced, mumbling audibly, "My self. Of course. Selling my self."

Against all expectations, that evening he left the hedge alone. Which was just as well, since it had been whittled down by the middle of summer to a series of three-inch sticks like miniature trees in a model railroad. They looked like skeleton fingers pushing through the dirt—appendages designed to scare off would-be intruders or trip up the mailman.

The next morning, at breakfast, he had an announcement to make. We knew he was about to make an announcement because he coughed into his fist. If it had been a spontaneous cough, he wouldn't have brought his fist to his mouth, but would have turned his head into his sleeve.

"Honey," he said, abruptly, "I'm taking the kids."

This had the effect of leaving our mother gasping like a carp hauled out of water onto a dock.

"Henry, what on earth can you mean?"

"I'm taking them," he stated, looking our mother levelly in

the eyes. "I've decided."

Our mother put her foot down—by stamping her heel hard on the yellow-and-orange checkered linoleum of the kitchen floor.

"We're not getting a divorce," she stated, curling her fingers into fists. "A divorce is out of the question."

"I didn't say anything about a divorce." Our father looked confused, the way a beagle might study the closed hands of its owner to determine which one held the treat.

"Nor separated."

I liked our mother's use of "nor." I thought it showed a touch of sophistication. She was actually very well educated. She had taken a six-month business correspondence course that had earned her a mail-order certificate with gilt edges. Plus, she worked in the local library part-time, so she read a lot. Just because she worked at a drive-thru by night didn't mean a thing about her level of intelligence. I only mention this because within a few weeks of her working there, most of the neighborhood kids had driven through with their parents and figured out she was my mother. Oh, the teasing I endured because of this one small misstep in her resume.

"I haven't said a word about separation," our father complained, feeling no doubt under attack, as he was.

"Because we're getting neither separated nor divorced." There was that "nor" again. Our mother seemed adamant.

"Of course not," our father agreed. I could tell that part of the concern in his voice had to do with the state of his Cornflakes, which were becoming soggier by the moment. If there was one thing he hated in the world besides having to work for a living, it was soggy cereal.

"I don't care how miserable we are together." This was our mother cementing the argument. "We're stuck with each other till one of us keels over or kills the other."

"Agreed," our father said, stirring his cereal so as to retrieve any flakes that hadn't turned into mush.

It turned out the separation our father had in mind was only temporary. He wanted to take us on the road as an experiment, thinking our presence would provide the boost of confidence he needed.

"It's what you said," our father explained to our mother, "about selling myself. What am I if not a family man? And what better way to prove it than to bring the kids along?"

"But just as an experiment," our mother reminded him the next morning, as he ushered us out the back door to the carport. She gave us each a hug and a peck and let our father spirit us away on a sales trip that took us due north in the newly acquired family Thunderbird.

Chapter 8

Thunderbird—the very name suggested a spirit, a soaring hawk or eagle, scouring the countryside. And this is how it felt, cruising along in a car with a hood so long I couldn't see the road in front of us without raising myself in my seat. Now that my sister was old enough to dispense with a car seat, our father had traded in the old, staid, steady, reliable family sedan for something far more adventurous. In fact, he plopped me into the seat beside him, which, adding to my excitement of being allowed to sit up front, was a bucket seat, letting me imagine I was a copilot buckled into a spaceship on its way to the moon.

But our first stop was Zanesville, an hour north of the Ohio River.

Our father wasn't buckled. Despite the broken collarbone he had suffered from our family accident, he decided he still didn't believe in seatbelts. But our mother had made him promise to strap us in safe and snug. And so my sister, as much as she wanted, couldn't lean forward into the space between the bucket seats from her position in the back, sitting smack in the middle of a seat as big as our living-room couch.

"Put something new on the radio," she complained. "I don't like this song."

It wasn't the radio, but an 8-track. Our father believed in keeping up with technology.

"Elvis?" he asked in disbelief. "You mean to say you don't like Elvis? Whose child are you anyway?"

"Yours," my sister responded, innocently enough. "And Mommy's."

"Of course you are," our father assured her. "But if you're

going to remain my child, you cannot *not* like Elvis. At least, you've got to give him a try."

"You mean like green beans?" she asked.

Ursie had an aversion to anything green on her dinner plate.

"Especially green beans," our father said.

If our mother had Jesus, our father had Elvis.

Our mother kept expecting Jesus to roll out of the sky on a bed of cumulonimbus, lightning flashing, thunder roaring, all the better to wake the dead and start a new millennium after a short, earthshaking Apocalypse.

It was all very fuzzy to my mind. I was never sure what was supposed to happen first. Did the dead arise and only then did the Rapture occur? Or were all the saved souls mysteriously plucked from what they were doing into the loving arms of Jesus with the waking dead following behind, shaking a misty grogginess out of their heads?

Our father's vision was clearer.

It was the Second Coming of Elvis Presley that kept our father in a state of heightened anticipation. Although the King had allegedly died the year before, like Jesus, there was a distinct possibility he had been resurrected from the grave. Like other Elvis fans around the country, our father had an eye out for his apparition outside the environs of Graceland.

"You know there have been sightings as close as Kalamazoo," he informed us once.

Thus, we had Elvis entertaining us on the 8-track all the way up along the Muskingum River.

Elvis provided a counterpoint to the drone of our father's voice, as he went over and over how much fun we would have— just the three of us. How it would be an adventure, of the character-building sort. How it would toughen us up. How it would—

"Hey, here's one I'll bet even Ursie likes. It's got animals in it."

"Again?" Ursie complained, covering her ears.

"You ain't nothin' but a hound dog," our father began singing along, encouraging Ursie to join in through the rearview mirror.

"Why can't we get a rabbit?" Ursie asked when the song ended.

It was only the twelfth time he had played the song that morning and the eleventh time Ursie had asked the same question, but I was happy, whatever the rationale for our trip. Flying along in the Thunderbird, I felt truly spirited away, as though by magic, from my mother's routines, which, so far this summer, had only produced bruises from bullies and uncomfortable moments with Mrs. Darnell's son, Walter, crouched before my sister and me in the hall. I was glad to be free of all of them for the time being and privately wished our father would continue to keep us until school started.

What I hadn't counted on was that the Thunderbird would not only serve as our means of locomotion but as our motel room for the night.

"It's just one night," our father said.

We changed into our pajamas and brushed our teeth and "went potty," as my sister still called it, in a filthy restroom at a Sinclair gas station. The toilet seat was grimed with a rim of what looked like volcanic ash. The floor tiles were littered with scraps of toilet paper folded into so many shapes of origami. The sink embraced a whirlpool of dried prickles from the beards of men who had used the restroom to shave. And the mirror was smeared with swirls of petroleum jelly.

"This place stinks," I heard myself complaining.

And it did. It reeked with a combination of skunk oil and tapioca, which was the fragrance our father sprayed from a canister that had been provided on the sink top until there wasn't anything left but ordinary air and he threw it into the waste basket overflowing with paper towels.

For dinner, we ate bologna sandwiches with mustard out of a cooler. Dessert was two Oreos apiece.

"Isn't it funny we're eating dinner after we brushed our teeth?" I asked Ursie, and she nodded her head vigorously, still chewing a bite of her sandwich. Our father ignored my comment, preferring to stare out the window into a drizzle of rain that he chose to swipe away with a flick of the windshield wipers from time to time.

We had encamped at a wayside park off a narrow two-lane road in the country, with just enough gravel to create a parking space for our car. The park had a picnic table, a single large tree that I recognized as a maple, and a wire fence surrounding it on three sides to keep the rows of knee-high cornstalks at bay. The sky, low and folded in blankets of stratus, was a collapsing gray tent, the kind my sister and I often strung on a clothesline, pegging its four corners with clothespins in the back yard.

"Lights out," our father joked, when the grayness had changed into a darker gloom that resembled the edge of twilight.

Each of us had a pillow and blanket he had brought out of the trunk. My sister had her favorite stuffed animals in the back seat, and I had mine—a penguin and a squirrel—in the bucket seat that reclined with the push of a lever like a dentist's chair.

"Aren't you going to tell us a story?" Ursie asked plaintively. "Mommy always tells us a story."

"I'm not very good at stories," our father answered. "Just try to go to sleep."

But Ursie couldn't. She woke up five times, by my count, in the night, whimpering for her mommy. I crawled into the back seat to comfort her, while our father snored.

"Don't worry," I whispered. "It's like a vacation. That's all."

But I have to admit, I was already feeling homesick, too.

———

In the morning, we discovered why he had brought us along. But first, we had to get ready.

There was a rusty water pump at the roadside park, and while our father pumped the handle, Ursie and I took turns putting our heads under the cold water to wash our hair and faces. Then it was my turn to pump while our father did the same with his hair and face. I could see as he stooped low that his hair was starting to wear out around the crown of his head in the size of a silver dollar. I stared at it as though examining a strange phenomenon under a microscope.

We moved from the pump to an outhouse with a crescent moon in the door. For toilet paper, we had to use pages torn from an old Sears catalog from 1967, which made me think the outhouse wasn't used very often. My sister was afraid she would fall into the dark hole in the seat inside, so I had to stand guard with the door propped open while I stared the other way, having told her I would rescue her if I heard a significant plop.

After this, all that was left was getting dressed, which we did in the back seat of the Thunderbird, one at a time. Our father, however, took his clothes behind a tall hedge of junipers, and when he came back out, he was dressed in a suit and tie.

I recognized the tie. It was the one we had bought him for Father's Day.

He had selected our clothes to match the formality of his.

Ursie wore a pink dress with a pink ribbon in her hair.

I wore—uncomfortably, I should add—a short-sleeved dress shirt with my usual clip-on tie. If I had known beforehand that I was going to get this dressed up, I would have begged to stay home with our mother, who would have dressed me just the same for her hospice visits.

"Well," our father said, slicking down a stubborn lock of my hair with a dab of saliva, "ready to make our first house call?"

"House call?" Ursie wondered aloud. "What the heck are we? Doctors?"

This was back when you still might expect your family practitioner to visit you at home if you were sick.

"Don't say 'heck,'" our father advised. "It isn't ladylike."

I have to admit, the same thought crossed my mind, as well.

After two house calls, it became obvious that my presence wasn't needed. The women—there were always one older and one younger, a mother-daughter combination—would invariably ooh and aah over Ursula as though she were a delicate ceramic doll they had just come across at a yard sale. I would get a curt nod, a pat on the head, an appraising look, as though they were trying to decipher in advance whether they should let me near anything breakable.

Speaking of things breakable, this is exactly what our father was selling, we came to find out. The young women were invariably brides-to-be, supposedly eager to set up good housekeeping. The idea was to make sure they put our father's chinaware on their bridal registry. He was like a Fuller Brush Man of fine china.

The delicacies that our father unveiled from chiffon wrapping in unmarked boxes were various styles of platters and plates and cups and saucers and bowls and gravy boats.

Once all of the samples had been unboxed, typically the bride-to-be (or baby-maker, as he referred to her in private) and her mother (the old crow, the mad hatter, the sorry sow—oh, our father had wonderful epithets for the mother) would sit side by side on the sofa, our father in an easy chair drawn up to the other side of the coffee table upon which the wares were displayed. His ultimate sales strategy was simply to sit there and stare, while the mother and daughter examined each piece, passing them back and forth—the daughter with an uncritical smile, the mother with a combination frown and eyebrow arch. Our father's goal was to turn the mother's skepticism into a sale. And that's where we came in.

"You're planning on children, of course," our father would interject like a wedge into a wide span of silence.

"Children?" the daughter might say. "You mean, kids?"

"Of course, _____ and I are looking forward to grandchildren," the mother would say, filling in the blank with the name of her absent husband, who might be in the other room watching sports at full volume or out in the yard gardening, having excused himself from the proceedings altogether.

"Did I mention these dishes are unbreakable?" our father would ask.

And here, the mother and daughter would exchange looks. As in: *Did he?*

"Go ahead, Sugar," he'd urge, handing Ursie a plate. "Go ahead and do your worst."

As coached beforehand, Ursula would drop the plate from above her head while standing—which, admittedly, wasn't all that high—onto a hard surface, such as a square of linoleum just inside the front door that served as a low-rent foyer.

The mother and daughter would spring back in their seats and gasp. You could almost see the exclamation marks sprouting from the tops of their heads. Our father would allow the plate to finish wobbling, and then he would pick it up, inspect it top and bottom, and hand it back to the bride-to-be's mother, who would dutifully examine the plate for flaws and, when satisfied, hand it to her daughter.

"What do you know," our father would remark, nonchalantly, as though discovering this feature of his dinnerware for the first time. "Kid-proof."

With Ursula and me in tow, our father's sales started booming. And so we began zipping across the map, until we reached

Toledo by way of Mansfield, Upper Sandusky, Findlay, and other points northwest.

All went well until a time when a more-than-usually skeptical mother (an "old bag," as our father called her afterward) asked for the plate to be dropped from a greater height. Not only did she insist that I, being shoulders and head taller than my sister, drop the plate in question, but that I stand tippy-toe on the dining-room tabletop while doing so.

"Yes, drop it, drop it, do!" Ursie shouted, clapping her hands beneath me, as though she were practicing a cheerleading routine.

I glanced at my father, nervously, but all he did was give a casual shrug.

And so I dropped it.

In my mind's eye, it defies the gravitational tug of the Earth. Instead of its fall being compounded per second by the standard laws of physics, it drops slowly, slowly—even more slowly than that, in case you're imagining the same scene—wobbling like an out-of-control UFO along its trajectory. When it hits pay dirt, it explodes into a thousand fragments, like shrapnel from a mortar shell. My sister claps even more fervently in evident glee. The onlooking daughter of the "old bag" claps her palms to her cheeks in a girlish gesture of disbelief. The mother nods in a caricature of smug satisfaction. I continue to stand with my arms rigidly outstretched in a state of shock. My father only shakes his head slowly from side to side while giving out a long, low whistle, like that from a distantly approaching locomotive.

"Some experiments are doomed to fail." This was all he said about the subject before asking for a dustpan and broom, which the "old bag" handily supplied.

From that time on, I was confined to the car.

Chapter 9

By the end of the week, we were used to our routine—all three of us. In the mornings, we would wash up, use the restroom or outhouse, change clothes, and eat breakfast, usually a bag of donuts or cookies.

Of course, with Ursula, everything was compared to the way Mom did things.

"Mommy never lets us eat cookies for breakfast," she stated once, a critical tone in her voice.

"I'm not Mommy, am I?" Dad replied, looking over the back seat.

"There's no nutritional value in cookies," Ursie countered.

"Where are you learning these things? From your mom?"

I have to admit, I was impressed by the level of vocabulary Ursula employed from time to time, although I was sure it involved sheer mimicry and had little more intelligence behind it than that of a parrot. Still, she came up with some interesting bits of information.

"There isn't any fiber in cookies," she stated flatly.

This was before nutritional labels were mandatory. We were on our own when it came to determining the health quotient of foods.

Mid-morning, we began making our rounds. Dad got the addresses the night before when he called in his sales for the day using a pay phone. These were long-distance calls, evident by the coins he had to keep inserting from the change in his pocket, while trying to write down notes in a ledger at the same time.

I imagined a mysterious entity on the other end of the conversation, a man in a swivel chair in shadows behind an enormous desk—like Charlie on *Charlie's Angels*—but Dad just referred to him as his "boss."

One or two more stops after lunch, and then we had free time, which consisted of finding a playground while Dad snoozed on a nearby bench. If it was raining, we sat in the car and told jokes or read books: picture books for Ursie, DC comics for me, the local newspaper for Dad.

On clear days, while Ursula entertained the customers indoors, and I was left outside, I began practicing spinning plates. I had grown tired of reading my three comic books over and over—by now, I had read each three times through. The dialogue had infiltrated my brain. I conceived of my thoughts as giant white balloons of newsprint in block letters emanating from a sharp point directly above my cranium.

First, it was a matter of finding sticks of an appropriate length and thickness. I decided on three as a sufficient number, since this was as many plates as I had been able to sneak out of the bottom of three different boxes. I knew that during his sales pitches, Dad never ever reached the bottom of a box. Basically, I think it came down to laziness. The more plates he removed, the more he would have to put back.

I had collected leaves as a project for the Cub Scouts the summer before, so I could tell a hickory from a willow. I knew a hickory stick was the toughest around. Isn't this what they made baseball bats out of?

"It's actually ash wood," my therapist tells me, looking up from her phone following a rapid keyword search. "At least in the twentieth century. Nowadays, at least according to AI, they're more likely to be made of maple."

Having snapped three limbs from what I *thought* was a hickory, I began a process of whittling away the smaller branches and twigs. This I performed with a handy pocket knife, also of Cub Scout origin, which was slightly larger in size than a pair of nail clippers—and about as threatening. This is why I was allowed to keep it.

I had to practice in secret, on the far side of the Thunderbird, in case Dad or Ursie peeked out a window—I knew what a tattletale Ursie could be if it meant cementing her relationship with Dad.

It took all of two afternoons to reach a reasonable level of proficiency. Coincidentally, I felt ready to perform on what was to become our very last stop. Timing the sales presentation with my new watch—a Green Lantern superhero wristwatch with a radium dial—I readied my performance. I planted the three sticks firmly in the ground, making sure they were plumb. Then I began spinning my plates. My timing was impeccable. As the third plate began its rotation, Dad and Ursie were stepping out of the house, backing down the front steps.

Backing down!

Their backs were to me!

This wouldn't do.

"Ursie!" I called out, and she turned, her eyes widening as large as the spinning plates, her larynx emitting a high, thin shriek.

"Daddy!" she called, pulling at his suit coat. "Look!"

I couldn't tell from the neutrality of our father's expression whether he was amused, alarmed, or approving. He was carrying his boxes of plates, stacked on top of each other, and peering over top as though spying from the watchtower of a fort.

But it was the woman behind him—a woman as thin as a fencepost—who provided the cue for our father's reaction.

She laughed and clapped her hands.

"Bravo!" she called out. "Perfectissimo!"

I didn't need a translator to know she liked what she saw.

She was dressed in a black kimono. Her hair hung long and rich and dark on either side of her shoulders, draping the robe like a stole. Her fingernails were painted black, as were her toenails, which emerged from a pair of black slip-ons.

It started to drizzle on my performance, and she invited us all back inside.

"A son," she said once we were seated in her small living room. "You didn't tell me you had a boy."

"We keep him in the car," Ursie told her. "He breaks things."

The woman gave a quick look around her surroundings. I saw that there were knickknacks on every shelf.

"Don't worry," Dad said. "He knows how to sit still."

And that's how I sat—very still—my hands on my lap in a gentlemanly manner, as she stepped into the kitchen to make tea.

It was like drinking amphetamines straight from a bottle. Mom never let Ursie or me drink tea or coffee or soda pop or even red fruit juice because she didn't want us to become "hyperactive." But Dad, I was discovering on this trip, was much more permissive. He let us do things that Mom never did.

I kept looking around for an older woman—the mother—but there wasn't one around.

"You know I'm expecting," she said calmly, her eyes sinking into her belly. I've seen photographs of my mother carrying Ursula that look like she has a breadbasket under her blouse. This woman might only have been concealing a water balloon.

"You don't say," our father said. He took a quiet sip of tea, unusual for a man who guzzled beers by the canful with loud slurps when at home or in the car of an evening, once all our driving was through.

"We don't know the sex, though," she said, and then her eyes began tearing up, and her eye shadow ran down her cheeks.

Dad brought out a handkerchief and offered to dab her cheeks. I couldn't imagine that the handkerchief was in any way antiseptic. I pictured it crawling with germs as thick as vermin.

"I say 'we,'" this woman said, "but there is no 'we' anymore. My fiancé —he was killed."

"I'm so very sorry," our father said. He was good at comforting other people, I was realizing, just not our mother. By the tone of his voice, he could have passed for an undertaker. "How did it happen?"

"It was all so quick. He left for work one morning as usual, and then I got a phone call saying he had been struck by a drunk driver." She raised her hands in supplication. "Can you believe it? He survives two years of rotation in Vietnam, but here he is killed by some maniac, already drunk at eight in the morning …"

Our father clucked his tongue and wagged his head.

"Jeremy, please take your sister outside. I'll join you in a moment."

"But Dad—"

I really wanted to hear more about this woman's fiancé. I was finding two things very curious: 1) that she was pregnant without being married and 2) that she and her fiancé had been living together—in "sin," as our mother would say.

"No 'buts,' boy, just do as you're told."

"Yes, sir."

I took Ursie outside by the hand, pulling her down the front steps. We sat side by side on the bottom step, counting cars. I was teaching her how to count from eleven to twenty. She was pretty good at it except for skipping thirteen, seventeen, and nineteen. Plus, she always wanted to call eleven "eleven-ty" and twelve "twelve-ty." Other than that, she tended to jump right from twenty to thirty-two, which she knew to be our father's age. We were never really sure how old our mother was.

It was the summer of '78—the age of disco and bell-bottomed jeans and platform shoes—but our mother still wore dresses, our father an open-necked polo exchanged for a sports team jersey on game days. Our mother kept her hair tied back in a ponytail, a leftover from her cheerleading days (I've seen the pictures of her in her sweater and skirt). Our father maintained a crew cut, sharp as a buzz saw. Eleven years had passed since the so-called Summer of Love.

Nevertheless, I do believe this is the summer our father fell in love, and his temptress was this woman—Evita—who had lost her fiancé to a drunk driver.

How do I know? For one thing, on this night, we were invited to stay in her house—the three of us. She showed us our rooms and ran a bathtub of hot water for Ursula first, me second, our father third. We came out one by one as shiny as freshly dipped Easter eggs. And then she lured us back downstairs with aromas that promised meat and potatoes in place of our ordinary bologna and peanut-butter-and-jelly sandwiches.

She had dressed up for the occasion—exchanging her kimono for a black satiny dress that was sheer enough to let the lavender color of her bra bleed through. Her bosom—that's what I called it at this age, usually followed by a snicker—was large and olive, like two plump melons showcased within a deep-cut "V." They were so gelatinous, I couldn't keep my eyes off them. Our father was having a hard time averting his eyes, as well. I thought if she bent any farther while refilling his goblet, they would slide right out of her dress like the Goop I loved to play with out of its canister.

That night, Ursie and I shared the single bed in the guest room. Evita advertised it as a queen, which boosted Ursie's feeling of self-importance and diminished my sense of pubescent manhood. I was only eight, after all. And besides, we had been sharing the back seat of a car for going on four, five, six … I had to add them up with my fingers … all of seven nights now. Seven nights meant tomorrow would be eight days, and I knew eight was one more day than a week.

"We should be home by now," I mentioned, using the open closet door to block Ursie's view as I put on my pajamas.

"I know, I miss Mommy too," Ursie said, settling her head against three pillows piled on top of each other so that she reclined at a 45° angle. Maybe this made her feel more queen-like.

"It's not that," I countered, climbing into my side of the bed and making sure the covers were tucked in such a way that there would be little chance of our grazing each other in the dark. "Mom said we would only be gone one week, and today makes a week. Tomorrow is the start of a different week."

"What day is it?" Ursie asked.

"Friday," I informed her.

"And what comes after Friday? Thursday?"

"No, Saturday."

From that point, I got sidetracked in giving her a lesson on the days of the week.

But before I got to Sunday, the room started shaking and the wall began pounding and we heard a series of moans and groans.

"It's an earthquake!" Ursie shrieked, sitting up in bed and clutching the covers to her neck.

"Don't be silly," I said, but I wasn't so sure. "There aren't any earthquakes in Ohio."

"Listen," Ursie said. She was right, there was nothing to listen to. The noises had stopped.

But then they started right up again.

"Oh, it's just Daddy and Evita jumping on the bed," I said. "Let's go to sleep."

"Daddy and Evita? Jumping on the bed?"

"That's right."

Having inspected the upstairs front to back and side to side, I already knew the house only had two bedrooms. And something told me our father wasn't sleeping on the couch. For one thing, after he tucked us in, I didn't hear his footsteps going down the stairs.

"Well, if they can jump on the bed, so can we."

It was impossible to restrain her.

As we started jumping, the noises from the other side of the wall stopped. Our father soon peeked into our room and asked us in his polite but firm voice to stop jumping on the bed—did we want to break it down and hurt ourselves?

We tucked ourselves in and turned out the light.

"We're like those monkeys," my sister whispered in the dark.

"Two little monkeys," I agreed, "jumping on the bed."

"One fell off and broke—"

"—her head!"

I gave Ursie a push, and she laughed.

My therapist will inform me on my next visit that, according to her research, the children's rhyme "Five Little Monkeys," to which my sister and my conversation alluded, derives from a nineteenth-century African-American song called "Shortnin' Bread" and that the original lyric used a much more derogatory term than "monkey."

"In fact, there have been calls for banning the poem from nursery rhyme books and kindergarten classes," she will tell me with folded arms. "What do you think about that?"

I didn't really have any thoughts about it. What was my therapist suggesting? That I go through my memories and modify anything that might be potentially insensitive? To whom? To her? To the imaginary audience inside my mind? Maybe she'd be happier with the alternative "Five Little Speckled Frogs" instead?

—

The next morning, our father put us on a bus for Parkersburg, West Virginia, the closest stop to our home.

"That's where your mother will pick you up," our father said.

"You mean like to hug us and give us a kiss?" Ursie asked.

"But she doesn't have a car," I protested, knowing what our father meant.

"Don't worry, she'll be waiting for you to take you back to Bellerophon. Kitty will be driving her."

Kitty was the name of our mother's best friend—our neighbor whose yard was separated from ours by a wire fence. Which was a good thing, because Kitty had a bulldog that hated children.

And that's exactly how we made it all the way home—like two little piggies.

Evita came along to the bus station in Toledo to give us hugs goodbye. She had prepared sack lunches for us for the return journey and fastened our names to our shirts with safety pins. The labels were done in big block letters. Our father got on the bus to make sure we found two seats side by side. Then I saw him slip the bus driver a $5 bill out of his pocket—which seemed an enormous amount of money, far more than the weekly quarter I received as an allowance—and ask him to keep an eye on us, throwing a thumb back toward our seats and speaking loudly enough so we could overhear his request.

The bus driver nodded but only kept his part of the bargain until we arrived in Columbus, when we changed drivers.

I don't think he let the new driver know about the arrangement, because the new bus driver ignored us, as he did everyone else, all the way to Parkersburg, even though we were right behind the driver's seat. The other driver had checked on us, every stop, asking how we were and giving us a treat: a peppermint or Hershey's kiss. He had a bottomless pocket of candies in his jacket. The new driver never so much as glanced at us in the rearview mirror.

We didn't arrive until a quarter past ten at night according to my glow-in-the-dark watch. We had left Toledo at half past eight that morning, making fifteen stops—I kept track with slash marks in the margins of a comic book.

When we got to our destination, I woke up my sister and we climbed off the bus. Our mother was there, but Miss Kitty wasn't.

We had been under strict instructions from our father not to mention Evita. He even gave us a whole dollar each to forget her name.

Our mother bunched us together in a smothering embrace beneath a single streetlamp in front of the bus depot, which looked to be closed.

"Where's Miss Kitty?" Ursie asked once the hugging was over and our mother held us at arm's length to get a good look at us.

The term "Miss Kitty" always made me laugh because it reminded me of *Gunsmoke* before it went off the air when I was younger, a program I hadn't been technically allowed to see because of all the shootouts. The only shows we were officially permitted to watch, in no particular order, were *The Wonderful World of Disney*, *The Waltons*, *Little House on the Prairie*, *Happy Days*, and *Lawrence Welk*. Off limits were shows of questionable decency such as *Three's Company* and *Hee-Haw*. Our father had a passion for *Charlie's Angles*, which annoyed our mother. She, in turn, became addicted to *Dallas* that year.

"Well, Miss Kitty—how can I best explain this?—she isn't here."

"Where is she?" I asked.

"Your bus was late, and so Miss Kitty had to drive back

home to be with her own children."

"Does she know Miss Evita?" Ursie blurted.

I was so surprised by the emission of her name that I gave Ursula a hard jab with my elbow, which unfortunately, given the difference in height between us, knocked her hard in the eye.

"Ow!" Ursie complained. "That hurt!"

Ordinarily, this would have earned a reprimand from Mom, but now she was all curious about this Evita woman instead.

"How will we get home?" I asked.

"Never mind that for now," our mother said, steering Ursula gently by the shoulder.

Home was a half-hour away by car, but we were on foot, it was late, and I was hungry. I supposed my sister was, too.

"What about bedtime?"

"Oh, well, we'll take a night off from bedtime."

Our mother led us into the only lighted building on the street, the fluorescent fixtures illuminating the yellow walls of an all-night diner behind the large plate-glass windows. Only two other customers were inside—an older man on a stool sipping a mug and a younger man in a booth studying a newspaper.

"Let's get you both something to eat," our mother said once we were situated in an adjoining booth. "Now," she said, peering over the top of her menu, "I'd like you both to tell me all about this Evita."

Chapter 10

All was forgiven—or seemed to be. In any case, nothing more was ever said of Evita.

Our father began working second shift in a manufacturing plant as a furnace operator. Our mother thought it best that he work somewhere stationary, as a means of curbing his instinct to roam. It helped that he was supervised at work and had to stay in one place. Their battles seemed fewer. At least, it was too cold for Dad to work on the hedge.

I couldn't imagine what a furnace operator actually did, since it seemed our furnace worked automatically, with minor adjustments to a thermostat. When I asked my father, he wasn't very forthcoming. "Turn knobs and watch a dial," is all I was able to get from him as a job description. It didn't sound very exciting. Until he added, "So the boiler doesn't explode," which restored my faith in the glamor of his profession.

My sister still had one more year to go before kindergarten while I attended third grade. At lunch, I sat with a couple of outcast classmates in the cafeteria—we were what you might refer to as a larval stage of nerd—but rarely spoke with anyone or raised my hand in class. I preferred to doodle in the margins of my notebook or stare out the window at a small courtyard of snow-covered benches beneath the prickly arms of hawthorns. Birds stayed alive eating the berries, and my doodles turned into comic strips with crudely drawn robins that had missed the fall migration.

My main interaction with kids on the bus was as a scapegoat for ear flicking from the seat behind. There was a girl—Melinda Ruiz—who sat next to me until the older kids made fun of us and tried to force our heads together into a kiss. After that, she changed seats and never sat next to me again.

My refuge was at home in the small bedroom I shared with my sister. An almost tangible line divided our room: Ursie's dolls and fairy princesses on one side and my plastic models and LEGO constructions on the other. Unfortunately, Ursie was going through a phase where she was growing bored with her dolls and began invading my collections of toys. And so we took trips through hyperspace with my Star Wars figurines (I only had two). Or else we dug through our laundry basket with a miniature backhoe in search of plastic dinosaurs we had buried, which we found and piled up in a corner as our archaeological finds of the day. Occasionally, I am embarrassed to divulge, she would get me to play dress-up, and we'd both raid our mother's closet and drawers for clothes and apply mascara and lipstick in the bathroom mirror and sit politely on either side of a small kids' table sipping imaginary tea poured from a toy plastic teapot into toy plastic teacups.

Saturdays were the best part of the weekend, of course. We could sleep in or, if we woke up ahead of our parents, we could charge into their room and bounce them awake on their mattress. They never seemed to mind. Our father would wrestle us out of the bed like a bear protecting its den, and our mother would wake with curlers in her hair to make coffee and a big breakfast: eggs, toast, bacon. The works!

Often, she let us eat in the living room while watching our favorite Saturday-morning cartoons in sequence: *Scooby-Doo*, *The Bugs Bunny/Road Runner Show*, and *Fantastic Four*.

Saturday afternoons, if the weather was foul, were spent on a couch watching black-and-white movies on our TV that sat like a cubic piece of furniture in a corner, taking up all that space, so that our mother used the top of it as a knickknack shelf with a doily. Late afternoons, we gave over the couch to Dad, who tended to watch sports with his eyes closed. But sneak up and try to turn the channel, his eyes would pop open in a flash and he'd holler, "Hey, now! I'm watching that!"

Saturday nights were family game nights served with deep dishes of ice cream with our choice of topping: melted caramel, store-bought strawberries, sugar-cookie sprinkles from a jar. The games we played were classics: *Life* (Ursie, with her preference for large families, enjoyed filling up her car with the little pink and blue pegs), *Monopoly* (even though Ursie had no concept of money higher in denomination than a quarter, she enjoyed moving the Scottie dog around the board and didn't complain when she sat out a turn in jail with her little pet for companionship), *Battleship* (I was captain of the sub, taking turns with Dad, who was admiral of the fleet, in calling out enemy positions), and even *Rock'em Sock'em Robots* (championship matches between the "guys" and the "gals" with each participant in control of one fighting arm). No matter the game, however, by the end of it, our mother would invariably accuse our father of cheating.

This accusation came up in *Scrabble* games too. Ursie, who wasn't old enough to form more than three-letter words, half of which she misspelled, paired off with our mother, while I teamed up with Dad to make the sides even. These games started off calmly enough, until Ursie and Mom started spelling words like C-H-E-A-T, S-K-U-N-K, C-A-D, and F-R-A-U-D, which Dad took personally, responding with words like S-C-O-L-D, N-A-G, S-H-R-E-W, and, lastly, B-I-T-C- Which was as far as he got before our mother swiped the letters from the board with a clattering backhand.

"Henry, the children!" our mother exclaimed, rising. "Their ears!"

This, despite no one had uttered the word aloud, a word Ursie couldn't read.

But she did have a good memory for letters.

"Daddy, what does B-I-T-C spell?"

"What?" Our father seemed distracted. "It's just a word for a female dog."

"Cur," our mother responded, stomping her way toward her bedroom, but Ursie didn't ask the meaning of that.

———

Sundays were the opposite of Saturdays: stiff and formal like ironed, starched collars. We suffered through church—even our father seemed bothered by it all, taking time out during the offering to go outside and smoke a cigarette. We couldn't see him through the stained glass, of course, but we could smell the tobacco on his clothes when he returned to our pew. By then, the collection plate had passed, and Ursula and I would have dropped the quarter each that our father had given us to donate, listening to the clink-clink with some head-lowering embarrassment, on my part, since it seemed such a paltry gift compared to the envelope-padded dollar bills that other children were giving.

On the way out the door, my mother always pushed me along ahead of her with her hands on my shoulders, as if I were a show dog being displayed at a contest. As we went past the minister, my mother would say, "Shake hands, Jeremy," as though I were to receive a blessing from the beaming face of the Pope. "Jeremy plans on being a preacher himself someday," she would boast every Sunday, as though our minister had never heard this prognostication before. I suppose it was something that bore repeating, as though to drill it into the top of my skull with a carpenter's awl. And it's true, the minister would nod and smile, going along with the threat of future competition to his occupation. I think it helped that he was a little deaf in one ear.

The only thing more uncomfortable than Sunday mornings were our hospice visits to elderly, dying Mrs. Darnell's house, which picked up again with our winter break from school.

The recurrence of these visits surprised me like a cavalry attack out of the woods. First off, it ran counter to what my idea of a winter break should be. I imagined sledding down vanilla scoops of snow, making snow angels in soft white confetti, packing and throwing snowballs at enemies either real or imaginary. Instead, we were inundated with a steady drizzle of rain that lasted all of four out of the five days leading up to Christmas Eve. And on two of these days, we made visits to Mrs. Darnell's.

The only difference from our summer visits was that we drove a family station wagon that my parents had purchased by trading in the Thunderbird. The reason we drove is that our mother had decided to take sole ownership of the vehicle, limiting our father's migrations from town. We dropped our father off at work in the morning and picked him up by dinnertime.

Walter, Mrs. Darnell's adult son who still lived at home, was overjoyed to see the both of us again—especially Ursula.

He knelt next to her on our bench in the hall, patting her hair as though she were a pet hamster.

"It's so good to see you again," he said over and over, the full sentence breaking into smaller chunks of discourse like a breakup of clouds: "So good … see you … again to see you … good … so good."

Based on the red circles around his eyes, it was evident he hadn't enjoyed a sound sleep in days. Who knew what calculations were going through his mind, keeping him awake at night?

The petting became stroking, and the discourse changed.

"Come to my room, won't you? I'd like to show you something."

Ursie threw me a worried look.

"I know!" I said, standing suddenly, my announcement much louder than I intended, so that it threw Walter off balance, making his arms flail out like a heron's wings to steady himself. Ursula took advantage of this momentary lapse to rush behind me, using my body as a pillar of safety. "Let's play a game of hide-and-seek."

Walter looked more confused than upset by the change in plan.

"Hide-and-seek?" he asked, as though he had never heard of the game before.

"We'll hide, you seek," I instructed. "Just close your eyes and count to a hundred."

"All right," Walter said slowly, his eyes moving inward, as though performing the math in his head. But then his eyes grew a crafty look. "I'll count to 100 by prime numbers."

"Sure," I said, shrugging my shoulders in lieu of my vague understanding of primes, "but make sure to cover your eyes."

Walter began counting before I was ready: "2 … 3 … 5 … 7 … 11 … 13 …"

And then I realized my mistake in allowing him to count by primes. I forgot it would let him skip a lot of numbers in between. At this rate, it wouldn't take him very long to reach 100. I should have made it 1,000.

"Sorry to interrupt," my therapist interrupts without needing the assistance of her phone this time. "But would you have known what prime numbers are at this age? I mean you were still only what? Eight years old?"

"Almost nine, but I was always good at math," I tell her and proceed before she can come up with a rebuttal.

"Come on," I whispered urgently to Ursie, yanking her to her feet and pulling her down the hall.

We tiptoed past Mrs. Darnell's room, which always smelled like boiled cabbage. My first impulse was to lead Ursie into this room, a room we had only visited once—Mrs. Darnell laying her hands on both our heads as though to give us a blessing. But the room was too dimly lit to read my comics, and Mrs. Darnell was in the process of dying with our mother beside her, an activity that seemed to require privacy, so we crept down the hall to the very last door on the left.

Inside was a large, sparsely furnished room. A cot—not a full bed—took up a small corner, as though to apologize for its function as a vehicle of sleep. An enormous wooden desk occupied the center of the room. On top of the desk lay various scale models of ships and planes and racecars and space rockets, including a miniature version of the Saturn V. I guessed this was Walter's room—a guess I was soon to find out was correct.

In another corner, behind the desk, sat the largest panda I had ever seen—larger than any stuffed animal I had ever longed to win at a carnival sideshow. Ursie broke free of my hand to inspect it.

"Look," she exclaimed, "there's a tag. Read it, Jeremy, please!"

To Ursula, I read, silently, *my very best friend in the whole world.*

"What's it say?" she urged.

"It doesn't say anything. It just says, 'Made in China.'"

"Uh-uh," she clucked. "That's a 'U,'" she insisted, pointing, even though it was in cursive. "U stands for Ursula. This panda's for me, isn't it?"

And with that, she put her arms around its neck and gave it a tremendous hug.

I looked with apprehension at the open door.

Why hadn't I closed it, locked it?

I was sure Walter was out of prime numbers by now.

"Quick, over here," I pulled my sister toward the only closet in the room, and she dragged along the panda. It was as big as she was, making for a tight fit for the three of us. As a harbor for clothes, the closet was barely functional. Immediately as you entered, you were confronted by a wall. To the left, shirts were hung crosswise, to the right, trousers. My sister turned right with her panda. I went left. These were the only hiding places. We had to wedge ourselves in like blocks of cheese. There was just enough room for our shoulders. Unfortunately, neither shirts nor trousers hung far enough down to cover our legs from sight, never mind the panda's, if Walter should open the door, which I had swung carefully back into place, leaving it a few inches ajar, just as I had found it.

"You couldn't have left the panda?" I hissed.

"It's mine," my sister hissed back. "It has my name on it. It belongs to me."

"Sh-h-h," I hushed, hearing the bedroom door creak on its hinges.

But there was no reason to hush her. She heard it too.

"It's Walter," she said. "We can't let him find us."

In her mind, she was playing a simple game of hide-and-seek. I wasn't sure what was in my mind, but it felt like a jumble of yarn that I was trying to untangle.

Through the crack in the closet door, I watched Walter enter quietly. He was a tall, thin man with short-cropped black hair smeared back from his forehead in a tight wave with gel. His eyes were magnified behind black horn-rimmed glasses. What made him seem so formal was that he wore a white dress shirt with rolled-up sleeves and dark trousers. His dress shoes made crinkling noises as he walked toward his desk. But before he reached it, he paused, turning toward the corner, where the folding chair that had held Ursie's panda stood empty. He contemplated its emptiness for a long time with his back toward us.

He turned, glancing around the room. He stared at the closet, and I inhaled sharply on instinct, which is to say, I gasped. Whether he heard me or not, to my relief, he declined to investigate the closet. Instead, he took a seat behind his desk and pulled open a drawer. From the drawer he removed a black revolver. I had never seen a gun in real life before—only in TV westerns and crime dramas.

Staring at the gun, Walter opened the chamber and placed a single bullet inside. Then he closed the chamber and spun it. When it stopped spinning, in one slick motion, he pressed the muzzle against his head and pulled the trigger. He did this without even closing his eyes. The trigger made a sharp click that made my body lurch in response.

"My bear!" Ursie exclaimed at the same time in a hoarse whisper.

"What about it?" I asked, irritated.

"It went down a slide."

"Huh?"

"A sliding board. It went down a slide."

"What are you talking about?"

This wasn't a playground. I was about to reach the conclusion that her imagination had gone haywire. But then she said: "I'm going after it."

And with a *whoosh* from her side of the closet, she was gone. I admired her devotion to secrecy. She hadn't even let out a scream. It was as though she had been swallowed whole in one definitive gulp.

I didn't feel confident enough to move from one side of the closet to the other. I was worried I had already given myself away with a swish of the long-sleeved shirts through which I was peering. But when I looked back through the crack in the door, I saw no trace of Walter. It seemed he had left the room—with or without the gun with its single bullet. In either case, it wasn't lying atop the desk. There was nothing on the desk except a ledger and a pen in a holder.

Cautiously, I crept out of the security of my hiding spot and pushed through the curtain of trousers hanging on the other side of the closet. It was too dark to make out anything, but when I put my hand forward, it encountered nothing—just air. Feeling around, I made out the edges of a rectangle cut into the wall. And lowering my fingers, I felt the smoothness of what seemed a sheet of metal—indeed, some sort of slide.

"Ursie?" I called softly into the tunnel. "Sister? Little Bear?"

No response.

There was nothing for it but to go after her. She had apparently slid down effortlessly, but it was a very tight fit for me. After some clumsy experimentation, I decided feet first might be best. I could only accomplish this, however, if I kept my arms raised over my head. I got stuck right away, even though I was tilted downward at a 45° angle. And so I began a laborious effort of shimmying and wriggling inch by inch down the tunnel with very little space above my nose—a fact I established by trying to move my head into a position by which I could peer ahead of my feet. No matter. Everything was dark—more accurately, black. As in pitch.

It was then that I became aware for perhaps the very first time of two major fears that would continue to haunt me: fear of tight spaces and fear of spiders. I hadn't encountered any spiders, although the sides of the chute I was slowly sliding through were dusty with lint. My breathing became rapid and shallow. I had a sudden sense of panic that paralyzed further movement. I couldn't see above me. I couldn't see below. I couldn't see anything. I just couldn't see. I had a horrible feeling that I was being squeezed into a container. My imagination ran to mason jars that our mother used for canning. Then a different thought entered my brain: What if I was descending into the bowels of a furnace? There was a good chance I would be roasted alive!

But wait … I recalled Walter's room being exceptionally cold, and I hadn't felt a draught of hot air all this time I was making my way down the slide.

Some slide …

Just as I was worried I would be stuck in place for good, one more wiggle brought my feet into empty space. There was no longer a bottom for my heels to grab onto to pull me along.

Then, instead of it being a matter of inching along, it became a struggle to keep from falling straight down into some bottomless pit. I had to brace myself in the tunnel with elbows and knees, so that I ended up in a vertical position, dropping by degrees, as I repeatedly relaxed, then tightened, my muscles.

It was a long drop, but then the tunnel made another 45° turn, folding me in half. Now it was time to return to my previous method of jiggling and wriggling, like a butterfly trying to free itself from its cocoon.

And then—a miraculous delivery! Someone pulling at my feet so that one of my shoes came off. Now I knew how miners trapped underground for days and days must feel when finally pulled free of the earth.

What alarmed me was that I felt not one but two sets of hands grabbing me, one pair on each foot.

When I popped out, I plopped onto something soft and squishy, which turned out to be Ursie's giant panda, mottled gray with dust from the duct.

"Why, hello, Brother." Ursie was there to greet me, holding one of my shoes in her hand. "This is Eva," she said, introducing me to the young woman who had just let go of my other foot, leaving my shoe intact. "She lives here. And guess what?" But Ursie divulged her secret before I could guess: "She's a princess!"

Chapter 11

The young woman did indeed seem a princess. She wore a taffeta gown edged with pink lace. In fact, everything about her was pink: her tiara, her magic wand, her smile. The room, too, was painted pink, although gray cracks bled out of the concrete blocks. There were pink balloons floating along the wooden joists of the ceiling, which had also been painted pink. The single light bulb overhead was covered with a pink shade.

The woman held out her hand, and I thought it was to help me to my feet, but as soon as I gave it a tug, she pulled it out of my clutch.

"No, no, no," she exclaimed, still holding her pink smile perfectly in place.

"You're supposed to kiss it," Ursie instructed.

Princess Eva held out her hand once more. Her fingernails were painted pink, and she wore a silver ring with a brilliant pink gem. I took her fingers more gently this time and gave them a reluctant kiss.

"Now you may rise," Eva said, waving her wand above my head. And so I rose, glancing around to try to make better sense of my environs. I must have looked a mess coming out of what appeared to be a furnace duct. The only thing missing was the furnace.

"Did you know Jeremy's a prince?" Ursie boasted to my chagrin. "When we play prince and princess together. Sometimes," she added to my further chagrin, "he even lets *me* be the prince."

"You mean to say you exchange roles?" Eva asked for clarification, which I didn't provide. "This would make sense," she said, surveying my stature from head to foot. "Your brother seems a bit on the scrawny side for a prince." At this, I took what could only be called, given the circumstances, umbrage.

"My mom says I'm bony—that's all," I said in my defense.

"And lanky," Ursie added. "Don't forget she calls you 'lanky' sometimes, too."

"Right," I admitted. "And lanky."

On the cusp of nine years old, I was ahead of my age group with a preteen gangly awkwardness I would never outgrow.

"Bony and lanky," Eva repeated, twirling away. "Hardly the physical qualifications of a prince, I daresay."

"Well, if you must," I said, still feeling insulted, "I guess you can go ahead and daresay it."

"Isn't she wonderful?" Ursie said, brushing the dust off her panda. "A real princess."

"Yes," I said, "wonderful."

Ursie followed Eva around as she tended to her dolls. Dolls lined every wall of the room. China dolls, plastic dolls, rubber dolls. Dolls with long hair, dolls with braids, dolls with ponytails, even bald dolls. Dolls in long dresses, dolls in miniskirts. Barbie dolls. Baby dolls. Dolls, dolls, dolls.

My sister was in heaven.

I followed along for a different reason. I had an irrepressible urge to pee. As Eva and Ursie fawned over virtually every doll in sequence, I searched the room for a bathroom. Aside from the way I had come in, there seemed no easy way out. A large iron door with rivets all around was too intimidating to offer easy access to a bathroom. Another small iron door had hinges on top and a latch below. It opened with a squeak that caught Eva's attention.

"Oh, that, my dear, is the old coal chute. But of course we don't use coal anymore. There used to be a coal furnace in this very room, but thankfully it has been removed."

That explained what Ursie had mistaken for a slide. It was

probably a heating duct or cold-air return, now dislocated from whatever furnace it had once been connected to. I looked up through the chute and saw a square of gray sky. A current of cold air blustered over my face.

"As you can see, it leads to the outside. Ah, the outside!" she remarked wistfully. "Now come, you must tell me all about what it is like on the outside before Walter arrives and takes you away."

"You know Walter?" I asked.

"Walter is my brother," she answered, frowning. "He is not a prince, nor will he ever be. But it is he who brings me my meals and empties my chamber pot."

"Chamber pot?"

"My royal chamber pot. It is beneath my bed. I give you permission to withdraw it if you have a need, as I can plainly see by your prancing about like a restless colt."

I hadn't even realized I was hopping from foot to foot in my anxiety to find a means of relieving myself. The chamber pot was, as she said, beneath her bed. It was essentially a large potty—the kind Ursie had outgrown only the year before. Except this one was made of metal and seemingly gold plated. Indeed, it seemed royal—a true throne.

I looked around in perplexity. I had no desire to unzip myself in the presence of two females, even if one of them was my sister.

"The screen," Eva said, pointing. "You may go behind the screen."

A Japanese screen hid a corner of the room from view, and it was behind this screen I trudged with the royal commode.

"All right," I said, peeking around the edge of the screen, "but please don't listen."

"We shall plug our ears," Eva said, closing her eyes at the same time. Ursie followed suit, although I was sure she would peek, as always.

When I was through, I set the commode by the iron door, per Eva's instructions. She told us Walter should be arriving any moment with her royal lunch.

"I am afraid I wasn't expecting guests," she said, pouting, "but I will share whatever fare I have."

"What kind of fare would that be?" I asked. My stomach was beginning to growl.

"Celery sticks and saltines," Eva replied.

"I'm not sure we can stay for lunch," I said.

But it wasn't because of the promise of such light fare. According to the Green Lantern, our mother's time with Mrs. Darnell was almost up, and I could only imagine how she would react if she found our hallway bench empty except for our coats and galoshes.

Without warning, a knock came from the other side of the large iron door: three metallic taps.

"Why, that will be Walter now!" Eva exclaimed, checking her own watch that she wore on a pink band around her wrist. "I must say, his arrival is earlier than usual."

"Hide us!" I pleaded.

"Hide you? Why, whatever for? Walter won't hurt you. He's a perfect dear." But then her smile flickered with uncertainty. "Except when he's in a mood. Oh, I do so hope he isn't in one of his moods."

"Under the bed," I instructed my sister.

I indicated the four-poster that occupied a majority of the room. It had a pink canopy, pink quilt, pink pillowcases, and, most importantly of all, a pink bed skirt that would hide us from view.

"We're playing a game with Walter," my sister told Eva. "Hide-and-seek."

"Oh, well, why didn't you say so? Of course, under the bed is the perfect hiding place. Walter will never suspect your presence. It's been so long since I've had guests after all. In fact, it's been a very long time—forever, I should say."

As we scurried beneath the bed, we heard Eva cross the floor and the door open.

"My panda!" Ursie gasped.

I reached out from under the coverlet and pulled it underneath just in time, as a shadow was thrown across the carpet, which I shouldn't need to point out was a brilliant pink—as thick and rich as a spilled strawberry milkshake.

"Brother!" Eva cried out, and I could see beneath the bed skirt that her feet left the floor as she gave him a hug. When her feet returned, she said, more calmly, "You didn't bring lunch?"

"It isn't time for that," Walter informed her with a neutral, deadpan tone. A silence went by. "Have you seen the children?" he asked. His feet began pacing widening circles around the carpet.

"Children? Oh, you're so funny sometimes, dear brother, I do declare. You know as well as I that I never have visitors."

The feet came to a standstill.

"Your bedpan seems rather full," Walter observed, as though he were a scientist collecting data.

"Yes, it is, would you please be a dear and empty it? You know I can't abide the odor. Phew!"

At this, Ursie broadened her mouth with a smile, but I clamped my hand over it to preempt a giggle. At the same time, I held my free forefinger in front of my lips to advise silence, a warning my sister agreed to with a nod.

"You didn't use toilet paper," Walter stated.

"Oh, but you're so observant," Eva said lightly. "I couldn't find any. I must be out."

"There's a roll on its spool, as usual," Walter said.

"Oh, is there? I must have been distracted."

Another silence went by. Walter's shoes began to traverse the carpet, coming nearer the bed, where they stopped and shuffled in place, as though infused with a nervous twitch.

"Would you like to look under the bed?" Eva asked, so abruptly it made my body flinch.

"Is that where they're hiding?" Walter asked.

"It's where I would hide if I were a child," Eva said. "Either there, or behind the screen. But I wouldn't look there."

"No?"

Walter's feet circled away to the other side of the bed.

"Only more dolls," Walter reported.

"The dolls are my children," Eva explained.

"Of course they are," Walter said, his tone softening. "You have so many children."

"I'm just like the woman who lives in a shoe," Eva said.

"Except you're not an old woman," Walter pointed out.

"No, that is true. And I'll never age, as long as I stay inside my room?"

"No, you will never age."

"I'll live forever."

"Yes, you will live forever."

"Oh, Walter, I do hope so. But if you should age, and I should not ..."

"Ollie-ollie-in-free!" Walter suddenly called out.

Ursie lurched as though to reveal her hiding place, but I held her back, pinching her arm. I believe Walter did stoop for one peek under the bed. At least I heard a sound that could have been knees crackling. But from that side, rows of shoes were piled three high from headboard to footboard, forming a visually impenetrable barrier. In any case, after a few moments, the iron door creaked opened and closed heavily, shutting us in.

Once more, we were captives.

Ursie gave me a push with her foot in my spine.

"It's safe, Big Brother. Time to get out."

Once we crawled out, Ursie ran to Eva and gave her a hug that brought her feet off the floor, just as Eva's had with Walter.

"Oh, I wish we could stay with you forever and never age," Ursie said. "I would so like to stay a little girl."

"Well, we can't," I said, using my Voice of Authority. The minute hand on my wristwatch was beckoning. "We need to find Mom."

But Ursie wouldn't let go.

"You go," she said, her eyes scrunched shut, her fingers clasped in a way so as to make them impossible to pry apart. I knew it was useless to try. "I'll stay here with Princess Eva."

"OK, you stay here," I said, opening the iron lid of the coal chute, our escape hatch from the Never-Never Land of Eva's kingdom. "I'm going to the car."

I peered up the chute. It was another 45° climb through a tunnel, but there was light at the end of it.

"Coming?" I asked, turning my head.

Ursie had let go of the princess, and Eva was stroking her hair.

"You must promise to visit me again sometime soon," she said, soothing her.

"Oh, we will! We will!" Then she turned to throw me a look of hopefulness. "Won't we, Brother?"

"Yes, of course we will," I stated, playing the adult who made the sorts of promises that seem made to be broken.

"It's so easy to visit," Ursie said. "Such a long, fun slide."

I couldn't bring myself to agree with her excitement about our method of entry.

"We'll rescue you," she added.

"Oh, but that isn't necessary," Eva said. "Someday, a prince— a true prince—will rescue me. But for now, I have Walter."

Eventually, we scrambled up the chute after a series of fare-wells: panda first, Ursula second, me last. On the outside, we peered back down at Eva's face. It looked like a distant mirror.

"Just look at yourselves," she laughed from below. "You're all covered in soot from head to toe." It was true, I saw, sizing up Ursula. I supposed I looked the same. We could have been chimney sweeps. The panda had gone from black-and-white to blacker-and-gray.

"Come join us!" Ursie called down. "It's easy!"

"It would ruin my gown. It's so much easier to go out the door down here. It opens from the inside."

"So you mean you're not trapped?" I asked, confused.

"Oh, no, not trapped exactly. Except, I know it sounds silly, but I'm afraid to go out."

"Afraid?" Ursie asked, looking up and around to inspect the gray sky and then back down. "Because it's so cold today?"

"Good-bye!" Eva called out to us one last time, and then closed the lid.

A wintry mix of drizzly rain and ice crystals was falling, as I took Ursula's hand and ran toward the car to wait for our mother, who would bring our coats and galoshes and deliver a double reprimand: (1) for making her worry what had become of us and (2) for getting so "filthy dirty."

Of course, there was the whole business of the panda bear, which Ursie kept as a parting gift. But after Mom asked her a few questions about it in private—I'm not sure what she replied, but they probably had something to do with promising never to take anything from people you hardly know—and after she had run it through the laundry, she let Ursula keep it on her bed.

In the meantime, I pondered what I was beginning to for-mulate as a life lesson: fantasy is pink and warm, reality cold and gray.

Chapter 12

Of course, you want your life to be like a story—any story will do. A fairy tale would be best, as long as it has a beginning, middle, and end. That's all that really matters. Not just your whole life either, but any part of it. That's what's called a chapter. And this chapter didn't end the way I thought it would. In fact, the ending cropped up before I was ready for it.

We promised Eva a second visit, and in fact we made several, except we marched down the stairs and through the massive iron door to her room rather than slide down the furnace duct. Now that we knew Walter was not his sister's prison warden—in fact, just the opposite, he functioned as her caretaker—we felt comfortable allowing him to escort us, bringing us down to the basement, and all four of us would have a lovely visit together, which generally involved the sipping of tea, the nibbling of biscuits, and the exchanging of pleasantries.

Walter was always the perfect gentleman, very attentive to his sister's need for perfection. He arranged the teacups just so in geometrical shapes: trapezoids and diamonds and rhombuses. Napkins were folded into triangles with fingernail-crisped edges, serving as the foundation of a lecture on right angles and hypotenuses. He allowed the tea to steep in its pot a precise amount of time as measured on his digital watch, and the sugar was delivered in dice-sized cubes. The only thing he wasn't much use for was conversation. This was Eva's department. She told us stories about castles and dragons, evil witches and kind magicians, knights and battles and quests. I admit, it was easy to get lost in the timelessness of her imagination, but Walter kept careful track of the time. And when our mother's hospice visit was five minutes short of being concluded, he announced it was time to go.

"Oh, must you, must you leave so soon?" Eva would complain, and each of our departures was accompanied by hugs and kisses and tears and promises to visit again. Walter would guide our departure with a hand on my shoulder, and his other hand on top of Ursula's head, where he softly petted her hair as he might a cat, a gesture that bothered me—and Ursula as well—on some level.

There might have been more visits and more tea parties, but old Mrs. Darnell decided to die one bright and shining day before the winter was through.

On our next visit, there was an estate sale with a sign out front advertising the whole house up for grabs. Windows had been boarded to prevent vandalism. It wouldn't be the first abandoned house to have rocks thrown through the windows—kids just being kids, breaking glass for kicks, as I well knew.

Our mother had her eye fastened on a jewelry box of Mrs. Darnell's. It's what she told us on the drive over. She described it to us in minute detail. Its color: a dark mahogany. Its interior: a deep velvet. Its ornamentation: a string of rubies all cemented in place on the lid. Its hinges: all brass.

And when you opened the lid, the loveliest music, making you think you had opened a small portal to heaven.

She was hoping she could place a bid on the jewelry box alone, but when we arrived, she found out it had been included in a larger lot of items displayed on a table in the dining room. While she pondered this dilemma, I pulled Ursie aside.

Walter was nowhere to be found. His absence made me worry about his sister.

"Let's visit Eva," I urged.

"Yes, let's do," she replied, clapping her hands. "We can go down the slide again … Whee!"

"No, let's use the stairs," I insisted.

"Oh, but I so miss the slide," she pouted.

The cellar steps creaked all the way down, making it sound like a descent of overgrown mice. Without an escort, the basement seemed brand-new to us. We were so used to following along in Walter's wake that we had never kept track of the twists and turns that led us to Eva's room. With the only light emanating from outside through small, high-up, cobwebbed windows, the basement was like a catacomb. All that was missing were the skeletons piled along the walls. Instead, there was a corner of the basement reserved for something that resembled a laboratory with table and microscope and a variety of utensils—pincers, scissors, scalpels, calipers, clamps—that seemed a preparation for either surgery or torture.

The light bulbs overhead were naked, without shades, screwed into their ceramic fixtures with cords that dangled just out of my reach.

"Hey, Sister," I said loudly, "how many psychiatrists does it take to screw in a light bulb?"

"What's a psychiatrist?"

"Never mind."

It was a joke that was going around I had picked up from my father, who maintained a dim view of psychiatric treatment.

Mostly, I was trying to lighten a damp, dank, dark atmosphere with what I thought was humor.

"Very funny," my therapist states in deadpan. "Amazing, isn't it, that this joke is still in circulation today. I had a fourth-grader tell it to me only last week."

"Sorry," I apologize, "no offense."

She stares at me levelly, the drawbridge of her eyebrows furrowing in concentration.

"And what are you hoping to change by coming here?" she asks. "What is it you want to change?"

It's a question for which I have no answer.

"Look," Ursie said, pointing through the cobwebby gloom. "There's her door."

Indeed, it was the only door made of iron. Not only that, it was the only door period. Oddly, it was locked.

I was able to reach the top two locks, which were just bolts that slid free of their holders, one requiring more effort than the other.

"Strange," I commented. "These were always unbolted before."

"Maybe we should knock," Ursie said, observing my efforts. "It's only polite."

And so we knocked, both of us.

"Miss Eva?" Ursie called. "Princess? Are you home?"

I unfastened the next clasp, which was held in place with only a rusted bolt instead of a padlock.

I thought I was through with the unlocking process, but as I pulled on the handle, it wouldn't budge. That's when I noticed that there was a keyhole inset below the handle. And that's what was missing: the key.

We tried knocking again, raising both our voices into a shout to resonate through the massiveness of the door. We pounded with both sets of fists, as well.

"Hey! You kids!"

A loud voice from behind: an adult voice. A male adult voice, connected to a flashlight that circled our heads as the man made his approach. He was dressed as a security guard complete with badge and holster.

"What do you think you kids are doing down here?" he

asked, a gruffness attempting to mask his curiosity, as his eyes bobbed around the cellar. It was extremely likely he was as afraid of the dark and spiders as we were.

"There's a woman trapped in here," I calmly informed him.

"A woman? What woman?"

"A princess!" Ursie clarified.

"Oh, a princess," he said, rolling his eyes.

"We're here to rescue her," Ursie insisted.

"Well, there isn't any princess down here that I know of. You'll have to come back upstairs with me."

"Wait," I said. "Just ask Walter. He can tell you."

"Walter?" he asked, pausing in pirouette.

"Mrs. Darnell's son," I explained.

"Listen, kids." And here he knelt in front of us with his flashlight lowered toward the floor. "You shouldn't be down here. Who are you with, anyway? Your mother? Well, she's bound to be worried, wouldn't you think?"

I appreciated that he was talking with us on our level, but we were out of rebuttals, and all we could do was trudge toward the stairs, as he prodded us along with his flashlight beam.

Upstairs, the small number of gawkers we had left had now become a throng, as they inspected various boxes and crates and tables of items with the inquisitiveness of woodchucks. Walter was not among them. We thought of looking for him upstairs, but the stairwell—a magnificent tower of wooden steps ascending the walls like the kind you'd find in a medieval castle—was blocked off with yellow tape.

Our mother hadn't been able to nab the coveted jewelry box.

"Well, now, come along, children," she said when she found us. "There's nothing else here within my meager allowance, I'm afraid." She always lamented the pitiful "allowance" she received from her share of whatever spending money was left over from her and our father's combined paychecks after utility bills, groceries, and the mortgage. Like a shepherdess, she herded us out the front door. An icy wind was blowing crystals that stung our exposed cheeks, making her hurry us toward the car.

"Wait!" I shouted through the scarf she had wrapped around my face. "I forgot something."

"Forgot something? What on Earth could you have brought with you that you'd have forgotten?"

"My yo-yo," I said. It was the first thing that entered my mind.

"Me, too," Ursie said. "I forgot something too."

"Don't tell me it's a yo-yo," our mother said, frowning at what she already suspected was our deviousness.

Ursie nodded gleefully, eyes shining between her scarf and stocking hat.

"I can buy you both yo-yos if that's all they are."

She had opened the back door, waiting for us to pile inside.

I was the first to run away, Ursie following at my heels.

"Jeremy, Ursie, wait! Where are you going?"

I knew exactly where. We ran around a corner of the house to the coal chute. With a glance at Ursie, I hefted the handle and opened the door. We crouched, peering down through the tunnel into blackness.

"Eva?" we both hollered down to the room below. "Miss Eva?"

Our mother came up behind us.

"Who on Earth are you calling for?" she asked. "Just who is this Eva?"

"A princess," I calmly informed her.

"Oh, only a princess."

"She's probably asleep," I said.

"Or poisoned," Ursie added, thoughtfully.

"A poisoned princess," our mother exclaimed. "My, what imaginations you both have."

"But it's true," Ursie protested. "We've met her. She invited us back to play."

I nodded in agreement, keeping a careful eye on my mother's reaction.

She studied us intently for several quiet moments, billowing loose ends of amber hair curling outside her brilliant red head-scarf, providing a stark contrast with her indigo eyes.

I do have to give our mother full credit for coming to our aid when she determined a crisis was real.

Before all was done, a police car had arrived with two offic-ers, and a squad of firefighters broke down the door with axes.

Inside, the pink walls and carpet were still in evidence, but all other traces of human habitation had been removed: the four-poster bed, the dolls on shelves, the Japanese screen, the silver commode.

The police assured us they would look into the matter, and that was enough for our mother to lead us away to the car.

I still have dreams in which I am a prince of some misfortune. There is always something wrong with my armor, something out of place, or else an itch I can't get to without removing it piece by piece. Undaunted, I proceed toward the cold, dank dungeon where a princess is held prisoner. I fight my way through small spaces. I hack through obstacles with a wooden sword. I shout, "I am coming! I am coming!" But there is something that always prevents me. A splinter in my vision. A stepped-upon nail that protrudes through my footwear. And then I invariably wake up before my rescue of the princess is anywhere near accomplished.

So much for epilogues.

Chapter 13

Some people were writhing on the cement floor. One woman was crawling down the makeshift aisle, dragging her legs behind. Others were gyrating in place, as though dancing to Elvis, arms waving over their heads. Our mother, standing between us, had her eyes closed, her head tilted back, her lips murmuring a string of inaudible words. Organ music pumped persistently through a crackling loudspeaker. The preacher, up front, was handling a large, long, twister of a snake, letting it crawl around his neck and arms, as he shouted and stamped and brayed. Several people were babbling out loud, a sequence of strange words—or not even words, just syllables.

To my ears, it sounded like the repetition of the refrain to an Elvis cover of a Little Richard song our father liked to sing in the shower: *A-wop-bom-a-loo-mah a-lop-bam-boom!*

If this was the Holy Spirit speaking, its language was incomprehensible, in dire need of a translator or bilingual dictionary. Yet that's what we were here to find: the Spirit. Or vice versa: the Spirit was meant to find us. A flame was supposed to erupt above our heads, a dove settle onto our shoulders. We would suddenly speak in an ancient language—Hebrew or Greek—our tongues wagging without conscious control, like a puppy dog's tail when its owner comes home. Anything could happen. Anything was possible. The important thing was to demonstrate a sign.

So far, my sister and I failed to exhibit one. We looked at each other around our mother's skirt, from our places beneath the low ceiling of the church. It wasn't even a proper church, more an abandoned warehouse by a set of railroad tracks on the West Virginia side of the Ohio River. A large room outfitted with a cloth-covered table that served as an altar, it held any number of folding chairs, occupied or rather ignored as most people were standing or writhing. Augmenting the fluorescent light fixtures, illumination came from rows and rows of candles. Asbestos clung in cottony clumps to exposed steel beams.

Our mother was dressed in an ankle length skirt, so unlike her ordinary attire that usually showed off a pair of slim legs rising to her kneecaps. Her hair, normally free-flowing, was tied in a tight bun on top of her head.

We made certain signs with our fingers and faces, Ursula and I, behind our mother's back, to express to each other how mysteriously entertaining church had become. Usually, our Sunday mornings were tedious, stuffy affairs, alleviated only by tic-tac-toe using the stubby little pencils on the backs of Request for Personal Information slips that could be found in special holders next to the hymnals. Our father, who attended these services, was tolerant of our private amusements, to the chagrin of our mother, who encouraged strict attention to the sermon, however long and dry it might be.

But this wasn't Sunday, and our father wasn't present. It was a Thursday evening in March. Dad was holding down the second shift at work. We would pick him up when the service was over.

Although we found Mom's trancelike state entrancing, it was the snakes that consumed most of our attention. When the snakes were brought out and introduced to the congregation, we climbed on top of our seats and refused to touch ground until the service concluded. We both feared the same thing: a snake getting loose and coiling around our ankles. One snake appeared to bite the hand of a man who was holding it, once the preacher had begun passing it around the room. Immediately, the man dropped the snake and went into a convulsive fit.

Fortunately, when the service was over, the snake was found

and returned to its terrarium with its wriggling, coiling brethren. The man who had been bitten recovered. People stopped writhing and babbling. And the woman whose legs wouldn't work seemed fully capable of locomotion on her way out the door.

"This is all so fascinating," my therapist remarks, showing an uncharacteristic display of enthusiasm regarding my monologue. "Do you know what kind of snakes they were?"

I couldn't conceive how the species of reptile would have any bearing on an episode that I would later interpret as more traumatic than inspirational. The traumatic part? The way the service had transformed our mother into someone strange, foreign, different—a zombie out of Night of the Living Dead, *which our father had selected from the video store for family TV night one time until our mother paused it before we even got to the shopping-mall scene and sent us kids to bed.*

"I mean, were they venomous? According to Wikipedia, *they're straight up real in these kinds of churches. But it would be a much better story if you knew for sure, no lie. You know, as an eyewitness. No faking it."*

In the hindsight of memory I think I recognize copperheads and/ or cottonmouths from my Cub Scout field manual, but they might have been innocuous black rat snakes for all I really knew. It's also possible I've superimposed a black-and-white documentary our class was shown about Pentecostal snake handlers back in middle school.

"OK," I agree for the sake of historical accuracy, if not drama. "Let's make them poisonous."

"Did you feel it?" our mother kept asking on the drive home. That was another big difference between Thursdays and Sundays, besides the writhing, gyrating, crawling, snake handling, snake biting, and speaking in tongues. Sundays were all about Jesus. Thursdays, it was turning out, were all about the Spirit—a Holy one at that.

"No, I didn't feel anything, did you?" I nudged Ursie. We were both sitting in the back seat.

"I think I felt something," Ursie said, to my surprise.

Our mother's eyes shifted to the rearview mirror, her eyebrows arching with anticipation in the light thrown by streetlamps as we rolled back home along a stretch of highway after crossing the bridge downstream at Pomeroy.

"Did you?" our mother asked. "What did you feel?"

"I felt my stomach rumbling," Ursie said.

"Oh," our mother sounded disappointed, "is that all?"

"I heard it too," I confirmed. "It seemed like it was trying to tell her something."

"Does tummy talking count as speaking in tongues?" Ursie asked hopefully.

Was she making a joke? She seemed kind of little to be experimenting with sarcasm. Then again, she would turn six in another week.

It wasn't speaking in tongues, but as a language of its own, it was much more decipherable. It meant the church service had caused us to miss our normal dinner time.

"Well, we'll just have to keep trying, won't we?" Mom said.

The bottom line was if we couldn't come up with some tangible sign that we had been touched by the Holy Spirit, we wouldn't be saved. Saved from what, we weren't sure.

"Maybe the snake," Ursie thought when we discussed it in private at bedtime.

The thought I was left with before falling asleep was how important it was to our mother to do something extraordinary, something so far from the norm, it could only be considered a miracle—an act of grace.

And so I began jumping.

The way I reasoned it with my ten-year-old brain, Jesus had

acrophobia. The Devil had tempted him to jump from the highest pinnacle of the temple, and He had declined. To my mind, that was the whole moral of the story: there were some things that even Jesus was afraid to do, proving He was just as much human as divine. It wasn't that He didn't trust the angels to catch him, He was simply afraid of heights. So I would prove my immunity to acrophobia by jumping. Maybe I wouldn't get as high as a pinnacle—I wasn't aware of any temples in the vicinity of Bellerophon, but a couple of church steeples might do—so maybe I could jump off our roof for starters and seek out higher places later. If I had enough faith, the angels would catch me in my fall. After all, wasn't that what angels were for?

My sister became my cheerleader. I started with the basement steps, and she stood at the bottom, as I raised the ante one step at a time, leaping like a frog from a lily pad.

I made it to the topmost stair. The pressure was on to meet or exceed my sister's expectations. She watched from the bottom with clasped hands.

I took a deep breath, as though preparing to dive under water, and jumped.

The first thing I felt was my head bumping hard against the ceiling that slanted in parallel with the angle of the stairs. The next thing I felt was a sharp stabbing pain in my right ankle as I crumpled into a heap on the cold concrete floor.

"Cool beans!" Ursie exclaimed, applauding. She was always hipper to contemporary slang than I was. Maybe she picked it up from school or TV. "That was gnarly."

One look at my ankle, and I could see that it was "gnarly" in a different sense of the word, meaning my practice sessions were over. I would never make it to the big-time by jumping from the roof. A bone was sticking out of my leg above my ankle at an angle. Blood was oozing onto the floor in a large puddle.

I don't remember if I screamed, but I must have blacked out, because the next thing I remember is waking up in a brightly lit hospital room with a doctor putting the finishing touches on a cast she was wrapping around my foot and lower leg following surgery to reconnect the broken ends of my fibula—technically the lateral malleolus that ends in a knob on the outside of the ankle.

My sister had a less clinical diagnosis: "Thigh bone's connected to the shin bone," she sang. "Shin bone's connected to the ankle bone. Except for Jeremy's!"

"What were you thinking?" This was Dad talking, his face leaning close to mine on the other side of the bed. "You're ten years old, don't you think you should have more sense?"

Somehow, my being in double digits was supposed to make a big difference in how I planned my accidents.

I was too surprised by my father's presence to answer.

"Shouldn't you be at work?" I asked, forcing out the question despite the throbbing pain that kept shooting up my leg as though to engage in a wrestling match with my upper extremities.

"Doctor," he said, bypassing my inquiry, "please tell me he's going to be all right. I mean, his ankle—will he be able to do sports? He'll still be okay for football, won't he?"

This was the first time I had even an inkling that my father planned a sports career for me, never mind football. But then, my father had been something short of a sports legend himself in high school: track and field, football, baseball, basketball. He had lettered in everything, except he had spent most of his career warming benches. Track and field was the exception. He had successfully competed in low hurdles, the long jump, and mile relay. Plus, he had a countywide trophy to prove it.

Still—sports! What was he thinking? Obviously, he hadn't played catch with me in quite some time in order to realize I hadn't progressed to the stage where I could consistently hit the broad side of a barn, despite my success with Mrs. Darnell's garage.

"Well," the doctor said. From experience, I knew any sentence starting with "well" wouldn't contain a completely positive prognosis. "It's too early to tell, but the bone set as neatly as could be expected."

"So he'll be able to play, then?"

I could tell he was worried. He didn't have a worry stone, but he did have a worry coin, a Walking Liberty half-dollar, which he rubbed between his fingers inside his trousers pocket whenever he was agitated. He would take it out from time to time and let me ogle it. Most of its features, front and back, had been worn away by worry and time, leaving a faint impression of the year it was minted beneath the eroded goddess's left foot: 1941.

This was the year his own father, having attained the draftable age of 21, had been called up for service during World War Two. Rubbing the silver half-dollar had seen his father—my Grandpa Earl—through one crisis after another during the war, including an assault on Juno, but then his luck had run out when he contracted bone cancer. He died before I was born but passed on the silver coin to his son as a keepsake, so my father could rub it between his fingers in times of trouble as though summoning a genie from a lamp.

"I would say with physical therapy—"

"Therapy!"

"Now, Henry," Mom cooed.

"This is the first I've heard mentioned the word 'therapy.'"

I was still quite out of it, but somewhere in that muddled conversation, I thought I heard the phrase "gimp for life," followed by a sharp gasp from our mother and her single reprimand: "Henry!"

My biggest complaint, which I wasn't to register until later, was that I had been unconscious during an ambulance ride to the hospital. A trip in an ambulance with lights swirling and siren blaring, and I couldn't remember a thing.

Mom and Ursula had met up with me at the hospital only after picking up Dad from work.

Imagine. An ambulance! What a story I would have had to tell if only I had been awake for it.

Chapter 14

I finished fourth grade wearing a cast. Classmates who had never paid me any attention now all clamored to sign it. I made a dozen friends before the end of first period. Girls who had made a point of ignoring me now asked how I was doing daily. The main subject of discussion was whether my leg was feeling itchy now that the weather was warming up as we headed toward summer break.

But once the cast was off and school was over, I went back to my usual life of virtual solitude, except for Ursula. Even though she had only graduated kindergarten and had turned six in March, she was still my only real playmate.

By the end of the school year, we had moved to a small rental home on a two-acre plot of land that we shared with our landlord, an older man with a bald head, what our father referred to as a "chrome dome." Our house was perched at the top of a dead-end road that wound down a hill past houses on wooded lots that grew larger and more expensive the farther you went, until ending in a cluster of what would come to be termed "McMansions" around a cul-de-sac. Each house contained a rather stuck-up kid or two, several of whom were my age, becoming snootier and snobbier with the size of the houses. They would have become friends—maybe not exactly close or dear—if not for an unbridgeable income gap between their families and mine. We were the poor kids at the top of the street, they the children of privilege at the bottom.

Even though the cast was off, I still walked with a limp that a weekly session of physical therapy was supposed to correct. But it didn't stop me from outdoor pursuits. Although I was advised to stay off my bike, I decided this advice didn't apply to coasting, so I coasted down the hill to hang around with the rich kids at the bottom of the street on my clunker of a bicycle. Our father had picked it out of someone's trash along a curb and brought it home tied to the top of the station wagon, as though it were the carcass of an animal brought down in a hunting expedition.

All I can say for it is it had two wheels that wobbled and a seat that had lost most of its cushioning, so riding it for any distance was an exercise in maintaining balance and enduring discomfort. The rich kids at the bottom of the street accepted me into their midst as an oddity, something eccentric to be approached with caution, probably on the advice of their parents. Nevertheless, we rode in circles around the cul-de-sac, staging races, me on my clunker, they on shiny bikes with high handlebars and gearshifts and hand brakes instead of coasters. When tired of racing, we turned one of the bikes over and pedaled it in place while feeding long sticks into the spinning spokes to take pleasure in the rattling, ratcheting sound. Do I even have to mention that the bicycle normally chosen for this activity was mine?

When we played tag, I was almost always "it." And since they knew the best hiding places, I almost never found anyone, but I would hear sniggers coming from behind bushes and trees— along with whiffs of tobacco smoke and, on one occasion, the aroma of something more exotic.

I did manage to make friends with one kid named Kevin. He seemed the "odd man out" and no doubt was appreciative when I took over this role from him. For instance, he didn't wear nice clothes like the other kids but dressed in jeans with tears in the knees that he said he had put there on purpose. He also wore tie-dye T-shirts with swirling purples and yellows and greens that were a mesmerizing variation from the casual tees with iron-on emblems and slogans that the other boys wore. Also, he was the only one of the bunch who went to public school, like me. He grew his hair long, almost to his shoulders. What's more, he even rode the bus! We hadn't ridden the same one, though, since he had just finished fifth grade, having put in a full year in middle school. I was fresh out of elementary.

And so, being older and more mature, he already had two major regrets in life:

(a) That he was born privileged and white rather than under-privileged and what he referred to as a "person of color."

(b) That he had missed going to Woodstock.

Regarding (a): I learned that the best poets, essayists, and nov-elists in his estimation were African-American—Langston Hughes, Maya Angelou, James Baldwin—and it was Kevin's am-bition to become a great poet, essayist, or novelist someday.

Regarding (b): I had only a vague notion of what Woodstock had been all about, but I knew it had occurred the year before I was born.

One day, Kevin and I were stalking through a nearby patch of woods for the ideal location of a treehouse hideaway. We thought we would borrow some lumber from the construction company that bordered our property at the top of the street. While hiking, we came across a blue heron, ankle deep in a swamp (although I can't say for sure that herons have ankles), preparing to spear a frog or fish it had its eye on with its long, narrow beak.

"Wow," I whispered, "have you ever seen anything like it?"

"Here," Kevin said, opening his billfold, a possession I en-vied, never having any bills to justify owning a wallet, "take a look at this and you tell me if you've ever seen anything like *this*."

What "this" happened to be was a neat, crisp, spanking-new, unwrinkled $100 bill. It was the first time I learned whose face stared out from it.

"Ben Franklin," I said in low-voiced amazement.

"Wasn't he a president or something?" Kevin shrugged,

handing me the bill as though it were a Kleenex I had requested to drain a runny nose.

Indeed, my eyes were watering ... with what I felt was a climactic moment in my life to that date. If I were to suddenly die on the spot from a cerebral hemorrhage (this is how our father's aunt died one day as she was pulling out weeds from her garden) or a lightning strike (this was how our mother's uncle died while confronting the Fates with an open umbrella on the back nine of a golf course in a thunderstorm), I would have gone out of this world with a satisfied smile.

I forgot all about the ignorance behind Kevin's question. Apparently, he paid less attention to history lessons than I did.

"It's a hundred-dollar bill," I muttered in my trancelike state.

"Keep it," Kevin said nonchalantly, as though it were a baseball card.

"For how long?" I asked, looking up, questioning whether the figure of Kevin possessed the insubstantial quality of a mirage.

"Forever," Kevin shrugged.

"Is this your allowance money?" I asked, trying to keep down an upsurge of jealousy.

"Not at all, I took it from a briefcase in my dad's office. He's got bunches of them. Hundreds of hundreds," he said with a smirk at his wit. "It's not like he's going to be missing one or two of them. I take out a couple from time to time if there's something I want to buy that my parents don't approve of."

"I don't think I can," I said, thinking of my parents' reaction, and handing it back.

"No, keep it, seriously," Kevin said, his hands pushing back my return of the bill with an invisible force.

"Well, I'll just hold onto it then," I said, thinking through options that might allow me to keep it both practically and ethically, "until you want it back."

—

While Mom was downstairs, working on a paint-by-number with Ursula, I took out her ironing board and steam-pressed the hundred-dollar bill between two sheets of wax paper to preserve it from harm, including spilled drinks, rips and tears, and wrinkles and creases—any of which could occur if subjected to the curiosity of an impetuous little sister. With it carefully layered between the sheets of wax paper, caught in an air pocket as though a dragonfly in amber, I punched three holes along the edge of the paper and fastened it into a three-ring binder that held a leaf collection using the same wax-paper preservation method I had all but forgotten about making the summer before. Neither of my parents was particularly interested in leaves. A leaf is a leaf is a leaf was their philosophy. And Ursie cared nothing for leaves until fall when she could leap into raked piles of them for fun.

So I complimented myself on finding what I thought was a safe hiding place—a permanent one, or so I thought at the time.

I saw Kevin's father several times but only spoke with him once. I don't know that he had a mother—at least she never called him in to eat, the way Mom would track me down with the station wagon when it was time for me to go home, much to my embarrassment in front of the kids I wanted so much to impress.

He was a tall, soft-spoken man who wore long-sleeved dress shirts in the summer with gold cufflinks.

The one time we engaged in conversation, he was pulling into the drive, and I had to move my bike to prevent its being run over. He asked my name, asked where I lived. Then he crouched down and took a good, long look at my bicycle. I thought he was mentally picking it apart for flaws, but he stood up, smiled, and said he used to own a bike just like this one.

"Make sure you practice bicycle safety." This was his word of advice before stepping into his air-conditioned foyer. Our house didn't have air-conditioning—just fans in one window of every room aimed toward the interior. The direction of the fan's air was another source of disagreement between our father and mother. Dad theorized that the fan should be facing outward so as to blow warm air out of the house. But Mom liked the feeling of a breeze circulating through a room, so her argument won out.

Later that year, Kevin's father was arrested for passing counterfeit money, namely fifties and hundreds. It had been the culmination of a yearlong sting operation conducted by the U.S. Secret Service—which made sense, the counterfeits being a secret.

It was Dad who pointed out the story that headlined the evening news. At dinnertime, it was his practice to read aloud snippets of news items that caught his attention while Mom dished out the meal.

"Imagine, a counterfeiter living right down the street from us," Dad said with a tone of admiration in his voice.

"Guess it just goes to show you can find crooks anywhere," was Mom's comment.

Ursie asked what "counterfeit" meant.

I studied my hundred-dollar bill for a long time that evening, trying to decide whether it was a product of Kevin's father's printing press that the FBI had confiscated from his basement, according to the article. Finally, after careful analysis, I decided it was easier to believe it was worthless. Not only did it ease my conscience, but it would have been next to impossible to explain to my parents how I had found or earned or saved enough money based on my meager 50-cent-a-week allowance to buy what I had set my heart upon: a brand-new bicycle.

That's right. It was the start of a new decade, and my weekly allowance had doubled.

Chapter 15

Except for the landlord's house next door, my sister and I lived in a sort of Eden. At least an Eden for two poor kids of unequal ages. A nearby construction lot provided all kinds of idle power equipment we could climb around on and pretend to drive or operate: backhoes, bulldozers, cranes. The orchard behind our house opened a kaleidoscopic array of pink and white flowers in late spring, which would have made climbing and sitting in the crook of an apple tree a mesmerizing way to pass the time if not for my bum ankle.

Behind the orchard was a small cemetery with older gravesites marked with deteriorating sandstone, making it hard to decipher dates and names, and newer graves saddled with more permanent granite of gray or salmon. The cemetery was simply another playground for us. We could climb on, leapfrog, or hide behind as many tombstones as we wished without fear of the residents getting annoyed or angry.

In the very corner of the cemetery, where it met the orchard, was a storm drain covering a square concrete catch basin with a heavy metal grille that could only be hefted with the combined strength of sister and brother, meaning Ursie and me. In fact, we needed extra assistance in the form of a makeshift lever I created with a rusty crowbar I borrowed from the construction company next door. After heavy rains, water rushed along the bottom of the drainage pit six feet below, pouring out of the opening of one small sewer pipe and emptying through the aperture of its cousin on the opposite wall. In between was a fun way to dispose of sticks or crabapples or pine cones, just to watch them race away out of sight.

Maybe the drain was there to catch runoff water from the cemetery to keep the graves from flooding, I theorized. My imagination drifted to images of water-logged coffins containing watery corpses—phantasms that I didn't share with Ursula.

A ladder—a series of U-shaped metal rods set into the concrete—led into the bowels of the catch basin, and once we lifted the metal grille, we took turns descending to the bottom rung, just to hang there like a monkey, contemplating the majestic force of nature in the form of water gushing along the open portion of the sewer.

This type of entertainment lasted only until Ursie lost her shoe. It went whizzing along like a toy boat on the surface of the deluge, disappearing through the aperture of the outlet pipe and leaving her with one damp sock in its place.

We wouldn't have gotten into so much trouble, except it was a brand-new shoe. Our mother gave us the usual reprimand about how much shoes cost, and didn't either of us know better than to risk our lives climbing down into a sewer, and how many weeks' allowance it would take both of us to make up the difference.

"Why me? What did I do? It wasn't my shoe," I complained.

"You're supposed to be the older, wiser brother who knows better," my mother responded with logic that was hard to argue against, mainly because she brooked no argument.

"But, but—"

Let's face it, any number of "buts" wouldn't propel me into a counterargument that would have scaled the fortress of my mother's crossed arms.

"Save your 'buts,' young man, until your father gets home."

"But who knows when that will be," I pouted.

"Seriously? Another 'but'?" Nevertheless, she looked at the calendar. "One week from tomorrow."

—

Our father had been laid off from his job as a furnace operator and had taken up lessons in trucking. Upon graduation from trucking school, he found a job hauling stuff—just stuff—medium distances at first that brought him home every evening, but then longer and longer trips that kept him on the road two, three, four days at a time. Eventually, we got used to his being away for one week, then two weeks. In between trips, especially the longer ones, he would spend a lot of time in front of the TV, watching game shows, or else sleeping, with clear instructions not to wake him unless it was an emergency. Approved emergencies came in only two forms: (a) fire and (b) a stranger at the door.

We almost never had to worry about (b) because our mother was usually around to answer the doorbell. Our father was making enough money so that Mom didn't have to go to work, and so she was free to pursue her altruistic activities. Except now that Mrs. Darnell was dead, she exchanged hospice visits for prison visits.

But first let me get back to the business of the storm drain in the corner of our landlord's property because it features later in this story. When our father found out—by means of our mother telling him—that we were crawling around in sewers, he blew up, as any misinformed parent might. In his view, we could be eaten by alligators that had been flushed down toilets as overgrown babies only to become outsized monsters of the deep. Or else attacked by a horde of rats, which wouldn't be as bad as alligators, except they carried all manner of disease, ranging from typhus to plague.

"Henry, please don't scare the children," our mother advised. "The plague hasn't been around for centuries."

"Maddy, you haven't read Camus," our father intoned. Did I ever mention our mother's first name was Madeline? Probably not. As kids, we never called her by her given name. It was progressively, Mama, Mommy, Mom. Neither did our father address her so formally. He used his own special pet name for her instead. As for Camus, I had no idea who he was or even how to spell his name. Its pronunciation—Ka-MOO—made him sound like a variety of cow. Overall, I was astounded by the range of reading material our father took with him to the bathroom.

And so, in due course, our father contacted our landlord who informed the public road department, who sent out a workman to fix the problem of easy access to the drainage ditch in question.

Ursula and I came across him one morning and watched him work. He took frequent breaks while working, sipping coffee out of a thermos or taking time to finish a cigarette, the ashes from which he tapped over the sewer grating he was modifying.

By lunchtime, he had welded in place two hinges on one side of the grating and a latch on the other. He closed the latch in place with a Master lock and affixed the key to an enormous ring of keys that hung from his utility belt.

"Well, that should keep you kids out of places you don't belong," he said, with one corner of his mouth raised in a smile that let us know he wasn't really upset with us.

"Why do people go down there?" I asked. "Grownups," I clarified, assuming the privilege of climbing down into the sewer was reserved for civil servants.

"Oh, sometimes it gets all clogged up, like a toilet. And then we have to run a snake through the pipes."

Our father had already warned us about alligators and rats, so a snake was something new.

"What kind of snake?" Ursie asked, staring through the grating on her hands and knees. "A copperhead?"

"Oh, no," the man laughed, "not a real snake." And then he described the kind of snake he had to use in such situations.

"Why do they call it a snake?" I asked.

But the man didn't have time to answer my question or

considered the answer too obvious to bother with.

In any case, Ursula and I didn't have much time left for rec-reation. There were only a couple of precious weeks of summer vacation left to us before August would come to a close with a flurry of purchases of new school supplies: three-ring notebooks, ballpoint pens, book bags, lunch pails. And then there was the business of buying new clothes, which involved entering and ex-iting a series of changing rooms to stand in front of three-way mirrors, while our mother stood behind us with a frown on her face, sizing us up.

I never relished changing in and out of clothes, but I always enjoyed looking at myself in a three-way mirror. You could pre-tend you were a stranger looking at the back of your own head. One time, I was placed in front of a mirror that happened to have another mirror directly behind me. I soon discovered with this type of arrangement that if you angled your face just right, you could see yourself receding into infinity as a series of smaller and smaller reflections. It made me think my life could go on forever, just as it was. But somewhere in my mind I was already beginning to appreciate that nothing in life really lasts for long.

"Do you mind a little literary criticism?" my therapist asks, leaning back in her comfy chair and setting her phone aside.

"Criticism?" I ask. In comparison, the couch reserved for clients has firm cushions and a straight back, hardly conducive to relaxation—and maybe this is the point.

"I was an English major before switching to psychology," she explains. "It's just that the symbolism, it's all so obvious: Eden, an apple orchard, a snake ..."

"It's not like I'm making it up," I defend my account.

My therapist replies with a calmness that unsettles me even more: "I didn't say that you were."

Chapter 16

The week before school started—I believe it would have been a Wednesday, but any day will do, you know how summers are when you're a kid, one day bleeding into another, each week a blur of images without consequence or merit—our mother took us on another volunteer expedition, this time to a nearby medium-security prison.

"There's nothing to worry about," Mom told us on the way over in the station wagon. "These prisoners aren't violent. They're just misguided."

And it was her job to guide them. The goal was improving their literacy in small groups of three or four. She would coach them on reading skills.

"Reading is so very, very important," she lectured us. "You can't do anything in life without being able to read. Anything worthwhile, that is."

"These are grownups?" I prodded.

"Yes, adult men."

"And they can't read?" I continued to prod.

"That's correct, weren't you listening?"

"Why can't they read?" Ursie asked.

"Well, now that's a very good question, a very good question indeed," our mother responded. In fact, it turned out to be such a good question, she didn't bother to answer it. This was something we were learning about the nature of questions. In any case, she had parked the car and was reapplying her lipstick in the rear-view mirror.

"Will we be sitting with the prisoners, too?" I wondered.

"Of course not," Mom said. "You'll be in a playroom."

"Far out!" Ursie exclaimed, using a phrase she had picked up from God knows whom—not me. We passed through a security checkpoint, where a guard gave us all a visitor's badge and phoned ahead to let someone on the "inside" know we were coming.

I didn't have to wonder how she would be helping them learn how to read. I took note of the book she held below her purse, the strap of which she had pulled tightly across her chest.

"You'll be having them read the Bible?" I asked, all innocence.

"What, Jeremy? Oh, yes. What better way to introduce them to the alphabet and God's grace at the same time?"

It was the same method she had used on me when I was in kindergarten. We had started with Genesis out of the New Revised Standard version, and I tried my best to follow the tip of my mother's forefinger as it roved slowly down the first column of the first page of tiny print.

I could only pity the poor prisoners who would have to suffer through the first six days of Creation as I had. It was almost enough to make you wish God had decided on doing the whole job in a single day. It's what I would have done. Then He would have had six whole days of rest and relaxation instead of just one.

Once we were inside the "pen," we were greeted by an assistant to the warden, a matronly woman in uniform, who escorted all three of us down a gray-painted, windowless hallway. At the end of the hall, a door opened to the left to the playroom. , which the assistant accessed with a key. It had a small square window high up on a wall—made of glass, I was disappointed to note, not bars. One wall was affixed with a mirror the size of a picture window. I had seen enough cop shows to suspect the mirror was see-through from the other side.

Our mother gave us each a peck on top of the head. I was

only ten, so I still didn't come up to her shoulder blades in height, although I was expected to undergo a growth spurt "any day now," according to my mom. Then she was handed off to a security guard who escorted her through a double-locked door at the very end of the hall.

The playroom didn't seem designed for play. There was a small circular table on three legs painted a dull green. A fourth leg was missing, which made it virtually unusable for playing board games or drawing with crayons without it tilting back and forth like a piece of unanchored furniture on a ship. Besides, the box of crayons had only five colors left, and these had been worn down to mere nubs. There were two board games: *Scrabble* and *Parcheesi*. Upon inspection, *Scrabble* was missing crucial consonants and vowels, while *Parcheesi* was down to just a handful of marbles that weren't enough to fill the board. A small green chalkboard on an easel stood nearby, with two large chunks of colored chalk—pink and purple—along with an eraser.

Three small chairs, which would have been fine for the baby bear of the fairy tale, and one large red beanbag were the only items of furniture designed for sitting.

A heavyset older boy leafing through a comic book was taking up the beanbag. I took the comic book as a good omen. It meant we had something in common. I only wished I had brought along one of my Green Lantern editions as a conversation starter.

A girl about Ursie's age sat at the lopsided table, vigorously filling in a page torn from a coloring book with dark purple, mercilessly straying outside the lines, indifferent to what should be the natural color of the rabbit that was the subject of her artistry. Her hair was as unkempt as her coloring, and she wore a ragged pair of shorts and stained T-shirt in contrast to Ursie's more formal calico dress. I was outfitted as usual for these charity visits of my mom's in short-sleeved dress shirt and clip-on tie.

Ursie went up to the chalkboard and wrote her name in screeching pink, pressing hard, as though to make a permanent impression.

When finished, she turned to the girl, who paused with her crayon.

"That's my name: Ursula," she beamed. "But you can call me 'Ursie' for short. What's your name?"

"Mandy," the girl said after a careful silence.

"That's a nice name," Ursie commented. "Do you know how to spell it?"

"Of course I know how to spell my own name," Mandy replied, somewhat crossly, not that I could blame her. I can't think of anyone who likes having their spelling ability challenged.

I turned my back on their embryonic getting-to-know-you conversation to introduce myself to my newfound friend. At least I hoped he would turn out to be a friend and not a nemesis. Based on the way he was glaring at me over the edge of his comic book, it was hard to be sure. If the latter, I was in for trouble. He had the build of a sumo wrestler in miniature with a cauliflower ear to match.

"So," the boy said, nice and slow, with a drawl straight out of a B-movie Western. "What's your dad in for?"

As a conversation opener, it had me baffled, but only for a second.

"Nothing," I said. "My dad's not in here for anything."

"Oh," the boy drawled, closing his comic but keeping his place with a thick thumb, "so it's your mom who's incarcerated, is it?"

I was so impressed by a five-syllable word coming from this boy's mouth that I failed to respond.

"Prostitution, I'll bet," he continued, overriding the arching of my eyebrows at the word. "Tell the truth. Your mother's nothing but a low-down, dirty whore. Which is bad news for you, being a momma's boy and all."

How was I to respond to this accusation? I was still stuck on the word "incarcerated," and now he was expanding my vocabulary with the use of the word "whore." I didn't have mental capacity left over to take offense by the term "momma's boy."

It was Ursie who piped up in our mother's defense.

"You better take that back," she said, breaking away from her conversation with Mandy, which had escalated into an exchange of insults, the more they got acquainted.

"Oh, yeah?" the boy said, half rising, but unable to get all the way out of the beanbag without recourse to gyrations that made him seem like a stranded turtle on its back. "And just what are you going to do about it?"

"Nothing," Ursie said defiantly. "But my brother will do something about it. Just see if he won't."

I found myself wishing she hadn't made such a promise.

"Hey," Mandy said, rising more nimbly from her chair at the table, "you can't talk to *my* brother that way."

It was the first indication I had that our two new acquaintances might be related by blood. The girl was as small-boned as a sparrow.

Oh, well, what was I to do except follow through on Ursie's threat, while it remained somewhat vague.

I took three purposeful steps forward, standing directly in front of Bean-Boy with my arms folded stiffly across my chest.

"You just wait," Bean-Boy said. "You just wait till I get on my feet."

"Yeah, like that's going to happen anytime soon."

Ursie snickered into her hand, which unsettled me with the realization I had spoken my thought out loud.

Mandy cut my sister's snickering short with a threat of her own: "If your brother does anything to my brother, I'll do the same and worse to you."

As I watched Bean-Boy struggle to get onto his feet, which I judged to be size 11s compared with my size 7s, a wave of sympathy overtook me. I thought about Jesus—yes, Jesus. What would Jesus do in a situation like this? Would He continue to observe the poor tortoise struggling to right itself? Or would He help it out of its predicament, even if it was a sworn enemy? Were tortoises even native to Palestine? And, if so, how big did they get? As big as this boy stuck in the bean bag in front of me? These were the questions that went through my mind as I reached out my hand. But instead of coming to his assistance, my hand took a different route with a will of its own and picked up the comic book, which Bean-Boy had set aside, unguarded, on the floor.

"Hey! You give that back!" he yelled furiously from Ground Zero.

"Archie Comics?" I asked in wonderment. "You read Archie Comics?" I hadn't leafed through one in years. I wanted nothing more than to spend the rest of the afternoon getting reacquainted with Archie and his pals: Reggie, Veronica, Jughead, Dilton … Of course! Super-intelligent, ultra-nerd Dilton Doiley, whose best friend and protector is ultra-strong, super-jock Moose Mason. There was no reason the two of us couldn't take our counterparts as role models and be friends.

"So what if I do?" Bean-Boy growled, which brought me to my senses: a Moose to my Doiley he was not.

And now it was Ursie's turn to yell.

"Hands off! You better give that back to me right now!"

Keeping one eye on Bean-Boy and one eye on the cover of the comic book, I was still able to record with my peripheral vision Mandy's snatching of a doll Ursie had brought with her and left on the eraser tray of the chalkboard. It wasn't exactly a case of baby snatching since the doll in question was a voluptuous Barbie—completely naked to boot, as Ursie had been interrupted in the process of dressing her.

As far as I could tell, we had arrived at a stalemate.

No blows had been exchanged, no wounds had been inflicted, no trips to an orthodontist or bone specialist would be required in the immediate future.

Speaking of the future, the clock on the wall read: 3:15. Our mother wouldn't be done with her literacy class until 4:00. That left 45 minutes to somehow defuse the situation at hand.

I've never felt that defusing a situation has been one of my strong points.

As Bean-Boy managed to get to his feet, Ursie placed Mandy in a headlock. In a way, they formed a center of gravity while my nemesis—now that his role had been confirmed—began to maneuver me around the room in a somewhat lumbering fashion, as though he were a polar bear on skis.

Despite a limp that several sessions with physical therapists never quite eliminated, I managed to stay a few paces ahead by placing obstacles in his path. Of course, there weren't many to choose from: two unoccupied kids' chairs, a chalkboard on an easel, and a beanbag. So I ran out of impediments rather quickly, although I meandered in a variety of loop-de-loops to keep my pursuer off guard.

Twenty minutes passed without an exchange of words.

"What's your name anyhow?" I finally asked between gasps for breath. I thought it might be a good idea to at least be on a first-name basis with my eventual executioner.

"What's it to you?" he asked, between gasps of his own, which I was grateful to hear were even quicker in succession.

"Well, What's-It-To-You," I mocked, "my name is" *huff* "Jeremy Hilary Jones."

"Hilary, huh? Isn't that" *huff* "a girl's" *huff-huff* "name?"

"I was named" *huff* "for the guy" *huff* "who was the first to climb" *huff-huff* "Mount Everest." I left out the part that my name had only one letter "l" compared to Sir Edmund's two.

"Oh, that" *huff-huff* "Hillary," he said. "I'll bet" *huff* "his sherpa beat him to it."

This was a sore point for me, as I had often wished my parents had named me after the indigenous guide who had helped Sir Edmund Hillary to the summit. He had a much cooler name. Think of it: Jeremy *Tenzing* Jones. Or just "Zing" for short.

"That's not" *huff-huff* "what the history" *huff* "books say."

On the verge of hyperventilating, I decided to do the manly thing—something you might not expect from a Hilary—and turn and face my pursuer while huffing in place. Bean-Boy stopped short, a look of utter confusion making his eyes blink repeatedly, and, so as not to be outdone, I suppose, he began huffing in place, as well. It was like we were both treading water, waiting to see who would be the first to go under.

Meanwhile, Ursie was clutching a lock of Mandy's hair, even as Mandy pulled at one of her pigtails, which she always referred to as "bear-tails," since she was our parents' Little Bear.

Finally, our huffing in place came to a halt.

"Anyway," I said, stalling for time, "are you going to tell me your name?"

"Toby," he said point blank.

"Ah, Toby," I said, as though the name held some deep significance for me.

"You better not crack any jokes," he advised.

"Like what?" I wondered. "Like 'Moby'?" The rhyme bubbled out of my subconscious without effort. "Is that what the kids at school call you? Moby—"

"Don't you dare," Toby warned me, and I didn't.

But Ursie did.

"Dick!" she exclaimed, pausing mid-headlock. "Like the whale."

As a comment on his girth, it was a verbal act of body shaming for which I felt tremendous embarrassment on Ursie's behalf—but not for very long.

"Hey!" Mandy erupted. "You can't call my brother that. Only *I* can."

Eyes narrowing into tiny beads of loathing, Toby took a baby step forward, and I took a baby step back. He took another baby step forward, and I took another one back. He took a third step, and I found myself pressed up against the door.

I tried the handle, but it wouldn't open. We were locked in.

Next to the doorframe was a red button with a typewritten note taped above it: Push for Restroom Only. Underneath, someone had scrawled in a kid's block letters: "OR EMERJENCYS."

Toby saw it at the same time.

What was this situation I had found myself in if not an emergency?

"Don't even think about it," he said. "Besides, wouldn't you need your mama to wipe your ass? I hear she's good at it."

"I suppose I have no choice, then," I said, with all the calmness I could muster.

"What choice?"

What choice indeed?

"Well, with my mother's honor at stake and all, I hereby challenge you to a duel."

"A duel?"

"Of course it would be of your time and choosing. And as for weapons—"

Before I could lay out the ground rules, he took a giant step forward, which would have closed the gap between us, except that, lacking a gauntlet with which to underscore my challenge, I reflexively flung his comic book at him. I had already read three-quarters of it while outpacing him anyway. Unfortunately, the trajectory had a tendency to strike him smack in the eye.

"Ow!" he yelled and then lunged, holding one hand to his eye, the other reaching, groping, stretching …

I closed my own eyes, bracing for impact.

But none came.

Instead, he pushed the red button by accident. Within seconds, the warden's assistant opened the door, and Toby brushed past her into the hall.

The lingering fear I had that I wouldn't live to enter fifth grade receded like a bad dream.

"Well," she said, looking at the three of us who remained. "That was certainly urgent. Anyone else need to go while the door's open?"

After assessing the situation further, the woman escorted the three of us to the lobby and left us to sit in hard, orange, molded plastic chairs. Ursie sat next to me, and Mandy sat across from us, where she made sure we could see her steady glare. Toby, I was happy to note, had been taken to the clinic.

It was a quarter past 4:00 when Toby rejoined us. His one eye was covered by a square bandage affixed by windings of gauze strips that gave him a sort of mummified look.

"To the death," his one eye seemed to communicate.

"To the death," he interpreted, in case there was any doubt as to the outcome of our duel.

"I would expect nothing less," I was able to reply with confidence derived from my certainty we would never encounter each other again.

"Where's Mommy?" Ursie wondered.

"I'm sure she won't be much longer," I tried reassuring her, even though I wasn't sure about anything at the moment.

But she was.

After fifteen long minutes, both our mothers hustled through the security door into the lobby.

Our mother came to our side of the room. The other mother went to her children's side of the room.

Our mother knelt down in front of us. The other mother knelt down in front of her children.

Our positions were so similar, I had the odd impression I was looking into a funhouse mirror that played tricks with our bodily forms.

In any case, we all stood up to sign out at the same time.

"Jeremy, don't you have something you want to say to Toby?"

And now I knew partly what our mother had been doing to cause her delay. She had been getting to know Toby and Mandy's mother.

"Here's your comic book," I said, extending it to him, a goodwill gesture that made him reflexively flinch.

"Keep it," he said. I wasn't sure if this was a gift in good faith or whether he simply didn't want to be reminded of the implement that had scratched his cornea, which is, medically speaking, what I later learned had happened to his vision.

"Besides that," my mother encouraged me.

"Oh, yeah. Well, you know, sorry," finally came out of my mouth after swimming around like a mindless goldfish in a bowl.

Apparently, Toby did not find my apology convincing.

"Dead," he mouthed, drawing his forefinger across his throat.

Soon after, we were buckled up in the back seat of the station wagon, Ursie and me, but our mother didn't pull out of the parking lot just yet. She sat there with the engine idling, staring at me, just me, through the rearview mirror. It was like one of those paintings that transfix you with the sitter's stare. I couldn't seem to make my eyes move away from my mother's.

"Well, Jeremy, I certainly hope you are better behaved when you see Toby again." Her eyes shifted suddenly to my sister, who instinctively looked up from her Barbie doll, whose hair had been pulled from its scalp, leaving her perfectly bald. "And that goes for you, too, Ursula Lee." The rare use of my sister's middle name let us know the gravity of the situation.

"But we won't be seeing them again, will we?" I said, a note of dread transforming into a whine.

"I hope not, too," Ursie said. "That Mandy was a total spaz."

"Ursie, language," our mother reprimanded gently. "As a matter of fact, I've arranged playtime for both of you this weekend."

I would have taken this information in stride, by striding away from it as quickly as possible. As it was, I was strapped in like a patient in a lunatic asylum, so all I could do was slink down in my seat to pull my eyes out of the rearview mirror.

———

We survived what would become popularized in another decade as a "playdate," but barely.

Our duel took the form of Lawn Jarts at 20 paces with our sisters serving as our seconds. Maybe you remember these? They were darts of a size and weight suitable for tossing long distances with the idea of their tapered steel noses making their way into a plastic circle like a Hula Hoop laid on the ground. Essentially, they were projectiles as lethal to juvenile play as a nuclear missile is to the goings-on of a city.

Toby and I squared off at a regulation distance at first. But then, the more we played, the closer we moved the Hula Hoops together until we were face to face. And that's when Lawn Jarts descended into a game of Chicken. Traditionally, as I learned in Cub Scouts, Chicken is played with open-bladed jackknives. The concept is to fling the knife as close to your opponent's foot— either one—as possible without actually inflicting damage. If you accidentally—through some error in calculation—strike your opponent's foot with the blade, you lose a point, more if your opponent loses a toe in the process. If, however, you come close enough to make your opponent flinch by jerking his (or her) foot away, you score a point. It's as simple as that. Except when played with Lawn Jarts, the probability for serious injury goes up a decimal place or two.

Despite my initial dread, I counted our playdate a success.

Ursie and Mandy had abandoned their roles as our seconds to resume their hair-pulling contest, ignoring the outcome of the duel, which took the form of an acute puncture wound between two tendons of my right foot—a wound that produced, to my disappointment, surprisingly little blood. It turned out to be a bad day to wear flip-flops. Nevertheless, it was a significant enough injury to preclude, in my mom's estimation, further encounters with my nemesis.

Yet in some odd way, I regarded my injury with pride. It meant I hadn't flinched. I had stood my ground and defended my mother's reputation—or at least had made the attempt.

"Did you know lawn darts were banned in 1988?" my therapist asks, glancing up from her phone. "At least the kind with metal tips. Too many injuries and deaths."

Sometimes I think my therapist is more interested in '70s and '80s nostalgia than in helping me come to terms with my childhood.

"I wish they had banned them ten years sooner," I tell her without so much as a smile.

Chapter 17

School began, and I wish I could say all returned to normal. Alas, it was a much different kind of normal than the normal we were used to.

Ursula began first grade, and I started fifth, which meant we rode separate buses. Our mother had joined a different church with a different set of rules and a different calendar of events, which interfered with our homework schedules. On Wednesdays, there was a candlelight service. On Thursdays, there was Bible study. On Fridays, there was evening worship. On Saturdays, there was another evening service in case you had missed the one before or wanted to do double duty. And then there was the regular church service on Sunday mornings preceded by Sunday school. At least there weren't any snakes!

In private conference in our bedroom at night, we both agreed we were getting more than our fill of religion. It wasn't that we wanted more time for homework. What we wanted was simply more time for ourselves, meaning "us"—taken together or separately. Also, we didn't much care for the way our mother fussed over our appearance before each event. For me, this meant shirt collar buttoned with a clip-on tie. For Ursula it meant reverting to dresses, which she had outgrown in favor of pants.

And so there we were, neck deep in the new normal, as though keeping our heads above water in a swamp.

Where was our father in all of this? Gone! He'd escaped through his new occupation of trucking. Ursie and I traced his whereabouts on a foldout map he had used to teach us the names of state capitals. We taped it to our wall and used stickpins from our mother's sewing kit to keep track of him. Two things we noticed about the pins. First, we needed more and more of them. The other thing was they kept getting farther and farther away.

Whenever our father did arrive home, the last thing he wanted to do was go to a religious service, and so he didn't. He was only home for a week or two he would complain. He didn't want to use up his time sitting on a hard pew when staying seated for long distances in the seat of his semi was plenty sitting enough. And so he would stay behind half-asleep on the couch with a newspaper folded over his head like a tent with the television on at low volume and the lights dimmed and curtains drawn. Our mother indulged us by letting us stay home with him since we hadn't seen him in so long, while she went off to church by her lonesome.

"Don't let your father turn into a couch potato," she would say before leaving.

"What kind of potato?" Ursie wanted to know. "Baked, mashed, or scalped?" These were the limits of our mom's culinary expertise with potatoes; "scalped" was Ursie's shorthand for "scalloped."

After she left, our father came out from hibernation, emerging like a springtime bear out of the cavern of his newspaper.

"Ready for an adventure?" he would ask, and we would jump right up from where we were playing a quiet game of checkers on the floor so as not to disturb him.

"Sure!" we'd both shout together.

"Okay, then, let's go."

And so we went on adventures. The nice thing about these adventures was they didn't involve snakes—except once when we came across a small, black garter, which our father assured us was dead by lifting it with a stick. We weren't surprised to come across it, though, since most of our adventures took place outdoors. Our father would drive us down to the river where we'd hike along the bank, wading our feet in the shallows, or skipping rocks toward the West Virginia side, without ever making it to the shore of our neighboring state, of course, the river being wider than a football field is long. Once we took the ferry, carrying our skipping stones in our pockets, just so we could say we got them all the way across. On the way back, he talked the captain into letting us sit in the pilot house, where we took turns steering.

"Ah, this is the life, isn't it?" our father would enthuse. "The life of the open sea."

But, as we both knew, it was only a river that flowed in a single direction, and mostly we spent our time hugging its banks.

Ursie was still small and light enough that Dad often carried her along trails on his shoulders, ducking so she wouldn't catch her hair in the branches of overhanging trees.

"You're going bald," she observed, uncharitably, from her perch up above.

"That's just my worry spot," our father assured her. This, as we knew, was our mother's pet name for it.

After thinking about it for a moment, she concluded, "You must worry a *lot*."

When it rained, we took our adventures indoors, more than once to a bowling alley, where I hopped along on my bad ankle, compounded by the Lawn Jart puncture wound, to throw one gutter ball after another.

"That's all right, Jeremy," Dad would say. "You'll knock them down next time."

And one time, by some miracle, I actually did.

Afterward, we'd divide up a pizza and he would tell us stories of his life on the road. He spiced them up with rescues of damsels in distress, dangerous crossings of troll bridges—

"Don't you mean 'toll' bridges?"

Dad looked at me as though I had asked something absurd.

"No, these were troll bridges with real, live trolls beneath."

"But not really," Ursie said, and I knew it was because she was afraid of something equally as sinister hiding underneath her bed at night.

To distract her, Dad popped a quarter into a slot and let us play pinball, the flashing lights and whizzing sounds and flapping paddles taking us into a new exciting world where the only danger was of the machine consuming your small, silver ball.

And so we would beg our father not to go back on the road whenever his time off was up and he climbed back into his rig. He'd lift us up into the cab and let us play with the buttons and wipers and blare the horn. Then he'd give us each a suffocating hug and lower us down to the ground. As one day led into another, we'd try our best not to miss him. Except for holidays. We truly found ourselves missing him most on holidays.

The first one he missed was Thanksgiving.

We didn't even know he wasn't going to be there until we sat down at table for the ritual carving of the turkey. What fooled us into thinking he was somewhere in the house was that a plate had been set for him at his place at the head of the table. We were expecting him to come marching downstairs to pick up the carving knife when the doorbell rang and our mother jumped out of her chair as though it were wired with a live electric cable to answer it.

The doorbell? On Thanksgiving?

Let me introduce Bill.

Just Bill.

Bill came into our lives the way an old-fashioned locomotive with a cowcatcher might surprise a real, live, cud-chewing cow sitting on the tracks.

His entire build, from head to toe, had something of the character of an old-fashioned steam engine. With thick forearms, a cider-barrel torso, a neck as big as a leg of ham, and a head shaped like a missile with tiny ears that would have been its guidance system and beady eyes peering through heavy lids overshadowed by a single dark eyebrow, he seemed built for heavy lifting or pushing things out of his way—both of which he did upon entering our homely abode. Obstacles were no match for him. As he moved through the small living room to the smaller dining room, he cleared a path for himself, rearranging our furniture as he went.

His most distinctive features, however, were a shaved head and handlebar mustache, neatly waxed and groomed.

"Sorry I'm late," he said. "Ran into a little traffic on the way here."

"Late? Who said anything about being late?" our mother said, seemingly flustered, about what or by what I couldn't be sure. "We were just sitting down to dinner."

Actually, she had set out all the fixings a half-hour before.

Bill startled us by taking a seat at the head of the table: our father's seat!

"You have children," he observed thickly beneath his thick brow. "I didn't know you had children."

"Bill, don't be silly," our mother said lightly. "Of course, I told you about the children. I even showed you pictures. Children," she said, turning toward her children, "I want you to meet Mr. Urchin."

"No, just Bill," Mr. Urchin insisted.

"And Bill, these are my children."

"Hello, kids," Bill said glumly.

We sat there, unresponsive. I, for one, was experiencing paralysis of the vocal cords. My mouth might have moved, but nothing came out.

"Children, be polite. When somebody greets you, what do you say?"

"Hello?" Ursie guessed, beating me to the buzzer.

"Why, yes," our mother enthused. "Hello is proper."

"Hello," I followed suit, my voice the meekest of whispers. If my voice were an animal, it would have been a mouse poking its whiskers outside the security of its hole.

"Thought you said it would just be the two of us," Bill stated flatly.

"No, no, you misheard me." I'd never heard our mother so flustered. "The two of them. I said it would be us and the two of them. The children!" she exclaimed, pointing in our general direction.

"Where's the dad?" Bill asked.

"Why, I told you that, too. He's in Alaska." At least this much didn't surprise us. Based on the latest positioning of sequins on our foldout map, our father had driven a semi all the way to Anchorage. "Well, now, should we start before everything gets cold?" Surveying the lack of steam rising from the mashed potatoes, the yams, the gravy boat, the creamed corn, and the green bean casserole, I surmised it was already too late for that. The only dish not affected was the one holding slices of cranberries from a can, which always amused me, the way they jiggled anytime the table was bumped. "Now, Bill, would you please do the honors?"

Based on the tattoos on Bill's forearms, I deduced he had recently been a prison inmate. Either that or a Marine. At the time, I associated tattoos with ex-Marines and ex-cons, mainly because one of our scoutmasters had been both and kept his tattoos on permanent display beneath rolled-up sleeves.

Bill picked up the long two-pronged fork with one hand and the long-bladed carving knife with the other. And then he proceeded to unnerve us, our mother included, by eyeing us one at a time around the table as though contemplating homicide. Finally, his eyes came to rest on the turkey—brown and glazed—on a platter directly beyond his plate. He glared at the bird as though it promised resistance, and then he dove in. His hands moved swiftly and deftly and, I might add, delicately—more so than I would have expected based on the density of his muscles. Within a minute, he had dissected the bird with the skill of a surgeon and sliced up separate piles of white and dark meat, with two large legs left intact on each side and a skeletal carcass in the middle.

His table manners turned out to be just as polite. One might even say impeccable. He prefaced his requests with "please" and followed up with "thank-you." Looks aside, in terms of his mannerisms, he could have been emulating Mr. Rogers.

Ursie took this as a challenge to outdo him, conveying her requests in triplicate, as in "Please, please, please pass the film."

"Film?" Bill asked, glancing around as though to search for a hidden camera.

"Oh, that's just Ursie's word for 'filling,'" Mom informed him, referring to her homemade stuffing.

"So what were you 'in' for?" I asked. At Bill's insistence, to "make a man" of me, I had been allotted a quarter goblet of red wine, so I suppose it was the alcohol that was doing the talking.

"Jeremy, don't be impertinent!" our mother reprimanded.

"No, no, quite all right," Bill said. "No offense meant, none taken." He looked directly into my eyes, a practice designed to see if I would flinch, I'm sure, which I did in hardly any time at all. "Possession of stolen property."

"Oh," I said, not bothering to mask my disappointment. "Is that all?" I was hoping for something more glamorous: bank robbery, armed assault, breaking and entering, murder!

"They gave me three years for that."

"But he was framed," our mother clarified. "Tell them, Bill. Tell them how you were framed."

"I was framed," Bill said, forcing a clump of mashed potatoes down his gullet.

"There were two friends of his," our mother added. "Two no-good friends—if you can even use the word."

"You can't," Bill agreed, moving onto a forkful of yams.

"They told him they needed storage space for a few personal items, so Bill graciously lent them one half of his garage. Isn't that right, Bill? Tell them the rest of it."

"Well," Bill said, washing down his yams with a tonic of wine. "It was like this, see—"

"How was Bill to know the items in question were stolen?"

"Hot," Bill said.

"Right," our mother agreed. "That's the slang term: 'hot.'"

"No," Bill said. "The beans. They're too hot."

"Oh, goodness!" our mother exclaimed. Bill had discovered the one dish I had overlooked that was still steaming: a crockpot full of baked beans. "Well, let's leave the lid off awhile. Let it cool."

"Water," Bill demanded, having guzzled the bottle of wine to the dregs.

"Jeremy, be a good boy and go fetch Bill some water."

"I-th," Bill said while diagnosing the extent of his burned tongue with the sensitive touch of a blunt forefinger.

"And don't forget ice, please," our mother translated.

After dinner, we retired to the "sitting room." Up until this point, I hadn't been aware we were in possession of such a room, but it turned out to be just the living room with a new name. As a sitting room, it wasn't exactly conducive to sitting. There was a plaid couch with sagging springs due to misuse serving as a trampoline for my sister and me. Aside from the couch, there were two folding chairs and a rocker that had lost its ability to rock. In general, we kids preferred to sit cross-legged on the floor.

And so we sat at Bill's feet, side by side, expectantly, watching him sip a brandy our mother had handed him.

"Well, kids, what would you like to know?" he asked, seeming to read our minds. "My days as a wrestler?"

"Sure," I answered.

"Yes," Ursie agreed.

Our mother glanced nervously from Bill to us and back, uncertain as to the appropriateness of the topic.

But Bill proceeded to tell us stories of his wrestling days. It turned out he had wrestled some of the greats, most of whom had strange, exotic names. The Baron, for instance, which made us picture a cape. Or Bruno Sammartino, which made me, at any rate, think of a sumo wrestler. Then there was Crazy Luke Graham, who tag-teamed with Dr. Jerry. Quite a dynamic duo, those two, Bill said. But nothing compared to The Sheik. With The Sheik, you had to be careful of the shiv he hid up his sleeve, because he'd use it to poke out your eye if you weren't on the lookout for it. But even that didn't hold water to Killer Kowalski, who'd rip your ear from your head if he could. And then there was Gorilla Monsoon …

"What was your name?" I asked.

"Baby Cyclone," Bill answered sheepishly.

"Baby?" Ursie asked, a question mark above her head. "You were a baby when you wrestled all these people?"

"But other times I was known as the Urchin," he announced with more pride. "I didn't last long in the circuit," he confessed. "It's like Brando said. I could've been a contender. And I *was*, actually, for a short while. Too bad it didn't last. Now I'm just a bouncer at a bar."

"Why didn't it last?" I asked.

"My hip was thrown out of joint, and that put an end to my wrestling days."

"Who did it to you?" I wanted to know. "Killer? Gorilla? The Baron?"

"Naw," Bill waved his empty glass, and noticing it was empty, extended it for a refill from our mother, whose hands, I noticed, were trembling. "Craziest thing, really. I was trying to catch a trolley and slipped."

"Well, that's all very ... interesting and ... enlightening," our mother ventured, "but—"

"Here!" Bill said, cutting her off and leaping to his feet. He moved several paces away, then turned, rotating his arms to loosen up stiff muscles. "On your feet, young man."

I looked at my mother, and she nodded doubtfully.

"Now come on at me, don't be shy. Come at me. Show me what you got, tough guy."

"You mean, just ... come at you?" I asked.

"Go on, Jeremy," Ursie said, getting to her feet, as well, "you can do it."

I took three steps forward, and Bill held up his hand, as though he were a traffic cop at an intersection.

"Whoa! Hold on a sec. Looks like we have something in common. My hip and your leg. You've got a bit of a limp, I see."

"It's nothing," I said, brushing it off, but grateful for the intermission.

"Jeremy hurt himself earlier this year," my mother said.

"He jumped down the steps and broke his ankle," Ursie put in.

"Ouch!" Bill said, wincing. "That had to hurt."

"He cried," Ursie just had to tell him.

"Yeah," I said, shrugging off her comment, "but it's all better now."

"Is it?" Bill asked, looking at my mother for confirmation.

My mother unhelpfully nodded her head.

"Hold out your arm," Bill directed, and I did as I was told.

Before I knew it, I had been lifted up, twirled around his neck from arm to arm, turned upside down, and pile driven into the carpet, where I ended up laid out on my back, staring at the ceiling, shocked I had lived to tell the tale.

"Now, tell me," Bill said, hovering over me, "did that hurt much at all?"

"No," I said honestly, sitting up. Bill helped me to my feet. "No, it didn't." And I was surprised it hadn't hurt—just like he said.

"Now that's how it's done if you want to put on a show and not really hurt your opponent," Bill said.

"Do you play with dolls, Mr. Bill?" Ursie asked, taking his hand. "I have so many dolls I want to show you."

"No," Bill said, pulling away, as though her hand were an asp. "Not dolls."

"Mommy!" Ursie wailed. "Please make Mr. Bill play with my dolls."

"Airplanes!" Bill countered brightly. "Paper airplanes. You got some paper, I'll show you."

Chapter 18

And that's how we spent the rest of the afternoon heading into evening, as our mother washed plates and silverware and glasses in the sink and tucked leftovers away in the fridge with Tupperware and tinfoil only to bring them back out again for a light supper of turkey sandwiches on Wonder bread. Meanwhile, Bill taught us how to manufacture all types of paper airplanes until we had assembled quite a fleet. There were standard-issue airplanes with pointed noses, wide-winged aircraft that circled in spirals, swan-like planes with long necks weighted with paper clips that arced toward the ceiling before nose-diving to the carpet, accordion-folded airplanes that wavered with uncertainty, small origami planes that performed graceful loop-de-loops.

This is how he had occupied his time in prison.

"Yes, now, Bill, about prison …" Our mother introduced the topic as a schoolmarm would. She even looked the part of a schoolmarm with her hair done up in a bun and reading glasses low down on her nose, and a long-sleeved dress with a hem that touched the floor, hiding her feet from view.

"Right," Bill said, "prison. I almost forgot."

And this is how we knew the topic had been prearranged between them somewhere in the space between dinner and supper.

Bill cleared his throat significantly.

Then, for good measure, he cleared it again.

"Prison," he announced. He looked at Ursula and me in turn. "You don't want to end up in prison."

He sat back in the rocker with his arms crossed, a smug look of satisfaction at having fulfilled an obligation.

"But Bill," our mother leaned forward, "won't you please tell the children about the horrors of prison?"

"Oh," Bill said, focusing on the TV, which was muted. The Cowboys were about to score. "It wasn't all that bad. Three square meals a day. The guards treated you well if you behaved. An hour a day for weightlifting. Not to mention the prison library, once I got the knack of reading." He cast a quick glance at our mother. "I got your mom to thank for that. All those reading lessons."

"Oh," our mother said, blushing. I don't think I had ever seen her blush before. "It was nothing. You were a good student, that's all."

"Score!" Bill yelled, leaping to his feet, then settling back down. The Cowboys had made their touchdown. "Had no idea the Bible was so full of big words," he continued, more soberly. "Like 'firm-a-net.' I still don't know what a 'firm-a-net' is."

"It's 'firm-a-ment,'" our mother corrected. "Not 'net.'"

"Right, well, I still don't have a clue on that one."

And that was something else we had in common.

"But Bill," our mother persisted, "firmaments aside, what an awful time you must have had of it in prison, wouldn't you agree?"

"Boredom, mostly," Bill said. "Fighting off boredom. Finding ways to keep yourself entertained."

"Like with paper airplanes!" I exclaimed.

I could tell by the look on our mother's face this was clearly not the moral she wished us to draw from Bill's lecture.

"Well," Bill said, "that's the game. Quite the blowout. Seahawks didn't stand a chance. Best be going."

He stood up to leave.

"Thanks, Miss Madeline, for a wonderful meal. Haven't had chow like that in years. Three to be exact, ha-ha."

He grabbed a bowler hat and black leather jacket from the coat rack.

Madeline—I wondered about his use of our mother's first

name. It was rarely I ever heard it spoken aloud. I was mainly
glad he hadn't achieved a level of intimacy that allowed him to
use our father's pet name for her: Maddy.

"But surely, Bill, you can't be leaving so soon?"

" 'Fraid, so. Got to make a quick stop by my parole officer's.
She wants to make sure I stuck around for the holidays, I imagine."

"Well, in that case—"

But before our mother could say anything further, Bill gave
her a hug that lifted her quite off her feet, revealing her heels,
and added a peck on her cheek for good measure.

"Oh, my!" Mom exclaimed before being set back down.

"You know where to find me, you ever need me," he said,
opening the front door.

"At the gym?" our mother asked timidly.

"Yeah, Daley's gym. Got a room upstairs. Nice and cozy.
Well, see you around, kids."

He gave us a broad grin, then stepped through the door into
a gray November evening.

———

At bedtime—and yes, I am embarrassed to admit, my mother
still tucked me in and gave me a kiss goodnight, but only because
I shared a room with Ursie, who was young enough to expect a
tuck and a kiss, and so she insisted on following suit with me, no
matter how much I squirmed … Believe me, I squirmed. I was
in fifth grade, for Christ's sake. I squirmed. I did!

"Mom," I said just as she turned off the lights. And before I
had even formulated the words in my head, I automatically asked
the profoundest question I had ever asked her to date.

"Yes, Jeremy?"

"Are you and Dad, like, separated or something?"

She turned the light back on, blinding us. Before my eyes
could adjust, she had taken a position next to my bed. I had the

upper bunk, so she was still standing. She had loosened her hair so that it curled, all wavy, down around her shoulders. She laid a hand—her left hand, the one with her ring finger—on the bedspread near my shoulder.

"Why, Jeremy, what makes you ask a question like that?"

Her voice was very soft, very quiet, very calm.

I half sat up in bed.

"Well, Dad didn't show up for Thanksgiving and Bill showed up instead and—" I let my sentence dissolve into a shrug of my shoulders.

"By distance, yes," Mom answered. "But that's all. Your father's busy in Alaska. He's working on something very important. A pipeline."

"What kind of pipeline?"

"An oil pipeline."

It pumps all that oil in Alaska all the way down here right into our gas pumps so we don't have to be so dependent on all those Middle Easterners for our energy needs, she explained. It's a top priority for our country's independence. President Nixon himself had authorized it several years back.

To me, her speech was less than reassuring. It sounded like something out of a textbook.

"When will we see him again?"

This was Ursie from her bottom bunk, her voice rising like a wisp of fog.

"At Christmas," Mom said, bending out of view to tend to her daughter.

"Not till Christmas?" I asked, lying back down, counting the days between now and then in my head.

"Your father promised he will be here for Christmas," Mom assured us. "Now please, both of you, try to get to sleep."

She turned off the lights, but left the door open a crack so the light from the hallway slanted inside, painting a yellow stripe on the wall.

"Do you think we'll see him at Christmas?" Ursie whispered in the dark.

"Sure," I said. "You know how Dad is with promises."

But I fell asleep trying to think of which of the many promises he had made over the years he had actually kept.

"Here you go," my therapist says brightly, placing two sheets she tore from a yellow ledger onto the coffee table between us as though laying down placemats: one for her, one for me. As far as I know, the ledger has been untouched from session to session. As a repository for handwritten notes, it remains unused, its pages left blank.

"What's this?" I ask, truly baffled.

"I thought maybe you could teach me how to make the specialty airplanes you flew."

"Is this some sort of test?" I wonder aloud, and privately: Of my memory? Of the veracity of my account?"

"Think of it as therapeutic," she says with a smile. "If you relive some of the good moments, you'll be better able to relive the bad."

I analyze this proposition for logical flaws. Is it based on some arcane psychological theory?

She leans forward, looking at me levelly and lowering her voice to a confidential tone. "I suspect there are some bad moments coming up, aren't there? I mean, that's why you're here, isn't it? Sharing your life story? It's all leading up to something bad, am I right?"

I don't answer, but this is how we spend the rest of the session: building and flying dozens of airplanes of all shapes, sizes, and aeronautical designs around her office, depleting her ledger.

"At least let me help you clean up," I offer when we are through.

"Don't worry about it," she assures me. "I have a ten-year-old coming in next who wants to be a pilot. She'll have a field day."

Chapter 19

Just as I had privately predicted, our father didn't make a showing at Christmas. Santa came just the same, even though our fireplace had been covered over with paneling by the landlord who lived next door. He didn't want us starting any house fires by accident. We did get packages, however, shipped from Alaska.

Mine turned out to be a pair of snowshoes. Ursula got an Eskimo doll. And Mom got a pair of fuzzy pink slippers.

"You do know that the preferred term became 'Inuit' following the 1977 Inuit Circumpolar Conference in Barrow, Alaska," my therapist points out to me with a flash of her phone. What could I say in response? With regard to political correctness, my family was very much behind the times.

Along with the presents, we got a Christmas card and a wallet-size photo of Dad holding up a gigantic fish on a hook. If he hadn't written "Love, Dad" on the back, I wouldn't have had a clue as to the fishmonger's identity. In the time he had been away, he had sprouted a full beard that looked like his neck had been attacked by a weasel. The card contained an additional note that apologized for his absence but tried to explain it was due to a trucking gig he had picked up that wouldn't let him take a Christmas vacation.

"What kind of job doesn't let you take Christmas vacation?" our mother complained.

My complaint was a little different. It had to do with the lack of an immediate opportunity to use my snowshoes.

"There's no snow," I said mournfully, looking out the window at an equally mournful drizzle of rain that had turned what little snow there was into a layer of slush.

My mother and I turned our heads toward Ursie in anticipation of the disgruntlement she would add, but she seemed perfectly happy with her *Inuit* doll.

In place of our father, Bill came over for Christmas dinner dressed in a Santa suit. He made no pretense of being the actual Santa, removing his beard, for instance, when it came time to eat. But he had a sack of odds and ends he had either bought at a second-hand store or picked out of a curbside van of stolen goods. I received a Slinky, the midsection of which was hopelessly tangled. Ursula got a small, stuffed mouse that seemed to be a cat toy, a fact confirmed when our mother sniffed it for an aroma of catnip and set it on the faux mantel out of Ursie's reach so she wouldn't get catty from the fumes.

We had been seeing a lot of Bill between Thanksgiving and Christmas. He turned out to be very good with tools, something our mother wasn't. It wasn't uncommon to come home from school and see him sprawled under the kitchen sink with a wrench and a bucket, or perched atop a ladder under a light fixture twisting exposed wires with a pair of pliers, or fixing the sofa whose underside had ruptured with the hernia of a coiled spring.

Whenever he was finished with whatever household project our mother had him working on that day, he would have dinner with us, and then, after dinner, he would wrestle me on the living room carpet, teaching me new moves with which to defend myself against surprise Ninja attackers, or he would lift Ursie onto his shoulders and prance around and snort like a horse while she yelled "giddy-up" with glee.

These were days I decided were worth remembering, but in the back of my mind, I knew they wouldn't last, and sure enough, Bill began to melt away with the rains that came as winter slowly merged into spring.

And that's when Angel arrived.

He made his entry on Easter for dinner. If ever there were a more appropriate time for an angel to show up, you'd have to assume Easter is it.

His real name: Angelo Ramaro, one of seven Ramaro brothers, four of whom were still in various correctional facilities, two of whom were out on parole, and one of whom was a missionary in Calcutta. Ursie and I had to page through a world atlas to find out where Calcutta was.

Despite his name, he didn't exactly fit the picture of our mom's "angel," the one who had rescued her years before when we had our family accident and she had flown as though by some miracle into a tree, where she ended up perching like an upside-down songbird. Instead of long, blond hair, Angelo's hair was dark and cut at odd angles, as though he had hacked at it with a steak knife. In place of tattoos, he had a birthmark in the shape of South America that extended down his left forearm, where it ended at Tierra del Fuego just short of his wrist, upon which was strapped a diamond-studded watchband holding an expensive-looking watch. In place of a leather jacket, he preferred suede with leather arm patches that made him look like an unkempt history professor. And rather than blue eyes that gazed out at the world with 20/20 vision, his almost-black eyes were as nearsighted as a rat's, presuming rats can only see what's in front of their noses.

Still, this is how our mother referred to him. In fact, this is how she introduced him to us, as Angel, minus the O.

It was Angelo who corrected her.

"Angel-o, actually. Short for Michelangelo. You know, like the painter."

As though to draw him from his scaffold, our mother took him by the arm and dragged him around to the far side of the dining-room table.

In between bits of conversation, he nibbled, his eating habits reminding me of a rat's as well. He had two slightly extended front teeth—not quite pronounced enough to be considered buck—and he held everything delicately with long, thin fingers with black-edged nails. His eating of corn on the cob was like the turning of a typewriter platen. He ate bread by nibbling away the crusts and leaving the middle. He raised morsels of ham on the tines of a fork as though for visual examination of flaws.

He was a good conversationalist, if by "good" you mean holding up his side of the conversation like a drawbridge holds up traffic. Basically, it was all one-sided. Compared with Bill's monosyllables comprising a vocabulary of twenty-odd words with never more than three or four in succession, Angelo was as loquacious as a thesaurus.

He talked about growing up in Hell's Kitchen, which seemed an odd place of origin for a person with a first name such as his. And he talked about how he had evaded the Vietnam draft by taking easy courses at a community college in air-conditioner repair and automotive repair and refrigerator repair—any kind of repair really; he was very good at repairing things—in which he was sure to get good grades even without having to cheat on tests. This was actually how our father had avoided getting called into service, as well, by attending college. After graduating, he went one step further by declaring a hardship exemption when his wife—my mother—became pregnant with me.

I was their hardship.

Anyway, back to Angelo.

Just as you might expect of an angel, he talked about Jesus: how he had found Jesus, or Jesus had found him, basically how they had found each other. It appeared they were on a first-name basis. In short, they had become great pals. The more he talked about Jesus, the more he made Him out to be a regular guy, the kind you'd find hanging out at a bar or sitting around a poker table or driving a taxi. This was just the kind of guy Angelo was—or had been. He used to like hanging out at bars and sitting around poker tables and driving taxis for a living. But that was all behind him now, except for the driving taxis part.

"And I owe it all to this little woman right here," he said between mouthfuls of baked beans, although "mouthful" is too big of a word, since he ate his baked beans one at a time.

"What little woman?" my sister asked. She looked under the table to see whether there might be a midget-size woman hiding under it.

"He means me," our mother said, blushing.

It finally dawned on me that Angelo had been one of our mother's pupils at the prison.

As with Bill, at the risk of impertinence, I asked what his crime had been.

The answer: fencing stolen merchandise.

"But that's all behind me now." He had pledged to our mother and Jesus to lead a clean life from here on out, an oath he had sworn on our mother's Bible.

"Maybe you knew Bill?" I asked.

"Jeremy, it's impolite to ask so many questions," my mother reprimanded me gently.

"Bill?" Angelo asked, suspiciously. "Can't say the name rings a bell. Should it?"

A few minutes later, the doorbell rang, as though a delayed cue for enter, stage left.

"Now who could that be?" our mother wondered with a dramatic flair that suggested she already knew who it was.

"I'll get it!" Ursie shouted, jumping out of her seat.

Ordinarily, our mother would have advised caution to a minor answering such a summons. Who knew who could be lurking on the other side of the door? Certainly not the Fuller Brush man or Avon Lady—not on Easter Sunday.

This time, however, our mother encouraged her.

"Yes, honey, why don't you? Why don't you get that?"

This made my sister stop in mid-stride as though she suspected a booby-trap.

"I'll get it," I volunteered.

"No, I want to get it," Ursie said, but she didn't move.

"How 'bout we get it together?" I suggested.

Ursie nodded, and we approached the door with slow, hesitant steps.

We pulled it open to find a large six-foot-tall rabbit taking up space on the welcome mat.

"Ho-ho-ho," it said, then corrected itself: "I mean, Happy Easter!"

"Who is it?" our mother asked sweetly from her place at the table.

"No one," I announced. "Just the Easter Bunny."

"Well, invite him in, won't you?" our mother said, rising from her seat. Angelo followed in our mother's shadow, like a child hiding behind apron strings.

"Won't you come in?" Ursie asked politely.

The bunny took three giant hops across the threshold, which placed it squarely in the middle of the living-room floor.

"Why, look what I have here, boy and girl," he said. "An empty Easter basket. Isn't that the saddest thing you ever did see?"

"Well—" I stalled, trying to think of something sadder. The bunny rabbit's ears were large and pink and stiff. The rest of his outfit was pinkish, as well, but more bleached out, like an old blanket that had been through the washer too many times. He wore large furry paws and had huge fluffy slippers for feet. His whiskers were two sets of soda straws taped under a pink button he wore on his nose, which exhibited a chronic twitch, as though he were stifling a sneeze. His voice was distorted by a set of false buckteeth that contributed to an exaggerated lisp. Despite the disguise, I could see something familiar in the musculature concealed within his suit. This was one well-constructed rabbit.

"And where do you suppose the Easter eggs could be?"

He paused only a moment to thump his right foot a few times on the thin living-room carpet, as though from impatience.

"Could be they're hidden all over the yard outside and that maybe they have chocolate in them …"

"Chocolate," Ursie drooled.

"… or maybe coins."

"Money?" I asked for clarification.

"Why don't you kids go looking for eggs?" our mother said, coming up behind us and giving us each a gentle push from behind.

We were about to move past the Easter bunny when he said, dropping his voice an octave: "Hold everything!"

"What is it? What's wrong, Bill?" Mom asked, startled. "I mean, Mister Easter Bunny," she corrected herself.

"Well, bust my britches if it ain't Mitch the Snitch!" the Easter Bunny said in a sort of snarl.

"Just a minute, Bill," Mom intervened, forgetting to use the Easter Bunny epithet. "This isn't Mitch. This is Angelo."

"Yeah, that's right. As in 'Mitch-Angelo.' But more familiarly known as 'Mitch,' as in S-N-I-T …" Bill hesitated, whiskers twitching.

"C-H," I helped him out.

"And that spells 'Snitch,'" Bill said, as though competing in a spelling bee.

"Wait a second," Angelo (or Mitch) said, peeking out from

behind our mother's dress. "I recognize that voice."

"And well you should."

"Bill Urchin," Mitch (or Angelo) said, eyes revolving in his head.

"The one and only," Bill said, taking another hop into the room. If not for the slim presence of our mother, he would have landed directly on Mitch-Angelo with his large, fuzzy feet.

"Now wait just a second, Bill," Mitch-Angelo said, back-tracking into the dining room.

"I always said, if there ever came a time you got out of the joint, I'd come looking for you, and here you are!"

"Hold on now, Bill. You gotta cut me a little slack. I never once for the life of me snitched on you."

"Yeah, but you sure 'nuff snitched on friends of mine, which is why I'm sure they gave you early parole like they did."

By this point, Mitch-Angelo had moved like a fighter in a ring to the opposite side of the dining-room table, circling one way, then the other, as Bill in his bunny suit didn't so much hop but clop around in his fuzzy slippers, trying to corner him.

My sister and I stayed on the sidelines, looking under our mother's outstretched arms that formed a guardrail, either for us, so we didn't get caught up in the potential fray, or for Bill and Mitch-Angelo to direct them out of the dining room so they didn't break any—

CRASH!

—plates.

Too late. Mitch-Angelo caught hold of a corner of the table-cloth and gave it a yank. Dishes went flying in Bill's general di-rection, splattering his bunny outfit with the remains of our Easter dinner so that he ended up looking like a Jackson Pollack on a pink canvas.

"My apologies, ma'am," Mitch-Angelo said, nodding toward

our mother. "Just send me a bill for the fine china."

He made a move to get past a corner of the table, just as Bill was recovering, having examined the damage to his costume as though enumerating the stains.

"And you can add in another twenty clams they don't end up taking this suit back at the costume shop," Bill said.

I was astounded to hear the word "clams" spoken aloud. I always thought it was just something crooks said in black-and-white movies. And here was a real-life gangster confrontation unfolding before my very eyes.

Mitch-Angelo lunged for the door, but Bill, in one big bunny hop, caught him by the arm and swung him back around, like an unwilling partner in a square dance.

But Mitch-Angelo was crafty. He took hold of Bill's furry paw and pulled. The paw came off, and Bill stared at it, his whiskers twitching irritably, as though his dance partner had actually removed his real hand. Mitch-Angelo dropped the paw on the floor and turned to make a quick getaway.

"Sorry to eat and run," he said gallantly to our mother, "but you know how it is in times like these."

He paused to make a slight bow—a fatal lapse. Bill was on him in a second, pouncing more like an enraged mountain lion than timid rabbit. He got Mitch-Angelo in a headlock that wouldn't come loose, no matter how hard his captive pried and pulled. Then he used his free arm to pick up his legs, and he began to turn them like a crank so that poor Mitch-Angelo's head began to twist around like a corkscrew. After he was done with this uncorking-the-bottle maneuver—one he had taught me in play, but now I was witnessing for real—he lifted his victim by his heels so his head was dangling only inches from the floor. Then he began spinning him around and around in a widening circle, like a Tilt-a-Whirl at a fairground, Mitch-Angelo's body rising from the floor into a near parallel position, a whirring feat of acrobatics that threatened to stir up enough dust to form a tornado. Ursie and I ducked every time Mitch-Angle came circling around, but our mother stayed just out of range, dancing to and fro in an effort to protect lamps and figurines and a row of decorative bottles on the windowsill.

"Bill, please," our mother kept pleading. "Put him down. Your behavior is—shameful!"

Gradually, Bill began to lose momentum. With a last flourish, he flung Mitch-Angelo against a wall, where he splattered like a bug, before sliding down the wallpaper onto the sofa.

Bill staggered backward like a drunkard—presuming a rabbit would have access to alcohol—and collapsed on an armchair. Two of his whiskers had come off in the struggle, and one of his ears was flattened. Otherwise, his costume showed few signs of damage except for the food stains.

Mitch-Angelo remained motionless, hands folded across his chest, as quiet as a corpse.

"Is he dead?" Bill asked hopefully.

Our mother leaned over him, and his eyelids fluttered as though animated by an electric circuit.

"Not quite," Mitch-Angelo answered for himself, springing nimbly to his feet and hurrying out the door.

Bill tried to go after him, but he was disadvantaged by his own lingering dizziness.

Our mother ran outside, calling, "Angel, Angel, wait!"

"He forgot his hat," I said, pointing to the coatrack as our mother walked back inside in a slow shuffle with her head down, her eyes focused on the floor. I could see through the window that her angel—a small snitch of a man she unaccountably liked well enough to invite to Easter dinner—had deserted her, arms flailing, down the sidewalk, where he hopped into the driver's seat of a yellow taxi and sped off in a cloud of black smoke that spit out of its tailpipe like a case of bad breath. "Maybe he'll be back for it."

"No, he's gone," she said, without looking up. "Bill, maybe it would be best if you were to leave."

"But the eggs," Bill said, his voice an oddly thin whine. "The candy. The coins."

"Yeah, Mom," I said. "We wouldn't want to cheat Ursie out of an Easter egg hunt."

I didn't mention the fact that I would be cheated out of it, too.

"All right," she said, standing with her head bowed in the middle of the room as though in shock or prayer. "But after that it's time for bed."

"But Mom, it's only four o'clock!" I pointed out.

"Is it?" she said. "It feels so much later."

"Madeline," Bill said, getting to his feet, clumping his way over to our mother in his furry slippers. "I swear, I'm sorry about all this—commotion." He put a hand on her shoulder—the one that had lost its mitten—but our mother shrugged it off. "At least let me help you clean up," he said, lowering his arm.

"No, it's all right," our mother answered, looking him up and down. "Why don't you take the kids outside and then just— just—oh—hop away home."

She ran up the stairs, and her high heels clicked across the ceiling until they stopped with a creaking of mattress springs.

"Well, kids," Bill said after a moment's silence. "How 'bout that Easter egg hunt?"

He sounded let down, disappointed perhaps that our mother hadn't chosen him as the object of her affections in place of his nemesis.

It was how we felt about it, too.

Chapter 20

After Bill left, we waited around downstairs for our mother to re-emerge, but no sounds came from her bedroom above. Finally, we decided to approach her door, which was half open, dark inside, the shades drawn.

"Mom?" I queried.

"Mommy?" Ursie asked.

We waited several heartbeats until our mother said, "It's all right, children, you can come in."

She turned on the bedside lamp. Her cheeks were streaked with tears.

"Are you all right?" I asked, taking a seat beside her.

Ursie curled up on her other side.

"Mommy, are you okay?" she wondered, too.

"Yes, dear, Mommy's all right, Mommy's okay," she assured us with a weak smile. She brought us both closer, her arms around our shoulders. Ordinarily, I would have squirmed out of such treatment, but this time, I thought it best to give in.

"When's Daddy coming home?" Ursie murmured.

"Yeah," I said, more forcefully than I intended, "when are we going to see Dad again?"

"Well, that's just the thing," our mother said in a gentle voice tinged with sadness, "I'm not sure he's coming back."

I sat up straight, breaking away from her embrace to face her.

"What do you mean?"

"Is he dead?" Ursie asked. The month before, we had lost a kitten to a traffic accident, so death was on her mind.

"No, no, my Li'l Bear, he isn't dead," our mother said, stroking her hair.

"Did he get lost?" she asked next. It seemed a logical follow-up to the topic of death.

"Is he still in Alaska?" I asked.

"No and yes," she said, "he's not driving a truck or working on the pipeline anymore. He's found a new love."

It took a moment for my brain to process this new information.

"You mean another woman?"

"Oh, no. Not a woman. Another adventure. He's found work on a boat."

"A boat?" I prompted.

"A fishing boat. He's going to be gone all this coming summer salmon fishing."

Salmon fishing. Well, it didn't surprise me. He had been trained as an ichthyologist after all. His first love had always been fish.

We stayed up later that night than usual. Bedtime, even in summer, was 8 o'clock for Ursula, 9 o'clock for me. But Ursie was almost always awake when I crawled into the top bunk, and if she wasn't, no matter how softly I climbed, my footsteps up the ladder would awaken her.

"I miss Daddy," she sniffled.

"I know you do," I whispered downward. "He's my dad too, you know."

"I know, but I really, really, really miss him."

I was waiting for the sniffles to break into sobs, but Ursula usually wasn't one for openly crying, not even when reprimanded. She had a way of expressing an offended air with a sharp upturn of her chin whenever our mother doled out a harsh word, which wasn't very often.

"How far is Alaska?" she wanted to know.

"Far," I told her.

"Farther than the moon?"

"No, not as far as the moon, but far enough."

"Farther than Detroit?"

Now I knew she was just picking names out of her head. We had never been to Detroit. I'm not sure under what circumstances she ever heard it mentioned. Maybe they were studying state capitals at school.

"We should go find him," Ursie said.

"Well, yeah, we should."

I was feeling tired. My eyes were starting to close, my mind starting to drift.

"We should go rescue him and bring him back home," she asserted.

"Yeah," I agreed, "we should."

"After school lets out?"

"You mean tomorrow?"

Tomorrow was Monday, the end of spring break.

"Not to-mor-row," Ursie said, drawing out the word as though to emphasize the idiocy of my question. "When school lets out for summer."

"Oh, right. Summer. Yes, we will. As soon as school lets out for summer, we'll go."

"To Alaska?"

"Yes, to Alaska."

It was one of those promises I was sure she would forget about by morning. I knew that I planned to forget about making it sooner than that.

"You promise?"

"Yes, I promise."

"Cross your heart and hope to die?"

"I'll cross my heart, but I don't hope to die."

It's how I always answered her when she made me take this vow.

"So you'll come with me?"

"Yes, I'll go with you. Now go to sleep."

I could hear her tossing and turning, fluffing her pillow, re-arranging her stuffed animals, pulling the blanket over her head to ward off monsters.

"Jeremy?" her voice emerged in the darkness.

"Yes?"

"Could this be all a dream?"

"Could what be a dream?"

"All of this."

I observed the shadows of her arms against the wall from the nightlight at the foot of her bed, stretching into a wide embrace.

"Yes," I said, "I'm sure that's all it is."

"I thought so," she said, sounding satisfied. "It's just like the song." Under her breath she started singing "Row, Row, Row Your Boat."

"Ursie, go to sleep."

"Okay, okay," she said impatiently.

And that was the last I heard from her that night, but I had a hard time falling asleep afterward. I remembered from our father's lessons that Detroit wasn't the capital of Michigan, but I couldn't think of what it was. Different cities went through my brain: Ann Arbor, Port Huron, Traverse City, Saginaw. Our father had taught us all the state capitals, and I had the feeling he would have been deeply disappointed by my forgetfulness.

And then all I could see was the outline of Alaska, disconnected from the lower 48 states, the way it appeared on our educational children's map of the U.S., just floating out there in the Pacific Ocean below Hawaii, as though it were a jagged island with a straight back. And it occurred to me how very, very far away it really was.

Chapter 21

"Jeremy, Jeremy, wake up!"

I felt jostled in my sleep, but the jostling became part of my dream wherein a mermaid was treading water next to me as I clung to a rubber raft on a turbulent sea.

"Jeremy!" A loud whisper.

And then I was awake. The shades had been rolled up. The dawn was unfolding behind a lacework of branches against a steel-gray sky.

"What time is it?" I asked, searching for the glow-in-the-dark dials on the clock on the dresser.

"Time to go," Ursie whispered urgently from the top of the ladder. She took hold of my hand and attempted to pull me out of my bunk.

"All right, all right," I said, taking her cue to speak softly. "But where are we going?"

"Alaska, don't you remember?"

"Oh, right," I groaned, rolling over in bed to face the wall. "Alaska."

It was the very first day of summer vacation. School ended the day before on a Wednesday, leaving today to be Thursday, but not a typical Thursday: a non-school-day Thursday, a summer-vacation Thursday, a special go-ahead-and-sleep-in Thursday.

"Jeremy!" Now she sounded adamant. I knew the tone she was using. There would be no dissuading her, no postponing her plans, no stalling.

"I suppose we'll have to pack," I said, crawling down the ladder.

"We're already packed!" she said brightly, holding up a

knapsack by its strap. I recognized it as an old rucksack of our father's, one he used when taking us fishing to hold sandwiches and bait, a leftover from his Boy Scout days.

"That's very efficient of you," I said, "but what all did you pack?"

I had turned eleven in January. Ursula had turned seven in March. Somewhere between six and seven, she had stopped seeming so much like a little animated baby doll and had transformed into more of a real-life person, just like Pinocchio had finally turned into a flesh-and-blood boy.

There was still something of the tomboy about her, though. For one thing, she kept her hair cut short. It was still bright blonde but never allowed to grow past the base of her neck. The bangs were cut straight across too, forming a bowl cut. I would tease her from time to time that she looked like Moe from the Three Stooges, but she would tease me back about my ducktail, telling me I was just an Elvis wannabe.

"I hope you don't mind, I raided your underwear drawer."

"You mean, you packed up my clothes? In the dark? How long have you been awake?"

"Not long. I packed two pairs of underwear. Do you think two pairs are enough?"

I pretended to think about this, while other thoughts swirled through my mind.

"Yes," I concluded. "Two should be enough. One for the trip out, and one for the trip back."

"Do you think we'll be back before dinnertime? I wouldn't want Mommy to worry."

She was still young enough to call our mother "Mommy," and this made me smile, while I pulled a shirt over my head in exchange for my pajama top. My bottoms would have to wait for a trip to the bathroom.

"We'll leave her a note," I said.

"That's what I thought, too."

I knew our mother would sleep in till noon, and I figured we wouldn't be gone long, probably not much past lunchtime. Our mother was going through one of her spells, which had been occurring more frequently since Easter. On school days, she would sleep in while we got ready for the bus. Before leaving, we would creep into her room and give her a kiss on the cheek, which she stirred awake long enough to accept.

The reason I knew she would sleep in so late is that noon was the time she finally awoke on weekends, so I didn't think weekdays would be any different. It was her migraines that were keeping her in bed so long. They arrived at night like a thief stealing into her brain and didn't let up until midmorning, but they sapped her of a good night's sleep, so she would try to catch up by midday before her part-time shift that she had resumed working at the local library. At least, this is how she explained it to us. It was like a blacksmith's shop inside her head: a steady beating of hammer on anvil.

We crept downstairs in the morning dimness.

"Wait," Ursie said, "we forgot our toothbrushes."

So we went back up and brushed our teeth and packed away our toothbrushes and a tube of travel-size toothpaste that had been stored away in the medicine cabinet in anticipation of a family vacation that never materialized.

Back downstairs we went and were just about to step through the door, when again Ursie called a halt.

This time it was her small stuffed animal Lambkins, so I had to go back upstairs with her because she was still afraid of the dark.

When we came back down, it was to retrieve our lunches—something Ursie almost forgot to do in our rush to get out the door. She had prepacked them the night before, knowing just how to do it from watching our mother prepare our school lunches. We stuffed them inside the top of the knapsack, which didn't feel very heavy, and this time I was the one to stop our proceeding out the door.

"What is it?" Ursie asked.

"Our note," I mentioned. "We better leave one."

"Oh, yeah, our note."

Ursula wanted to write it, which she did, very slowly and carefully, in big block letters:

DEAR MOMMY
WE R GOING TO ALASKA TO SEE DADDY
LUV
LITTLE BEAR

"Mind if I add something?" I asked, looking it over.

"Sure, go ahead."

She sat up on a chair to watch me at the kitchen table. I drew an arrow at the bottom of her note and flipped the piece of paper over. Then I wrote out in cursive:

We won't be gone long. We should be home by the time you wake up. Don't worry if we're not. We're just playing for fun.

"What's it say?" Ursie wanted to know, since she hadn't learned cursive—that wouldn't be until second grade the following school year.

"It just says, 'We'll tell Dad you love him and bring back a salmon for you.'"

"Oh," Ursie said, climbing off her chair, "that sounds nice."

Now we were ready to depart through the kitchen door, but this time, we both hesitated at the threshold. Birds were calling back and forth through the trees. Crickets were chirping, winding down their nightly chorus. A hound howled in the distance.

"Well," I said, "shall we?"

"We forgot about money," Ursie said.

"Right, we'll need money for …" I couldn't imagine what for besides maybe a soda pop at a drugstore.

"Bus tickets," she answered. "You don't think we can walk all the way to Alaska, do you?"

She was already starting to develop a sense of sarcasm, which I was learning to tolerate, but I appreciated her foresight. We trooped back upstairs where Ursie emptied her piggybank—fortunately, it had a rubber stopper on its belly that negated having to break it—and I added the allowance money I had saved up, but in Ursie's estimation it still wasn't enough. So we emptied our mother's cookie jar—a hollow ceramic figure of a headless chef; the head had fractured long before—of its contents. This was her "rainy day" money—whatever was left over from the amount our father sent her biweekly in a big Manila envelope to pay our bills and buy groceries.

Pooling our resources amounted to twenty-three dollars and forty-one cents.

"Think it's enough?" Ursie asked.

"It should be plenty," I assured her.

"We'll pay Mommy back of course," she said, watching me stuff the money into my pants pocket.

"How?" I wondered aloud.

"Daddy will give us money to pay her back."

She seemed to have thought out her plan with precision, leaving very little to chance.

Back at the threshold, Ursula tucked her hand inside the crook of my arm, and we stepped out the door. Somehow it seemed a significant step.

"One small step for man," I said, quoting.

"And one giant leap for Little Bear," Ursie followed up with a hop and a skip down the driveway that led to the road that would lead to Alaska.

"No more school bus," Ursie mentioned as we walked along the shoulder of the road. Our only close neighbor was our landlord. A light was showing in an upstairs window, indicating he was an early riser, too. We still didn't know him very well—just a kind, older man with a red face that showed up whenever our mother was behind on the rent, which was often of late. We walked along past the construction company with its rusting dump trucks and bulldozers and backhoes. We crossed the railroad tracks that led to our first intersection, where we waited for the light to change.

Turning right would take us down to the Ohio River and the heart of Bellerophon. This is where the town's single bus would stop every half hour. But this bus, barely functional relic that it was, wouldn't take us far enough. We needed the out-of-town bus, but to get to that bus, you had to go to the next town over, as we learned when coming home from our trip to Toledo. Parkersburg was closer than Marietta, so we decided on that.

Bikes were ruled out. Ursula's still had training wheels and a bell with a basket in front. The tires on my old clunker were flat from disuse. Besides, there wouldn't be a sidewalk along the roadway to Parkersburg, and we were always instructed never to ride our bikes out on the street. And if we made it to the bus depot, we certainly weren't going to leave our bikes behind for anyone to come along and steal.

But to get all the way to Parkersburg meant either hailing a taxi, which would be hard to do, since our town only had a couple of those, as well, and you had to order them by phone. Or it meant walking.

And so we walked.

Chapter 22

I don't think Ursula had a good concept as to how far thirty miles really is or how long it would take to walk it. The main highway traveled largely north of the Ohio River, but we chose a road less traveled—although somewhat of a shortcut—only two lanes, that wound around hills through dense woods that opened suddenly onto vistas of terraced farmland nestled in valleys and dells. The shoulder, edged with thistles and briars, was wide enough, at times, to let us walk side by side. In other places, it narrowed to a single-file footpath. Every once in a while we came across a raspberry bush and paused to pluck the berries, even though most were pale and immature.

We were forewarned of vehicles climbing hills with heavy engines or descending hills while downshifting long before we saw them, and when we did, we motioned with our fists for the drivers to honk their horn, which they usually did, often with a smile, as though providing us a special service. This honking of the horn never failed to make Ursie skip with glee. I admit it amused me, as well.

I doubt we had gone more than two miles before Ursula's legs began to tire. She stalled every few steps, pausing to let a daddy longlegs cross her path, prod a motionless grasshopper back to life with a stick, or question whether a toadstool on a rotting stump was poisonous.

After a while she begged for a ride on my back. The sun was hovering in the branches of trees, the birds were quieting, and a squirrel chattered above us, encouraging us to move along. I told her I would have a difficult time carrying both her and the knapsack, so she volunteered to strap it on her shoulders, and I heaved her onto my back. She was as light as butter, but even so, I couldn't carry her for long without needing a break.

I dropped her off at the entrance to a cove in the trees. There was something enchanting about the way the sunlight streamed down through the treetops and lit up a small grass-carpeted circle that could be perceived between the two thick tall trunks serving as a gateway. The grass was only ankle high, free of noxious weeds or poisonous ivies. Surrounding the circlet of grass was a border of dark-green ferns that wavered in the slight breeze like gestures of welcome, and so, feeling invited, we entered.

We had about half a water bottle left. The ice inside had melted. And we each took a small swig so as to conserve the rest for the long march that still lay ahead. A sudden shaft of light haloed Ursula's head and lit her up like an angel.

"Do you think fairies live here?" she asked, handing back the bottle.

"You're too old to believe in fairies," I responded, starting to withdraw the brown bags that contained our lunches.

"Is it lunchtime already?" she asked. I looked at my watch. I had graduated from my Green Lantern watch to a digital Timex. It was only ten o'clock.

"Are you hungry?" I asked.

She nodded her head vigorously.

"Starving!"

"Then it's lunchtime," I said and proceeded to unwrap our sandwiches.

"I packed cookies too," Ursie informed me.

"Chocolate chip?"

"Is there any other kind?" she asked slyly. Again, I wondered how long her sarcasm had lain incubating, waiting to hatch.

We ate in silence for a while, listening to the sounds of the woods, the occasional truck growling past.

"Do you think God visits here?" Ursie asked.

"I don't see why He wouldn't," I answered. "It's as nice a place as any."

We investigated the perimeter of the clearing, overturning fallen logs, lifting up heavy rocks, to see if there were any worms or bugs crawling around underneath. Plenty of bait for fishing an invisible creek we could hear gurgling through the trees.

"I should have brought my fishing rod," I lamented.

"You don't like to fish," she reminded me.

Tiring of our investigation, she lay back in the tall grass, holding a cookie above her head, ostensibly to eclipse the rising disk of the sun.

"Is God bigger than the sky?" she wanted to know.

"Well, I guess He would have to be, wouldn't He? I mean, the sky—it's only so big, but the universe, well, it's a whole lot bigger, so it just stands to reason He would be bigger than the sky, and then after that, you'd have the orbit of the Earth, I suppose, and then the orbits of all the other planets, all the way out to Pluto ..."

"Pluto was still a planet back then," I assert with a smugness derived from a well-established fact in my memory.

"As it still should be," my therapist agrees. "I was traumatized when it was downgraded. I was only six at the time. I even mailed a letter to Neil deGrasse Tyson in protest."

It's the first inkling I have that she harbors sympathy for the underdog, same as me.

Ursie let me ramble on for a while unchecked, as I regurgitated as much fifth-grade astronomy as I could recall from science class, including references to various constellations, the small and large Magellanic Clouds, the Andromeda Galaxy, our nearest spiral neighbor, and on and on, until I noticed she was asleep.

I pulled her Lambkins from the knapsack and tucked it under her arm, then stretched out beside her and stared up at the clouds, imagining what I thought prehistoric people must have imagined: an invisible man in the sky reining the cumulus like steeds.

I must have dozed because when I opened my eyes, Ursie was shaking me awake.

"We need to go," she insisted. "We don't want to miss the bus."

"Right," I said, sitting up in the tall grass. "About the bus," I started to say, but she gave me such an anticipatory look of hopefulness that I couldn't disappoint her. Instead, I packed up the knapsack without returning her gaze as I put back in a couple of the items that had fallen out: flashlight, toothbrush, comb, and hand mirror. I was touched to see she had packed a Batman comic book for me to read, probably for the long bus ride ahead of us.

I wanted to tell her that even if there was a bus with destination Alaska, we wouldn't be able to afford it—not with just twenty-three dollars and forty-one cents. I doubted that amount of money would buy us even a single one-way ticket to Columbus in the middle of the state. All packed up, I stood up in the grass, and pulled her to her feet.

"You're right," I said, "we better hurry if we're going to make it."

She started off down the road at a fast pace so that I had to lope like a leopard to catch up. Then she stopped—so suddenly I had to put on the brakes to keep from running smack into her.

She turned to look up at me, her eyes clouded with thought.

"What is it?" I asked, somewhat startled.

"I don't think we should bring Daddy back home when we find him," she said solemnly.

"No?"

"I think we should just visit him and leave him there in Alaska."

"Why's that?"

She hesitated for a moment.

"Because of something Mommy said."

"What did Mom say?"

"She said if ever Daddy comes home she would kill him for leaving her alone so long with the kids."

"She told you this?"

She shook her head no.

"Is it something you heard her say?"

She shook her head yes.

"To someone else?"

"On the telephone. I don't know who it was."

"Well, I'm sure she didn't mean it."

"You don't think she'll really kill him?"

I gave my shoulders a shallow shrug.

"Probably not."

She stood there a while longer, staring at her feet, digging the toe of her second-hand Keds in the gravel. A truck breezed by, catching us in the draft that blew along after its wake.

"Look," I said, "if you want to turn back …"

She shook her head from side to side, still staring at her feet.

"Keep going?" I asked.

"Keep going," she answered.

And so we kept going, but only a dozen or so steps before she stopped again and turned.

"Do you think God forgives murderers?"

"I don't know. Probably. I suppose He would. If they're sorry."

"Because if Mommy really does kill Daddy, I don't want her ending up in the Bad Place if we go to the Good Place. I want us all to end up in the Good Place together."

"I don't think she's going to kill anyone," I said.

"Swear?"

"I swear I don't think she's going to murder Dad," I said, and this seemed a good enough answer to start her walking again.

"Are you ever afraid you'll die in your sleep?" she asked as we trod along.

"Because of the prayer?"

Every night we still recited the age-old prayer: *Now I lay me down to sleep, I pray the Lord my soul to keep. If I should die before I wake ...*

"How would you know you had died if you're asleep?" she asked.

"Well, maybe you would wake up in a different place and so you would know," I answered.

"Lambkins!" she shouted.

She stopped suddenly, and this time I did bump into her.

"What?"

"When I woke up, I had Lambkins, but I can't remember if I put him back in the knapsack. Oh, please check to see if Lambkins is there, Jeremy! Please!"

I pulled off the knapsack and opened the flap. Ursie took it and rummaged through it, saying, "Oh, no, oh, no," and started to cry.

"We must have left it back in the clearing," I said. We hadn't gone that far. "I'll go back and get it."

"Oh, would you? Please!"

She gave me a hug around my waist that wouldn't let go.

"All right, but you have to promise me you'll wait right here, won't you?"

"Of course I'll wait right here."

And she sat on a boulder by the side of the road to prove it.

Chapter 23

In hindsight, I should have insisted she come back with me to get her stuffed animal. It wasn't such a good idea to separate, even by the length of a hundred yards, on a strange road winding through unfamiliar territory with woods on either side.

But I knew her legs were tired, and my ankle was starting to throb with an odd twinge, a reminder of its fracture. I wasn't going to be able to carry her on my back this time if her legs gave out.

I found Lambkins right off, hiding in the tall grass, but when I came back out of the clearing and looked up the road, I saw a brown sedan parked on the opposite shoulder with its rear driver's-side door opened and my sister standing beside it. She was looking back along the road toward me, and when she saw me emerge, she gave me a little wave over top of her head. On impulse, I waved back, and then the unexpected happened: she climbed into the car and closed the door.

The strange thing was, instead of running toward her, I froze in place, although "froze" is probably the wrong word. It was more that my insides began to melt and drain down out of my bowels through my legs and out through my feet, as though to reach down into the ground through the gravel and root me in place like a tree. At the same time, I felt my face flush and the hairs on the back of my neck rise like porcupine quills—a sensation that spread all over my scalp. I stood like this for a moment, locked in place, as though straitjacketed by a strange dream. This couldn't be real, this couldn't be happening. That must be some other little girl. That must be someone else's little sister.

I couldn't even find my voice.

"Ursie," I said meekly, tentatively, as though learning to speak.

And then the car pulled casually away from the shoulder and into the right-hand lane, heading away from me. It took no time at all for it to round a curve and become lost behind trees.

That's when I started running—or hobbling, actually.

No! my brain screamed without sound.

No, no, no, no, no!

It was as though my identity—my entire sense of self—flew out of my mind like a bird. I reached the place where Ursula had climbed into the car. I stared at the rock across the road I had left her sitting on. I looked for some trace of her, some evidence that had been left behind, something concrete to hold onto, but I saw nothing. Just the tire marks in the gravel, letting me know the car—a brown sedan, a brown four-door sedan, a brown four-door used sedan, a brown four-door used sedan with corroded fenders—had been real. I kept repeating its description in my head, willing myself to add more details, anything I thought I could remember about it. The car had been too far away for me to read the license plate, and I don't know if I would have thought to do this even if I had been close enough to make it out. I spun in a circle, feeling helpless, alone, invisible, or worse—nonexistent. I could only think of what my mother would say.

Shit! I thought. And then I said it: "Shit!"

A bad word. A cuss word. One of a handful of words our mother had warned us never to say, although I had overheard her uttering it once when the lid of a tin can of tomato paste she was opening had sliced open her index finger. But she had immediately crossed her heart for forgiveness.

What to do?

What to do?

Wait for a car to come along and try flagging it down? But what if its driver were to abduct me in the way Ursula had been abducted? But *had* she been abducted? Now that I thought of it, it seemed she had stepped into the car freely, under her own will. But how could that be? Why would she have done something like that? And why had she waved? What was the meaning of her wave? Was it a wave good-bye or a wave to motion me to hurry up and join her? I tried recreating her wave in my mind but couldn't decide which kind of wave it had been.

"Shit," I said again, under my breath, and turned around to begin the long walk home. It seemed the most logical option—not that my brain was thinking logically. What had happened seemed surreal—beyond reason—something apart from ordinary reality.

I would have to run the best I could, despite my sore ankle.

I kept telling myself: *It's only two miles ... I can hoof it easy ... I'll be there in no time ... See? I'm already down the first hill ... And now I've made it to the birch tree with its peeling bark ...*

And so on, as I picked out markers as milestones to run to—personal goals by which to pace myself—and then a new marker once I reached the one I had picked out.

But in the forepart of my brain I kept worrying: *What will Mom say?*

As my mind began to clear, I wondered whether to go home first or go directly to the police station. Our town only had a handful of police officers. The station was really just a single room with a dispatcher's desk. The room shared double duty with the post office, and the dispatcher also served as the mail clerk. I could picture a line of people waiting at the counter to mail packages. I could imagine their looks as they eavesdropped on my report to the dispatcher, and this helped me make up my mind.

A brown sedan, a rusted-out brown sedan—there was something in my memory about a brown sedan, but I just couldn't place it. I thought about it, trying to jiggle my memory, all the way to our kitchen door, which was our ordinary entrance and exit, since it abutted our drive.

I walked briskly, full of purpose, through the door, then stopped abruptly. Mom was sitting at the small vinyl kitchen table, still in her bathrobe, clutching a mug of coffee with both hands. She looked up as I entered, a loose curler dangling from a strand of hair alongside her face.

"I got your note," she said. She didn't seem bothered by our absence, rather the opposite. A thin smile suggested she had even been humored. "So did you make it to Alaska?"

A joke—a definite joke. This was unusual, my mother joking. It was such an odd thing for her to do, I didn't know how to react. I didn't laugh. I didn't smile. All I could do was stand there.

"Jeremy? Are you all right? Where's Li'l Bear?"

I couldn't move. I couldn't speak. I couldn't even gesture. It was as though my central motor system had decided to switch itself off to conserve energy.

My mother's eyes widened. She pulled the curler from her hair, apparently only now becoming aware of it.

"Jeremy?" she said more seriously. "Where's your sister? Isn't she with you?"

No words came out of my mouth. I didn't even attempt to make my mouth move. I hadn't rehearsed any sort of announcement. I didn't know how to even broach the subject of Ursula's disappearance.

"Jeremy, what's wrong?" my mother said, standing, pulling her robe more tightly closed.

"She's gone," I finally managed to say. The words sounded odd to me, as though it were some other voice using my vocal cords the way a ventriloquist would a puppet.

"What do you mean 'gone'?" she demanded. She took a single, interrogative step in my direction, then changed course to lean out the doorway, hands on the doorjambs, as though expecting Ursula to pop up like a weasel.

"She got in someone's car. I don't know whose."

"Jeremy, what is this, some sort of joke?" she asked, spinning around. "If this is a prank you and your sister devised to play on me—"

I shook my head.

"Not a joke. A brown sedan. She got into a brown sedan."

"Jeremy!"

My mother rushed over to me and took me by the shoulders. Then she took my head in her hands and braced it firmly, tilting it so I couldn't help but look into her eyes no matter how hard I tried to avert my own.

"Tell me exactly what happened," she said, her voice only starting to quiver.

I took a breath. I swallowed hard.

"She was sitting on a rock. I went back for her Lambkins. And then I saw this brown sedan. And she was standing next to it. The back door was open. And when she saw me, she gave me a wave. And then she got in the car. And the car took off."

My mother kept my head in a vise grip, her eyes locked on mine.

"Christ," she said, "oh, Christ. How long ago was this?"

About an hour I told her, maybe more, I hadn't been keeping track of the time.

She went to the phone. Her hands were trembling as she held the receiver. She dialed zero (9-1-1 had yet to be instituted statewide) and waited for the operator, then calmly asked to be connected with the police.

My body felt strangely calm, as though it had entered a shallow sea. I swayed back and forth on my heels as I listened to my mother report Ursula missing to the dispatcher. I had a feeling of buoyancy. I wouldn't have been surprised to lean back and float on a cushion of air. But then my stomach lurched and I ran upstairs to the bathroom. I leaned over the toilet, my insides retching, but only spittle drooled out. After that, I went to our bedroom. I stared at my sister's bunk a long time, and then I climbed into my top bunk and pulled the covers over my head, wishing for it all to be over, whatever it chose to be.

Chapter 24

My sense of refuge below the covers didn't last long. My mother called me back downstairs. The dispatcher was sending both officers on duty to our house to take a report. They would need me to answer some questions.

I now have a sense of what purgatory must be like. It must be a surreal period of anticipation without an outlet, as though you are sitting in a doctor's waiting room without an illness and with no real expectation that the nurse will ever slide open the translucent glass window to call your name. Just this ongoing sense of uneasiness percolating through your system ...

My mother shuffled around the house while I sat at the kitchen table, waiting on the officers to arrive. We didn't talk, we didn't interact. Every time I felt the urge to apologize, to say how truly sorry I was, something inside my brain thought better of it. For my mother's part, she found what she wanted: a shoebox full of family photographs. She sat opposite me at the table, sorting through them, not looking at me, not speaking, as though to pretend I wasn't there. But every now and then, her head would sag and her face disappear within the tent of her hair, and a stifled wail would clog in her throat, before she regained her composure and continued sorting.

She finally laid out two photographs of Ursula: one was a wallet-size photo of her first-grade school portrait, but it had been taken last fall, so it was several months out of date. The other was more recent, taken outdoors with Ursie and me in our Sunday best perched on either side of a pale rose, leaning in to smell it together. Without glancing up to see how I might react, she took a pair of scissors and proceeded to cut the photograph in two, effectively snipping me out of the picture.

The front doorbell brought in the two officers. One was a serious older man with a crewcut and close shave, the other a just as serious younger woman with blonde hair done up in knot. She was Bellerophon's first female police officer, the first in the county, in fact—this I knew from the news it had made the year before when she was hired. The male cop wore a very stern, unsmiling expression. The female cop seemed just as grim-faced, which sort of threw me. In the TV shows I watched, one officer was always the "bad cop," the other playing the "good cop."

We all took seats in the living room, where the female cop asked my mother questions about Ursula's physical appearance—any telltale marks, such as moles or birthmarks or recent scratches or black-and-blue marks that might set her apart. She wanted to know whether Ursula knew her address and phone number, which my mother thought that she did. All the while, the male cop stared at me, chewing a piece of gum. I wondered if it was Bazooka Joe and, if so, what he had done with the wrapper.

All of a sudden, my mother startled us all by remembering her manners. She leaped out of her armchair and asked if the police officers would be interested in coffee.

Both declined, and the female officer continued asking questions. She wanted to know about Ursula's father: where he was, what he was doing, when he had last been seen, what kind of car he drove.

Mom told them everything she knew: that he hadn't been in town since the summer before, that he had made his way to Alaska by driving trucks longer and longer distances, that the last she had heard he had boarded a fishing boat—the *Argo*—as an engine operator and crew hand, that it had left port a couple of weeks ago and all communication was relegated to shortwave radio with no opportunity for direct phone calls, and finally that she didn't believe he had a car to his name at the moment, since he had left us the family station wagon for our own needs.

The female officer wrote all of this down in a small notepad with a flurry of blue ink, while the male officer continued to stare at me chewing gum, like a heifer chewing its cud. At this point, there was a pause in the interview, and my mother burst out with: "But shouldn't we be doing something? Shouldn't we be out looking for her? It just seems the longer we wait—" And here she broke down into sobs.

The female officer reached out a hand to her knee, which she patted to reassure her that this part of the process was vitally important, that the more groundwork they covered, the better the chances of finding her daughter. And besides, she added, they had already issued an alert for officers to keep a lookout for a brown four-door sedan last seen traveling east on Highway 61.

"Has your daughter ever run away from home?" the female officer asked.

My mother shook her head.

"No, of course not. No. Except—" The female officer held her pen in suspension, waiting for my mother to continue. "Well, there was a time awhile back she was always pretending to run away, any time one of us got angry with her, me or my husband, but she never went far. I don't believe she ever made it to the end of the block. Jeremy always convinced her to turn back home. It was never serious."

At this point, as though triggered by the mention of my name, the gum-chewing male officer spoke directly to me.

"Jeremy, is it?" His demeanor took on a kindlier aspect. Ah, so this was the "good cop," after all. "Tell me everything you can remember, son, beginning with what your sister was wearing."

I hesitated, waiting for him to pull out a notebook and pen, as his cohort did.

"Go ahead, Jeremy, don't be afraid," my mother encouraged.

When no notebook was forthcoming, I began. I told them everything I recalled.

"Could you make out a license plate?" the male officer asked.

I answered in the negative.

"Was it an Ohio plate?"

I said that I thought that it was, based on its color.

"And what color was that?"

"Red letters on a white plate," I said, but then my mind played a trick on me so that it seemed it could have been the other way around. "Or white letters on a red plate."

The female officer, I noticed, wrote this down in her notebook.

"And your sister—you say you remember her waving at you? Can you show me what kind of wave it was?"

For this, I stood up and tried to duplicate what I could see in my mind's eye, her body only half-turned toward me as she stood near the opened rear door on the driver's side, her arm coming up over her head in a loose C-shape and her tiny hand rotating back and forth on its wrist—a royal wave, the kind of wave a queen would make, or princess.

"And then she stepped inside the vehicle?" the officer asked.

"Yes, that's right. She stepped into the vehicle."

"Of her own free will? Or did somebody force her?"

"Of her own free will," I said, and then, less confidently, "I think."

"Could you make out anything about the driver?"

I squinted my eyes, trying to recall any form or semblance from memory.

"No," I gave up. "I don't think so."

"For instance, was the driver a man or a woman?"

"A man, I think. I'm not sure."

"Was there more than one person in the car?"

"No, I think there was only the driver."

"But you're not sure."

This was more of a statement than a question, but I shook my head anyway.

"And you weren't aware of any coercion?"

I raised an eyebrow, not quite understanding the word.

"Nobody grabbed your sister from inside the car?" the officer elaborated. "There wasn't a gun? Some other weapon?"

"No, sir," I answered. "Not that I can remember."

A long silence ensued, neither officer moving, just sitting still, looking at each other as though to communicate telepathically.

"Mrs. Jones," the female officer addressed my mother, "is it all right if Jeremy comes with us. We'd like to have him revisit the crime scene."

A crime scene—I hadn't thought of that curve in the road in this particular way until now.

My mother nodded her head.

"Of course. Should I come along?"

"No, that shouldn't be necessary," the male officer said, rising. "We won't be gone long, I shouldn't think."

"Besides," the female officer said, "we'll need you to stay by your phone, in case your daughter or the kidnapper calls."

This was the first time I heard the word "kidnapper" used, and I could see my own shock at the word mirrored in my mother's alarmed expression.

"So is that what this is?" my mother asked. "A kidnapping?"

"Kidnapping might not be the right word at the moment," the male officer corrected his partner. "We're treating it as an abduction."

They explained they would need to find out if the driver crossed the state line into West Virginia before involving the

FBI. Rest assured, they had the county sheriff's department on the case, as well as the State Highway Patrol. In fact, the sheriff's office was sending over a negotiator in case the abductor called with any demands. It would be good to have a professional on hand, guiding the process if this should occur.

"But kidnapping," my mother mused, standing, her gaze beseeching an explanation from either officer. "Demands. Like ransom? It's not like I have—we have—any money, any savings."

At the mention of money, I dug into my pocket and brought out the twenty-three dollars and forty-one cents. I handed this over to my mother, who accepted it with a bemused look.

"It's from your cookie jar," I explained. "Part of it, not all," I felt the need to clarify. "I was going to put it back."

"We can't overlook any possibility," the female officer said, overlooking this transaction, while the male officer took me by the shoulder and escorted me through the door.

"Jeremy?" my mother said with a pleading tone as I crossed the threshold, and the officer let me stop to await the rest of her query, but none came. Her question, if there was to be one, went unspoken.

Chapter 25

I rode in the back of the police car behind an iron cage that separated the front seat from the back. Every once in a while, the radio erupted with static. An occasional voice burst out of the static to state something or other in code. Once the female officer, who wasn't the one driving, picked up the intercom and said, "That's a 10-4," to some inquiry that I found unintelligible.

I imagined that this was maybe the biggest thing to happen in our town in quite some time. In my short lifetime, there had never been a murder, only an occasional robbery, usually of a gas station, a couple of car break-ins, but no assaults or batteries except for barroom brawls and domestic disputes. This I knew because our father, when he lived with us, would read the police beat out of the local newspaper, a weekly rag of only four or six newsprint sheets folded in half. It wasn't much of a paper. As for local news on TV, we picked up a Marietta station with difficulty because it was UHF. There were a couple of VHF channels that arrived out of Columbus, but the capital was so far away as to seem a foreign city. Our landlord hadn't wired our house for cable.

Overall, our community seemed a remarkably safe place, especially for kids, who, in the summer, would run around loose and unsupervised until dusk or their parents called them in, whichever came first. My parents made me aware of some of the vandalism that occurred in town—a shop window broken, some graffiti spray-painted on the side of a building—as they drove us about town. Except for a couple of break-ins, a stolen car or two, that was about it in the arena of crime

"What is that you've got going there?" the male officer said, smiling into the rearview mirror, "a little bit of a late Elvis look? You an Elvis fan, Jeremy?"

"My father likes him," I said. I wasn't sure how to respond to the officer's attempt at small talk. I was sure that in his eyes my ducktail compared unfavorably with his own military-style haircut. Besides, there wasn't much I could do about it. My mother had trained my hair into a cowlick through years of Brylcreem.

"Now all you need is the sideburns," the male officer said, laughing at his own joke. It was obvious they had switched good cop-bad cop roles.

"This the right way?" the female officer asked, throwing me a look over her shoulder.

We were winding through woods, climbing along widening spirals weaving through the hills.

"Yes, ma'am," I nodded my head.

"Just let us know when we reach the spot where you saw your sister get into the car."

The male officer began to take the hills more slowly, lowering the dial on the speedometer to 20 ... 15 ... 10 mph, a good thirty-five miles an hour slower than the road allowed.

"Do you mean where she got into the car or the spot from where I saw her?"

The officers exchanged looks in the front seat. It seemed they hadn't considered these alternatives in perspective.

"Let's start with where she got into the car," the male officer said, sizing me up in the rearview mirror.

We drove for a time, but all of the curves through the woods—and there were several—looked the same. I couldn't recall any distinguishing marks except for the large rock my sister had sat upon while I asked her to wait, but large rocks along both shoulders were characteristic of this stretch of highway. I had learned in school they had all been deposited by glaciers during the last Ice Age and bulldozed out of the way 12,000 years later to make a road. Besides, the whole landscape looked different under the light of late afternoon. The dawn had produced subtle variations of grays and greens, but now all the leaves looked brighter, the trunks of trees more distinct. Plus, it was different looking out a car window instead of directly in front of my two feet.

The police car began to slow around another wide curve.

"Did you come this far?" the male officer wanted to know, a keynote of impatience underlying the question.

"Maybe not this far," I said. "I think it might be easier to look for the clearing."

"The clearing?" the female officer said. Once more, she exchanged a glance with her partner—a questioning look that I failed to interpret.

I explained I had gone back to a clearing to get her stuffed animal for her and it was when I emerged from the clearing that I saw her step into the brown sedan.

"All right," the male officer said, pulling the car around with a violent tug at the wheel that made the front wheels crunch into the gravel on the first leg of a three-part U-turn. "Let's see if we can't find that clearing."

It didn't take long.

"There it is!" I said, waving my finger through the cage in my excitement. It was just as it appeared this morning, although by now, this morning seemed as if it had all taken place in some other era. It felt like something you might imagine yourself doing after reading about it in a history book—not something you personally experienced.

The male officer jerked the police cruiser to a stop. I made a move to get out of the car, but the locks made a clicking sound, and I couldn't open the door.

"We'll check it out," the male officer said. "You wait here."

And so I waited, staring at them as they approached the entrance to the clearing cautiously, stepping lightly. I never felt so much like a prisoner in a cage as I did then.

They dissolved into the shade of the trees, and I waited, resting my chin on my arms on the panel below the side window, feeling very drained and tired. I thought I could fall asleep then and there, and it's possible I closed my eyes for longer than a few seconds because the sound of the door locks unlatching startled me awake.

The male officer was back behind the wheel, but the female officer was next to me, bending to look at me through the door, which she had pulled open.

"All right, Jeremy, let's you and I take a walk down the road, okay?"

I got out of the car, feeling disoriented for only a moment, as to which way we were to walk. But she pointed me in the right direction. As we walked along the left shoulder, against the traffic, which was virtually nonexistent, this time of day, the patrol car followed slowly behind us by several yards in the right-hand lane. Its red lights on the roof were swirling, although its siren stayed silent, and the on-again-off-again color added a surreal aura to the scenery.

To be more certain, I counted off my steps and when I got to a hundred, I stopped. There was the rock—almost boulder-sized—where I had left my sister waiting. Automatically, I lifted my arm, aiming it across the roadway at the place where I believed she had stepped into the stranger's car. I felt as limp and as empty as a scarecrow.

The female officer kept hold of my arm, preventing me from crossing the road, while the male officer stepped out of the patrol car and inspected the mud-slicked shoulder, kneeling to check it over, then unfurled a roll of yellow tape from the trunk of the car to form a barrier. Meanwhile, the female officer radioed in to request someone from the county crime lab to come to the scene. Immediately I thought of Barry Allen, better known as The Flash, who worked as a police scientist as his daytime job when he wasn't fighting criminals and arch-villains. At this time, the term "forensics" hadn't entered common vocabulary. I also knew in the comic books he had a sort of reputation for always arriving late to a crime scene.

Sure enough, I waited in the backseat of the squad car until about a half-hour later, a police scientist showed up in the form of a small, rotund man with a gray broom-style mustache and round wire-rimmed glasses—nothing like The Flash. He wore a tweed jacket with a wrinkled shirt, the collar fastened primly with a bowtie. Overall, he reminded me of Captain Kangaroo. He drove a van with county plates that he parked on the opposite side of the road. After conferring with the two officers, he bent low to inspect the tire tread impressions in the mud. Then he went back to the van and came back with a kit for making plaster-of-Paris molds.

We didn't wait around for Captain Kangaroo to finish—or even start—his job. Instead, we drove back to the police station.

The police station? This took me off guard. I thought they would take me back home. Why were we stopping here? There were just a few more questions they wanted to ask, was their reply.

"You're not opposed to answering a few more questions if it will help us find your sister?" the female cop asked, sweetly— maybe a little too syrupy—as she opened the door for me. "You wouldn't want to impair the investigation, would you?"

"Impair" didn't sound right to my ears. I knew she meant some other word, but it didn't come to me until later, long after there was a time for rebuttal. "Impede," I thought long afterward. She had meant to say "impede."

"Watch your head stepping out," she cautioned.

Inside, there was a line at the post office counter, as I had worried there might be, but the line was longer than usual, and it didn't seem that all of the customers were there to buy stamps. Some were already facing the entrance when we pushed through the glass door, as though they were expecting my arrival. I'm sure word had already gone around about my sister's abduction, so I shouldn't have been surprised to see so many people standing around waiting for new information. The dispatcher's radio was no doubt more entertaining than an afternoon soap. Even as we trekked across the small lobby to where a section of the counter was raised on hinges to admit us into the area behind it, the radio spit out several blurbs about Ursula, a continuous crossfire of police voices.

I tried to avoid the gaze of the onlookers as I was led into a rear hallway. We turned left and came right away to a solid gray metal door that was half open. The officers knocked and a man's voice within said, "Enter"—not "Come in" or "Who is it?"— just "Enter," as though he possessed kingly authority over those he considered subordinates, sort of like the Wizard of Oz.

Chapter 26

Behind the gray steel door was a small storeroom, not much bigger than a broom closet. Boxes were stacked ceiling-high on three-tier metal shelving units against the walls. In the middle of the floor was just enough room for a small card table with folding chairs propped open on the near and far sides. A tall, thin man in a white dress shirt with rolled-up sleeves and a loose tie stood up as we entered, taking a last glance at a couple of items of paperwork on the table before turning to greet us. He had a narrow, pale hatchet of a face with bleary-looking eyes in small sockets like colorless gemstones set in milky-white gauze.

"Hello, I'm Detective Sergeant Barber," he said, holding out his hand. "And you're …" He took another quick glance at the paperwork on the table, "Jeremiah Jones, is that correct? Do you go by Jeremiah?"

"No, sir. Jeremy."

"All right, then, Jeremy …" Letting go of my hand, he motioned me to take the chair on the opposite side of the table, which I managed to do only by squeezing through the narrow pathway between the table edge and the shelves. "Make yourself comfortable," he said, not without some irony, I thought. "I'll be back in just a moment. Officers …" He motioned to the two police officers. And with that, he closed the door.

A moment took five minutes, ten, twenty, a half-hour.

So this was to be my interrogation room. Overhead was a single fluorescent light in an exposed fixture. On the table sat a bulky reel-to-reel tape recorder with a built-in microphone, similar to the one that sat largely unused in our school library for learning second languages. It was plugged into the light fixture outlet with a long white extension cord that curled into a loop like a noose.

My therapist voices skepticism at this version of events. She finds it odd that I was placed in a janitor's closet instead of a regular police interrogation room. Perhaps there is something symbolic in this choice of locale? Or is that maybe too cliché? It lacks officiality. For example, it seems unlikely a tape recording without a parent present would be admissible in court, if the case were to go this far. It all just seems so unprofessional, the entire experience surreal.

It was a small town, I remind her. The detective was probably bored on his ass half the time. This was the kind of case that could advance his career.

Besides, this is how I remember it. I was eleven, I inform my therapist— old enough to tell the difference between fantasy and reality—but she simply adds a note into her phone and nods for me to proceed.

"Thank you, officers," Detective Sergeant Barber said, returning through the door with his back to me. "That'll be fine," as a way of dismissing them. He shut the door but took a moment before turning around to take his seat, which he did wearily, as though he needed an afternoon nap.

"That's a nice watch you got there," he said suddenly, his eyes sharpening, becoming interested. "Mind if I take a look at it?"

I held out my wrist, noting the time: 3:32 p.m. It didn't seem possible it was only mid-afternoon. It didn't even seem it could be the same day. Again, I had the sense that all that had happened that morning belonged to the distant past.

"How about a closer look?" he asked, letting go of my wrist and holding out his hand. It took me a moment to realize he actually wanted me to remove it and hand it over. I did so, reluctantly, taking time with the buckle. "Thanks, Jeremy," he said casually, as though this were an ordinary transaction. He set the watch on the table face down.

"Are you hungry, Jeremy? Thirsty?"

I nodded my head. Now that I thought about it, I hadn't eaten or drunk anything since earlier this morning—not since Ursie and I rested in the clearing. I wished I could go back there. I wished I could rewind everything that had happened all the way back to that single point in time. In hindsight, I would have done everything so differently. I wouldn't have left Ursie sitting by herself on a rock.

"I'll see if I can't rustle you up something," he said, making a vague effort toward a smile. He didn't seem the type of person to whom smiling came naturally. I expected him to leave the room, but instead he spoke into a transmitter on his wrist.

"Just like Dick Tracy," I said aloud, when he was done.

"You like comic books, Jeremy?"

"Yes, sir." I mentioned The Flash and Green Lantern as favorites.

"What about baseball cards?"

"No, sir." I knew other kids who collected them, but they weren't for me.

"You like sports? Play any?"

I had to reply in the negative on this one as well. I wasn't very good at sports, something I knew from the second-grade playground. I was always the last one picked for kickball and then placed far out in the outfield where it would be unlikely the red rubber ball would ever be launched.

"What about games? I hear Dungeons & Dragons is popular with kids your age."

I shook my head without telling him the reason. For that kind of game you need a group of friends, and I didn't belong to any cliques.

"Would you say you've got a lot of friends?"

I didn't answer at first. I was so astonished by the question, I suspected him of reading my mind.

"No, sir. Not a lot."

"Any girlfriends?"

"No," I smiled, cringing with embarrassment, "not yet."

"You spend a lot of time with your sister, don't you?" he asked, point blank, more of an in-the-know statement of fact.

I didn't say anything to this, not sure what he was getting at.

"Jeremy, I'm going to start tape recording our conversation, just in case something comes up that might help us find your sister." He switched on the tape recorder and I watched the reels begin to turn. "Could you state your name for the record?"

"Jeremy," I said, my mouth feeling suddenly dry, so that my name came out as a whisper.

"A little louder, please," he said, "and use your full name, your legal name, okay?"

I cleared my throat and stated my formal name, in full, as he requested.

"Good, and also for the record, I have here a form—a release form—signed by your mother, allowing us—that is, the police department—to ask you a few questions. I'm now showing it to you so you can verify your mother's signature."

My mother's signature? I'm not sure how the detective expected me to recognize my mother's signature, since the birthday cards she gave me were always signed, "Love, Mom." But I accepted the signature at face value: Madeline Jones. The J formed a wide, graceful loop, as though filled with helium. It might lift the rest of the letters right off the page like a balloon. Far from reassuring me, her signature struck me as a form of betrayal. But I had other, more physical, concerns at the moment.

For one thing, I was wondering how long it would take for a

snack and a drink to arrive. But more than that, I was growing concerned about how long this questioning would take and when I could go home. It seemed important I should be with my mother, although part of me just wanted to crawl into a cave and hibernate until Ursula's case was resolved—one way or the other. I didn't want to think of the other.

He asked about my home life. We talked about my relationship with my mother and father. He asked if I missed my father and when was the last time I had seen him. He wanted to know how well I had done at school and if I was looking forward to sixth grade. He told me he had two kids of his own and even showed me photos he had of each in his wallet: an older boy with red hair and freckles, a girl somewhere between Ursie's and my age with darker hair and glasses. He even told me their names, not that I would remember them.

And then we talked for a while about my hobbies (model building) and interests (comic books). He wanted to know more about my friends—what kind of kids I hung out with on the playground or after school. I told him about some of the rich kids down the street from us, but how there weren't a lot of neighborhood kids to play with on a regular basis. He thought that must make things quite lonely at home, and was that why I played with my sister so often? I answered that it was more that I would hike around and climb trees and that Ursie would sort of tag along—not that I ever minded.

He asked if it bothered me that we shared a room, and I said, truthfully, not much. Ursie was still scared of the dark, so she liked having someone to talk with before she fell asleep. And I was able to stay up later in my upper bunk with a flashlight reading comic books.

He brought up the subject of religion and asked how often we went to church. When I told him three times a week, he raised his eyebrows, as though this were shocking news. Sometimes four, I mentioned, and this raised his eyebrows even higher. He asked how I felt about going to church so often, and I told him I didn't mind, except that it interfered with homework and playtime.

He wanted to go over my relationship with my mother, and I told him about the migraines my mother was having and how she was having a hard time of it without my father around.

In some ways, I enjoyed our conversation. It moved along at a relaxing pace. It was flattering, an adult taking such an interest in my personal life. I didn't mind confiding in him. Except for the difficulty he had smiling, he seemed a gentlemanly sort of detective, the kind who wore his badge loosely. I wasn't sure how any of this was going to help locate my sister, but I didn't mind talking with him.

Then, before I knew what was happening, the conversation took a more serious turn. It was right after the dispatcher brought in a snack: three chocolate chip cookies on a paper plate with a Dixie cup of milk to wash them down. I attacked the cookies with gusto and slobbered down half the milk. I wasn't sure how much time had elapsed since the snack had been promised, but it seemed it could have been hours.

I became aware of the detective sergeant watching me scarf the cookies as though cataloging the eating habits of an exotic animal, and so I slowed down.

He adopted a position of leaning forward, elbows on the table, fingers clasped as if in prayer—a stark contrast to his former attitude of leaning back against his chair, at times, with his hands folded behind his head.

He asked me to go through the whole story of Ursula's disappearance, starting with the very moment we awoke. I told him I had already divulged all of this to the two police officers who had driven me to the site of the abduction, but he said he'd like to hear it all over again—my side of it—just for the sake of getting it all on tape.

When I was through, he leaned in closer toward me as though about to confide a secret.

"Jeremy," he said softly, "there are some things about your story that are kind of—well, how shall I put it?—bothering us."

"Oh?" I responded, savoring the crumbs of my last cookie. What he said wasn't registering. "What story?"

"Take the business of your sister's waving to you just before she stepped inside the car. You say you're not sure if it was a wave to indicate a good-bye or to invite you to come along. Is that right?"

"Yes, sir."

"So you're not exactly sure what kind of wave it was."

"No, sir, I guess not," I answered slowly, carefully, still chewing, as though I knew I was giving an incorrect response in a history quiz.

"For another thing," he went on, disregarding my puzzlement, "there's the business about the car—the brown sedan. How did you know to call it a sedan?"

"Oh, that's because my dad—well, we had one growing up—and that's what he always called anything with four doors: a sedan."

"But you weren't sure about the license plate." And here, he was looking over some notes. "You thought they might be red letters on a white background or white letters on a red background." Now he looked up. "That's quite a difference. Red letters on a white plate make sense. That could very well be an Ohio plate. But white letters on a red background—that would make it a diplomatic plate." A corner of his mouth twisted into a smirk. "Do you think it was maybe a foreign dignitary driving a rusted-out brown *sedan* around these parts?"

He let a moment go by while I washed down the remnants

of my cookie with a final splash of milk, draining the Dixie cup to its dregs.

"You know, we've issued a statewide bulletin on the car in question," he said, sounding very detective-like of a sudden. "Even West Virginia authorities are searching. But so far, there aren't any reports of missing or stolen vehicles matching the description you gave us."

"So maybe it wasn't stolen," I said, trying to be helpful, while wiping away my milk mustache with the back of my hand. There was still something about the car that was lodged in a recess of memory—far, far back. I had an odd feeling I had seen it before, parked somewhere. But I decided not to bring this up with the detective. The rust spots were new though. I couldn't place them in my memory.

"What were you doing out on the road so early in the morning?" he asked point blank.

I felt a little foolish in answering, but I told him the truth: "We were going to Alaska."

"Alaska!" he exclaimed, in the same manner a scientist might declare, "Eureka!" or a parachutist, "Geronimo!"

I told him all about Ursie's plan to hike to Parkersburg so we could catch a Greyhound to Alaska to visit our father, even though all I had was twenty-three dollars and forty-one cents in my pocket from our mother's cookie jar and both our allowances combined.

Detective Sergeant Barber listened to this without smiling, but without frowning either—something in between.

"Alaska aside, Jeremy, there's this whole business of the clearing," he said, making it sound sort of suspicious. "You say you took your sister into this clearing—the one you pointed out to the two officers."

"Yes, sir. Although I wouldn't say I took her into it."

"No?"

"It was more like we went in together, you know, to rest, have lunch."

"And about what time was this?" he said, studying his notes again. "Around ten o'clock or so?"

"Yes, sir. I think it was around then."

"A bit early for lunch, wouldn't you say?"

"Yes, sir." Something about the way his tone was changing made me keep calling him "sir"— as a safeguard. "It's what I thought at the time, too, but we were hungry."

Detective Sergeant Barber sat back in his chair and studied me for a long time in silence to the point where I began to feel very uncomfortable. I had never been looked at with this much scrutiny before—not even by my mother making sure I had washed behind my ears after a bath.

"And you both came out again," he finally said, making me work hard to remember the most recent subject of our conversation, which was beginning to feel more like an interrogation as it progressed. "But only you went back in."

"That's correct," I said; then remembering, I added, "sir."

Now the detective sergeant leaned forward again. I had an urge to use the bathroom but thought it might be wiser to hold it a while longer. Something about the detective's change in demeanor made me think he might use my sudden need to urinate against me, as leverage.

"Jeremy, is there anything you want to confess?"

"Confess?"

"About your sister? It would be a lot easier if you were to confess now before something is—discovered."

I had to turn this over in my head for a minute, trying to work out a proper response. The only confessing I ever did was in church, and that was only for minor sins, like forgetting to turn in my homework or saying something mean to a classmate or not eating all my vegetables. There wasn't anything I was prepared to confess about my sister.

When I failed to respond, the detective changed tactics.

But first he had to pause the tape recorder and exchange reels, a somewhat tedious process that made him curse when the tape crimped and he had to touch the ribbon of tape to smooth it out. Then I had to state my name all over again—just for the record.

"Let's run through a couple of scenarios," he suggested, focusing on the tape to make sure it was rotating on its reels. "What say we put our heads together and use our imaginations to come up with some different versions of events? Are you with me?"

I wasn't sure, but I nodded my head anyway. I just wanted this whole situation to be over and done—the faster, the better.

He leaned forward with a sudden jolt, as though launched by a spring.

"Is that dirt under your fingernails?"

I looked at my fingernails as if for the first time in my life. I noticed the dirt, too, and answered yes, it must be.

"Do you know how you got that dirt under your fingernails?"

"No, sir." And it was true, I wasn't sure at first how it had got underneath both sets of fingers, even the thumbs. Then it occurred to me. "It might be from pulling up rocks and logs to look for bugs."

"Bugs," the detective sergeant said flatly.

"Ursie liked searching out bugs, you know, just for fun, so that's probably all it's from, turning rocks over for earwigs, pill bugs, that kind of thing."

"And this was in the clearing you did this—looking for bugs?"

"I think so," I answered. It was such an inconsequential,

everyday activity, typically done without fanfare. There was nothing memorable about it.

He brought out a Polaroid camera from nowhere, like magic, and asked if it would be all right if he took a photograph of my fingernails. I agreed, although I couldn't see the point of it.

"I notice you said 'liked,'" he said, setting the camera back in its hiding place.

"Sorry?"

"You said that your sister 'liked' to dig for bugs. You didn't say 'likes.' You used past tense, not present."

I knew my tenses from countless school lessons. He didn't have to remind me. But it made me think—was I already starting to think of Ursie as the sister I used to have?

"Let's go back to our scenarios, shall we?" Detective Sergeant Barber said, sounding someplace between impatient and enthusiastic.

"Okay," I said, hesitantly, not sharing his mood in the least but feeling tired, drained. My thoughts were becoming muddled. If my brain were a body of water, it would have been a swamp.

"Scenario One," he announced, with the promise of more to come. "Let's say you're walking along, it's just breaking dawn, still a little dark out, your sister stumbles, slips maybe, and falls into the road, just as a car—a brown sedan, let's say—comes swerving around the curve. It doesn't slow down. It doesn't stop. It hits your sister and keeps on going. Are you with me so far?"

I nodded my head. As pure story, it was dramatic enough to hold my attention.

"You cry out, but there's nothing you can do. And there's your sister. All the life snuffed out of her. What do you do? You feel responsible for her safety. So you pull her off the road, maybe into a clearing, and you decide to bury her body."

This part of the story shocked me, and maybe it showed.

"Can you imagine it happening this way?"

"But that's not what happened!" I protested.

"Still, you can imagine it, can't you? Happening like this?"

"I wouldn't just bury her," I said. "I wouldn't just leave her."

"You were panicked. You were afraid of what your mother would say. You didn't want to get into any trouble, so you made up this story about her being abducted. It would be easier this way, your mother holding out hope that her daughter—your sister—is still alive. It would get you off the hook in a way."

I shook my head. It's true, I could imagine what he was describing, but it just sounded too awful to contemplate.

"Jeremy? Is that how it happened?"

"No," I said, but my voice sounded tired.

"But you can imagine something like that happening, can't you? Just for the sake of argument?"

"Yeah, maybe," I let slip. I just wanted our conversation to be over. I just wanted all of the questions to stop.

"Scenario Two," he said languidly. "It's the first day of summer vacation. You're excited to sleep in, to do things with your friends—maybe go fishing. Do you like to fish?"

No, I thought, not really, but I nodded anyway. I always felt a little sorry for the fish.

"But you've got this sister who wakes you up, pestering you to walk with her to Alaska—of all places. So, being the good brother you are, you play along with her, and you hike along, knowing there's no way you're ever going to reach your destination, and you could only see in your future any number of these kinds of excursions—all summer long. Is this making sense to you?"

In a strange way it was, so I had no trouble nodding my head, going along with this second scenario.

"And with your mother having migraines every day and you

having to take care of your sister so often, you become a little irritated, let's say. Are you following me?"

"Yes, sir," I answered, although I could sort of see where this was heading. Just as with Scenario One, it didn't seem to be moving in a direction in my favor. It was starting to feel like a Twilight Zone episode. It was just easier to keep answering "yes," just bobbing my head along with the flow of the narrative.

"So, let's say, just hypothetically—you know what it means to speak hypothetically?"

Another nod of my head: yes, yes. I knew what a hypothesis is: an educated guess. It was something we practiced forming in science class. A prediction. How long will it take for a chick to hatch from an egg? How long for a tadpole to turn into a frog? How long for bacteria to breed in a petri dish? How long for this interrogation to be over?

"Let's say it was an accident. You didn't mean to do it. It was just something that happened. Maybe you threw a rock in her direction. Maybe you pushed her into the road just as a car was driving past."

He let a moment go by to let these possibilities sink into my brain, like ingredients stirred into a bubbling stew.

"Is that what happened, Jeremy?" he asked softly, leaning closer across the table. "Was it an accident? Something you didn't mean to do?"

I just sat there, numbly, unable to answer.

"It doesn't matter how it happened," he said, leaning back against his chair. "It could have happened any number of ways. But the fact is, it wasn't your fault. You were acting from emotion. Frustration. Irritation. Sort of like a reflex. A doctor taps your knee with a rubber mallet, and your leg moves. That sort of thing."

Another round of silence went by without my being able to respond, but this time, it seemed that a response is what the detective was waiting on.

"Jesus, I didn't kill her," I said solemnly, looking down at the table, studying the slowly spinning reels of the tape recorder. The feed reel was running low on tape, as the take-up reel greedily consumed it. I was hoping he wouldn't have to change reels all over again.

"I'm sure you wouldn't have meant to," he said, as though it were an established fact, "but you can picture it, in your mind, how it might have played out this way?"

"I didn't kill her," I said again, but my voice was losing its certainty.

"No one's saying you did. But you can appreciate how some-thing like this could have easily occurred, can't you? It's within the realm of possibility, wouldn't you agree?"

He waited a moment, but I couldn't respond.

"Jeremy? Are you still with me on this?"

"Yes," I said, forgetting the "sir." I put my head down, let-ting it rest in a cradle formed by my arms, crossed on the table.

"It's okay, Jeremy," the detective sergeant said, reaching over and putting a hand on my shoulder—a hand I was too tired to flinch away, although this is what I felt like doing, the way I would a mosquito. He waited another long moment, and then he asked, "Did something happen, Jeremy? Something you didn't mean to do?"

"I didn't murder my sister," I mumbled into my cave.

"Was it an accident, Jeremy?" He drew his hand away. Is that how it happened? An accident?"

"No," I said, but without conviction.

"Did you hurt her, Jeremy?"

"No."

"Jeremy, did you hurt your sister?" he prodded softly, sym-pathetically.

I lifted my head but found I couldn't say anything. My voice seemed locked deep inside. The room looked watery, the detective's face all blurry. I just wanted to go home. I wanted to rest. I wanted to see my mother.

"It's all right," the detective said, patiently. "It's just that it would go easier on you, if you were to tell me what happened to your sister—what really happened. I have officers searching the clearing right now. It's only a matter of time before they find something."

Something?

And then I remembered something I could say—a stalling tactic that people being interrogated used on TV.

"I want a lawyer," I stated.

The detective frowned.

"I don't think there's any reason to bring in a lawyer. Not at this point."

"I want a lawyer," I said again, more firmly.

The detective stared at me, narrowing his eyes, scrutinizing my own.

"All right, Jeremy," he said. "If that's what you want."

He paused the tape recorder and rose to his feet. He gave me a long parting look, then left the room, closing the door behind him.

I felt an enormous sense of relief. It was almost as though I had to convince myself that I hadn't done anything wrong. I wasn't a criminal. I hadn't killed Ursula. I hadn't been charged with her murder. Did this mean I was free to go? If I tried to leave, would they let me? Or would they make me wait until they brought in a lawyer?

Finally, I couldn't wait any longer. I had to use the bathroom—bad. I stood up, but my legs were wobbly, so I had to hold onto the table edge for support. I worked my way around the table and took two steps toward the door, when it opened and I collapsed into the arms of the detective sergeant. He propped me up under my armpits. His arms, although wiry, were as strong as steel struts.

"It's all right, Jeremy," he said into my ear. "You can go home now."

"What?" I said into his shoulder. "Why?"

He held me back at arm's length, still keeping me upright.

"They found her," he said, evenly, without emotion, neither smiling nor frowning. "They found your sister."

He let go of me and I sat down, collapsing onto the folding chair he had sat in to interrogate me.

And then it occurred to me to request more information.

"Alive?" I asked, tentatively, not daring to look up.

The detective waited a heartbeat, as though to take a breath before replying.

"Yes," he said, "alive."

I noticed my watch and turned it over, face-up.

It was 7:37 p.m.

Chapter 27

Our house was full of activity. The lights were all on when we pulled up to the curb. Bill Urchin (aka Baby Cyclone) was holding off a news crew—complete with shoulder-held camera and an on-the-scene newsman with microphone— the way he would as a bouncer at a bar, probably at my mother's request. With his shaved head, thick, tattooed, crossed arms, and planted feet, he seemed as immovable as a fire hydrant. The news crew appeared as predators denied fresh meat, but because the detective's car was a plain, unmarked Crown Victoria and because he left me off at our landlord's house, I was able to sneak past and around the yard to the kitchen door without being bothered.

As I made my way inside, I found the house bulging with people. I recognized Church Congregationalists, stout middle-aged women of the Ladies Aid. Parents of rich kids from down the street who were setting foot in our house for the first time since we moved in. A troop of Boy Scouts was packed into a crevice of the dining room. It seemed everyone in town had shown up for one reason or another: some to offer comfort, hope, a sense of community, others to hold forth, kibitz, pontificate. And maybe more than a few were there the way vultures flock around a carcass or drivers rubberneck at an accident. Also likely was the prospect of a free meal.

The dining-room table held a buffet of baked goods, hors d'oeuvres, candies, tinfoil-covered dishes, and pies, pies, pies. Hungry as I was, I didn't feel like eating just then. I passed by the table as though it held nothing but the bowl of wax fruit, its typical centerpiece.

No one appeared to notice me as I passed through to the

living room. Only our landlord, baldheaded Mr. Jenkins, standing silently in a corner eating a slice of three-tiered chocolate cake
on a paper plate, acknowledged me with a sympathetic nod. A
cluster of first and second cousins from both sides of the family
stared at me as though they should recognize me, as I did them,
but neither they nor I made a move to reintroduce ourselves. We
hadn't seen each other in years.

Otherwise, the mood in the house was buoyant. Everyone
was talking excitedly in small groups about the good fortune of
finding Ursie alive. From eavesdropping on a couple of conver-
sations, I gathered it would still take an hour or more for her to
be delivered to our doorstep. She had been found at a Tasty
Freeze in North Carlton, about sixty miles north, sitting in a
booth with a strange man, eating a chocolate sundae.

Members of the Ladies Aid were gossiping in a low tone between sips of tea:

"Do you think she was …?"

"Oh, let's pray not!"

But something in the way they leered made me wonder
whether they weren't secretly hoping that she had been—whatever it was they were imagining.

"But to think of it—Mrs. Darnell's son …"

"Surely, Walter wouldn't have done anything."

Walter!

The name made me stop cold. I felt a wave of anxiety riffle
through me. This is where I had seen the brown sedan. It was
always parked in old, dying Mrs. Darnell's driveway whenever
Ursie and I tagged along with our mother on her hospice visits.
Two or three harsh Ohio winters must have rusted it out more
than I could recall.

In the living room, my mother was pacing a trough in the
threadbare carpet. She only paused to inhale furiously on a long

menthol cigarette, something I had never seen her do. For all I knew, she had only taken up smoking today.

The minister stood at one end of her runway, blocking her from taking off into the air, I supposed. An assortment of sympathizers lined her path on either side, watching her glide back and forth as though she were a ball in a tennis match.

It became immediately apparent that I had stumbled onto a theological argument.

My mother asked the minister why God is punishing her: first her husband, then her daughter?

"It is not for us to ask the wherefores and whys," the minister calmly replied. "We must all accept the judgment of the Lord."

But why, oh why, *her*, my mother wanted to know. What did she—meaning herself—do wrong? Was there some sin she was being punished for?

"We are all of us sinful creatures," was the minister's response. "We must all seek forgiveness. None of us is exempt from the wrath of God. We can only do what we can to deserve His love—meekly, with submission."

"But what kind of love is that—letting my daughter, my only daughter, be abducted—missing—for so long?"

She took a ferocious drag on her cigarette, and blew the smoke upward, above the minister's head, toward the ceiling, where it hung in an oblong circle, like a halo. The effect seemed to take my mother by surprise, as well as me. It was apparent she hadn't realized she was capable of such a trick as blowing smoke rings.

"The Lord works in mysterious ways."

This was the minister's standard response.

My mother began pacing again.

"Well, why does He have to be so goddamned mysterious all the time?" There was a collective gasp from the Ladies Aid.

"Pardon my French, Pastor. But why can't He just come out in the open once in a while and let us know why it is He does what He does?"

"It's not for us to know or say. It's God's will."

My mother stubbed out her cigarette in the nearest available saucer.

"Oh, I'm so tired of hearing about God's will. Yes, I'm thankful my daughter's alive, but I still don't know if she's okay—who knows what's been done to her? Nobody can tell me. Is this God's will to leave me in doubt? And if she had been found dead, murdered—would this have been God's will? And what kind of God would allow something like this to happen in the first place? And my husband not here. And my son—Jeremy! Where on Earth have you been?"

She rushed toward me and hugged me close.

"Answering questions," I murmured into her neck.

"What?" she asked, holding me at arm's length to take a good look at me. "All this time?"

A half-hour later, a swirl of red lights against the living-room curtains announced the arrival of Ursula.

All talking in the house ceased. My mother went to the screen door. The news crew muscled its way past Bill and followed the officers—two sheriff's deputies, both of them male, not the pair of male/female officers from town—escorting Ursula all the way up the steps of the porch, determined to capture the reunion of mother and daughter on camera.

They weren't disappointed. No one was. Ursie rushed into our mother's arms and hugged her as she stooped to greet her.

"Oh, Mama, Mama," she cried, reverting to her babyish term for her mother, I noticed. "I'm so sorry I'm late getting home. I kept asking him and asking him to take me home, but he wouldn't take me home!"

Instead of hugging her back, our mother pulled her away and, grasping her firmly by the shoulders, shook her gently as she scolded her: "Don't you ever, ever, ever get into some stranger's car ever again. Do you understand?"

It was quite a performance—all caught on camera. We watched it on the 11 o'clock news on WTAP out of Parkersburg that night, our mother appearing quite chagrined.

"Oh, Mama, it was only Walter," Ursie said tearfully. "You know I wouldn't get into just any stranger's car." And then she broke into sobs.

"It's all right," our mother said, holding her daughter close, rubbing her back and stroking her hair. She squinted up at the bright lights of the news crews—there were more of them now—whose reporters began pestering mother and daughter with questions all at once so it was impossible to make out what they were asking.

"Please," our mother begged, and Bill, arriving at the top of the steps, reached in and pulled the living-room door closed on the broadcast.

"Show's over, folks," he explained sternly.

Seeing me over our mother's shoulder, Ursie broke away and leaped, her arms outstretched, so I had to catch her and return her hug.

"Oh, Jeremy, I'm sorry I left you behind. I wanted you to come with, but he told me to get inside the car and he would wait. He didn't want me to get run over standing in the road. So he told me to get in the car, but he didn't wait like he said."

It was our mother's turn to take her by the shoulder and spin her around.

"Did he hurt you?"

"Walter? Oh, no. He wouldn't hurt me."

"Did he touch you anywhere?"

"Just to hold my hand once."

"And that's all?"

"Yes, it was just to hold my hand when he took us to visit the princess."

"What princess?" our mother wanted to know.

"Why, Princess Eva. You remember her, don't you, Jeremy?"

All eyes turned toward me.

"Walter's sister," I explained.

Everyone within earshot nodded, seeming to understand.

Apparently, almost everyone in town, except us, knew about the fate of the formerly aged, currently deceased, Mrs. Darnell's daughter Eva.

Later, Ursula told us all about her visit, which she reported in glowing tones as a marvelous adventure—if you ignore the bit about the kidnapping. It appeared coincidental that Walter had been on his way to visit his sister early that morning, just stumbling across Ursie sitting on a rock at the side of the road and inviting her to go for a ride. Princess Eva, Ursie said, still wore a pink chiffon dress with billowing folds. Her head was still crowned with a tiara, and she still waved her magic wand around as though to transform others into magical creatures.

There were others where she was staying, but they all seemed ogres and trolls in comparison, confined as they were to wheelchairs and hospital beds and wearing the most drab, colorless gowns and slippers. In comparison, Eva glimmered like a goddess out of mythology. She lived in a large furnished room in an enormous mansion—in actuality, a private sanitarium for patients of means—with wide lawns and cobblestone patios.

She had had a most wonderful visit. Eva had been so happy to see Ursie, she had missed her so much. They had a tea party on one of the patios overlooking a pond and afterward had fed the ducks and geese bits of bread from a bag that Walter had brought along. After visiting hours were over and they hugged their goodbyes—Eva making her promise to visit again some-time soon—she got back in the brown sedan with Walter and asked very politely to be driven home, but this Walter was reluc-tant to do. Wouldn't she rather have a bit of dinner with him, and, feeling hungry, she had said it would be okay if only she could call her mother first to ask permission. But there wasn't a phone anywhere to be found, and so they had gone to a Tasty Freeze, and Walter had splurged on a cheeseburger and fries.

"Not a pay phone even at the restaurant?" our mother asked.

Eventually, it came out that Ursula still didn't know her phone number. Later, our mother would sit her down and have her write it out a hundred times to memorize it.

"And so Walter would have called here if only you knew our phone number?" our mother asked.

"Yes," Ursie answered, "if it hadn't been for the police."

They were just beginning to enjoy their dessert when two police officers came into the restaurant. One officer drew his weapon and aimed it at Walter in their booth, while the other took Ursie by the arm and pulled her to safety. I only wished I had been there to see it.

At present, the two deputies who had entered behind Ursula informed our mother an ambulance was waiting. They said it was procedure to take Ursula to the nearest pediatric unit, which hap-pened to be at Marietta Memorial where she had been born, to be checked over for evidence of trauma.

But our mother refused. She told them her daughter had been through enough for one day, and besides, she believed her when she had told her she hadn't been inappropriately touched.

Well, then, they would still need to stop by in the morning to take Ursula in for questioning at the county sheriff's office. In fact, they let slip that this was where they were going now, to deliver Walter, who was handcuffed in the back of their squad car. Ursie had sat between the officers in the front seat on the ride back to town.

"I'd like to talk with him," our mother said.

The deputies informed her this would be unorthodox, not to mention ill advised.

"I'm going to talk with him," our mother insisted. "You're going to let me talk with him."

And so the deputies relented.

Walter, as it turned out, had been living in a group home for men with disabilities. He had been off his medication—his meds—this day when he got it into his head to visit his sister in her sanitarium. Even though diagnosed with schizophrenia, he still had driving privileges as well as access to his deceased mother's sedan.

Murmurs circulated around the house as our mother climbed into the back of the squad car, its lights idly swirling, the camera crews following along like a pack of starving dogs. She sat with him for ten full minutes. The glare of the lights from the cameras bounced off the glass, making it difficult to distinguish their faces, but from what I could see of their silhouettes, our mother did most of the talking with plenty of animated gestures, while Walter, for his part, sat impassively.

When she returned to the house, the camera crews at her heels, Bill trying to keep pace, fending them off, the officers assumed she would want to press charges, but somewhere in there, she had a softening of heart.

"Charges won't be necessary," she said quietly. "He meant no harm. All is forgiven."

The sheriff's deputies seemed somewhat put out about this. They told us they would be taking Walter to the sheriff's office in any case—if only to hold him while they figured out which

District Attorney's office would want to press charges of its own, since in their travels, Walter had taken Ursula across county lines.

"We can't have someone like that driving around town picking up stray girls, now, can we?" the one officer said, making it sound like Ursie had been a lost puppy on the side of the road.

That night, back in our bunk beds, we stayed quiet for a long time, although I could hear Ursie's breathing, steady but light. Sounds of conversation still rose like the cooing of doves from below, as our mother finished herding out leftover guests who were loath to depart. Earlier, she had tucked us both in extra tight, although it was a mild summer night. Even so, she shut and locked the window as a safeguard. She spent an extra-long time sitting on the edge of Ursie's bunk, not saying anything, but humming a bedtime song. I only knew she had left when the humming had stopped.

Just when it started to sound like Ursie was asleep, she whispered up to me in the dark.

"Jeremy, you awake?"

"Yes," I said. "Are you all right?"

"Uh-huh."

A long thread of silence spun out like a line off a fly reel.

"Do you forgive me?"

I rose up on an elbow.

"Of course, I forgive you. There's nothing to forgive."

Another spool of silence unraveled.

"Do you love me still?"

"Yes," I said, "now try to get some sleep.

For my own part, I was exhausted.

"Seems this whole episode would have been quite the life-altering experience," my therapist comments, rather coyly, I think.

"Yeah, I guess so," I reply, somewhat drily, in return.

I shift my position on the couch on my side of the small, cramped office. I cross and uncross my legs. I am feeling suddenly uncomfortable, like J. Alfred Prufrock, grown older and slightly bald, sprawling on a pin. It must be her gaze, now that it's left her phone and is concentrated solely on my reactions.

"For both you and your sister," she points out, encouraging me to agree with a slight nod of her head, and I do. "She's OK? Your sister?" she asks. "She survived the trauma? She turned out all right?"

"Yes," I assure her, as well as myself. "She turned out OK. She turned out fine."

"And you?" my therapist continues to prod. "It was probably even more traumatic for you. But you survived it? You turned out all right, too."

This comes across as more of a statement of fact, and I give myself a minute to think about it, to mull it over, as though I've never really taken time to contemplate the current state of my own well-being before. Then it occurs to me: maybe I haven't.

"I suppose so," I finally decide.

"So this is where the story ends?" my therapist prompts, leaning forward in her chair, hands clasped, elbows on knees, eyebrows furrowed. "You both lived happily ever after?"

"Not exactly," I confess, letting out a pent-up sigh. "There's more."

Chapter 28

At the beginning of the school year, with the salmon fishing done, our father arrived for what was meant to be a short visit, but our mother talked him into staying through Christmas. Then he would go back to Alaska by bus, leaving us the family station wagon, as usual. He would spend the winter driving a semi, hauling equipment and hardware and supplies back and forth along icy roads between Anchorage and an oil refinery. And then he would go back to salmon fishing with the spring thaw, rejoining his crewmates on the *Argo*. The money was just too good to pass up, and our mother, realizing money as one of a growing family's essential needs, gave him her blessing.

His appearance had changed. Just as in the photograph he had sent us holding up a fish as long as he was tall, he had a ruffed grouse of a beard and moustache that hid the lower half of his face. But he was more liable to wear flannel shirts with sleeves rolled to the elbows rather than his former attire of Browns and Indians jerseys. His dresser drawer dedicated to Chief Wahoo remained unopened. Even though we lived near the river down south, not the lake up north, he was still more of a Cleveland fan than Cincy or Pittsburgh. In this regard, he was still our father.

"When do you think it became improper to call Native Americans 'Indians?'" my therapist asks without consulting her phone this time.

I shrug away what I consider a rhetorical question.

"All the way back in the 1960s," she asserts, settling into her side of the office with a sly grin. "Part of the Civil Rights movement."

"Is that so?" I respond. "Still, you have to admit, Cleveland Native Americans doesn't exactly roll off the tongue."

"Agreed. 'Guardians' is a much better name."
"Right, like Guardians of the Galaxy."
I appreciate these rare moments when my therapist and I are in accord.

During the months he stayed with us, Ursie and I had school, of course, so we didn't see as much of him as we would have liked to. But even when we came home from school or stayed home on weekends, being with our father was sort of like hanging around the mummified remains of King Tut. He hibernated a lot. Basically, he lay on the sofa watching TV or reading the newspaper. On more than one occasion, the newspaper would fold over his head like a pavilion, and from within we would hear a regular vibrato of snores.

When he first saw me—we were all there to greet him at the bus station in Parkersburg—the very first thing he said to me was, "Hey, you got glasses."

"Yes, sir," I answered. I had just got the prescription, in fact, the week before, for nearsightedness. It was when I couldn't decipher the number of the license plate on the brown sedan that had abducted Ursula from a distance of only one hundred yards that I knew the inevitable was in store: eyeglasses in sixth grade.

"How are you going to fly jet airplanes wearing glasses?" he asked, hefting his duffle bag onto his shoulder from where it had been disgorged from its compartment under the bus.

I couldn't be sure if this was my father's typical veiled criticism of my shortcomings or just a joke. I took it for the latter and let out a laugh.

"Seriously," he said, "if they start calling you 'four-eyes' at school, you let me know, okay?"

"Yes, sir."

"I'll go right over to that kids' parents and let them know just what I think of that kind of verbal abuse."

"Yes, sir."

"And what's with all this 'sir' business?" he asked. So I made an effort to refrain from calling him this, even though there was something new and—I don't know—sort of formal about his demeanor. He had the air of an Army lieutenant.

On weekends, our mother would periodically stand near the sofa, hovering over him, her arms crossed, staring down at his newspaper-covered face, as though she were keeping watch over an ill child. As the day progressed, her frown would gradually deepen, her eyes narrowing, her forehead creasing.

"Henry," she would say, "why don't you get up and do something with the children? You know you're going to miss them."

And so he would grudgingly emerge like a bear from the den of his newspaper and sit on the edge of the couch, leaning forward with elbows on knees.

"Okay, okay, Maddy," he would say. "No need to keep harping on the same old theme." Then turning to us, he would ask, kindlier, "All right, kids, what'll it be?"

Sometimes, it was a walk around the block or a bike ride to the park. Other times, it was playing catch with a red rubber kickball. He would kick it high in the air and expect one of us to catch it without flinching. I'm embarrassed to say, but my sister was much better at this game than I was.

One time, our mother suggested lawn darts.

"There's that set in the garage that hasn't been touched for over a year now," she mentioned.

But I told her I wasn't all that keen about playing.

Occasionally, our father would ask, "How about a trip to the zoo?" But we knew, then, he was joking. Bellerophon didn't have a zoo. The closest one was in Cincinnati, far down the river.

In this way, with our mother's stern encouragement, we got to see more of him than we would otherwise. But he still held himself aloof, seeming more like a kindly uncle—sort of the way Bill had become.

For the months our father stayed at home, we saw very little of Bill. Except one Sunday, our mother invited him over to watch football. We didn't know what to expect. We imagined a competition. A wrestling match. A duel to the death with faux fireplace implements. Instead, the two got along passably enough. It happened they were both Browns fans, which helped smooth over any tension involving the struggle for male dominance.

I knew in any physical contest, our father would be the loser. The contrast between the two men as they sat on opposite ends of the couch, reaching over to snag popcorn from the same bowl, slurping down cans of Iron City and Schlitz when the Iron City ran out, was very evident. Our father was scrawny, slim, wiry. Bill was built to lift loads in the manner of a forklift. Apparently, our mother had rigged this encounter as a way of allaying any worries our father might have about her fidelity.

The only odd thing I noticed was how they didn't utter a single word to each other, all through the game. They communicated by grunts and groans and yells and occasional high-fives to indicate their approval or disapproval of the way the game was unfolding. Only at the end, when they shook hands with Bill's departure, did they say to each other, "Good game," even though the Browns had lost once again.

I'm not sure what our father and mother did together when we were in school. Sometimes, we'd come home and catch them smooching on the couch. They would sit up in a hurry, our mother blushing, our father tucking in his shirt. One night, I got up to investigate a noise that sounded like burglars trying to enter our house by hammering a hole through a wall, but as I listened outside my parents' bedroom door, I identified the noise coming from behind it: a loud pounding of mattress springs.

I was going on twelve, but I was starting to form vague images, deduced from discussions in sixth-grade health class, of what men and women might do together when the kids were in bed. I knew from rumors and hints on the playground that some of it might involve the shedding of clothes—pajamas, nightgowns—but that's as far as my imagination went, before it dissolved into mist.

At the beginning of January—a day after New Years's in fact—despite protests from our mom ("So soon? You couldn't stay until Jeremy's birthday at least? It's only two weeks away."), our father got back on the bus for Alaska. It would take five days and several layovers and transfers. On the platform, as our father's duffel bag was being loaded, we said our good-byes. We gave him hugs—Ursie and I—at the same time, my embrace higher than my sister's, but in terms of responsiveness, it was like hugging a tree trunk.

Our father patted our heads, and then he gave me the same instruction he did every time we parted ways: "Take good care of your sister."

Our mother, in her wisdom, had decided against telling our father about Ursula's abduction, and since our father rarely left the house except to make visits to the hardware store or go fishing, it was fairly easy to keep the incident secret.

What made it even easier was our mother giving up setting foot inside a place of worship while our father was home. Not that our father complained. We always had the feeling he merely suffered through church services only to please our mother. But now there was no chance that some member of the congregation would refer to what our mother and Ursie and I referred to among ourselves "The Incident." In the short time Ursie had gone missing, police were never able to reach our father directly, and so he hadn't received the kind of news that probably would have induced him to hurry back home. For her part, our mother didn't want our father to think we couldn't take care of ourselves while he was gone. Was it that our mother didn't want our father to have second thoughts about leaving? Did she really, deep down, *want* him to leave?

Had I known this would be the last time we would see him, would I have given him an extra hug? Would I have said, "I love you"? Would I have clung to him like life itself? It's hard to say. He promised he would see us again that autumn, so I had this to look forward to, but as September rolled through October and then into winter, his promise slipped through like a trick knot, and his presence failed to materialize. Instead, once again, we had Bill over for Christmas dinner, sans Santa beard, and Easter dinner, sans bunny ears. He was becoming more and more a solid fixture in the house, as dependable as the washing machine, which only occasionally broke down, or the kitchen faucet, which only required a washer now and then to stop a drip.

Our only complaint? Ursie and I were gravely disappointed our father hadn't even remembered us with a Christmas gift.

"No Eskimo dolls this year," Ursie lamented.

"No snowshoes," I added to her lament.

"Bastard," our mother muttered, loud enough for us to hear. We didn't dare correct her assessment of our father's negligence. We might have said the same, had we been permitted.

———

Just like the year before, Dad missed my birthday, except this time he failed to recognize it with so much as a card.

I wasn't exactly thrilled about turning thirteen, the way others in my class were about their birthdays.

I knew high-rise hotels and buildings delete the thirteenth floor altogether as unlucky. And that's how I felt about turning thirteen years old. Why couldn't I just skip over it right into being fourteen? I had a sense of foreboding as it approached, and I didn't consider myself any more superstitious than the next fellow.

But it felt as though I were being pushed forward into a new era of living that I wasn't certain I was quite ready for.

"Out of your tweens and into your teens," was how my mother phrased it, trying to make it sound as jolly a transition as a Dr. Seuss rhyme.

But, to me, I could only recall the fight-or-flight terror I experienced when my father pushed me off the end of a diving board into the deep end of the town's municipal pool, when I clung to it with my toes curled around the edge, staring down at the twelve-foot depths in a profound state of paralysis—the same fear I imagined pirate victims must have undergone when being forced to walk the plank.

"Come on, Jeremy, you're holding up traffic," my father had complained.

And when I refused to budge—not so much out of conscious reluctance but an uncontrollable frigidity of my nerve fibers—he came right up behind me and, with a shove, sent me to my doom.

And so I turned thirteen with a sense of nostalgia for the good old days of twelve, which later I would translate as a wistfulness for puberty versus adolescence.

My therapist interjects with a "fun fact" again without recourse to her phone: Did I know the whole gangplank business is only a myth? Is this something she learned watching a MythBusters *episode? And on that note, I consider terminating our relationship. I have been seeing less of her anyway, letting a session lapse here and there, as my memories sort themselves out. Their folds and wrinkles have smoothed into a wide, checkered plain upon which individual events sit isolated like chess pieces. I can move them now, rearrange them, without ending up with two or more pieces on any one square.*

—

Aside from seeing Bill, we visited Princess Eva in her wellness home in the country, our mother serving as chaperone. Just as Ursula had described her, Eva wore a pink chiffon gown and sparkly tiara and waved a magic wand with a silver star made of tinfoil on the end. She seemed just as enthused to see me again as she did Ursie, and our mother left us alone to enjoy our tea party—or in my case, put up with it; I felt more than a trifle old for such things—while she visited some of the other patients and chatted with the nurses.

She even made a visit to Walter once to see how he was coming along in his new group home, but she wouldn't let us go with her, not that we wanted to. She just wanted to make sure he was getting the psychiatric treatment he needed and that he was taking his medications per his new regimen.

That left Bill as our only regular adult friend.

Bill worked by day as a trainer at Daley's Gym in a warehouse district near the train tracks on the far edge of town, and by night as a bouncer at the Knotty Pine Bar and Grille in what was called the Uptown. So he wouldn't have had any free time to babysit us, even if our mother had felt him qualified to do so.

And so enter Judith.

Chapter 29

Judith came into our lives like a beacon to moths. She was the flame about which Ursula and I fluttered.

This was after our father died. He wasn't officially dead—just presumably dead. Our mother, for one, didn't believe a word of it, even though his death would have explained the months he had been incommunicado, not to mention the months our family's portion of his paycheck had ceased arriving. Death would have been preferable to negligence. Nevertheless, she was certain he was still among the living.

"If he were dead, I would know it," is all she would say. This was after she came out of her bedroom, into which she had sealed herself for three full days after she learned the news. She kept herself in darkness, the shades drawn, and Ursie and I took time off from school—which was winding down toward spring break anyway, filled with silly games in my sister's classes and boring movies in mine—to tend to her needs, bringing her tea and toast as her only requested form of nourishment. Somewhere during those three days of near-isolation, she had come to the personal conclusion that her husband, our father, was still alive.

According to the telegram, the wreckage of his ship had been discovered clinging to an Arctic ice floe by a trawler that was mapping icebergs in the Bering Sea. No survivors were found, and the life raft hadn't been deployed. The telegram had been sent by the port of call from which our father's boat, the *Argo*, had been launched for one last salmon run late in the season the previous October. We received a more detailed letter along with a news clipping about the incident from the State Department by mail.

"Now I know why he didn't remember my birthday," Ursie sniffed sadly.

We never held a funeral service. And so, in our minds—our hearts, as it were—we had to side with our mother in her belief in our father's still being alive: his aliveness, as we thought of it. We pictured him on an iceberg, like a polar bear, surviving by plunging his head into arctic waters, hunting for seals. He was out there, somewhere, in a wide, expansive sea of icy flotillas, snow-encrusted patties that resembled frozen pies.

This meant no more early morning ventures to Alaska.

It also meant our mother, migraines or not, needed to increase her hours at the library to full time. Her savings were dwindling, and the death benefits from Social Security weren't immediately forthcoming. Apparently, there was significantly more red tape to work through, requiring extra forms to fill out, in the case of a spouse who was merely missing as opposed to dead with an actual corpse for proof. All of this added up to one long delay in her receiving Social Security checks. Mr. Jenkins, our landlord, was sympathetic about allowing the rent to lapse, but even when the payments began to kick in, they barely covered our household expenses.

With the end of the school year approaching, we needed a babysitter. At least this was our mother's view of the matter. The incident with Ursula's abduction, two summers before, was still fresh in her mind. She didn't trust me, even at thirteen years of age, to look after Ursula, age nine. Anything could happen when she wasn't there to prevent it. Household fire. Vicious bite from a feral raccoon. Broken arm from falling out of a tree. Severed artery from mishandling a sharp knife at lunchtime.

And so in due course she hired Judith. The warmth of her presence was like a spring thaw, even though it was the start of summer vacation.

She was just seventeen, between her junior and senior years. We fell in love with her instantly. She had a warm smile that could melt ice cubes. She had long, braided hair that was tied off with beads, and she wore loose-fitting tie-dyes that were either long shirts or short dresses. Her toenails peeking out of her sandals—genuine Birkenstocks!—changed color almost daily. Plus, her collection of necklaces, some beaded, others plain silver or gold, made it look as though she had raided the jewelry case at the local Murphy Mart.

She wasn't exactly Julie Andrews—in fact, she told us she couldn't sing a note on key—so we weren't expecting Mary Poppins. But that was all right by us. There were lots of other things she could do. Like make origami out of dollar bills in the shape of geese and elephants. Or blow enormous soap bubbles from a loop of yarn tied to the end of a stick that we would chase all over the yard. Or teach us the Electric Slide. Or play Monopoly on a kids' level, letting us build up real estate on Park Place and Boardwalk.

One time, she took an interest in my collections, and so I showed her my box of rocks and my jar of old coins and my old leaf collection, the leaves all iron-pressed in cellophane and arranged in a three-ring binder.

"What's this?" she asked. "A hundred-dollar bill?"

It was the last page of my collection, and I had forgotten all about the fake $100 at the end. I let her know it was counterfeit, but she didn't deflate with disappointment. On the contrary, she seemed impressed I had come by one.

Then there were our games. Playing hide-and-seek in the cemetery. Picking unripe apples and seeing how far we could throw them. Dropping pinecones through the storm drain at the far corner of our lot into the water below, a rivulet that was sometimes trickling, sometimes gushing, depending on the rainfall, as it coursed through the open sewer. The wrought iron cover still had the lock that our father had had placed on it, keeping us from opening the grating and climbing down the ladder into the deep, dark bowels below. I wondered where he had put the key. The township road crew worker who had welded its hinges and latch had given a spare key to our father, in case we should drop something of value into the catch basin and no one at the township was available to unlock it. Had he placed the key somewhere in the house? Or had he taken it to a watery grave in the Arctic?

By the time Judith became our babysitter—or just "sitter" in my case; I openly protested the prefix "baby"—we had grown accustomed to thinking of our father as missing but not gone. He was still a part of our world, not in an afterlife with an invisible barrier that would keep us from ever seeing him again, at least in this lifetime.

Our sitter was a mirror opposite of Eva. If Eva was a princess, Judith was a gypsy.

"Um," my therapist interjects. "The correct term is—"
"Roma," I say quickly. "You don't have to tell me. I know."

Nevertheless, she wore rings on her fingers and rings on her toes. We had never heard of toe rings before, so these were a novelty. One of the rings on her fingers was a mood ring, and from time to time, she would share it with us, just to see what our mood was that day. Yellow meant somber, and black meant troubled. Mine was invariably black.

One time, we all watched in amazement as Ursie's turn with the ring produced fluctuating colors, which Judith said was highly unusual.

"Are you feeling a little mixed up today?" she asked Ursie. "Your aura is all over the place."

I wasn't sure what she meant by "aura."

In the cemetery, playing hide-and-seek, Judith was almost always the seeker, not very often the hider. When seeking, she would eventually give up and call "All-ee, all-ee, in-free!" This would coax us from our hiding spots behind tombstones.

Once, I decided to hide in a freshly dug grave. Hopping down into it was the easy part, but getting back out was more difficult. Hearing the call to come in to home base, I scrabbled up the sides but only succeeded in loosening the dirt, which began breaking away in chunks and cascading down into the pit to the point that I became alarmed by the possibility of being buried alive. But Judith heard my yells for help, and having Ursie sit on her feet as a counterweight, she leaned over the firmest edge and dangled her belt—a beaded leather strap—for me to grab onto, and with our combined effort, I managed to scramble out of an early grave.

"Bet you won't be hiding there anytime soon," was all Judith said with a laugh. She found many things in life—things our mother would have disapproved of—a source of personal amusement.

As I've mentioned, I was only thirteen, but it's fair to say I was in love with her—despite the seemingly unbridgeable gulf of four whole years between our ages. One of the things she taught us was how to play chess. Until this point, my main capability lay in checkers. Chess seemed as far out of my league as college. Ursie caught on faster than I did. I always had to curb a tendency to hop over my opponent's chessmen, so the only pieces I truly understood were the knights. But Judith told us chess was simply a game of wits, a way of sharpening your strategizing skills. It didn't matter if you won or lost; it gave you practice in sensing patterns. I never fully bought her argument—mainly because I didn't understand it. For me, the object of any game—an attitude my father had inculcated—was connected with winning.

On sunny afternoons, you might find us perched in an apple tree in the orchard, pretending it was a pirate ship.

Rainy afternoons we might spend in the garage with the door wide open so we could view the slants of rain. We'd unfold a sheet on the grease-stained concrete floor for a picnic and idly eat our lunch until the rain let up, and if it didn't, we'd dare each other to see how far into the rain we would run until we turned back for the safe haven of the garage.

But this was only Monday through Thursday. Our mother had the day off on Fridays, and on Saturdays and Sundays she alternated weeks but only worked for three hours of an afternoon. These were test sessions to see if I could handle the responsibility of overseeing Ursie without tragic outcomes, like abductions or kidnappings. Surely, our mother figured, I could manage a three-hour shift without incident, but just in case, I always had her work number at her station at the reference desk handy. Sometimes, for fun, I'd call and disguise my voice and ask the most obscure spur-of-the-moment questions I could think of, often with Ursie's help:

"Yes, excuse me, please," in a professorial tone, "I am in dire need of information about how a porcupine goes to the bathroom without prickling itself."

Or: "Hello, do you have any references on home remedies for flatulence?" in the wheedling tone of an old woman. "Yes, you heard me correctly, Missy, flatulence. Do you need me to spell it out for you?"

Or: "Does the library have any books on the premature balding of gerbils?" This in the voice of a distraught teenager. "We've had Karl for a month and he's starting to lose all his hair."

We would try to laugh in pantomime at these prank calls that momentarily flustered our mother, but I'd often have to cover the transmitter with my hand so she wouldn't hear us break out into open guffaws and titters.

Ursie would try her hand at it, too, but our mother almost always saw—or heard—through her disguised voices immediately. Plus, her questions bordered on the bizarre:

"Do you have any books made of whipped cream?" she might ask.

Or: "Do chickens get chickenpox?"

Or: "Are purple cows as purple as eggplants?"

Subjects like these our mother caught onto quickly.

Except with Ursie's questions, she pretended to take them seriously, and she would provide replies as equally absurd:

"Yes, we have two flavors of whipped-cream books, vanilla and strawberry. I'm sorry, but we're fresh out of chocolate."

Or: "We don't seem to have any reference material about chicken illnesses, but we do have books about sheep with measles."

Or: "It depends where they live. In Australia, for instance, purple cows are lavender, but in Brazil they lean toward mauve."

———

Strangely, after our father's presumptive death, we'd given up on churchgoing. We tried out a Universalist church for a couple of Sundays and then a Christian Scientist church for another Sunday before our mother decided against attending church altogether. It wasn't a vocal decision. It was just something she let quietly slip from our Sunday routine. This opened up new habits and routines for Sunday mornings. For one thing, we got to hang out in our pajamas the whole morning before our mother announced it was time to brush our teeth and throw on some clothes.

In place of religion, our mother was discovering other practices: yoga, for one. It wasn't unusual to come across her balancing on her head on a pillow with her feet propped against a wall. Meditation was another. For these sessions, she sat cross-legged on the living-room carpet with her thumbs and index fingers pinched in circles on her knees. She would hold this position for thirty minutes at a stretch, emitting low humming sounds. She never lay on a bed of nails or walked on coals, but she did experiment with pyramids and crystals, which she placed on her belly as she lay outstretched on her bed. She explained once that this was all part of a process of self-healing.

We found the concept strange.

"Why would you need to heal yourself if you aren't hurt?" Ursie asked. "It's not like she's got a scratch or broke her leg." I just was as perplexed and, for once, didn't have a readymade answer.

And so the days of summer passed by with Judith as our guide. Everything was perfect, but one thing I was beginning to learn was that perfection doesn't last. And as it goes with such things, it started before I was fully aware of what was happening—with one of the rich kids, a boy about my own age, from down the street waving as he rode past on his bike.

We were in the front yard, the three of us, taking a break from Duck-Duck-Goose, which is an exhausting game when played with only three participants. Instead of riding on past, Alex Hoyle braked hard, did a U-turn, and parked his bike at the foot of the drive, just laying it down without a kickstand.

"Hey, Jeremy, whatchya doin'?"

"Hey, Alex." He had ridden his bike past us hundreds of times the summer before without stopping once.

"Who's this?" he asked, as though Judith were something inanimate, without sensory organs, such as a garden gnome or, in her case, a nymph.

I made the introductions, and he sat down with us uninvited.

"Mind if I join you?"

It was already too late to refuse. He couldn't take his eyes off

Judith in her low-cut halter top, and Judith modestly averted hers, knowing full well what he was staring at.

That's when I suggested we all go inside for lemonade. It was the first time Alex Hoyle had ever stepped inside our house, and this, as it turned out, was my first mistake—if I were to take the blame for everything that followed, which I do to this day.

Word soon got out that we were harboring a beautiful babysitter at our house, a seventeen-year-old goddess with long legs, full breasts, and luxurious brown hair that swung in braids past her shoulders.

The next day, Alex brought a friend of his along to play—or "hang out," which was the more mature term for it—and the day after that, this friend brought two friends. The following day, seven kids showed up at our door. Their numbers, I nervously realized, were growing exponentially.

"Where's Judith?" Alex wanted to know.

I told them it was Friday. Judith had the day off on Fridays because our mother was home.

"Oh, well," Alex said, staring at the toes of his tennis shoes, shuffling his feet on our mat, "see you around then, Jeremy. Maybe next week, huh?"

"Sure," I said. And this, it turned out, was the very worst thing I could have agreed to.

Chapter 30

On Monday, they were back again—nine kids total—this time with a couple of older brothers, who were playing tag-along, scoping out the center of attention, from a distance, as though feigning indifference. They were much too cool for direct stares, preferring indirect glances that they hurriedly buried whenever Judith looked in their direction. It was like watching a mating ritual on Mutual of Omaha: a bunch of males and one female. Two, if you count Ursula, but she was only fresh out of third grade, so she didn't count. Mostly, she was left alone to pursue her own interests, which lately involved creating her own stick-figure comic books based on the adventures of Wonder Woman and G.I. Joe. I was too busy keeping an eye on the older males of the herd to pay her any attention.

Mostly, they shuffled around a tetherball pole with a deflated ball. Mr. Jenkins, our landlord, had set it up the summer before, thinking it would be a perk that Ursie and I would enjoy. We had batted the ball around a little, but neither of us displayed much aptitude or interest.

What disturbed me most was that Judith seemed remotely interested in the older males. They came close to brushing shoulders a couple of times but exchanged only a few words that, to my ears, sounded like low grunts uttered by the males and a light, flutelike laugh emitted by Judith at whatever it was they were saying. What bothered me even more was a feeling of neglect in that Judith was abandoning her duty to "sit" with Ursie and me.

The neglect intensified when Ryan McNeil showed up on a skateboard that he usually rode up and down the street all summer long, to check out the "action"—what little there typically was. He was well known as someone who didn't like to be left outside the circle of any action taking place. He had longish hair parted down the middle and actual sideburns. He always wore a tank top to show off his muscles, which were of a different order than Bill's—not bulging so much as lithe and firm. Like Judith, he was seventeen, going into his senior year.

His forte was hockey, and he wielded a mean stick, even when riding his skateboard. I had seen him play in a game the winter before that Bill, in fact, took me to, thinking exposure to sports might do me some good. I was impressed by the amount of "checking" Ryan did. Bill explained the concept as simply a way of trying to take an opponent out of action by driving him into the glass. It must have been a legitimate tactic because he was able to avoid the penalty box, unlike a couple of his less fortunate teammates.

Overall, there was something dangerous about Ryan. He was a jock, but a special kind of jock. He didn't play any other sport, just hockey, so this left him free to spend his summers on a skateboard even though he had the keys to a red Mazda RX-7 coupe that his father had bought him.

"Sweet ride!" my therapist observes with an outburst of enthusiasm that catches me off guard. "You're not going to believe this, but my high-school girlfriend drove a used RX-7."

I want to remind her that these sessions are meant to revolve around my reminiscences, not hers.

"Or maybe it was an RX-8," she reflects, seemingly disturbed by the uncertainty as she sinks back into her padded chair. "Come to think of it, it might not have been a Mazda at all. Maybe a Nissan 350Z?"

She appeals to me with a hopeful look, as though I might offer an answer, being such an expert on cars.

We all came up to the car to gawk. Ryan revved the engine a couple of times before stepping out and leaving the door open so we could take a look inside. It had a new-car aroma that was clean and ammoniac and waxy all at once. It was an early graduation gift, he told us. A whole year early, I thought, since I knew he still had his senior year ahead of him.

"It doesn't have a back seat," Ursie observed, as he showed it off to us, as though it were a display model on a car lot. "Where am I supposed to ride?"

"You're not," Ryan snapped. He held the passenger door open for Judith, but she declined with a toss of her braids. Miffed, he lifted the hood to show off the engine to a cluster of drooling males.

"Show's over," he said, slamming the driver's door shut but leaving the keys in the ignition.

All I knew about his home life was that his mom and dad were trying to divorce each other, but the Church—with a capital "C"—was morally opposed, since there was no motive other than lack of interest in each other as a couple. This must have created tension at home, but Ryan's father was a respectable figure in town, serving on the school board, for instance, so I doubt their dissatisfaction with each other ever came to physical blows.

On his very first visit, he arrived by stealth, as we were all hanging out on the wide front porch, wasting time. By some miracle of locomotion, he rode his skateboard right up the curb, pulling a wheelie that propelled him into the air, where he did several twists and turns before returning to Earth. Flipping the skateboard up with his foot, he caught it, tucked it under his arm, stared straight at Judith, and said, "Hey."

"Hey," she said back before turning her attention back to a magazine—one of those girly, gossipy ones—she was paging through on the porch swing, a cushioned glider with enough room for three.

Later, I learned they had lockers side by side at school but rarely spoke to each other, inhabiting, as they did, different worlds, belonging to different cliques. In fact, Judith had already boasted she was more or less clique-free, preferring to mingle with individuals instead of stereotypes and oftentimes skipping a school dance in favor of reading a book in her room, typically something on Eastern philosophy or poems by Rilke. She was fluent in two languages, Spanish and German, and it was her ambition to become a translator, perhaps making it all the way to the United Nations someday.

"Wouldn't that be cool?" she had confided in me once.

The other males gave Ryan room as he approached, forming a gauntlet of shifting knees through which he climbed the three concrete steps to the top of the porch where Judith sat on the glider, with Ursie on one side and me on the other, as she rocked us idly with the heel of one sandal, creaking the chains like a metronome.

She was reading aloud columns out of her magazine—fashion tips, letters to the editor, dating advice—mainly to entertain Ursie, but all the boys on the steps pretended to be rapt with attentiveness. Except Ryan. He marched right up to her and said, "After you're through with that rag, I've got something better we all could be doing."

Judith closed the magazine on her lap, keeping her index finger in place.

"Yeah?" she responded, sounding intrigued.

"Be right back."

And with that, Ryan jumped back on his skateboard, somehow lifted himself right up onto the metal rail, and slid down onto the sidewalk, speeding off down the street and out of sight around the first curve in a road full of them.

He was gone less than ten minutes, but instead of coming back on his skateboard, he arrived in his red sports coupe, pulling right up against the curb with a screech of tires that made Mr. Jenkins, clearing a gutter of leaves, almost fall off his ladder. Suspicious, our landlord turned his head, then went back to his work.

The something better turned out to be a 12-pack of Corona.

"Got it out of the old man's stock," was all he said about it, breezing through the front door as though he were sole proprietor and owner. We all followed him inside, Judith and Ursula ahead of us—ladies first. In the living room, he began to distribute cans of beer, handing them out to the ring of boys.

"How 'bout you, little man?" he asked, when he came to me. I could feel every boy's eyes on me, waiting for my response.

"Sure," I said blithely, as though beer-drinking were an everyday occasion with me. "Although I usually don't start this early in the morning," I added, as a mark of sophistication.

"Judith?" Ryan asked, politely, holding out a beer.

"I'm not sure about this," she said. "Their mother's due home in a couple of hours."

"We'll have the place cleaned up by then, won't we, guys?" Ryan said nonchalantly, and everyone, me included, nodded their heads.

"I don't think Mommy will like this," Ursie said, and started up the stairs.

Halfway up, she paused and turned.

"Coming to work on our puzzle, Judith?" She had a 1000-piece jigsaw puzzle—a scene by Monet—that took up half of our bedroom floor. She and Judith had been working on it for the past few days. I had to hopscotch across half-formed water lilies to get to my bed.

Some of the boys sniggered, but Ryan kept a straight face.

Judith glanced once at Ryan, and then turned her attention to Ursula.

"Not right now, sweetie," she said. "Maybe a little later, okay?"

Ursie trudged up the rest of the stairs, pounding her feet on each step to indicate her level of disgruntlement.

The boys began a game of cards, taking turns at euchre around the coffee table. Sometimes the game was spades or hearts. One time Ryan suggested strip poker with a nod and wink at Judith, but she just rolled her eyes.

The only complaint was that our living room lacked a video-game console.

"No Atari?" was the cry of disbelief among newcomers.

The only video game we had was the original version of Pong, which "Santa" had delivered as a Christmas present a number of years prior. But this was 1983, and even I got tired of watching the pixelated ping-pong ball zig and zag in slow motion across the green screen.

Television wasn't much better. We still hadn't opted for cable, despite our landlord lifting the prohibition from our lease. This limited us to a couple of fuzzy channels that required a certain finesse when wiggling the bunny ears that sat on top of the set.

"No MTV?" was the common criticism.

And so there were cards.

Of course, when bored with cards, there were always plenty of belches and farts to go around. It was all part of a contest for male predominance—except for one female. Ursie enjoyed participating in these competitions, amazing her competitors by coming in second place for belches and earning honorable mention for farts.

Once the routine had settled indoors, it was almost impossible to get anyone to go outside, not even to toss a Nerf ball around.

A few of the boys accepted cigarettes from Ryan's pack of Camels—Judith declined, as did I—and pretty soon there was enough smoke clouding the room, even with all of the windows open and a floor fan blowing, to make anyone think the house had caught fire. Except for the intensity of three or four cigarettes going at once, I didn't think our mother would notice the smoke, since she had taken up smoking as an indoor activity herself. Plus, she always had a spray-can of Lysol around to deodorize the place when she was through.

Once the boys all departed, following Ryan's cue, they left behind more of a mess than they had promised to help clean up. Judith and I spent a half-hour emptying ashtrays and crumpling empty beer cans into a trash bag, which Judith closed with a twisty-tie and placed in the trunk of her mother's old VW, which she affectionately referred to as the Bug. (Our father would have added the prefix "Slug.") Her mom wasn't allowed to drive it for six months because of a DUI, so Judith had it all to herself, except for when her mother needed her to run errands—mostly to refresh her supply of alcohol from the local carryout with a fake ID.

I found it interesting from an engineering perspective that the trunk of such a vehicle was in the front. The back, where a trunk normally would be, stored the engine, which Judith showed me when I asked. It was barely larger than a lawnmower engine and sounded like one, too.

I enjoyed Judith taking me seriously enough to show off her car, but it was nothing compared to the giddiness I felt at my inclusion in what I had always regarded as a rich kids' club. Which was why I had to make Ursie promise and hope to die if she divulged any of the beer-drinking and cigarette-smoking goings-on to our mother.

But Mr. Jenkins ratted on us, informing her about a disturbing trend he had been observing of late: as many as seven or eight—and at one time, twelve!—boys coming to the house every afternoon.

"What about this, Jeremy?" she asked.

Ursie gave me a look from the other side of the dinner table that said, "Told you so!"

"Nothing," I said, mustering an air of nonchalance. "They're just friends from down the street."

"Friends? Really?"

She was so taken aback by the concept that I might actually have friends outside of Ursula or Judith or Bill that she promptly dropped any further inquisition she might have been planning.

"Oh, well," she said, beaming, "if they're just friends of yours."

Ursie shot me another look as though to say, "Oh, brother!"

It turned out all Mr. Jenkins was worried about was damage to his property.

"You know how kids can be," he said.

But our mother allowed him to inspect the place, and after running his finger along baseboards, tapping different spots on the papered walls, and testing various floorboards with the toe of his shoe, he emerged satisfied that no harm was being done.

Our landlord wasn't the only one who was concerned. Judith on one occasion said to me, shortly after she arrived one morning and Mom went to work, "Maybe you shouldn't have your friends over so much."

But I just shrugged off the suggestion with, "Yeah, maybe." For one thing, I knew I didn't have the cajónes to stand up to a bunch of boys, most of whom were older and bigger than me. I could only picture myself shooing them out of the house like flies.

A couple more get-togethers passed. Alex Hoyle, the original group member, as I thought of him, was always a presence, but the other boys varied. One thing remained constant: it was always boys who gathered, never girls. Ryan was sometimes a no-show, but more often a "show," although always making a point of being the last to arrive. He liked making grand surprise entrances, I observed.

Another thing he started doing by stealth was approaching Judith. He would come up behind her when she was changing a record on the turntable or switching a channel on the TV set. (Our family had an old Zenith Space Command 600 push-button remote control, but it had stopped working in 1979.) Or if she was stacking dishes in the sink or opening the refrigerator. It was always from behind. He would clasp his arms around her waist and nuzzle her neck or pull on her braids so as to turn her head so he could aim a direct kiss.

But the one thing that never varied was Judith's responses to such advances. She would squirm out of his embrace, or compress her lips together and squint her eyes and turn her face so that his attempts at a kiss generally went awry and landed on a cheek. She would pull his fingers apart, with difficulty—he held on so tightly—and duck out of the wreath formed by his encircling arms.

"Oh, come on," Ryan would complain. "What's the problem?"

From what I could tell, the main "problem" was that Judith didn't care for an audience of gaping-mouthed adolescent boys.

No one else made any attempt at "romancing" Judith, as I termed it in my head. It was as if everyone had silently agreed to the proposition that Judith was hands-off, property of one Ryan McNeil.

Chapter 31

A couple of weeks passed before it was proposed that something different than beer and cigarettes be consumed. It was Ryan, of course, who did the proposing.

"Got any pot?" he asked Judith.

She seemed reluctant to answer at first, but then she slowly nodded and said, "Yeah, in my purse."

Her purse was literally a work of art, all macramé and beads, a large handbag, almost as big as Dad's old Boy Scout knapsack, the one Ursula and I had packed for our excursion to Alaska. She dug out a plastic baggie and we all, Ryan included, watched in fascination as she expertly laid out a string of crumbled twigs and leaves along the length of a cigarette paper, like the fuse of a bomb. She rolled it up and licked the seam, long and slow with a pointed tongue, her eyes taking everyone in, then twisted the ends and pulled out a lighter.

"We better do it out back," she cautioned. "And not everyone at once. Just two at a time. Whoever wants to," she added, giving me a direct look that let me be excused, like a genie granting a wish.

I knew about marijuana only from a theoretical perspective based on what our health teacher taught us back in sixth grade. Actually, all she did was show us a movie on the subject and ask if there were any questions at the end. But the class had been too mesmerized by the fantastical images portrayed in the film of what people saw when stoned on dope—or maybe it was LSD— to raise our hands. In the film, an ordinary hot dog could turn into a laughing troll—one of those small plastic naked ones with a shock of purple or green or orange hair that were popular at the time. There were some other exotic images, but the laughing troll/hot dog was the one that stuck.

Ryan was in the first pairing to go out, of course, and when he came back, he handpicked others, two at a time, to go around the corner of the house, where they couldn't be spotted by Mr. Jenkins on his ladder. Our landlord was still full of suspicion and had taken to finding all sorts of chores to do around his house that required an aerial perspective. Finally, it came down to me and Alex Hoyle. He was about my age, and he had been over so many times that I was starting to think of him as a true friend.

"All right, you two, go!" Ryan commanded, as if we were paratroopers about to jump out of a plane on a dangerous mission.

Alex went out, grim and unsmiling, ready to meet his fate. I could tell from his expression that it was his first time, too. I went around the backside of the house with him just to watch. Judith seemed to understand. I handed the joint back to her after Alex passed it to me, and she stubbed it out in the grass without taking a puff herself.

In the days that followed, the group showed reluctance to go outside, mainly out of laziness. It took too much effort, all that going and coming, as though rotating through a volleyball match. Judith protested at first, but then she just gave up and bought an extra can of air freshener out of her own pocket money.

It was when a joint was being passed around in a circle in the living room that I was teased, or rather taunted, into taking a short puff.

"What's the matter, Jeremy, scared?"

"Yeah, Jeremy, afraid you'll go crazy or something?"

"You wanna be part of the group, don't you? Nobody likes an outsider."

I held the smoke in my cheeks, pretending to enjoy it, and when I let it out, I brought up a series of coughs, in imitation of some of the other first-timers, just so they all thought I had really taken it into my lungs. I guess it fooled them, or they were just too far gone to notice or care.

"Good goin', Jeremy," they said. "That's the spirit."

And everyone laughed.

I may have appeared overzealous in my attempt to fit in by raising the joint to my lips again.

"Hey, don't bogart it," Ryan reprimanded. "Pass it around."

Mostly, when stoned, the guys would just sit around and stare at the ceiling or act dumb and break into giggles over nothing at all. They gave up card playing, which was their usual standby when things got dull. Instead, they went through all our record albums, Dad's Elvis and Mom's Everly Brothers—they had stopped buying vinyls in the '60s and never graduated to cassettes—even a couple of Disney soundtracks meant for Ursie. Then they went to work on some of the albums Judith brought over. These were leftovers from the 70s: Grateful Dead, Mott the Hoople, Lou Reed. While listening, they munched on whatever our kitchen larder could provide.

Even our mother started to notice.

"My word, but your friends certainly go through a lot of snacks in a day," she said once. "That's a bag of potato chips and a carton of Graham crackers that I thought would last most of a week. Better tell them to slow down. I'm not made of money, after all."

So I tried hiding the snacks one day, but the gang just rooted around in all the cupboards until they found them anyway—in the bathroom closet behind a stack of fresh towels. Then they played a game of keep-away with an assortment of Hostess Ho-Hos they had discovered.

This is when things started getting weird—once the gang started running out of new things to do.

The next day was a Thursday, and it seemed to me it was just out of boredom, but someone started picking on me, just for fun. The rest of the gang joined in, and then it went on and on from there.

They started up a round of "your mama" jokes, but I couldn't respond. I didn't know how to play the Dozens, as I learned it was called. And so they just went around the circle anyway, seeing who could come up with the raunchiest, crudest joke involving my mother. My blank expression must have added to their amusement. And when Judith asked them to stop, they simply ignored her.

Then Ryan broke the pattern with Truth or Dare, a game I was a little more familiar with, except I was the only contestant. Given the mood of the crowd, I stuck with Truth. I didn't want to find out what they might make me Dare.

"Hey, Jeremy," Ryan asked on his turn, "you ever kiss a girl and make her cry?"

Someone else said, "Yeah, like Georgie Porgie." All of a sudden, this became my new nickname—not one I particularly liked.

Ryan suggested, "Someone go up and grab his sister. What's her name again?"

"Ursula," I said quietly, using her formal name to make her seem more grown up.

"Yeah?" Ryan said, seemingly surprised that someone so young could have such an adult-sounding name. "Someone go get her. Why should she always miss out on all the fun?"

A couple of kids obliged, like soldiers following orders.

Judith said, "Oh, come on, Ryan, do you really have to drag her into all of this?"

But Ryan only smiled in an odd, cryptic sort of way.

"What is it?" Ursie asked when marched down the stairs ahead of her escorts, holding her place in a Word Search puzzle book with one hand, a red ballpoint pen in her other. Lately, she had developed an avid interest in puzzles and mazes of all varieties. She had begun stacking a collection of brainteasers the way I had comic books.

"Hi, Ursula," Ryan said, "wanna play Truth or Dare?"

"I don't know," Ursie said, "how do you play?"

"Well, if you pick Truth, you have to answer truthfully, and if you pick Dare, you have to do whatever we say."

"Okay," Ursula said indifferently. "Dare."

"Dare it is," Ryan said. "Go on over and give your brother a kiss, why don't you?"

"Oh," she said brightly, "is that all?"

She was used to giving me a kiss on the cheek every night before bedtime.

I let her kiss me, and everyone laughed—all except Judith, who sat with her arms crossed, wearing an indelible frown.

"Now, be polite, Georgie Porgie, and return her kiss," Ryan said. A couple of the guys snickered at the command.

I just sat there, dumbly, not knowing how to wriggle out of the situation.

"Come on, Georgie Porgie, be a sport," one of the older kids said.

"But I didn't say 'Dare,'" I remembered.

"You've been playing Truth too long," Ryan pointed out, "and all of your Truths so far have been—how shall I put it?"

"Boring," someone suggested.

"Yeah," Ryan agreed, "boring. So let's give your sister a little kiss."

And then they started chanting, "Georg-IE, Georg-IE, Georg-IE!" until I complied and gave Ursie a quick peck on the cheek, which made them all burst into applause and cheers.

Except Ryan wasn't satisfied.

"Not like that," he said, seemingly cross. "Full on the lips."

I must have hesitated too long, because he came over and, taking the back of our heads with each hand, mashed our faces together. A couple of the other guys hovered over us, scrutinizing our resistance, until our lips, hers as compressed as mine, came together. I thought that would be it, but Ryan held our heads in place until I heard Judith say, "Hey, that's enough, come on!"

"Aw, what's the matter?" Ryan asked, letting us go. "Don't like a little romance?"

"Can I go now?" Ursie asked me, and I said, "Sure."

But Ryan said, "Not so fast. Your sis could probably teach *you* a thing or two, Georgie. She probably got plenty of lessons from that creep who picked her up—what was it, two summers ago? Don't tell me you never heard about it, Judith. It was all over the news."

"Yeah, I heard of it," Judith said, "now leave her alone."

Despite my proximity—I was sitting right there on the floor beside her—I remained mute. I couldn't locate a voice that would defend my sister. For her part, Ursie went back to hunting for words in her puzzle book, which she spread flat on the coffee table, finding a space between beer cans, either crumpled or being used as ashtrays.

"I'm sure he taught her plenty," Ryan said, ignoring Judith, kneeling on one knee near Ursula, who circled a newfound word, ignoring him. "Let's go with a Truth this time. Where all did he touch you anyway? Did he touch you here?"

Ryan jabbed a finger at the top of Ursie's head.

"Hey," she said, "that hurt."

Refocused on her word search, she waved her arm as though to ward off the buzzing of a mosquito.

"Ryan," Judith said, "this isn't funny."

"Relax, would you? I'm just messing around." And I'm sure,

from his perspective, this is all he was doing.

"Well, I don't like it, and I doubt very much that Ursie likes it either."

"Or maybe here?" he asked, going back to his game.

This time, he took a poke at her shoulder blade, which Ursula shrugged off.

"Ryan, stop!" Judith called, coming closer, but it seemed a voice at sea, for all the effect it had. "You're going too far!"

"Jeremy," Ursie echoed, looking up from her puzzle book, "make him stop."

"Or maybe a little lower?" Ryan asked, preparing to jab her again, but before he could launch his finger, Judith lashed out and slapped him hard across the face.

"Jesus!" Ryan stood up to face Judith. "I wasn't actually going to—"

But Judith slapped him again, even harder, cutting off his sentence.

Both appeared stunned: Ryan that he had been hit, Judith that she had hit him. They stared at each other for a count of one, two, three … and then a strange smile started to stretch Ryan's lips like a rubber band. Judith made a move to strike him a third time, but he grabbed her wrist and held on tight, twisting it.

"Ow," Judith complained, "you're hurting me."

"So that's how you like it," Ryan said, "playing rough?"

"Let me go!" Judith said, as Ryan dragged her to the stairway.

She grabbed onto the banister with her free hand, but Ryan pried her fingers apart, one at a time. Standing behind and above her, he formed a harness across her chest with his arms and began lugging her up the steps.

"Jeremy!" Judith called out, "do something. Please!"

But I couldn't move. I could only stare. I felt cemented in place.

"Call the cops!" she pleaded before being jerked around the landing and up the remaining steps to the second floor.

The protests continued, loudly, beseechingly.

"Ryan, stop! Please! Don't!"

We all listened in silence to the thud of footsteps across the floor in the direction of the front bedroom, which was our mother's. There was the loud slam of the door that made me lurch. The sound brought me to my senses, and I got up to make a move for the phone. But one of the older boys pulled it off its cradle and dangled it like a lazy pendulum from its cord.

I thought of going to Mr. Jenkins's house to get him to make a call, but my way out the door was barred. The only recourse I had was to go up the steps to try and interfere with whatever Ryan was doing, but another kid grabbed me around the waist, pulled me onto the floor, and knelt on my chest, both knees digging hard into my ribs. By the way he so easily manhandled me, I assumed he was a wrestler.

"Just hold still," he kept saying. "Just hold still, okay?" But his voice sounded less than confident.

I twisted my head around to give Alex Hoyle a pleading look, but he pretended not to notice.

One boy said, "Someone turn up the volume." He meant the record player, but nobody moved.

Upstairs, there was the thump, thump, thump of the bed and the repetitive creaking of springs. It seemed to last forever, but it couldn't have been more than a minute or two. Throughout it, a voice kept shouting, "No, no, no, no, no!" But I didn't think of it as Judith's. It was easier to accept them as the cries of some anonymous woman.

Finally, the thumping stopped and there was a short period of silence, followed by sobs. Then, through the sobs, came an accusation, loud and sharp: "Bastard!" Something hit the wall, as though flung. Whatever it was, it shattered. And then Ryan came slowly down the steps, head down, shoulders slumped. He stopped at the bottom. His gaze seemed preserved in a state of shock or disbelief—maybe denial.

"Jesus, Ryan," one of the older boys said, "did you really—?" But he left his question dangling.

"What if she calls the cops?" another boy asked.

"She won't call the cops," someone said. "Her Mom's in AA and Ryan's dad's on the school board. Who are the cops going to believe?"

"Ryan?" a younger boy asked. "You okay?"

Ryan jerked his head up. He looked around the room with a dazed look, as though becoming aware of an audience for the first time, the way a deer might slowly appreciate its being surrounded by wolves. Without saying a word, he left quickly through the screen door. By the sound of it, he hopped right on his skateboard and sped off down the sidewalk.

There were still sobs, loud and steady, coming from upstairs.

The boy who was pressing my chest with his knees stood up and said, "Come on, everybody. Let's go."

They all filed through the door—nine boys of varying heights and ages. Alex Hoyle was the last one out. He turned at the threshold as I pushed myself into a sitting position on the floor. He threw me a meek smile, accenting it with a shrug.

"Sorry, Jeremy," he said, and then he followed the others.

—

The phonograph record had stopped playing, the needle scratching the runout groove in an endless circle, failing to return to its cradle.

Ursula was staring at her Word Search book. She was crying silently, the tears streaming down her cheeks. I had my own tears to deal with, wiping them off with the sleeves of my T-shirt. The crying from upstairs slowed, quieted, ceased, but I didn't think it a good idea to go up to her—not yet.

"Come on," I said after a time, "we better start cleaning up. Mom will be back soon."

"Is Judith okay?" Ursie asked when I came back into the room from the kitchen.

"I don't know," I said, honestly, picking up trash and placing it into a fresh garbage bag.

"Should we go up to her?"

I emptied an ashtray and cleared off the coffee table with the back of my hand, while Ursie held open the mouth of the trash bag.

"We better wait a while," I said. "I'm sure she'll come down."

But she didn't come down. We were through cleaning up. Ursula was a good helper. As a finishing touch, we freshened the room with lavender and vanilla from two spray cans. Afterward, we sat on opposite ends of the couch. I had removed the vinyl from the record player and placed it back in its sleeve. And so we just sat there, silently, waiting. Finally, I could hear stirring from above, footsteps on the floor of our mother's bedroom.

"Wait here," I said to Ursie, and she seemed to understand.

I crept up the stairs quietly, afraid of what I would encounter. Looking down the hall, I saw our mother's door was only half-closed. I tried proceeding noiselessly, but a couple of creaking floorboards gave me away. I stood at the door, gathering courage to knock.

"Come on in," Judith said softly. When I entered, she was facing away from the door, holding the sheets from our mother's bed all bunched up against her chest. "Watch your step," she cautioned, still not looking in my direction.

I stepped carefully. There was a photograph on the floor, fractured glass shards fanning out and away from a broken frame.

"Draw the blinds, would you?" she asked, and I did as she requested, dimming the room. It would have been hard making out Judith's features even if she hadn't kept her face averted.

"Don't worry about the sheets," she said, her voice sounding distant, detached. "I'll start the laundry." We had an old washer down in the basement that clanked repeatedly every time it was operated.

"Are you all right?" I asked, but my question sounded so soft to my ears I might only have imagined asking it.

"Yeah," Judith said after a pause. "I'm okay." But her response was hesitant, unsure, as though weighted down by lead. "You?"

She still wasn't looking at me, but I nodded my head anyway.

"I'll come back up and sweep up," she said, shuffling slowly past me through the door with the sheets all crumpled up in her hands. I thought I saw bloodstains, but the dimness made it hard to tell.

"No, that's okay, I'll get it," I offered, but she was already gone.

After she left, I looked at the picture on the floor—the object she had flung against the wall on Ryan's departure. It was a photo our mother kept on her nightstand. The glass had splintered. Inside the frame was a black-and-white glossy of Mom and Dad. It looked like it had been taken a long time ago, before I was born. Inside the photograph, they were holding hands. They were smiling.

Chapter 32

We didn't know what to expect come Monday. All weekend, Ursie kept urging me to "tell Mommy" about what happened to Judith. But from her perspective, all that had happened was Judith had been dragged up the stairs by a brute of a guy the way cavemen in the cartoons were always hauling their wives around by their hair. I just told her to "hush" whenever she brought up the topic. "Judith is a big girl," I'd tell her. "She can sort it all out, I'm sure."

But I wasn't sure if she would show up on Monday. I had my doubts. After all, why would she? I didn't expect the gang to turn out, and they didn't, not even Alex Hoyle. When Judith didn't show at 8:30 a.m. per usual, I gave up the situation as lost. But then our mother said Judith was running just a little late.

"Surely, you can take care of each other for a half-hour while I go to work?" she asked.

Otherwise, it was an ordinary Monday morning.

There were some differences. Judith kept her distance all morning, speaking to us only when necessary. We didn't play games. We didn't take walks through the orchard. There was no hide-and-seek behind tombstones. There was no helping Ursie separate the pieces of a new jigsaw puzzle she had spread out on the coffee table.

Ursie asked, "How come?"

But Judith just turned away with, "Maybe later, okay?"

She wasn't wearing her ordinary attire. The tie-dye halter-top/miniskirt combo had been traded for a pair of denim shorts and a loose-fitting T-shirt that hid her contours. She had cut her hair, too. It reached the base of her neck, but there wasn't enough for so much as a ponytail, Ursie observed. The braids were gone, as well.

It was after lunch that we had what I term The Talk. It wasn't the sort of talk my dad was supposed to give me but never did because he wasn't around ever to give it. As early as fourth grade, though, I had asked how babies are born and my mother had handed me a book on the subject, part of a science series for kids. It showed a diagram of a squiggly sperm approaching with determination a round egg. I got the theory down pat: sperm meets egg. I just wondered about the logistics. I imagined a microscopic ICBM missile flying through air, seeking its target. When I asked how the sperm actually made it all the way from the man to the woman, my mother blushed and said, "Ask your father." But Dad just said, from behind his newspaper, "That's something for later."

And now it was later, but the person giving me The Talk was a seventeen-year-old babysitter—or just sitter—and the contents of the conversation were much different than I would have supposed them to be if it had been my parents providing the lecture.

We were sitting side by side on the front porch steps, where I joined her after lunch, taking my seat tentatively, not sure if she wanted to be bothered. She was smoking a cigarette, but her hand was steady—nothing like the trembling agitation our mother showed whenever she smoked a cigarette, which she generally reserved for times of stress. Needless to say, these were often.

We sat in silence for a while. Birds were chirping in the oak tree overhead. There was an undercurrent of other sounds, cars passing, a dog barking. Ursie was inside, behind the storm-door screen in the living room, humming a song to one of her dolls, which she was tucking in for a nap. At nine years old, she hadn't quite outgrown her baby-doll phase.

"Guess your friends aren't showing today," Judith said, giving me a sideways glance.

"They aren't my friends," I stated firmly.

"I wasn't sure about coming over, but I had my escape plan all set if they came around. First, I would have kicked that bastard right where it hurts, then I would have driven both you and your sister over to the library and told your mom what's been going on at her house."

The word "bastard" rolled right out of her mouth with ease. I didn't know how to respond to this volley of words, but I was glad the guys from down the street had stayed away and that Judith was still here, sitting beside me.

"I didn't figure it would be like him to show up and apologize or anything," she said. "That would be too much to ask."

I knew she was referring to the "bastard," but still I kept quiet.

"Guys like that never apologize," she said, snubbing out her cigarette, then drawing another one out of her pack. She continued to look straight ahead, speaking as if to an invisible auditor. I might have only been an eavesdropper, no more of a presence than a mouse.

But after lighting a fresh cigarette, she cast a sidelong look, taking me in.

"You're too young to appreciate this, but a girl wants her first time to be special—with someone special. It doesn't have to be all handsome prince and fairy dust and bed of roses or anything. A girl just wants it to be something she can remember—you know, without regret."

"Was this your first time?" I asked without thinking. Immediately, I felt my cheeks and forehead flush with embarrassment. I knew I had overstepped my bounds without even knowing exactly what I was asking.

"No," she said, levelly, "it wasn't. There were a couple of other times—not like this."

"Were they special?" I asked. I didn't feel in control of my words. They just came out without premeditation, from some secret part of my psyche.

This time, she gave me a long look before going back to her cigarette.

"No, not really," she said. "But at least I didn't have to keep saying 'no.'" She took a deep drag and then released a long stream of smoke. "Listen," she said, "this is very, very important. I don't expect you to understand right now—you're what, only twelve?"

"Thirteen," I corrected her, yet feeling hopelessly younger than I wanted to be at that very moment.

"But when a girl says 'no,'" she continued, "I'm not saying in every instance—but way more often than a guy likes to think—'no' really does mean 'no'!"

She ground out her second cigarette with her foot and started to pull out a third, but decided against it, tapping it back into her pack. She stood up to go, and I said something I had been planning to say all along—I just didn't know how to broach it—but now I wanted to keep her from going back into her silence inside the house.

"What if you could get back at him?" I asked, knowing it sounded abrupt.

Judith looked down at me, mulling the proposition.

"Like revenge?" she asked, unsmiling.

"Yeah, maybe," I said.

"You can't get revenge on someone like that. He's too well connected. His father has too much clout."

She started to climb the steps, moving past me.

"But what if you could teach him a lesson?" I asked, standing up, trying to halt her retreat with mere words.

This made her pause at the top of the porch steps, although she didn't turn around.

"A guy like that—he doesn't learn lessons. And that's the whole thing really. He's been spoiled all his life into thinking he can get whatever he wants. It's always been handed to him. He doesn't think twice about taking something without asking."

She crossed the porch toward the door and halted with her hand on the handle.

"Still," she said, half turning to face me, "it'd be nice if he did think twice the next time he decides to try something like this. What did you have in mind?"

"I have a plan," I said.

"A plan?" She sounded intrigued.

"Yeah, just something I've been thinking about. I'm not sure it would work."

"Okay," she said, walking back to the steps, where she took a stance above me, crossing her arms. "Let's hear it."

I suddenly felt sheepish and small.

"It would mean you'd have to see him once again."

"Oh, no," she said, lowering her arms and turning away. "I'm not seeing that bastard again—ever!"

"But it would be the last time," I said, more loudly than I intended. It almost came across as a shout. "It's the only way it'll work. He'd have to think you want to see him."

"No," she said, "absolutely not! He can go to hell for all I care."

I took a deep breath and let it out.

"But that's just where I want to send him!"

Chapter 33

It would only be a temporary hell—not the permanent kind, if there is such a place. I had been thinking about what had happened all the rest of Thursday and into Friday morning. I hadn't slept well. I just kept feeling I was to blame somehow, for not foreseeing it, forestalling it, and I wanted to make amends—with my own conscience, if nothing else.

It's odd how it all started to work out in my brain—almost without conscious direction. It was a plan that came into being slowly, like an ectoplasm out of a bog.

Its gestation occurred when I was organizing my part of the bedroom, putting things in order so our mother could vacuum the threads of our thin throw rug. I was operating in a trancelike state, just going through the motions of my Friday routine, the way a zombie or robot would.

I came across my leaf collection that I had shown Judith and flipped back to the cellophane-pressed counterfeit bill.

"Who wouldn't want a hundred dollars?" I might have said aloud. And then I wondered whether it would be enough money to interest a kid whose parents were already rich and who probably got a hefty weekly allowance just for being their spoiled brat of a son. Would it serve as a lure? As bait? But for what?

I kept this thought on hold until I decided to take a walk, just to take my mind off the day before. Ursie said she would like to tag along, but I told her no, I just wanted to be alone. I was planning to cut through the orchard into a field accessed through a gap in the hedge that bordered its farther side. There was a path through the field that led to a quarry that was technically off limits to us kids, so I thought it might be a good place for sitting and pondering life's imponderables.

But I never made it past the orchard. I stopped to ponder instead the grating of the storm drain in the far corner, bordering the cemetery. It covered the concrete drainage pit with the open sewer at the bottom that had so intrigued us to the point our father asked the county engineers to have it welded on hinges and clasped with a heavy-duty lock.

I stared through the bars of the grille a long time, as though I were captive of an extraordinary dream. A black trickle of water crawled along the bottom of the catch basin, out of one drain and into another. The openings of the drainpipes were small, only a foot or so in diameter, room enough for a basketball to float through, but not much bigger. Except for the ladder, a series of U-shaped iron rungs embedded in the cement wall, there were no other forms of escape. The iron bars on top made it look like an inverted dungeon.

I stood in place like a scarecrow, turning my head to take into consideration the immediate environs. There was a gravel road that led to the cemetery entrance, marked by a pair of crumbling brick structures that must have long ago held a gate. The road was edged by a border of raspberry bushes. One thing about the cemetery, the tombstones were so ancient—the oldest going back to the early 1800s—that hardly anybody visited. Once in a great while, there was room for a fresh grave, but most of its inhabitants were long ago deceased.

As for the orchard, occasionally kids stopped by to pluck a few apples, but harvest season was still a couple of months away.

I decided this would serve as a perfect penitentiary, if only I could locate the key.

And so I spent the afternoon searching. First stop was my father's jewelry box—except it wouldn't be called that for a man. I just couldn't think of any other word for the small chest in which he had stored his valuables: a collectible Hank Aaron base-ball card, a set of gold cufflinks he had worn on his wedding day, an old driver's license, several old nickels and dimes that pre-dated World War II, and a set of toenail clippers. The toenail clippers were a source of nostalgia. Our father had notorious corns on the soles of his feet as well as ingrown toenails, and my sister and I would find it fascinating to watch him dig into the nails and excavate the corns, which he always did on the living-room couch, in full public view.

But alas, no key.

That's when I thought of Bill, our standby fix-it man. There was almost no problem he couldn't handle with a trip to the hardware store or a look inside his trunk for the proper tool.

This meant going down to Daley's Gym, which I decided to visit on Saturday afternoon, when it was my turn to watch Ursie while our mother worked a library shift. It wasn't a very far ride by bike, but Ursie's still had training wheels—she couldn't bal-ance without them—even though she was fresh out of third grade! She had never learned to properly ride a bike, a fact that only now struck me, like a footnote in a school textbook. Our father had never been around long enough the past several years to teach her. And now that he was presumed dead—another item that our family regarded as a mere footnote until proven factual—I suppose it fell on me to teach her. But today wasn't the day.

And so, with our mother tucked away behind her reference desk at the library, we slowly made our way to Daley's Gym.

It was our first time inside. The first thing that struck me was the smell of sweat—a mildew smell that would have signified mold in any other location, like a basement. There was a boxing ring with a couple of boxers going at it with protective headgear and gloves. A few exercise machines were scattered around an enormous punching bag. And a couple of other guys were lifting free weights of a size that looked like they must have been low-ered into the gym by a crane.

Bill was sitting ringside, leaning in on a chair with his arms folded on the canvas below the ropes. He was studying the moves of one of the boxers intently, shouting out encourage-ment or instructions from time to time.

"That's it, that's right, guard your left, move your feet, come on now, get a punch in, give 'im the ol' one-two"—and so on until his running monologue stopped short when his prizefighter got knocked down by a punch square to his forehead despite his helmet. Then it was: "Come on, pick yourself back up, get up on your feet," which the fighter, a kid who looked maybe eighteen or nineteen, was loath to do.

"Hey, kids!" Bill beamed, taking note of us for the first time. "What brings you around?" Then he said to his fighter, "Take five, Murphy. Better go put a beefsteak on that eye while you're at it."

He herded us over to a vending machine where he plugged in a couple of quarters—one for each of us—for a pop. Soda pop was something our mother never let us drink at home. She considered it unhealthy for minors. Plus, she reasoned it would only encourage us to drink other fizzy drinks, ones with alcoholic content, later in life. She didn't know anything about the beers I had consumed the past couple of weeks at our house.

"You've heard of a glass jaw, I presume," Bill said. "Kid's got a glass forehead. It's his one weak spot—his Achilles' heel, you might say. Now what can I do for the two of youse?" he asked, bringing up a stool so he could talk with us on our level.

I explained the nature of my quest: how could someone cut through a thick padlock?

"Are you thinking of breaking into something?" Bill asked. "You better watch out for those old refrigerators they throw away." He knew there was a junkyard by the quarry near our house. "They got a chain and padlock on them for a reason. You'll suffocate in there, you get shut in."

I assured him it had nothing to do with refrigerators. It was just that I needed to remove a bike chain whose combination I had forgotten. As a lie, it seemed both harmless and reasonable. And to my relief, he bought it.

"Well, I've got a bolt cutter in my trunk, you go out back." I knew his car, a white Buick, from his frequent visits to our house. "Tell the truth, I have a pet name for it. I call it my nutcracker." He held up his hand to forestall my question. "Best not to ask."

He brought out a set of keys and pinched the one that would unlock his trunk between a beefy finger and thumb, handing it over. "You'll recognize it straight off. You see a pair of pliers looks like they're meant for a giant, those are them."

We found the bolt cutter—or nutcracker—all right. It was heavy, too. I had to drag it across the parking lot, lugging it back so I could return Bill's keys.

"Keep it as long as you need it. I'll pick it up at your house when you're through, okay?"

He gave me a friendly nudge against my cheek with his closed fist and Ursie a kindly pat on the head.

I was able to get the bolt cutter back home by balancing it on the seat and handlebars of my bike, turning it into a dolly that I pushed all the way up the road from town to our patch of ground on the outskirts and then down the gravel lane to the cemetery entrance. Ursie followed me all the way there. She got off her bike, which she was pretending was a pet stallion named Sheba. Commanding Sheba to stay, she followed me as I pulled the massive set of pliers around behind the raspberry patch to the iron storm-sewer grating. It was as unwieldy as a dead body.

"I just don't get why Bill calls it a 'nutcracker,'" Ursie mused.

"It looks nothing like the nutcrackers we set out at Christmas."

It took some finesse to position the jaws of the bolt cutter so it would grip the metal loop of the lock. Trying to force a cat to take hold of it would have been as easy. I wish I could say the lock snapped as easily as a toothpick, but it took more pressure than that. Eventually, through a combination of foot stomping and butt plopping against the upraised handle, with the other handle firmly set on the ground, the pliers cut their way through the metal and the lock popped loose. The clasp was rusted but movable, and with Ursie's help, I was able to pull open the grating on its hinges, equally rusty, but which remained intact. In fact, it was easier lifting than I remembered. I could just about manhandle it myself unaided—a hopeful sign I was getting stronger as I got older.

"Wow!" Ursie said, staring down into the cubical pit formed by four concrete walls. "It sure is dark down there."

"Yeah," I said, remembering our childhood excursions into its depths. "It sure is."

My next stop was the hardware store, and I didn't even have to bring Ursie along. I made up some excuse about visiting a couple of friends down the street. Our mother, having returned from the library, was so relieved these "friends" wouldn't be coming to our house for once and consuming all our food, she granted instant permission.

A young clerk, with a prematurely balding large head, so that he reminded me of Charlie Brown, directed me to the aisle that had a small assortment of padlocks, hidden amid drill bits and levels and tape measures, so I would have missed them altogether if he hadn't pointed them out.

"Got some valuables you need locked up?"

"Baseball cards," I answered casually, and he nodded his head, knowingly.

"Must be some pretty good ones," he said before returning to the display of batteries I had pulled him away from restocking.

Well, there went almost five dollars of my allowance I had been saving up for weeks (ten to be exact, at 50 cents a crack). I had my heart set on buying an Estes rocket from the hobby shop next door to the hardware store. I was finally old enough in my mother's estimation to build one and set it off without losing any fingers or setting my hair on fire. But now I used the money to buy not one, not two, but three locks.

Two were of a flimsy nature, all brass, looking more for decoration than security—the kind you might lock a toy chest with. The third was more substantial—stainless steel—of a quality similar to the lock I had cut through. They also carried combination locks, but I didn't want my prisoner, should I capture him, to spend his time trying to figure out the sequence of numbers that would spring him free.

The reason I bought two of the flimsy locks was to make sure I could break one apart using a large rock. It only took three tries, but I had to hit it pretty hard. Ursie, who had joined me for this exercise back at the Orchard Bar & Grille (as I was starting to refer to my makeshift prison), clapped her hands, impressed.

"Wow, Jeremy! You're strong!"

I took the compliment with grace. Maybe I really had grown stronger.

"But why do you have to be so destructive?"

This was actually one of our mother's lines, something she used whenever we had torn the house apart to build forts out of couch cushions, for instance.

Now that I was sure that this type of lock was breakable, I could proceed to the next phase of the operation: setting the bait. But this would have to wait till Monday. I had to get Judith on board first.

Chapter 34

And she wasn't.

Let's rewind to the moment I divulged that I had a plan.

Judith lowered her head, giving it a moment's thought. Like a snared rabbit, she had been taken by surprise.

But then she just walked away, saying only, "I'll need to think about it."

I studied her face all the rest of the day for signs of softening, but her features were inscrutable.

Monday evening after she left, I took my $100 counterfeit bill out of its hiding place in my leaf collection and, with Ursie tagging along—actually, her tagging along was essential, as she was a key element of the plan—we lifted the grating on its hinges and peered down into the gloom. Good thing we brought flashlights.

The bottom of the pit was better lit earlier in the day, when the sun shone high in the sky, angling its beams straight down. But, for now, I could make out a pile of dark, rotting leaves.

This was just a test run. I wouldn't actually need to set the $100 bill in place until the day Judith "invited" Ryan to come over—if that day should ever arrive.

This excursion was just to see if it would be possible to make it seem as though the counterfeit bill had floated through the bars and got snagged on something—but what? The pile of leaves was too soggy. As a test, I pasted the bill against a large rock I placed at the bottom, but I couldn't be sure it wouldn't peel away and float downstream through the drainpipe.

The best bet turned out to be a bramble of raspberry bushes I plucked from the hedge that bordered the orchard. It would seem natural for it to have wormed its way through the grating,

having been blown there by wind, and it made a convincing resting place for the $100 bill. It would seem it had simply floated
along until snagged by a couple of barbs.

On Tuesday, silence reigned. It was as though our house had
been transformed into a library. I decided to play it coy by reading a book. I found myself re-reading the same paragraph over
and over again. I couldn't help but follow Judith over top of the
page, as she fussed around the house, dusting and rearranging
and vacuuming and cleaning, pausing every now and then to look
at me with her arms folded before moving on to a different task.

At lunch, I continued to play it low-key, not bringing up what
I was starting to think of as the Plan with a capital P, and Judith
never mentioned it either. Instead, we listened to Ursula summa-
rize the latest mystery she had spent the morning reading. She
was a voracious reader of Nancy Drew. It went along with her
passion for puzzles. My books were all about journeys to the
center of the Earth and invisible men.

After lunch, Judith decided she would try reading a book of
Mom's, some romance or other. Ursie went upstairs to play. And
I took up my spot in the corner, exchanging my book for a Ru-
bik's cube that Ursie had solved in record time but had me
stumped.

Every time Judith glanced up, I looked away, and vice versa.
And this is how our afternoon proceeded up until the time for
Mom to come home, when Judith set her book aside—I noticed
she had only read two or three pages—stood up and advanced
toward me with a furrowed brow of determination.

"Okay," she said, and that was all I needed to hear.

———

After dinner, I worked up enough courage to set myself in motion on my old clunker of a bicycle down the street to the rich
kids' cul-de-sac at the bottom. I still look back at this with

amazement at my bravery. No knight in shining armor faced any greater foe than I did with Ryan McNeil. Fortunately, my mission didn't entail challenging fire-breathing dragons head on. All that was needed was one tablespoon of slyness, a pinch of stealth, and one heaping cup of patience.

I marked out his house based on the red RX-7 parked at the bottom of a luxurious driveway, where Ryan and two other kids were shooting hoops, facing the backboard attached to the garage.

I rode my bicycle around the cul-de-sac once, twice, thrice, passing Ryan's driveway each time. On the third time, the ball dribbled down the drive toward the curb, and I braked, dismounted, and picked it up.

One of the kids had chased it down, but when I handed it over, he hollered back, "Hey, Ryan! Look who it is!"

Ryan came walking up dressed in cargo shorts and a tank top. He seemed so nonchalant, so carefree, all I wanted to do was slug him as hard as I could in the face with enough force to break his nose or teeth, but I knew I was outmatched. One Ryan McNeil had enough upper body strength to manhandle three Jeremy Joneses.

"Georgie Porgie," he said, and the other kids laughed. "What brings you down this way?"

"I dunno," I said, shrugging. "Just looking around for Alex."

I meant Alex Hoyle, my main point of contact with the gang, but I knew he wasn't home because he had already told me he and his family were going on vacation this week—destination, Ocean City—which was something one of the kids playing with Ryan mentioned.

"Oh, well," I said, getting back on my bike.

"Hey, wait a second," Ryan said. "You wanna play?" He twirled the ball on his forefinger, awaiting my reply.

"I'm not very good," I admitted.

"That's okay, we need a fourth, so come on."

And just like that I was in the game.

I was hoping he wouldn't want to let me go so soon without finding out something about Judith, but I wasn't going to be the one to bring her up, if I could hold out so long.

It's true what I said about my basketball skills. Not only was I not very good, I was terrible. I really, truly stunk. Throw me the ball, and I'd drop it. If I passed the ball, it was almost always picked off. Dribbling, I'd trip over my feet. Shooting, my shots were always blocked, and if they weren't blocked, they fell hopelessly short of the rim—a perfect swish through pure air. Layups were beyond me. I'd charge the basket, toss the ball high up in the air, and hope for the best. My best efforts resulted in the ball coming straight back down and bopping someone's head—usually mine.

The two other guys playing with us—even the one on my "team"—laughed, joked, and smirked at my clumsiness, but Ryan kept a straight face. It was a face he aimed in my direction even when I didn't have the ball. It was as though his expression contained an overwhelming question that he kept in a jar with a tight lid, afraid to let it out or it would hop away. I think he chose to be on the opposite team so he could keep his focus on me. My other opponent roughed me up from time to time, blocking my shots, setting a screen hard into my ribs with an elbow, once even knocking me flat on the concrete. But Ryan went easy on me, letting me take shots, never picking off my passes, always giving me room to dribble around him.

No surprise, my side lost the match, 10 to 2.

"Play again?" Ryan asked.

"Naw," I said, glancing at my watch. "I better be getting home."

I started walking down the drive toward my bike, but Ryan caught up with me.

"Hey, wait a sec," he said. "I want to ask you something."

I waited, as he requested, but stared straight ahead, without looking at him.

"How's Judith?" he asked in a low voice so the other two kids, back to taking turns playing H-O-R-S-E, wouldn't overhear.

"Good," I lied. "In fact, she's been asking about you."

"Really?"

"She said she'd like to see you again. She wants to know when you're coming over."

"Oh yeah?" Ryan responded. His voice sounded incredulous but edged with hopefulness.

"But if you come over, she wants to see you alone."

"Alone?" he asked. "Really?"

"She said she'd make it worth your while," I said.

By this time, the other two kids had joined us to see what the holdup was all about.

"What's so hush-hush?" one of them asked.

"Georgie Porgie got a secret?" the other one prompted.

"Guys, cut it out," Ryan snapped. "Give us some space."

He shepherded me down the rest of the drive out of range of his friends' ears.

"She wants to make brownies," I said. "She says she has a special recipe."

"Oh yeah?" he repeated, that same skepticism underlining his response.

"Tomorrow okay?" I said. "Just so I can tell her."

He pondered this for a moment, as though suspecting a trick.

"Not tomorrow," he said. "Maybe the day after."

"Bring your skateboard," I told him. "She said she wants you to teach her a few tricks."

Ryan smiled in a funny way, not sure how to take this last remark.

"Okay," he said, "skateboard it is."

And with that, he went back to his friends, who ribbed him and joked and whistled and laughed.

My therapist has been relatively quiet of late. Ever since my recounting of the rape, she has allowed my narrative to proceed virtually uninterrupted in subsequent sessions, not even using her phone except for the occasional tap-tap-tap of a note or two—highly unusual behavior for her. Even more unusual, she has been concentrating intently on what I've been telling her, the drawbridge of her eyebrows alternately rising and lowering in reaction, to the point of unnerving me.

"Looks like we're out of time," she observes with a sigh.

"Do you want me to come back?" I ask. This may be a measure of my own insecurity. Is there value in my coming here? Is there a point to these visits? Are the events of my memory trivial? Are they not worth exploring? Am I boring her?

"Of course!" she answers with an enthusiasm that takes me aback. "You've got me hooked. I've got to see if the bastard gets what's coming to him."

I inwardly smile at the unprofessionalism of her language. Maybe not so inwardly because she follows up with, "What? We shrinks are human too."

"Well, I could just tell you now." And save myself the expense of a session, I think unkindly, being well able to afford it.

"Don't you dare," she admonishes, covering her ears. "I hate spoilers."

Could it be she has a vested interest in how this all pans out?

Chapter 35

Wednesday, we spent in a state of high anxiety.

What if Ryan showed today unexpectedly?

Judith paced circles. I spent a lot of time in the bathroom (my stomach kept turning over, making me think I was about to vomit). Only Ursie seemed completely relaxed, playing make-believe with her dolls. Finally, I suggested a game of chess, just to take my mind off the prospect of Ryan's arrival. Judith played, as well, and Ursie won both matches, whipping us soundly.

On Thursday, we put the Plan in action. I kept the $100 bill in my pocket, while hiding with Ursie behind a grape arbor that bordered our property with a view of the driveway. We whiled away our time catching and releasing a cricket we had found in the grass. It was going on lunchtime, when Ursie announced, "I'm hungry," and stood up. My stomach was growling, too, but I begged, "Just a few more minutes," and pulled her back down.

Coincidence? Luck? Precognition? Within the few more minutes I requested, Ryan pulled up in his red sports car, parking it around the back of the house, as though embarrassed to leave evidence he was visiting the poor kids at the top of the street in public view. It wasn't the skateboard I had asked him to arrive on, but when he exited the car, he held his skateboard at his side as he climbed the front steps.

"Okay," I said, "let's go."

And we went, running all the way back to the grating, which we lifted on its hinges so that I could climb down and affix the $100 bill to the thorns of the raspberry bush at the bottom. I positioned it in the middle of a sunbeam that flooded the drainage pit with light. Then I climbed back up. We shut the grating, and I locked it with the flimsy toy-chest lock I had kept for this very purpose.

Then we hurried back to the house. I had assured Judith we wouldn't leave her alone with Ryan for more than ten minutes, and we made it back just in time, both of us panting for breath, so that it really did seem we were full of excitement when we burst through the screen door.

Judith leapt immediately to her feet. Ryan was sitting on the opposite end of the couch, keeping a wary distance, leaning forward, hands clasped between his knees. Was he suspecting a trap?

"Jeremy! Ursie!" she shouted. "What's wrong?"

"Nothing," I said, out of breath. "I just came in for my fishing pole." I really did have a fishing pole, a gift from Dad, that I kept in the back of my closet, from which it rarely made an appearance.

"I thought you said you found a way to get rid of the kids," Ryan said, scowling at us.

"What do you need your fishing pole for?" Judith asked.

"Oh," I said, reticently, "nothing really."

"Money!" Ursie declared, right on cue.

"Ursula," I said, sternly, "shush!"

"Sorry," Ursie said, playing her part perfectly, "it isn't money. It's fish."

"Just where are you going to find fish around here?" Ryan scoffed. "Your mom's freezer?"

"We found some money down a drain," I admitted, starting to climb the stairs to our room. "That's why we need my fishing pole."

"How much money are we talking?" Ryan asked, leaning forward, amused. "A dollar?"

I stopped on the stairs.

"Yeah," I said, "just a dollar."

"Oh, it's more than that!" Ursie said, coyly, her hands behind her back, doing a two-step back and forth.

"What?" Ryan said, intrigued, "five dollars?"

"Higher!" Ursie exclaimed.

"Ursula," I reprimanded from the stairway, maintaining my formal tone, "would you please just be quiet."

"It's got a president on it," she said, reciting her lines. "Benjamin Franklin."

"Franklin isn't a president," I corrected her, as planned.

"Franklin!" Ryan said, standing up. "Why, that's a hundred dollars!"

"Yeah, well, it's ours, soon as I get it out of the drain," I said and ran up the stairs to grab my fishing pole.

By the time I came back down, Ryan was at the door, offering help.

"Judith?" he asked—tentatively, quietly, almost sheepishly, I thought—"you coming along?"

"No," she said, divulging her excuse. She had to wait by the phone in case our mother called. She wouldn't want our mother to worry if no one answered. Earlier, as we planned our ruse, she had thought it would be more convincing if she didn't join us. She didn't want to raise Ryan's suspicions.

"Well, I'm sure we'll be right back," Ryan told her. "Let's go find Ben Franklin," he joked, following us out the door.

Halfway across the orchard, his pace slowed.

"I don't think she's that into me," he said, more to himself it seemed than to us. He came to a stop beneath a tree and reached up to pluck an unripe apple. "Guess I can't really blame her." He rubbed the tiny green fruit between forefinger and thumb before letting it drop. "Are you sure she said she wanted to see me again? For real?"

"Come on," I urged, ignoring his inquiry, alarmed by this change in momentum. "We're almost there."

The $100 bill was right where I'd left it, snagged on a raspberry bramble in full sunlight, Ben Franklin clearly visible and staring up at us like a prisoner locked in a cell.

"You weren't kidding," Ryan said.

Crouching on the other side of the grating, I lowered the fishhook through the bars but had trouble snagging it, just as I'd planned. What I hadn't foreseen was Ryan taking over the fishing pole and trying to hook it himself. He caught an edge of it, dislodging it from the bramble. It floated down the trickle of water, lodging precariously against the lip of the outpouring drain.

"Whoops!" Ryan said. "Any better ideas?"

"Maybe we can break the lock," I suggested.

"Yeah," Ryan agreed, sizing up its flimsiness. "That might work."

He found a large rock that just happened to be lying nearby and, just as I had hoped, he lifted it up to bring it down hard on the lock.

But he hesitated, then handed the rock to me.

"Here," he said, "you try. It's your money after all. I'm not going to be the one getting in trouble."

Easy said, easy done—or so I thought. Just as I had practiced, I pummeled the lock with one, two, three herculean blows. But it didn't shatter like it was supposed to.

"Lock's not as flimsy as it looks," Ryan commented.

Unnerved but not undaunted, I lifted the rock above my head and brought it down—hard.

Still no luck.

One more try, and then another.

Ryan began whistling. I could tell he was losing patience.

I took a deep breath for one more effort. *Please*, I prayed, *please*. I closed my eyes and, using both hands, willed the lock to succumb.

"Yay!" Ursie shouted, clapping.

"Finally," Ryan said.

Ryan helped me lift up the grating on its hinges, and all three of us stared down into the pit at the $100 bill, still stuck to its bed of wet leaves.

"Looks like you can get it now," Ryan said. "I'll see you back at the house, but if you don't mind"—and here he gave me a nudge and a wink—"go ahead and take your time, okay?"

"Wait a second," I said, panicking. "We might need a hand."

"Why?" Ryan asked. "Either one of you should be able to climb down there and get it."

"I can't!" Ursie shrieked, as prearranged. "There might be spiders."

"Ursula's terrified of spiders," I elaborated.

"Well, guess that leaves you, Georgie—I mean, Jeremy."

"Okay," I said, "but can you wait in case I need help climbing back out?" I pointed out my bum ankle that still caused a bit of a limp.

"All right, but make it fast," Ryan said.

"Just a minute, I've got to find a tree."

"A tree? Can't it wait?" Ryan barked. "I mean, seriously."

"It's the excitement," Ursie confided.

I grabbed my crotch and loped off to the far side of an apple tree, just a few paces away. I unzipped my pants, only pretending to remove my equipment. I peered around the tree at Ryan, who seemed impatient, pacing back and forth, looking at his watch.

"Hey, Jeremy!" he called out. "What's taking so long?"

"Just another minute," I yelled back. "Almost through."

"Oh, for Christ sake. Okay, I'm going down, but if I get hold of it, it's finders-keepers, agreed?"

"It'll just be a minute, I swear!" I called from behind the tree, as though desperate. Peering cautiously around the trunk, I watched Ryan climb into the sewer. As soon as his head disappeared from view, I ran back and heaved at the grating. It took a few moments to lift it, but fortunately Ryan was looking down, not up. I tried lowering it as softly as I could, but my muscles gave way, and it fell with a thud. Then I clasped it with the heavy-duty lock I fished out of my pocket.

Prisoner secured!

Ryan didn't realize he was anyone's prisoner yet. He had bent down to examine the $100.

"Hey," he complained, holding it up to view, "I should have known. This isn't a real hundred dollars. It's counterfeit. See? The ink is all smeared."

He looked past the bill to the grating above, where Ursie and I were kneeling as though to observe a raccoon in its cage.

"What's going on up there?" he said, climbing up the iron rungs of the ladder. Reaching the top, he pushed against the grating. "What is this? Some kind of joke?"

"No," I said, "no joke. You've just become our prisoner."

"What the hell are you talking about—prisoner? Let me out of here."

He gave each of us a puzzled, one-eyed look, only beginning to catch on to the reality of his situation.

"Oh, Christ," he said. "Oh, shit."

He had a few other choice words for us as well, but we just stood there, looking down at him.

"Cover your ears, Ursie," I instructed.

———

Back at the ranch, so to speak, I announced: "Mission accomplished!"

But somewhere in there, Judith had experienced a change of heart.

"How long are you planning on keeping him locked up that

way?" she asked.

It was a fair question. I hadn't really thought past the "taking him prisoner" part of our plan. I was so self-satisfied with the outcome I hadn't considered the "*keeping* him prisoner" part of the equation.

"Just until—" I said, stalling for time.

"Just until he says he's sorry," Ursie filled in for me.

"Yeah, that's all. We just want him to apologize to you."

Judith took a deep breath. She didn't really want to go visit him in his cell as a part of our little "revenge play," as she termed it, as though it were a middle-school stage production. She didn't relish the thought of seeing him again. But she was willing to go out and gather up an apology on the condition I set him free.

When we arrived at the stormwater pit, Ryan was standing in his cell, staring up at the grating, as though he had been anticipating our reappearance.

"Ah," he said, "so there's the real culprit. Satisfied, Judith, that your little accomplices pulled off their little prank?"

"Look, Ryan," I said, boldly, "all you have to do is apologize and we'll set you loose."

I used the term "loose" on purpose, as though he were some sort of rodent caught by an exterminator.

"Apologize?" he said. "For what? You invite me out here only to pull a stunt like this? It's you who should be apologizing to me."

"You know what for," Judith said solemnly.

This made Ryan pause.

"All right," he said, "I'm sorry. There! Are you satisfied?"

"You don't sound very sincere," Judith said.

"I'm sorry, I'm sorry, I'm sorry. How many times do you want me to say it?"

"I want you to mean it," Judith said.

"Look," he said, defiantly, "I'm not going to apologize for something I didn't do. You wanted it. You know you wanted it. And now you want me to apologize for you wanting it? As soon as I get out of here, I'm going straight to my dad. He's got a lawyer, and it'll be me who'll be pressing charges against you! What do you think, you can just lock someone up for the hell of it without facing consequences?"

It was an eloquent speech, I'll give him that, but not the words Judith wanted to hear.

"You're making this very difficult," she said down to him.

"Difficult?"

"On yourself," she said. "Come on, kids. Let's go."

"Hey!" Ryan yelled. "You can't just leave me here!" He climbed up to the top of the ladder so his fingers were sticking out of the grating between the bars. "Come back here, bitch! Where the hell do you think you're going?"

But it was too late. He had said all the wrong things, including the b-word, which Ursie informed us was a term for a female dog. Why he had called her a female dog, she hadn't a clue. Meanwhile, Judith was like an object set in motion in a beeline back to our house. And, as Newton pointed out, a body in motion stays in motion until some outside force acts against it.

Except in this case, there was no outside force. Her course was predetermined.

"We'll see if he changes his mind on Monday," she said. Monday was four days away.

"Of course, there's the evidence," I mentioned.

"Evidence?" Judith asked.

"We'll have to dispose of it."

"His skateboard?" Ursie wanted to know.

"No," I answered, "the car."

We couldn't leave his red RX-7 sitting in our driveway, but

we didn't intend to dispose of it so thoroughly. We had one-half hour until Mom came home, so we acted quickly. We didn't think driving it on a regular road was such a good idea, especially as we would have to go past Mr. Jenkins's house. Even though he had given up his ladder, now that the gang wasn't coming over, he was still prone to peeking out windows. Also, Ryan's car, being new and red, was well known around town. Any number of people might wave and, looking more closely, think it strange to see someone other than Ryan in the driver's seat.

So we drove it down the gravel road toward the cemetery. Judith was at the wheel, driving slowly. I was riding shotgun, and Ursie sat on the stick-shift console between us. At the cemetery entrance, Judith paused, and, with the windows down, we could hear Ryan hollering for help, just barely, from his prison on the other side of the raspberry bushes. He must have heard the car and figured it was a visitor paying their respects. His pleas acted like a siren's song, and I could see doubt begin to quiver Judith's lip. So I rolled up the window.

"Let's keep driving," I suggested. Taking up my suggestion, Judith took us down to the far side of the cemetery where there was just enough room provided by the gap in the hedge for the car to squeeze through. In the field beyond, we were treated to a bumpy ride at higher speed. Judith shifted up from second to third gear once we found a dirt road with deep wheel ruts on either side of a long ribbon of weeds.

"Hold onto your seats everybody!" she shouted.

"When did you learn to drive a stick shift?" I asked.

"My dad taught me."

It was the first time she mentioned her father. I knew she lived with her mom, who needed help managing her diabetes. So it must not have been too long ago that her dad had given her driving lessons.

"Where's your dad?" I asked, hollering above the roar of the engine and the grinding of tires along the dirt road.

"Dead!" she shouted. "In fact, he's buried back there." And with that, she pulled up sharply at the edge of the quarry filled with a deep, green pool, the mirror of its surface stroked by a steady breeze. Our mom had forbidden Ursie and me to venture this far, and this was the first time we had been close enough to appreciate its beauty, stark and sheer. A fifty-foot drop, almost vertical, ended in water. It was this drop that I knew was popular with kids with guts enough to dive. And it was this same drop that made our mother declare it taboo territory.

Judith shut off the motor and had us all get out of the car. A couple of vultures spiraled overhead beneath a blanket of high soft cumulus clouds. A breeze was setting dust devils in motion along the rim of the quarry.

"I used to swim here," Judith said. "When I was younger."

No one was swimming there at present, maybe because it was getting late in the day.

"It's toxic now," Judith explained. "Something about the algae. You can't swim in it. You'd get sick."

"Or die?" Ursie wondered.

"Maybe," Judith said.

Now that she mentioned it, I did see a sign off to the left, its warning against swimming dissolving into rust.

We stared into the quarry for a while, the wind whistling around our ears. The pool rippled like a restless eye.

"There's something you should know about manual transmissions," Judith said. "Never park them in neutral."

And with that, she gave the rear bumper a gentle push with her foot. The car cascaded right over the lip of the cliff and plunged down the fifty feet into the quarry with a loud noise that sounded less a splash and more an object smacking concrete. We peered over the cliff edge to see the RX-7 spin once around and then go under with a thick gurgling sound, emitting a number of large bubbles that popped as soon as they broke the surface. A series of ringlets spread across the water, lapping the encircling shore.

"Hooray!" Ursie shouted, clapping her hands.

We never did dispose of the skateboard. I have it to this day, as a memento, I suppose. In reality, I never had an opportunity to return it.

"Come on," Judith said, putting an arm around each of us. "It's a long walk home."

Chapter 36

It was a long four days, too. But Ursula and I did our best as jailers, preferring a humane approach with the goal of rehabilitating our prisoner.

To sustain his nutrition, we fed him hot dogs right out of the package—raw because we weren't permitted to activate the stove unsupervised—and chocolate chip cookies for dessert. To quench his thirst, we airdropped Capri Sun juice pouches through the grate. I can't say he felt grateful for the menu items, but it was the best we could do. Our mother, though, wondered why we were running so low on hot dogs. Hadn't she just bought a pack of Oscar Meyer? Or had the grocery store clerk failed to bag it?

We also delivered various sundries: a travel-size tube of toothpaste, a new toothbrush still in its wrapper (compliments of a recent trip to the dentist), a comb, a half-roll of toilet paper (slightly mushed when it was forced through the bars), a hand towel, and a couple of out-of-date issues of *National Geographic*.

It was sort of like taming a wild animal. We were looking for remorse, but ended up with a series of mood changes.

Thursday evening was a period of adjustment—for him and us. He was still bitter, angry, upset. But as all he had to offer were accusations and threats, we left him to his solitude. He told us when he got free of his dungeon, none of us would be safe. He would first kill Judith, then me. These would not be quick, merciful deaths but ones drawn out by various means of torture. And I shouldn't think my little sister would be exempt.

Once he was through murdering the three of us, he would get his father's lawyer to bring up charges that would send us to prison for life. I reminded him that we could only be held until we were

21, since we were underage, but this didn't faze him. He would make sure all of us were prosecuted to the fullest extent of the law. There was no dissuading him, although I did point out how difficult a time he would have incarcerating us if we were already dead.

"Boy, what a meanie," was Ursie's assessment. "He needs to take a chill pill." She was under the impression that such a sedative actually existed as a brand name for prescription downers.

Friday morning, and his mood had become sullen, withdrawn, unresponsive. Conversation was out of the question.

"Boy, what a grump," was Ursie's commentary.

Friday evening it rained, and we spread a plastic tarp over the bars to keep him dry, weighing the corners down with rocks.

Did this improve his mood? Let's just move on to Saturday.

Saturday morning dawned bright and clear. The rain from the evening before was still emptying through the storm sewer. The trickle from the opening of one drainage pipe to the other had widened to a steady stream, and Ryan was straddling it spread eagle to avoid getting wet—or wetter. He was leaning against one wall of the concrete pit with his arms crossed and his eyes closed. It seemed he might be asleep, so we hollered down to him, only to find his mood sour and sore. Yet it seemed he was somewhat resigned to his lot.

"Don't you have anything better than raw hot dogs?" he asked, plaintively, holding up one from his fingertips like a scientist might a lab specimen by its tail.

"You don't like them bare 'n' naked?" Ursie asked, using her pet term for cold wieners outside the bun.

"Can't you at least zap them?"

"Like with a ray gun?"

"Let me guess," he jeered derisively. "No microwave."

We returned with a P&J sandwich in a baggie that I lowered on a fishing line. He ate it sulkily in a damp corner of his cell.

"He didn't even say 'thank-you,'" Ursie observed.

On Sunday, we slipped a couple of waffles through the bars.

"Better not l'eggo your Eggos," Ursie joked, but Ryan didn't find this amusing.

"What?" he said, sarcastically, "no syrup?"

"Still a grouse," my sister commented. I believed she meant "grouch" but didn't correct her.

"Well, at least you had the decency to toast them," he noted.

As we stood up to leave, he called out, "Wait! Hold on a sec." His voice sounded desperate, so we complied, bending low to hear what he had to tell us. "What would you say if I gave you a hundred dollars … each? Huh? I'm talking real money—not counterfeit. Just think what you could do with a hundred dollars."

I admit it was a tempting offer. I could see innumerable dolls and doll dresses and Barbie and Ken accessories flickering through my sister's eyes like moving pictures. As for myself, I pictured a brand-new bike, a sleek ten-speed with drop bars curving like ram's horns, but I shook the image out of my head.

"No," I said, "there's only one thing that will free you."

"What's that?" he asked, chagrined.

"An apology to Judith. Tomorrow."

"And promise never, ever to bother her again," Ursie added, with an extra "Ever!" for good measure.

He thought this over for a minute or so, and as it appeared he had nothing further to say, we stood up to go.

"Hey, wait! I'll make it two hundred apiece. How's that? It's my final offer."

"Geez," Ursie told him, "you could just say you're sorry and save yourself a whole lot of money."

If Ryan wasn't prepared to show remorse, Ursula and I were beginning to develop guilty consciences.

It started with Sunday's paper. The front-page headline was

all about Ryan's mysterious disappearance. The police were on record as suspecting foul play. Ryan's parents were quoted as saying how terribly they missed their son, how they hoped he was safe, and how they were prepared to offer a substantial cash reward for information regarding his whereabouts.

It was the main topic of conversation when Bill stopped by for Sunday dinner, as well as to pick up his nutcracker.

"Probably just took out on the road," Bill theorized. "It's the thing to do these days. Wouldn't be surprised if he's in L.A. by now, surfing the waves, a young chap like that. It's what I'd do."

"The poor, poor parents," our mother lamented, casting a lingering look at Ursie. "I know just what they must be going through."

That afternoon, back home from his vacation, Alex Hoyle stopped by.

"Hey, Jeremy."

"Hey, Alex."

"You know anything about Ryan?"

"No," I lied. "You?"

That evening, Ryan's parents came over. They were on a neighborhood crusade to hand out mimeographed flyers about their son's disappearance. The flyers were done in purple ink, giving the photograph of Ryan an Andy Warhol sort of look, as though he were a subject for modern art. Our mother offered them tea and comfort, but they declined. They were determined to hand out a flyer to every inhabitant of Bellerophon.

"Did you know our son, Ryan?" his father asked me on his way out the door.

"Just a little," I answered. "Like, from a distance."

"He never came over here?" he asked with a dubious look.

"Jeremy had some friends stop by from down the street earlier this summer," my mother intervened, "but the only boy he ever mentioned was Alex."

"You're sure you don't remember him?" Ryan's father asked, pointing to the purple portrait.

"Not really," I said.

"Everyone knew Ryan," his mother insisted, dabbing her nose with a Kleenex. "He was a very popular boy. Well-liked by all."

Two police officers—the same male/female team from two years prior—stopped by with their notepads, asking similar questions as they had about Ursie's disappearance. Their main reason for their visit was that they were trying to find a starting point for setting loose a posse of hound dogs to sniff out his trail. There had been sightings of Ryan's RX-7 parked at the top of our street over the summer. I'm not sure I fooled anyone with my claim of ignorance ("Maybe he was visiting the cemetery," I volunteered as a hypothesis), but the mere threat of bloodhounds made my stomach drop with the force of a block of cement.

"We can't hold him much longer," I whispered to Ursie in the dark at bedtime that night.

"Yeah," she agreed. "I guess we'll just have to let him go."

But letting him go wouldn't be that simple, now that there was a full-scale investigation into his disappearance that included segments on the nightly news coming from not only Parkersburg but as far away as Columbus and Cincinnati. I could only picture our mug shots once he was found. Our mother, standing in line at the post office to mail care packages to us in prison, would be ashamed to see our portraits on the bulletin board next to those of common criminals.

Of course, Judith's mug shot would be pinned right next to ours, keeping us company. It's true what Ryan so rudely informed us: if we weren't careful, we could end up in "juvie" as a result of this whole affair. Would it be possible for the three of us to end up in the same cell all together? I wondered.

Chapter 37

Judith was careful, however. She had the same fears about prosecution that we did. She had read the papers, too.

This is why she brought a small, battery-powered cassette tape recorder along with her on Monday. The recorder was a novelty to us. We had to take turns, Ursie and I, talking into it and playing our voices back. My voice sounded alien to my own ears, muffled, as though I were speaking underwater.

"How's our prisoner?" Judith wanted to know.

We gave her our status report.

"Still a grumpus," Ursie said. "He thought he could bribe us."

"Unrepentant," was my official word of the day.

"Well, then," she said, after rewinding the tape in the recorder to its starting point. "Shall we?"

We traipsed through the orchard for one more visit to give our prisoner one last bid for freedom. I, for one, felt confident he was ready to apologize. That's all Judith wanted was an apology—except it had to be on tape. This way, she explained, he wouldn't be likely to pursue the matter in court or seek retaliation.

The only problem with the tape recorder was its range was poor. It had a built-in microphone, so you had to speak directly into it to achieve the best audio. We had experimented with various distances and discovered that speaking from more than two feet away resulted in a voice that was tinny, scratchy, and soft, even on the loudest volume level. So Judith would have to literally set the recorder on the bars of the grate in order for Ryan to be fully audible from his position down in the pit.

This meant there would be no secrecy about the recorder. It

would be in plain view.

After establishing the protocol—"This is Judith Radcliff interviewing Ryan McNeil on July 25th, 1983"—she began by recording her version of the events from the week before, while Ryan stood silently below.

She got to the part where Ryan dragged her up the stairs, and then she asked me to cover Ursula's ears.

"… and this is when you raped—," Judith began, but then she took another look at Ursie and me. "When you forced me to have intercourse with you," she said flatly, revising her delivery. Her voice held no emotion, as though she had rehearsed this as a newscaster would. "Do you agree to this version of events?"

It didn't take Ryan long to respond: with total silence.

I was still holding my hands over Ursula's ears, needlessly. It became clear he wasn't going to say anything that could incriminate himself.

Judith paused the tape.

"Jeremy, maybe you better take your sister for a little walk," she requested. "This might take a while."

"Come on," I said, pulling Ursie by the hand.

We walked once, twice, three times around the cemetery, following the oblong loop of the narrow gravel road.

On the third time around, Judith was standing, holding the tape recorder at her side. She looked over at me, shaking her head.

When we approached, I could hear Ryan going ballistic. With the tape recorder off, he had launched into a tirade with frequent lobbing of f-bombs.

"Those aren't very nice words," Ursie said. "We should give him a bar of soap."

She was referring, of course, to the bar of soap our mother threatened to use on us for uttering in her presence bad words we had learned from our father.

"You want me to say I'm sorry?" Ryan spewed. "Okay, then, here goes. I'm sorry I ever laid eyes on you! I'm sorry I ever laid a hand on you! I'm sorry I ever laid you!"

Judith started to walk away from the grating and motioned us to follow.

"What did he mean 'laid you'?" Ursula asked. "Like down for sleep?"

She must have been thinking of our nighttime prayer.

"It doesn't mean anything," Judith said.. "He's raving."

In fact, he was still going strong as we departed.

"Hey! Come back here! I'm not through with you yet!"

But Judith was through with him. He had remained silent during her attempt to draw out a confession, or at least an apology, even though she had promised him she wasn't going to do anything with the tape. It would just serve as an insurance policy. But apparently Ryan didn't trust her.

"So now what?" I asked when we got back to the house.

"I guess we just let him go," Judith said, "and hope he doesn't follow through with any of his threats."

But I had a different brainstorm.

"What about intimidation?" I asked.

"Intimidation?" She laughed at this. Sizing me up, she said, "No offense, Jeremy, but I don't think you'd be all that intimidating to someone like Ryan. I watched him play hockey once. The guy's a brute on the ice. He'd snap you like a toothpick."

"Not me," I said. "Somebody else."

"Who?" she wanted to know.

"I know," Ursie said coquettishly.

"Yeah?" Judith said.

Ursula had already guessed.

It was time to bring in Bill.

—

And so Bill re-enters our story as a deus ex machina from a Greek tragedy: a god, descending on wires, to bring the play to an end when the playwright has run out of options.

Recruiting Bill involved another bike ride to Daley's Gym. I left Ursula at home this time with Judith.

I divulged the whole sordid tale to Bill at ringside, but I wasn't sure he was listening. He nodded his head and repeated obligatory "Uh-huhs" at key moments, but most of his attention was focused on his prizefighter with the glass forehead, who kept getting knocked down by his sparring partner.

"Come on, kid, get back on your feet!" he would yell from time to time, and then come back to me with, "Sorry about that. What were you saying?"

I finally got to the part where we were afraid to let Ryan out of his dungeon for fear of retaliation or incrimination or both. Pensively, I waited, while Bill followed the footwork of his fighter, issuing instructions … directives … commands, which consistently resulted in the inevitable knockdown.

"So," I ventured to say, "do you think you can help?"

"Don't worry about it," he said, keeping his eyes on the prostrate body of his fighter and thumping his hand against the ring for the ten-count. "I'll take care of it."

"You will?" I asked, amazed at his ability to keep two things in his head at once.

"The kid's hopeless," he said, turning around to face me.

And then he asked for the key.

"The what?" I responded, baffled.

"I presume you've got the key to the lock? I'd hate to use my nutcracker, if I don't have to. Wears out the blades."

I dug the key out of my pocket and handed it over. In my role as prison warden, I had forgotten I had the means of releasing Ryan from his cell all along.

That evening, when Ursie and I went to check on him, we found the drainage pit was empty, but the lock was still in place in its latch on the grating. Either Ryan had discovered Houdini-like skills of escape, slithering snakelike through the narrow bowels of the storm sewers, or Bill had come by.

It turned out to be Bill, of course, but we didn't learn the details until the next day, when he made a special trip to our house to deliver them.

He had made it all seem very casual and natural. For all intents and purposes, he had driven his white Buick up to the cemetery entrance, pretending to be a visitor, and, just as he anticipated, Ryan began screaming for his release as soon as he heard the crunch of tires through gravel, followed by an idling engine.

Bill had gone to investigate and found a drowned rat of a human being standing in the sewer, staring up, saying, "Thank God, thank God." As the saying goes, foxholes and sewers make believers of us all.

Bill brought his nutcracker out of the trunk of his car and pretended to use it to snap the lock as he secretly opened it with its key. Setting the implement aside, he helped haul Ryan out of his pit of despair.

"Here, fella," Bill had said, offering him a flask, "looks like you could use a stiff drink."

Ryan hadn't bothered to ask about the contents but guzzled it down. This is what Bill had been hoping would be the case, as the flask contained a knockout drug, an oral variant of the doping liquid that boxers sometimes smeared on their gloves when facing a superior opponent. The drug had its effect. Although Bill drove him down the street toward his house, as Ryan had requested, he had no intention of taking him anywhere except the gym. By the time they reached his driveway, Ryan was completely knocked out in the passenger seat.

This made packaging him much easier.

"Packaging?" Judith asked. We were all clustered around the kitchen table, listening intently to Bill's drawl of a story.

"A couple fellas at the gym and me, well, we sort of boxed him up," Bill explained.

"In one piece?" I asked. I was well aware via news accounts and movies of the Mafia's practice of slicing up their victims like cuts of prime rib. And I couldn't be sure that Bill wasn't connected with the Mob.

"Of course in one piece," Bill answered.

"Alive?" Ursie wanted to know.

"Of course alive," Bill averred. "That's what the airholes were for."

The way the story ended for Ryan—whether deserved or not—is he was kept drugged all night to ensure he would remain unconscious for his trip out of the United States. According to Bill, he was flown out this very morning as an express package, special handling required, as part of a "supply run" in a private Cessna to an address in Central America of a friend who owed Bill a favor. If his friend were to follow the instructions enclosed in the attached letter, Ryan would be stretched out on a beach in Costa Rica with an ounce of heroin on hand. And if all went well from there, this is how the local authorities would discover him.

"Heroin is a narcotic," Bill explained.

"I know," I said. After all, I had watched the sixth-grade film on the perils of addiction.

"What's a narcotic?" Ursie asked.

"A drug," Judith told her.

"A highly illegal drug," Bill elaborated. "I hear the penalties for having heroin in your possession overseas are much harsher than here in the good ol' U.S.A. Chances are good he'll be locked up in a foreign prison for some time to come."

"Jesus!" Judith exclaimed, but it was hard to tell from her face, the way her lips were pursed into a half smile, if she was feeling pleased, remorseful, or something else.

We all sat in silence, as we took in Bill's forecast of Ryan's fate.

Finally, Judith interrupted our thoughts.

Glancing at the clock, she pointed out it was long past time for lunch.

Bill said he could stay and asked what was on the menu.

"Anything but hot dogs," I said.

"Sometimes a hot dog is just a hot dog," my therapist points out with a smirk, misquoting Freud's quip about cigars. I'm surprised at her allusion, given the psychoanalyst's chauvinism.

I try to find her joke amusing, but I have to confess my disappointment that this appears to be her only reaction to the success of Ursie's and my quest for revenge. It feels so underwhelming—anticlimactic, in fact.

"Nobody, I mean nobody puts ketchup on a hot dog," I quote Clint Eastwood in rebuttal, putting on my best Dirty Harry impersonation.

"Touché!" my therapist laughs. "Seriously, did you know, contrary to popular belief, hot dogs don't contain mystery meat?" she tells me, having disgorged this factoid from her phone. "Apparently, it's all right there in the label."

"Guess it pays to be frank," I add, immediately embarrassed by the lameness of the pun.

"My job would be so much easier if people came with labels," my therapist reflects. "What about you?"

"Me?" I react, genuinely surprised.

"Is there a mystery you're hiding somewhere inside?"

Chapter 38

My fourteenth birthday was a nonevent, celebrated only by my mother, Ursula, Judith, and Bill. "Celebration" is the wrong choice of word. It passed mournfully, and we allowed it to expire quietly. As with Thanksgiving and Christmas, this was another family occasion that our father would miss through no fault of his own. It wasn't until winter began ebbing into spring that an event occurred that our mother conceived of as a good omen, which counterbalanced my anxieties. It came in the form of a certified letter sent by a law firm out of San Diego.

"All the way from California," our mother mused, examining the envelope front, back, and upside down, as though to reveal its secrets through clairvoyance.

"Aren't you going to open it?" I asked.

"Open it, open it!" Ursie enthused. Fourth grade hadn't necessarily enhanced her maturity level.

"All right, then," our mother said, taking a deep breath before unzipping the envelope with a steak knife in lieu of a letter opener. You'd think she was preparing to commit hara-kiri.

She read the contents silently, several times through, turning the letter from front to back to front again.

"Well?" I asked.

"What is it?" Ursie wanted to know.

"Uncle Eugene died," she said solemnly, folding the letter back into thirds.

"Who's Uncle Eugene?" I wondered.

"He's your great uncle," our mother responded unhelpfully. "Or was."

"What was so great about him?" Ursie asked.

"Yeah, why was he so great?" I pitched in with my new four-teen-year-old insolence I had decided to begin cultivating.

Shrugging off our inquiry, our mother divulged the bare facts of his existence: how he had lived a virtual hermit's life all these years as a retired surfer, a beach bum eking out a living with a metal detector, an existence hermetically sealed on the Pacific coast from all contact with relatives, never, ever attending any family reunions, for instance, but, on the other hand, never inconveniencing family members with a visit that would require an extra plate and fresh sheets.

"Very odd," our mother said, continuing to keep us intrigued.

"What is?" I asked.

"He left an inheritance to you," she said, looking up with an air of perplexity.

"To me?" I rebounded brightly. Was there a chance my Great Uncle Eugene had been a deep-sea diver? I imagined doubloons hoarded from sunken treasures he had discovered as a hobby.

"And your sister," she added.

"Oh," I responded, deflated by my sister's inclusion. I was a full-fledged teenager now. I expected all familial ties with my sister to more or less cease or at least be reasonably diluted

"Yippee!" Ursie exclaimed. Then: "What's an inheritance?"

Our inheritance, it was reported in the letter, was nonspecific. In fact, there wasn't any detail about the exact nature of it. All that was required was a parent's or guardian's signature on a form to be sent by presorted envelope and the inheritance, whatever it was, would be shipped as soon as possible.

"Shipped?" our mother questioned, as she reread the letter, this time aloud. "Why shipped?"

She would have preferred the inheritance to arrive in the form of a certified check—ideally an amount in eight or nine digits to stem the low tide of our family's receding finances.

And, to be honest, I was anticipating my fair share of a small fortune, as well.

"Why us?" I wondered aloud, engaging with a sudden doubt that this was all some terrific mistake. I had experience being disappointed by broken promises before, after all.

Mom gave the letter another once-over, front and back. "It doesn't actually say," she concluded. "But I suppose there must be some reason or other. Uncle Eugene—he was always so full of odd notions and quirks."

The whole notion of a surprise inheritance—something truly out of the blue end of the spectrum—kept all three of us guessing for three weeks, while the details of the estate were being worked out to the satisfaction of the other parties involved. What other parties? As far as our mother knew, her uncle had remained a bachelor through life. More unknown relatives, it appeared. The West Coast clan, as our mother referred to them. The kind of cousins and aunts and uncles you might visit once in a lifetime, typically in early childhood, and then never see again, possibly getting an annual birthday or Christmas card with a stenciled write-up of the Year in Review—if that.

Our mother dug through the "family archives," an odd assortment of Manila folders and envelopes she kept in a box in the bottom of her cedar chest beneath piles of mothproofed sweaters and afghans. But with regard to Great Uncle Eugene, she came up with only one item that had been preserved: a small postcard from Monterey Beach addressed to our mother's mother, a grandmother I had never met because she died before I was born.

"Surf's up!

Love, Eugene."

And that was it. Eugene was our grandmother's brother. The image I had of my grandmother was a blank slate, but my great uncle I could distinctly picture, trotting out to the waves with a surfboard under his arm, background music provided courtesy of the Beach Boys.

Even Judith and Bill got in on the guessing game, taking wild stabs at the nature of our forthcoming inheritance. It was almost in the form of a riddle: What was it that needed to be shipped that would be suitable for children?

"Something PG," Judith quipped.

I rather resented being referred to still as a child, lumped in with my sister.

"PG-13," I might have noted, to set myself apart, if only it were a couple months later when this addendum to the rating system came out.

Judith had enrolled in Oberlin College up on Lake Erie and would be attending that fall. She was finishing up her senior year at a private school. Her mother had died during the winter due to complications arising from a diabetic stroke, and Judith was staying with us part of the time, sleeping on the couch, to avoid the isolation of her empty childhood home.

"Maybe it's a computer," Judith suggested. The new Apples were coming out and known to be big and bulky.

"Or a surfboard," Bill suggested. Although where in Ohio we would use it, we didn't have a clue. The Ohio River as it flowed past Bellerophon was almost as still and stagnant as a lake, except during spring thaws.

It finally arrived in April, three weeks past Ursie's birthday, too late to be considered an official present. It was delivered just ahead of our school bus, and Mom let us both stay home that day, the event seeming so momentous. Judith and Bill came over, too.

It took two parcel delivery workers—a driver and helper—to lift it out of the back of the truck. It was a huge wooden crate with square sides longer than it was tall, so it wouldn't fit on a dolly. The instructions on each side of the crate were very clear on this point: KEEP UPRIGHT!!! The message was bracketed with arrows so you couldn't make a mistake as to which way was "up." It was vitally important that the crate remain vertical.

The airholes startled me. I was immediately panicked thinking Ryan had been delivered back to our doorstep. My fear was more visceral than logical, however. I knew, as did everyone else in our town, that Ryan's parents had sold their house and moved to Costa Rica to be close to their son while he worked out his legal troubles. This was one positive effect of Ryan's overseas incarceration, postponing his parents' divorce by bringing them closer together in the common cause of orchestrating appeals for their son's release.

Our mother signed off on the paperwork, and the delivery workers hung around to see what was inside the crate, which was starting to move across the front lawn in a series of determined jerks.

"It's alive!" I cried.

"Maybe it's a bomb," Bill surmised. "Or a Tasmanian devil."

"You've been watching too many Warner Brothers cartoons," Judith teased.

"Everyone stand back," our mother commanded, "until we find out what it is."

She examined the letter that had arrived with the crate.

"It's addressed to you and Ursie," she observed, handing the letter to me. "Why don't you read it out loud?"

"I can read, too!" Ursie complained.

But I did as instructed and unfolded the letter, climbing the front steps to use the porch as a podium. I pointedly cleared my throat, as I knew public speakers were wont to do, then began in a speech-delivering style I hoped was suitable to the momentousness of the occasion. All the while, though, I kept one eye on the crate, which was continuing to move with lurching starts and sudden stops, like a Monopoly piece.

"Ahem!" I began.

"Oh, just read it already," Bill groused. He had to get back to the gym.

"'Dear Jeremiah and Ursa …'"

"Ursa?" Ursie exclaimed. "He got my name all wrong."

I wasn't all that happy with the spelling out of my formal name either, but I proceeded with my oration.

"'Dear Jeremiah and *Ursa*,'" I emphasized to my sister's annoyance. "'This is your Great Uncle Eugene coming at you from the other side of the grave—if there is another side, which I doubt. Either there is or there isn't, and I'm sure I'll adapt either way, which is beside the point. In any case, by now, my ashes have been scattered in the Pacific blue, per instructions to my solicitor.

"'The real point, however, is this: I am naming both of you the beneficiaries of my lifelong companion, Bigelow Paine. You will find him to be a pleasant enough life mate. And I mean life mate in a literal sense, as he has had the impudence to outlast me, his best friend, and will no doubt outlive both of you.'"

"My God!" our mother said. "It's a person."

"It can't be a person," Judith said doubtfully, peering alongside Ursie through one of the air holes.

"Be careful," our mother cautioned. "You might get your eye poked out."

Judith decided to play it safe and back away from the crate, pulling Ursie back with her.

"Your mother's right," she agreed. "Extreme caution would be wise at this point."

"Ahem," I coughed to regain everyone's attention. "'He is by my measure fifty-two years old. I first fell in love with him as a young surfer of twenty-five when I found him washed ashore, just a small dude then, and so I had no idea of the type he would turn out to be. But I've since had experts examine him to confirm his variety. Not a Galápagos, as I first thought, but a Sulcata from the Sahara. Can you imagine how he traversed two oceans?'"

I paused, as though I were a medium preparing to transmit an answer to Great Uncle Eugene from the attendees of a séance. But it was regarded as a rhetorical question, so I continued with my delivery.

"'He can easily live to be 150 years old,'" I continued reading, "'which, by the way, is about how much he weighs in pounds.'"

I wait for my therapist to add more "fun facts" that she is able to glean from her phone, facts I had to look up in an encyclopedia at the local library at the time: that "sulcata" is Latin for "furrow," which describes the multiple grooves outlining its armor plates; that it can drink 15% of its body weight in water when thirsty; that what it has in common with other tortoises and turtles is getting stressed when picked up by only its shell so that it's "swimming" in air—which is how I'm feeling now, as my therapist remains silent, letting the moment pass without interruption.

"'I am attaching a list of instructions for his care, but his needs are rather simple. Just a head of lettuce a day, but his favorite diet is apples. He'll also need a fence for an enclosure. Not chain link, else his head might get caught. And it will need to be sunk deep into the ground, as he is a very good digger.

"'But really all he needs is what any of us craves.'" And here I inserted a dramatic pause. "'A little love and affection.

"'I am entrusting his care to you because you are the only two relatives I have that are young enough to raise him to middle age, as it were, and pass him on, if necessary, to your own children, which I hope you have.

"'Please give my love to your mother. She was always my favorite niece, although I've only had the pleasure of meeting her twice when she was small. Nevertheless, I did appreciate the birth announcements she sent for each of you and the family photos at Christmas. I am only sorry I never came out East for a visit.

"'Peace and love,

"'Your late, great uncle Eugene'"

We all paused for a moment, reflecting on our deceased relative's words.

And then our mother commanded, "Well, let's not just stand around. Let's open it and see."

She sounded as enthusiastic and as anxious as I felt and I was sure Ursie felt too. Maybe even Bill and Judith.

"Careful," our mother said, "we don't want to harm it."

"Him," I reminded her. It was important to get his pronouns right, whatever he was, although I had my suspicions.

Bill took charge of pulling off the top of the crate with a crowbar from his trunk. Immediately, all four sides fell down flat, revealing an enormous reptile with an armor-plated shell; four large, scaly feet; and a round, green head on a probing neck.

"A turtle!" Ursie shouted. "Hurray!"

"Tortoise, more likely," I said, having studied the difference in school.

"Tortoise, shmortoise," Bill said. "Fact is, he's getting away!"

And it was true. Bigelow Paine didn't wait for the courtesy of making introductions. He began clawing his way across the yard toward our landlord's house—more specifically, his newly cultivated bed of red and yellow tulips.

"I can't get a good hold on him," Bill said, his every wrestling maneuver thwarted by the tortoise's persistent beeline for Mr. Jenkins's yard.

"I'll stop him!" Ursie cried out and hopped on his back with a running leap. "Yippee!" she yelled, twirling her arm as though handling an invisible lariat.

Bill backpedaled ahead, and I followed closely behind, having to trot to keep up. Judith and Mom brought up the rear along with the two delivery workers, who had stuck around with as much curiosity as the rest of us.

I was amazed at how quickly a tortoise this size could crawl. There was no stopping it. As soon as Bigelow Paine made it to the flowerbed, he stopped, lowered his head, and began munching.

Mr. Jenkins came out and, massaging his bald head, contemplated the trespasser ruining his garden, which had only just burst into bloom, after careful cultivation, the week before.

That evening, we discovered that tulips are toxic to tortoises. Bigelow expressed his internal torment with a series of low groans and frequent vomiting. It took us half a listing of Yellow Page entries to find a veterinarian within a 50-mile radius who had expertise with reptiles and was willing to make house calls. The vet delivered a purgative along with a prescription for a diet more congenial to a tortoise's wellbeing. We were surprised to see raw meat as one of the permissible foods.

But at this moment, we all stood around watching the tortoise with Ursie still on his back, as though she were a cowgirl giving her stallion permission to graze.

"Permanent or temporary?" Mr. Jenkins asked at last.

"Permanent!" I shouted.

"Temporary!" our mother countered at the same time.

"Well, as soon as you decide, let me know, and I'll adjust your rent accordingly."

With that, he went back in his house, leaving us to figure out a way to get Bigelow back to our yard along with a method of keeping him there—at least for the time being, until Ursula and I could persuade our mother to come around to our way of thinking of him as more than just a temporary houseguest.

"I'll start on the fence," Bill said.

"I'll go buy some lettuce," Judith offered.

"Maybe you should get some hamburger, too," Ursie reminded her.

"We'll see," is all our mother kept saying about the situation, her typical refrain to Ursula's and my plaintive pleas. "We'll just have to see."

But at the time, she seemed to be of the opinion that, the damage to Mr. Jenkins's flowerbed having been done, she might as well let Bigelow enjoy the rest of his tulips.

At the end of this session, my therapist holds me in place with a sad-eyed lady of the lowlands sort of look, as though I have let her down in some way and not just shared one of the happiest memories of my childhood.

"Is something wrong?" I ask, experiencing an awkward reversal of roles.

There is a note of despondency in her voice as she informs me she's done a little research into the facts of one Ryan McNeil. She has found holes in my account as large and as many as the holes provided to keep Ryan alive on his parcel-post journey to Central America or the airholes in the crate containing Bigelow Paine.

According to her findings, the Ryan McNeil she came across had graduated cum laude and earned an athletic scholarship to play hockey as a forward for the Marietta College Pioneers. There is nothing about his missing in action for four days or being incarcerated in Costa Rica for drug possession.

"Maybe this was some other Ryan McNeil," I tell her.

"Another Ryan McNeil? In the small town of Bellerophon during this time period?"

I maintain the steadfastness of my account.

"None of that means it didn't happen the way I remember it."

"Remember it? Or imagine it?" she asks.

"Is there a difference?" I wonder aloud.

Chapter 39

Our father's homecoming was much less dramatic than the arrival of Bigelow Paine. It began with a visit by a State Department official, whom I mistook at the door for a new Fuller Brush Man, although he hadn't stopped by in years. He wore the same sort of frumpy suit and carried the same kind of traveling case.

My sister and I were home for spring break. Easter was as good a time as any to resurrect the dead, and that's exactly what the State Department official proceeded to do.

But first, he sat us all down—Mom, Ursula, and me—in the living room. We were scrunched together on the couch, our mother between us, while the State Department official, who introduced himself as Mr. Brown, sat in a foldout chair opposite the coffee table, upon which he opened his briefcase and drew out a sheaf of forms that he arranged in separate piles as though preparing to read a set of tarot cards to predict our fortunes.

"You're familiar with the ship *Argo*," he said, a statement, not a question.

"Yes," our mother said, "my husband's boat."

"We have reason to suspect it was torpedoed," Mr. Brown stated as a matter of objective fact.

"Torpedoed!" our mother exclaimed.

"By a Russian sub. About a year and a half ago in the fall of '82." As he explained the circumstances, Mr. Brown kept his eyes on his paperwork, which he sorted and resorted, forming different arrangements. "It appears the *Argo* may have accidentally strayed into Russian—or more correctly, Soviet—territorial waters, and, assuming it didn't respond to commands to identify itself, was, shall we say, blown out of the ocean."

And here he looked over the top of his black plastic-framed eyeglasses to gather our reactions. I'm not sure that we actually had any, as we each of us remained mute, slowly taking in what Mr. Brown, in his officious way, was divulging.

"We were told there weren't any survivors," our mother recalled, then timidly asked, "Were there?".

"I'm getting to that," Mr. Brown said straightforwardly without the least bit of impertinence. It was clear he was a professional at delivering this sort of news. "Have you heard of the Chukchi Sea?"

"Well, no," our mother said, as though she were being accused of something indecent, "never."

"It's just the other side of the Bering Strait. You know about the Bering Strait?"

And here, Mr. Brown looked directly at me, as though testing my grasp of geography.

"Yes, sir," I answered confidently. "It's where the land bridge used to be that Indians used to cross over to North America before they became Indians."

"Correct," Mr. Brown said without the astonishment I would have expected at the rapid facility of my answer. "Except the correct term is 'Native Americans.'"

"Jeremy has always been very good at science," my mother boasted with maternal warmth.

Mr. Brown failed to acknowledge such praise as he was in the process of unfolding a world map, spreading it out on the coffee table, covering all of his papers.

"Here you see the Chukchi Peninsula," he said, pointing to the map. We all leaned forward to see more closely what lay just outside the ridge of the squarely trimmed nail of his forefinger. "There are a number of settlements along the peninsula and on offshore islands. The settlements are those of the Yupik."

"Yupik?" our mother echoed.

"Siberian Eskimos," Mr. Brown explained.

"I didn't know there were Eskimos in Russia," I said, absorbing the seriousness of the lesson.

"We have Inuits," Mr. Brown said.

"Inuits?" Ursie asked, surprising us all—even Mr. Brown—by deciding to jump into the discussion.

"Another name for Eskimos," Mr. Brown said, sweetening his tone for Ursula's benefit. "The Yupik are theirs, the Inuits ours."

"I see," Ursie said, as though the distinction helped clarify a sticking point in Mr. Brown's lecture. "Inuit" wasn't a commonly used term at the time.

"Ursie, please," our mother said, "let Mr. Brown continue. Mr. Brown?"

"Yes, well, here's the thing," he said, looking at us each in turn with a three-second stare that seemed to be assessing our emotional readiness for the summation that was to follow. "We have reason to believe that Henry Jones, your husband," he said to our mother, "your father," he said to us children, "was the sole survivor of the wreck of the *Argo*."

Our mother let out a gasp. As for myself, I had the opposite reaction, preferring to hold my breath.

"There, you see," our mother said, as though she were reminding us of a diagnosis she had made about an illness in advance of its confirmation by doctors, "I knew it all along."

"Furthermore," Mr. Brown went on, "we believe he was rescued at sea by a whale-hunting crew of Yupik and that he spent considerable time living among them in one of their villages."

"No!" our mother said, registering a note of disbelief.

Mr. Brown chose to disregard her objection, folding up his map and bringing out a black-and-white photograph, which he laid on the coffee table so that it appeared right-side-up from the point of view of our mother.

"Is this your husband, Mrs. Jones?" Mr. Brown asked, point blank.

Our mother stared at it. Ursula stared at it. I stared at it. The photograph appeared to be a mug shot, based on the way a set of white numerals arranged on a black rectangular board dangled like a necklace from the man's neck. I tried to discern the outlines of a face entangled within an overgrown shrub of a bushy beard and enclosed between curtains of long, straggly hair. I convinced myself that I recognized my father's eyes and nose, as these were the only facial features available for inspection. But I left it up to our mother to make the determination.

"Well, yes, it might be," our mother said, hesitantly, tilting her head one way, then the other, so as to examine the photograph from different angles. "It's possible. There's a resemblance. Children? What do you think?" she asked, turning to us for support.

"It's Dad," Ursie said with conviction.

"Jeremy?" our mother asked, turning toward me.

"I think so," I answered, less certainly.

"For the sake of argument, we'll assume the affirmative," Mr. Brown said.

"But this photograph," our mother began, tentatively. "Was he arrested or something?"

Mr. Brown nodded his head gravely.

"I am afraid this is the case," he said. "Detained, more accurately. He was discovered by a routine policing of Yupik settlements and placed in a detention camp."

"A gulag?" our mother asked, expressing a high note of fear.

"Well, they don't call them that anymore. But now that the KGB are involved, he's been transferred to Moscow a few weeks ago, for processing. Apparently, the assumption among Soviet authorities is that your husband is a spy."

"A spy!" our mother said, half rising from her seat.

"Please, Mrs. Jones," Mr. Brown said, his tone softening, "we do not think your husband is a spy, but try convincing the Soviets. This is the inherent problem. However," and here he paused for dramatic effect, "I believe the State Department has come up with a solution—or at least a proposition—that will get you your husband back. And your father," he added as a footnote for Ursula's and my benefit. "One of theirs, for one of ours."

"But," our mother started to say, pausing a moment to arrange her thoughts, "if this is my husband, and he isn't a spy, why—"

"—would we make such an exchange?" Mr. Brown finished her question for her. "We plan to trade a—"

"Double agent," I interrupted. It was the only explanation that made sense. Otherwise, why trade a spy for someone who clearly wasn't anything of the sort?

Mr. Brown considered me with a creased brow.

"But," I continued, contemplating the exchange of prisoners, "if the Russians suspect Dad isn't really a spy, then they would have to know that our prisoner is a double agent. That way it's an even tradeoff. It's how the Russians can save face."

Mr. Brown cleared his throat.

"You have a very bright boy here," he said, turning toward my mother, neither confirming nor denying my hypothesis. "Has he ever considered a career in public service?"

This made my mother think for a moment.

"Jeremy has never expressed an interest in any type of career. He's only fourteen."

"Yes, of course. Well, unfortunately, I can't reveal any of the specifics of the operation. In the interest of national security, you understand. Here," he said, handing her a thick packet of forms all hinged together with an industrial-strength brass staple in the corner. "I just need you to initial the bottom of each page as indicated, and sign off on the document at the end."

"But what is it?" our mother asked, taking hold of the document as though it were a chalice or holy relic. The last time I had seen a document this thick, it had been the lease Mom and Dad had signed when renting our house from Mr. Jenkins next door. Either that or the Yellow Pages.

"Simply a release form," Mr. Brown said. "It authorizes us— meaning the State Department—to engineer the exchange and absolves us of all responsibility should something go wrong."

"What could go wrong?" our mother asked.

I imagined spotlights, guard towers, machine-gun nests, shots fired in the night, but Mr. Brown declined to elaborate.

"Oh, any number of things, but let's not worry about that for the moment. It may take a while for you to read through the form. It's a long document, but important. And I wouldn't want you to skip anything." He paused, inhaling, and I braced myself for an important addendum to the proceedings. "Would you happen to have any coffee?" he asked.

"Of course," our mother complied. "As long as you don't mind instant."

"Instant is fine," Mr. Brown said.

I was given this as a task to complete.

"Jeremy, you know how to put the kettle on?"

And so like Sookie out of the nursery rhyme, I departed for the kitchen.

Mr. Brown joined me and, while stirring granulated sugar into his instant coffee—black, no cream—happened to look out the kitchen window.

"Is that a Galápagos tortoise I see in your backyard?" he

asked casually, clinking his spoon as it revolved in the mug.

"No, sir, not exactly," I dared to contradict him. "It's a Sulcata. From the Sahara."

"Not that it's my department," he said, "but you'll want to make sure you obtain a permit for it if you haven't already. It's considered an exotic animal."

And with that word of warning, he went back to join our mother in the living room.

———

It took a full month for the paperwork to go through and the arrangements to be made. Finally, we received a call toward the end of May, a week before summer vacation, that Dad was being delivered stateside direct from Moscow. First, he would have to spend a week in Washington for purposes of debriefing. Only then would he be ready for reception by his family.

The only downside to the whole business, from our mother's perspective, was that not only would the continuance of death benefits cease, but the government expected her to pay back the full amount of all the checks she had received, although they tried to ameliorate hard feelings by setting up a repayment plan.

"Oh, the unfairness of it," our mother complained when she was notified of the situation by certified mail. "Not that I'm unhappy your father's alive," she hurriedly added.

Nevertheless, it would take a full three months of red tape to bring our father back to life in the view of the U.S. government. During those three months, he would exist in a purgatory of forms, forms, and more forms, each of which had to be filled out in carbon-copy triplicate on our new Smith-Corona electric typewriter.

We held a small, informal celebration at our home in the wake of Mr. Brown's visit with only Bill and Judith as invited guests.

"It's like Lazarus, right out of the Bible," Bill said, raising his bottle of beer as a toast. The rest of us were sipping champagne. Even Ursie and I were permitted a sixteenth-goblet each—despite our mother's previously expressed fear that a single sip could lead one to alcoholism—just enough to whet our thirst and feel its fizziness on the way down our throats. "Am I right, Madeline?"

Apparently, our mother's reading lessons at the prison had paid off all these years later.

"Absolutely," our mother confirmed.

"It's too bad the government can't bring the dead back to life the way Jesus could," Judith remarked. "You know, like—" She snapped her long, delicate fingers with every nail painted a different color with a unique design. "Instantaneously."

"Well, even Jesus waited four days to perform his miracle with Lazarus," our mother corrected her.

To bring a dear one back to life—one I haven't seen in years—if only through thoughts, memories, words.

I allow myself to slump forward, elbows on knees, and stare at the carpet. For the first time, I appreciate that it's shag, as though lifted right out of an '80s home décor catalog. If I squint my eyes, I can picture its purple and red weave as beads in the locks of long, braided hair. Closing them, I can see her face, her smile. I'm sitting beside her on the glider, pretending to take an interest in the glamour shots of models as she pages through the Cosmo *on her lap. On her other side, Ursie follows her painted fingernail down a column of love advice.*

"She was a Tuesday's child, full of grace, and this was the day of the week she died, only six months ago," I tell my therapist without raising my head. "Breast cancer. She died alone in hospice. Well, maybe not entirely alone. No family, but she was always good at making friends. My sister sent me the obituary that someone sent her. It didn't say she was survived by a partner or children." I lift myself back into a sitting position. "We'd kept

in touch with her over the years—well, Ursula more than I had. We didn't even know she was sick." I look steadily into my therapist's eyes, as though for the first time, seeking out the meaning behind her steady gaze. "I should have been there for her. We both should have. I just wish it could all have been different."

"But you were," my therapist tries to assure me. "You were there for her."

Her eyelids close and open with deliberate slowness, just once, like a cat will do to express trust and reassurance. The drawbridge of her eyebrows has been raised to allow the passage of what I interpret as compassion.

"No, I wasn't," I tell her. There's something more I need to add, but I can't bring myself to return her gaze to share it. "It wasn't just Ryan." My admission comes out as a murmur from deep within my throat.

The room becomes so still, so quiet. I hear my therapist's slow intake of breath, and then the slow relaxation of her exhale. "Oh," she voices softly, and this is all I need to hear to know she's comprehended what I've told her. This one simple utterance is like a trigger releasing a spring, and it all comes out in a rush:

How Ryan takes charge at the top of the stairs, directing—no, commanding—each boy to march straight up the steps, two or three at a time, as though the complicity of others, his so-called friends, will absolve him of his crime. How I struggle, pinned to the carpet, wanting to believe they'll have the decency to abstain, as if their voyeurism would make it any better. And then, when the last group is through, how Ryan looks over the banister and, staring straight at me, asks with a knowing grin, "Who hasn't had a turn?" How, with that, I find myself hauled to my feet and dragged up the stairs and down the hall into the dimness of my mother's room. If only I could put up more resistance. If only I could fight harder, but there are too many hands clutching, grasping, pulling. And then—and then—before I even know what is happening, my pants are down around my ankles, underwear too. And I am being forced onto her—her nakedness, my skin against hers—pushed, prodded, held in place until ... until they see that I won't. Not just won't—

can't. And then they all laugh and joke and I hear their laughter descending the stairs and parading out the door. And all I can think as I pull myself off her and slump to the floor is that I am so, so glad her eyes remain closed. She might be drugged, for all I know. Someone must have drugged her. But this is all I can think and feel at the time: how relieved I am that her eyes are still closed.

I don't know how much of this comes through. By the end, my chest is heaving, and I am leaning far forward, sobbing into my lap, head clamped between my hands, embarrassed for my tears, that I couldn't relate the horridness of what had happened calmly, rationally, dry-eyed.

But the adult has dissolved into the child. I am thirteen years old all over again—helpless, scared, confused.

"I just wish we could do something," I express without conviction, but I am telling this to Judith, sitting cross-legged on the floor across from my position on the couch, a coffee table between us littered with empty beer cans and cigarette butts, as we contemplate our options, having sent Ursie out of the room. "To get back at him—at all of them. For what they did."

But there will be no retribution. Judith declines to report the rape, declines to press charges. She doesn't want to involve my family in legal proceedings that she knows would get ugly. She anticipates the victim-blaming that would occur if her case were to go to trial. How the defense would portray her as the enticer—given the drugs and alcohol on the scene. And with me as her only witness—DNA evidence is still three years away—there isn't much I could testify to support her allegations, having not been present until the god-awful part I played at the end.

At this moment, she is outwardly calm, composed. The flashbacks, the nightmares—these will come later. She will wake up screaming from her "bed" on the couch, fixated on our house as a temporary abode—a deliberate means of exorcising her demons, a path that will lead, so she hopes, toward healing. It's an unrelenting trauma that compounds my guilt.

"It wasn't your fault," my therapist tells me, her voice almost a whisper. She is leaning toward me, head hovering over the blank slate of the coffee

table, hands reaching out where I can see them. I notice her nails, painted glossy purple, each with its own design stenciled in white filigree. They remind me of Judith's self-manicures, serving to anchor my pain.

"That's what she told me, too. That she forgave me." I labor to sit up, head still lowered, unable to meet my therapist's gaze. I accept the box of tissues I am handed, grudgingly, thinking how insufficient they are as a remedy. "That's the worst of it. She forgave me."

"But you haven't forgiven yourself," my therapist states gently, as a matter of genuine fact, and I respond by shaking my head, meaning agreement. "Have you told anyone this? What you've told me?"

I continue to shake my head no.

"Not even your sister?"

The question upsets me.

"Of course not my sister. Especially not her!"

I stand up to leave, but my therapist beckons me to wait.

"You haven't finished your story," she has the temerity to remind me.

"There isn't any more," I tell her, firmly, suppressing a sudden upsurge of anger. "That's where it ends. That's where it always ends."

"I don't believe it," she says, rising. She takes a single step forward, captivating my attention with wide, hazel eyes, her eyebrows in a level, neutral position, like flags at half-mast. "You can't let it end there."

I take hold of the door handle, and she touches my arm, the lightest of restraints. It feels like first contact.

"Jeremy," she says quietly, and I realize this is the first time she has spoken my name. "Please. This is important. Tell me. How does it end?"

I take in the question. I permit its entrance. I let it revolve inside my mind for seconds, minutes, finally allowing it to settle, like a dead weight into a flood of emotions.

"Maybe next time," I tell her, unable to conceal the edge to my voice.

"Sure" my therapist says. A smile graces her lips that I find undeserving, however slight its expression. "Till next time then."

Chapter 40

But there isn't a next time, not right away. I let weeks go by without a visit. My work is keeping me busy. I absorb myself in my work like a sponge— a Breadcrumb Sponge (Halichondria panicea), if I'm going to be specific.

As I am coming back to shore on the ferry from my research on the islands, my attention is riveted by a solitary lobster boat returning from its morning haul—first one back to the harbor, which could mean the crew was very efficient at emptying and rebaiting the traps, or the pots were half-empty when winched from the ocean floor. Probably the latter. The crew is already going about its business of readying their craft for the next day's run out to sea at the "crack ass of dawn," as the expression goes: captain at the wheel and two crew hands, one sternman still sorting the "roaches" by size and weight, the other cleaning the craft, swabbing the deck, removing all the grime and goo—the kind of stuff my occupation regards as specimens. There will be tons more when the boat is drydocked—barnacles, tubeworms, algae— scraped in mass quantities from the bottom of the hull.

I wave, but they are too busy to notice. Besides, they are too far away for me to ask about their catch. It's then that I think of my father heading out to sea on his doomed salmon-fishing boat and of the time he returned home from his exile abroad, reuniting with his wife and us kids. Before reaching the dock, I call my therapist to set up an appointment as soon as her schedule permits.

"Long time no hear," she tells me brightly over the phone.

"I know how it ends now," I let her know, perhaps a bit breathlessly.

And that is all I need to communicate for her to bring up her calendar right away—on her phone, no doubt.

"But Jeremy," she says, a note of caution in her voice, "the truth this time."

"Agreed," I assure her, raising my right hand in a three-fingered vow, a Boy Scout's promise, even though she can't see it. "Nothing but the truth."

—

On the day of our father's homecoming, we made the trip— Mom, Ursula, and I—from Bellerophon along Route 35 all the way past Xenia, where the tornado had leveled the town almost a decade ago, to Dayton, where we would greet him at Wright-Patterson Air Force Base. This was particularly exciting for me, since I knew this was the facility where the military was secretly storing the aliens they had autopsied after the Roswell crash. Not to say I wasn't as excited about seeing my father again.

We greeted him on the tarmac in a light drizzle that demanded umbrellas, under which we huddled, as the plane pulled in and braked. It was a huge military transport plane painted a dull mustard color with two large propellers under each wing.

Our father was excreted from the rear of the plane, which transformed itself into a ramp, down which rolled jeeps along with an assortment of Army soldiers in drab green. I easily identified the plane as similar to the one I had glued together as a replica out of a Revell model kit. Dad was distinguishable by his civilian appearance. He had maintained his beard, although it was more neatly groomed than in his most recent photograph. He wore khaki trousers and a blue dress shirt.

The first thing I noticed, aside from his clothes, was how round and chubby he was, like a jolly old elf, except that his beard was dark brown instead of Santa-Claus white. His weight gain could be attributed to a steady diet of whale and walrus blubber, he would explain to us later. Six months in a Siberian prison camp had actually slimmed him down to his present size, he claimed.

"You should have seen me before I went in," he told us.

His face, however, had remained raw and puffy and red, the result of being overexposed to the snow and cold of a long winter's night.

Upon disembarking from the cargo plane, he approached us

with slow, hesitant steps, somewhat unsteadily, a slight wobble in his gait. He came halfway across the tarmac and stopped, surveying us. The propellers were slowing, like windmills, and, following our mother's lead, we all strode forward with long steps headlong into the rush of noise and air to embrace him.

But there was something in the way he held the three of us—wife, son, and daughter—that made me sense the moment wasn't quite right. Something was amiss. It wasn't the heartfelt explosion of feeling I had been anticipating, from whichever direction I considered it, neither giving nor receiving.

No matter how tightly we held onto him, his return embrace was loose. Instead of a hug, he patted us lightly on our heads. I could sense the urgency in our mother to cling to him, to squeeze some more life out of him, but eventually she had to surrender, and we all took a step backward.

Ursula and I took his hand on either side to lead him into the terminal, following our mother, who hurried backward through the glass doors, afraid to take her eyes off her husband.

Our father's hands, though fleshy, were limp and passive, barely returning our grasps. I noticed, though, how rough and leathery the texture of his fingertips felt. I wondered if he had been forced to do hard labor in the Siberian detention camp or if it resulted from his outdoor life among the Yupik.

For the first few days of what I came to view as his hibernation with us, Ursula and I assaulted him with questions, as he sat in a new Lazy-Boy recliner our mother had bought for him as a coming-home present. Although it never seemed we were bothering him or taking him away from anything important, his answers were consistently reticent. It might take him minutes to work up a reply to any single inquiry, and just about when we were turning away without hope of a response, he would call us back with a long, drawn-out, "Well …"

We asked about a walrus-shaped figurine he wore on a leather strap around his neck.

It was an amulet, he explained. Sort of a lucky charm. Carved out of a walrus tusk. Meant to ward off evil spirits.

We asked if he had lived in an igloo.

No, not an igloo, but a wooden yaranga, he clarified. Inside was a smaller hut draped with reindeer skins and packed with tundra grass for sleeping. You kept warmer this way, a layering method transferred from clothes to habitation.

How strange, I thought, to have a house inside a house, but the idea intrigued me. It made me reconsider the architectural possibilities of our rental home.

I asked if it was true that Eskimos—whether Inuit or Yupik or other—had thirty different words for "snow," as I had been taught in social studies.

Not only for "snow," but thirty words for other things, too, like the sky, the sea, the ice, love.

Ursula asked him to say something in the Yupik language, and a long, interminable sentence rolled out of his mouth with lots of whistles and clicks of his tongue and sucking, slurping sounds.

"What does it mean?" Ursie asked.

"You are my friend," our father translated. "Now please let me have a piece of whale blubber if you're willing to share."

He told us the kind of whales he had helped hunt were orcas. It was a new word for us. We had previously known them only as killers. The name "orca" made us feel a little sorry for this type of whale, as though they had done nothing to deserve such murderous treatment at the wrong end of a harpoon.

There were other things we learned, too, sometimes without even having to prompt him.

For instance, he told us the Yupik, shortly after he had been rescued from an icy sea, had christened him with a new name that loosely translated as Reborn Man with Baby Face. This was because the local shaman was convinced he incubated the reincarnated spirit of an elder who had died just the day before. Plus, his beard had failed to conceal the essential softness of his cheeks.

Eventually, we ran out of questions, and our father exhausted his gamut of stories, and so we began quietly drifting away from him, as in a life raft from a marooned ship.

Our mother, however, had other questions for him, ones not related to his past life with the Yupik but to his present life with us.

At first, she coddled him and treated him gingerly. Making a refuge out of his recliner, our father had very few demands. His diet waned, as his body slimmed. He let his beard grow out, however. It seemed he had exceedingly little interest in the goings-on of family life, preferring to idly scan the headlines of the daily news or passively flip through television channels—there were dozens to choose from now that we had splurged on cable—with a newly acquired, fully functional remote control. The few times he got up were to stretch in place or attend to bodily functions.

When he ventured outside, it was to observe Bigelow Paine, our tortoise, in his corral constructed by Bill of deeply embedded boards. Holes in the earth around the perimeter indicated the places where he had tried digging escape tunnels, and claw marks on the boards showed where he had attempted climbing out of his enclosure. Our father seemed mesmerized by the tortoise's otherwise lack of activity, except for munching on apples and heads of lettuce and slabs of ground beef. Was he observing its behavior through his new set of eyes borrowed from the Yupik, seeing the tortoise as a source of fresh meat?

I tried helping him reconnect to reality by taking an interest in the baseball games he would watch, listlessly, passively, never once yelling or throwing things at the screen the way he used to.

"Seems the Indians are having a pretty good season," I tried engaging him. "Except for their losing streaks against the Tigers, Yankees, Blue Jays, Angels, and White Sox." I had been following their win-loss record in the local paper.

"So nothing's really changed," Dad responded, glumly.

At night, I was disturbed to note that our father was just as likely to fall asleep in his recliner as he was to make the hike upstairs to join our mother in their conjugal bed.

By this time, Judith had moved out to attend college, so she wasn't there to help mediate our parents' discussions. Bill became a rare presence as well, relinquishing his alpha male status in our household to that of our father.

As time progressed from days into weeks and then months, our mother's inquiries regarding our father's plans, hopes, and aspirations became less cushioned and more caustic.

Early on, you might hear her ask, "So what are you planning to do with your old self today?" in a jocular mode of delivery.

Within weeks, this transmuted to, "So have you given any thought to looking for work?"

This was because the death benefits had ceased, as the government was in transition from deciding our father wasn't dead enough for our mother to keep receiving assistance to officially acknowledging that our father was alive enough to have his Social Security card reactivated. In the meantime, our mother had gone back to working fulltime, whereas prior to our father's reappearance she had been able to scale back her hours.

Eventually, toward the end of the summer, our mother's questioning became more direct: "Are you going to get your lazy ass out of that recliner today or what?"

I can tell you it was a shock hearing our mother, ordinarily abiding by Christian values of charity and goodwill, using such language on the hapless, prostrate figure of our father.

In late August, she set up an appointment for him with a psychologist in Marietta.

"The psychologist says we're to start with you," she said. "Then me. Then the two of us together. Our marriage needs work."

But it was hard to tell if anything our mother said imprinted itself for long on our father's consciousness. Whenever she addressed him, he was more given to averting his half-lidded eyes to a point on the ceiling past her head, as though running his gaze through the grooves of a familiar crack. There were many to choose from.

"Henry, are you even listening to a word I'm saying?" she would frequently ask, a question which our father always answered in the affirmative by giving his head a slight nod.

Our parents never made it all the way to full marriage counseling. In fact, our father never went back to the psychologist for a second visit. One trip, in his estimation, was enough.

Following our father's single visit, the psychologist had a long talk with our mother over the phone. After she hung up, she took us kids apart into the backyard where Bigelow Paine was starting a new hole near a fencepost, making another bid for freedom.

"According to the psychologist," our mother said, recounting the gist of her phone conversation, "your father is suffering from the reverse of midnight sun sickness."

"Sun sickness?" Ursie responded, clutching her throat. "How can the sun make you sick? Is it catchy?"

"No, it's not catching," our mother said calmly. "It's what happens to people who live for an extended time above the Arctic Circle, as your father did. Except, according to Dr. Friedman, your father became so used to the idea of a sun that almost never

sets, at least during the peak of the summer, and to the idea of a
night that almost never quits, at least during the height of winter,
that he is suffering from a reverse phenomenon."

I was amazed at how erudite our mother had become about
the syndrome and wondered if, in addition to talking with Dr.
Friedman, she had memorized the content of an entry in a med-
ical encyclopedia. I knew she harbored a Merck Manual for quick
diagnoses of family illnesses.

"So the reverse is … what?" I asked, trying to understand
our father's condition.

"The reverse is that your father is having trouble adjusting to
days and nights of more or less equal length. It's upsetting his
circadian rhythms."

"What do cicadas have to do with it?" Ursie asked, staring
around at the trees, which were bristling with the sounds of sev-
enteen-year locusts.

"Not cicada," our mother corrected, "circadian."

"Oh," Ursie thought she understood, "because he lived next
to Canada."

"No, not Canadian," our mother tried to convey, then gave
up. "Oh, never mind."

I gave my sister a nudge.

"We'll look it up later," I said. We had entered a period where
Ursula was aggressively adding to her vocabulary by consulting
Webster's for the meaning of multisyllabic words on an almost
daily basis. She was also doing the "It Pays to Expand Your
Word Power" quizzes out of our mother's *Reader's Digest*s.

"But anyway," our mother sighed, "that seems to be the
whole problem with your father. His rhythm is out of whack."

This did seem to account for his overall passivity, but it still
didn't explain, in my view, the guilty, evasive looks he emitted
whenever he spoke at length with our mother.

Eventually, it came out that he had left behind in Siberia a Yupik wife who was pregnant at the time he was incarcerated by the Russian police.

For years afterward, all our mother said in reference to this liaison was summed up as a euphemism, "He rubbed noses with an Eskimo woman." But, of course, it takes more than rubbing noses to produce a child.

In all fairness, our father hadn't even realized he had become a second husband until Mr. Brown, the State Department official, poked around and discovered that the shamanistic ritual, which had involved lengthy recitations in Yupik with celebratory dancing as he held hands with the woman he had impregnated, was considered legal matrimony in accordance with Russian tolerance of indigenous native customs.

It was also Mr. Brown who arranged a visa for our father's return visit to the Chukchi Peninsula. The double agent he had been exchanged for had been assassinated by a poisoned hypodermic needle, clearing a path for our father's emigration. Apparently, there were certain conditions to which our father secretly agreed, but these were only ever hinted at, never spoken out loud.

Only later in young adulthood did I learn the truth about our father's matrimony. At the time, following his confession, which involved much yelling and shouting on our mother's part behind the closed door of their bedroom, accusations which were met with somber apologies spewing from our father, our mother simply informed him, "It looks like you have a decision to make."

A couple of years prior, a group calling itself The Clash came up with what would eventually emerge as a hit single, "Should I Stay or Should I Go?" This summed up our father's conundrum in a nutshell.

In the end, our father went. But not before saying good-bye.

—

Of course, good-byes aren't always forever. In the ensuing years, we saw our father two other times: once, after Glasnost melted the Cold War, when my sister and I made a visit to our father's village and were introduced to our step-mother and half-brother, and a second time at our mother's funeral, which our father was granted permission by Russian authorities to attend.

At the airport, on the morning of this, our father's first departure, our mother stood apart, refusing with crossed arms to give him anything more than a curt nod of her head. But more often than not, forever after, she was given to shaking it slowly, from side to side, observing in a laconic way, "Your father, he might as well be another Oswald, taking a Russian wife and defecating to Moscow."

She meant to say "defecting," but I'm not sure whether her word choice was a simple mistake or deliberate, and I, for one, never thought to correct her.

Before he boarded his flight, my father tousled my hair, and I waited for him to state his usual parting command: "Take good care of your sister."

But this time, he brought us both together in a bear hug and, releasing us, told us, "Take good care of yourselves."

Just before exiting through his gate, he turned, and, as an afterthought, added, "And each other."

There was only one member of the family he left out: Bigelow Paine.

Through the years, no matter where we migrated—Ursula out West to become a software developer raising a family in Silicon Valley, while I opted for a Cannery Row style of existence engaged in solitary research as a marine biologist along the New England coast—we shared duty, shipping him back and forth across the miles between us, taking care of our tortoise, who was destined, we knew, to outlive us both.

Postscript

"Here's something interesting," my therapist comments, glancing up from her phone. "Did you know the last sardine cannery in the U.S. was a processing plant in Maine that closed shop in 2010 after one hundred years of operation? Tragic, don't you think?"

"All except for the fish," I point out.

And with this fresh factoid circulating in my head, I arrive at the conclusion that it may be time to move on.

ACKNOWLEDGMENTS

As with my previous two novels, I heartily thank my mentor, Katherine "Kathy" Burkman, author, director of Wild Women Writing, and Professor Emeritus of The Ohio State University, for a favorable review that encouraged me to pursue publication. My spouse, Miona Jansen, a keen writer in her own right, provided sensitive editorial commentary and direction. My friend Rusty Geiger, recently retired from his job as an editor for the State of Ohio, applied his eagle eye to a draft that uncovered a number of grammatical errors, factual inconsistencies, and unintentional anachronisms. Any remaining issues are his fault (just joking, Rusty!).

I am also grateful for the feedback I received from the following readers: Margaret Anich, Ann Boucher, Maureen Cefalu, Anne Marie Drew, Fiona Forsyth, Elaine Graham-Leigh, Lalainya Goldsberry, Adrienne Mylander Grier, Tom Miller, Olga Núñez Miret, Frank Parker, Linda Thompson Sabo, Melissa Kraus Shockley, Justin Simons, Samantha Verba, and Clay Woomer. Additional support came from Dale Beckman, Amy Bennett, Gary Chrislip, Jill Geiger, Maureena Andrews Renner, and Joe Sabo.

Lastly, I would be remiss if I didn't mention the love and support of my sisters, Brenda Anne Conklin and Karen Marie Toothman, as well as that of our mother, Annemarie Conklin, née Lutsch.

ABOUT THE AUTHOR

A native Ohioan, B. Robert Conklin (he, him, his) lives, writes, and works, not necessarily in this order, in Columbus, where he and his spouse nurture the ambitions of their three Gen-Z kids, who seem determined to take less-traveled paths of their own. In support of loved ones, he is an advocate for trans rights, eating-disorder recovery, and autism awareness. In a different medium, he is resolved to keep posting original cartoons to his Tumblr blog until his followers beg him to stop.

Visit him at www.brobertconklin.wordpress.com

QUESTIONS FOR REFLECTION AND DISCUSSION

1. In what ways is Ursula a major character in the novel? Or do you find the title a misnomer?

2. How would you describe the bond between Jeremey and Ursula? Close? Competitive? Codependent? In what ways does Jeremy succeed as a protector of his sister? In what ways does he fall short?

3. What are the major dysfunctions of Jeremy's family? What are its redeeming features, if any?

4. Do you find the novel to be an accurate representation of the mid-70s through early 80s? How does it accord with or differ from your experience of this time period or your understanding of it based on others' recollections or media accounts?

5. Do you find any parts of the novel to be too farfetched? If so, can this be attributed to the narrator's overactive imagination? Or is some other factor at play?

6. Do the attempts at humor in the novel work for you?

7. How would you describe the therapeutic relationship between the adult Jeremy and his therapist? In what ways is the relationship helped or hindered by the generation gap between them?

8. How would you characterize Jeremy and Ursula's father? Do you view him as a deadbeat dad or something more? Something less? What about the mother? How did you respond to the way she is portrayed?

9. What role does religion play in shaping the story arc?

10. Do you find Jeremy's and Ursula's reactions to the rape of their caregiver believable? Is their revenge plot plausible? How are we to respond to this portion of the novel given the revelation of Jeremy's therapist about its veracity?

11. Is the adult Jeremy suffering from early onset dementia? Or is some other psychological factor responsible for the tricks his memory plays on him?

12. In light of so many novels being banned in schools for containing mature issues and themes, do you view the novel as appropriate for young adult readers? Or do you view the novel as strictly for adults? How would you define its target audience?

13. What do you like or dislike about the small-town setting? How would the novel change if set in a big city?

14. What do you find believable about the mother's reaction to the abduction of her child? Is there anything about her response that does or doesn't ring true?

15. What role do mental health issues play in the novel? How are these issues portrayed?

16. How did you respond to the ending of the novel? Did the novel come to a satisfactory close? Was anything left open-ended?